UNDER A BLOOD RED SKY

Richard A. Collins

Authors On Line

Visit us online at www.authorsonline.co.uk

An Authors OnLine Book

ISBN 0 7552 0154 X

Authors OnLine Ltd
40 Castle Street
Hertford SG14 1HR
England

This book is also available in e-book format, details of which are available at www.authorsonline.co.uk

This book is dedicated to my father,
Christopher Robin Collins (1942-2004),
whose kindness and generosity I struggle to emulate.

Acknowledgements

I would like to thank some of the people who have provided help and guidance over the years. First, my parents, for their constant support; Dr. Linda Fothergill-Gilmore from the University of Edinburgh; Dr. Meihan Nonoyama, Dr. Akiko Tanaka and Dr. Patrick K. Lai from the Tampa Bay Research Institute; Prof. Tzi Bun Ng from the Chinese University of Hong Kong; Prof. Albert Cheung-Hoi Yu and Dr. Terence Lok-Ting Lau from Hong Kong DNA Chips Ltd, for enabling me to work at the forefront of biotechnology; and last but not least, my wife Laam and children Jade Elizabeth and James Andrew, who make the struggle worthwhile.

The events described in this book are based on fact.

Email: bloodredsky2004@yahoo.com
URL: www.underabloodredsky.com

Prologue

The hand of the Lord will bring a terrible plague on your livestock in the field, on your horses and donkeys and camels, and on your cattle and sheep and goats.

Exodus 9:3

Late November

The rumble became louder and more distinct as the convoy of vehicles approached the stadium. Inside the vast concrete arena, huddled together to protect them from the bone-chilling cold, sat three thousand members of the elite work units – those privileged enough to be allowed the morning off to attend the rally. The crowd shuffled their feet and blew into cupped hands in vain attempts to keep warm.

A forest of national flags fluttered in the stiff dry wind that tumbled down the northern flanks of the Tian Shan. At nine hundred metres above sea level, the wind chill made the usually tolerable minus ten degree Celsius air feel like minus thirty.

Only one side of the stadium was filled with spectators. The rest of the seats were empty. After an hour of speeches, pep talks and cheering the rally was nearing its climax. The crowd waited anxiously for the main attraction.

Urumqi, capital of the Xinjiang Uygur Autonomous Region, was quiet today. The city, once an important centre on the Silk Road from Europe to ancient Cathay and now an industrial powerhouse of the People's Republic of China had a centuries-long heritage. It became an Uygur stronghold in the eighth century A.D. following periods of tenuous Chinese control during the earlier Han and T'ang dynasties. It came under Chinese control again in the 1760s as part of Eastern Turkestan, and in 1884 the city was made the capital of the newly created Sinkiang Province. Numerous mosques in the city testified to the continued importance of Islamic influences on the million-strong population.

After the formation of the People's Republic of China in 1949, the city had expanded greatly as the region's vast mineral wealth had been ruthlessly exploited. Because of unchecked growth and pollution, Urumqi was now hailed as the ugliest city on the face of the earth.

Urumqi's native population, mostly Uygur, with Kazakh, and Kyrgyz minorities, reflected the long history of interaction along the caravan route from Central Asia. In the decades that followed the formation of the People's Republic they had been marginalised and overlooked in the race for prosperity by the hated Han.

Shipped in to conquer the western provinces after the revolution the number of Han, natives of the northern and eastern coastal provinces, had increased nearly ten-fold since 1949 where they had carved a comfortable niche for themselves as the administrators and ruling elite of the increasingly important province.

Yet for every kilometre of road hewn out of the unforgiving terrain west of Beijing, a thousand Han political prisoners and pioneer zealots had perished. Today's relative comfort was paid for with history's misery, terror and blood.

Pushed aside in the race for underground riches – oil, gas, coal, beryllium and copper – the native Uygurs had grown swiftly resentful. Intimidated by the crushing of the neighbouring Tibetan revolt in 1959, the Uygurs claim for a homeland of their own had never been formally acknowledged. Even writing or speaking the name of the imaginary Eastern Turkestan or independent Xinjiang was a crime. Bolder moves by the natives were dealt with even more ruthlessly.

The Uygurs had been cowed by both the weather and the news, yet today it was the ruling Han who lived in fear. In the preceding weeks they had been warned not to go out alone or at night as vigilante gangs and suicidal loners from the oppressed minorities vented their anger. They told themselves that if they lived through today everything would be all right.

On some unseen cue the stadium gates opened and the convoy roared inside, the noise of their engines reverberating around the three-quarters empty arena. Blue streams of diesel fumes belched from the tailpipes as the vehicles circled the pitch like covered wagons in a modern wild-west show. After circling the pitch the ten olive-green army trucks came to a halt.

With a clang the tailgates dropped open and uniformed soldiers jumped down. They looked up expectantly into the black bowels of the vehicles. From inside four men in plain clothes were shoved roughly from the back of each truck on to the frost-hardened ground.

Each man was handcuffed and chained at the feet so that they stumbled awkwardly as they hit the ground. They hunched up instinctively as blasts of crisp arid wind blew in their faces. Behind them more uniformed men alighted and stood behind the shackled prisoners. Cold, lost and afraid the forty souls looked around as the silent crowd stared back.

Colourful silk banners were strung out across the back wall of the stadium. In gold letters on red backgrounds they spelled out the slogans of the conquerors:

STRIKE HARD AGAINST CRIME
ONE CHINA FOR ALL
THE PENALTY FOR SECESSION IS DEATH
LOVE THE MOTHERLAND

The prisoners, grubby and unshaven, were forced into a line facing the crowd. The soldiers stood behind them in two neat rows, stiff in freshly pressed khaki. A single white-gloved hand rested gently on the right shoulder of each captive. The soldiers did not need to use force to restrain their charges.

Terror was enough.

A six-axle WZ901 Armoured Anti-Rioting Vehicle was parked in one corner of the football pitch. The turret of the black and white painted vehicle housed a 7.62 millimetre Type 59 machine gun – aimed directly at the prisoners. The commanding officer did not seem to notice or care that if the prisoners attempted to flee a large portion of the watching crowd would also have been mown down if he had ordered the vehicle to open fire.

In the centre of the grass pitch, ridiculous in its isolation, stood a small wooden desk behind which sat an elderly man in uniform. The three stars of his insignia indicated that he was *shang jiang*, a general. He was flanked by a group of younger officers. A man in a dark blue uniform stood close by with his own entourage. The Director-General of the Public Security Bureau had come to see that justice was being served. A short distance in front of the desk stood a microphone; its black power cable snaked across the pitch and disappeared into the depths of the stadium.

After a few seconds surveying the audience and the convicts in turn, the general rose and approached the microphone. He tapped it with his gloved hand and a muffled boom echoed around the stadium. Bending forward slightly he addressed the crowd, reading from a piece of paper.

"The men standing before us today have committed serious crimes against the People's Republic of China," the man barked. His words were shrill and full of menace. "These crimes include treason, secession, causing explosions, possession of explosives, and murder," he continued. The phrases rolled around the stadium, bouncing off the vacant concrete bleachers before being lost to the icy breeze. "The crimes were committed this year in Yining City in Korgas County of the Xinjiang Uygur Autonomous Region." The man paused for effect and raked the standing spectators with his glare. "Each of the accused has been tried in accordance with the law and found guilty. Each man shall have his property confiscated and be executed. The sentence of the Ili Prefecture Intermediate People's Court will now be carried out."

The man turned to face the row of prisoners and nodded to one of his junior officers. On command the men were herded back into the convoy of trucks. One man dared to resist the pushes and shoves of his guards and struggled free.

"God is great! Freedom for Xinjiang!" he shouted.

The two soldiers nearest to him pulled him to the ground and stamped on his face and head. Bruised and bloodied he was thrown into the back of the truck.

"Anangga ski Hanzular!" screamed the man from inside the truck. The soldiers scowled at the other prisoners as they looked on with mute hatred.

The fleet of trucks gunned their engines and left the stadium heading slowly out of town. The broad straight boulevards of the modern city were cleared of traffic for their passage. After a few kilometres the column left the metalled road and took a series of dirt tracks until they were deep into the pasturelands south of the city.

Soon the convoy approached a large area of flattened grass. An olive-green military car waited by the side of the road; a soldier rested against the bonnet. As the convoy closed to within a few hundred metres he snapped to attention. The trucks stopped a short distance away and the waiting man marched to the passenger side of the lead vehicle.

"First Lieutenant Zhang, sir," he said, saluting smartly to the officer who had alighted from the truck's cabin.

The man nodded. "Right, let's get this over with. Your first time, son?"

"Sir?"

"An execution. Your first time?"

"Yes sir!" the young man grinned.

"I hope you remember it," the man replied grimly. "Right," he said turning to the long line of vehicles behind him. "Get them out!" He waved his arm in a wide arc.

The tailgates clanged open once more and the bedraggled prisoners were shoved out onto the dirt track. Two soldiers pulled each man to his feet and stood on either side of him as they formed themselves into a long ragged line.

"I have taken the liberty of arranging the order of the execution," the young officer beamed holding an open notebook. "With your permission, sir?"

The elderly officer looked back incredulously and shook his head. "Just count the bodies when you've finished, son. If there's any missing you'll know you've screwed up." He looked at the front of the line of prisoners. "You first," he called.

A pair of soldiers yanked the first convict in the line upright and half-dragged half-carried him toward the elderly officer. The man studied the prisoner for some seconds. With a sideways tilt of the head he indicated the area of flattened grass next to the dirt track.

The soldiers brought the man to the place indicated. A sharp kick to the back of the leg brought the prisoner to his knees. Both soldiers stooped slightly preventing the man from rising by gripping his shoulders firmly, effectively pinning him to the ground.

The elderly officer pulled a QSZ-92 pistol from beneath his thick woollen trench coat, unlocked the safety catch and cocked it. He approached the kneeling man from behind and aimed for the base of the skull. From thirty centimetres away the 5.8 millimetre bullet would pulverise the brain before exiting the skull on the other side. By shattering the medulla oblongata at the base of the brain, death would be instantaneous, almost merciful. It was the most efficient way Colonel Huang knew of killing someone.

The prisoner coughed as though trying to say something. He slumped forward unable or unwilling to resist - limp like a rag doll.

The crisp cold air was pierced by a sharp crack as Colonel Huang squeezed the trigger. The prisoner arched his back slightly in reflex before keeling over.

The two soldiers lowered him gently to the ground before standing to attention. Dismissed, they rejoined the convoy by the side of the road as the next prisoner was marched to the place of execution.

The second prisoner saw his fallen comrade and began to struggle kicking his feet wildly, resisting the attempts to make him kneel. Overwhelmed by the strength of the soldiers the man eventually succumbed. Whimpering slightly and clenching his eyes tight shut the second shot rang out clearly.

As the fifteenth body was laid to rest Huang paused to reload. He surveyed his handiwork. The corpses were arrayed almost neatly in a single row. Some of the bodies gurgled as the nervous system's control of the smooth muscle was relaxed. Steam rose from the recent dead as the involuntarily ejected faeces of the corpses began to cool.

Overcome by the stench of death First Lieutenant Zhang grimaced. Clutching his mouth in his gloved hand he ran to the edge of the road and retched violently. The Propaganda Department photographer took the opportunity to move in for some close-ups of the bodies.

"Next!" called Huang, resuming the production line of death.

At last the shambolic figure of the final prisoner was dragged to the flattened grass, now bloodied and shimmering wet, as the morning sun hung low in the winter sky.

The young man, perhaps thirty, looked older. Aged by experiences sane men would rather forget, he stared ahead, mute in his acceptance of the inevitable. But he was no plains sheep. He would die like a man. Pulling himself erect he shrugged off the guiding hands of his uniformed companions and walked stiffly yet defiantly onto the grass. As he crossed the verge where the dirt road met the grass he turned and looked behind him. Despite the beating in the stadium, in the distance he could see the empty truck at the end of the dirt track through his swollen and half-closed eyes. He smiled grimly.

Zhang barred the way. His index finger jabbed the prisoner's chest.

"You see! You see!" he said, his voice rising so that it bordered on the effeminate. "You will never win! This is what will happen to you and all your kind."

"What you do in the name of your Motherland, so I do in the name of mine," answered the man wearily.

A flicker of hope flashed in the dishevelled man's eyes.

"Sir," he said to the young officer, "would you do me the honour of telling me the time – the exact time?"

Zhang looked at his watch. "You will die at precisely two minutes past nine," he replied with obvious relish.

Three minutes. I need three minutes.

"Sir," the man asked again. "As I am the last … guest, at this gathering, might I be permitted to smoke a cigarette?"

Zhang backed away nervously as the man was brought to his knees like the others before him.

"Sir?" he asked, turning to the colonel. "Is it okay?"

Huang narrowed his eyes and squinted at the pathetic creature kneeling before him. This was the great Sidik Kadeer. The Leopard. Cornered now but how dangerous was he still?

Following his capture, Kadeer had been interrogated for weeks but had not revealed anything, even when some of the Public Security Bureau's more inventive techniques had been used on him. Apart from his screams of agony he had not spoken a word. Colonel Huang admired him for that.

Huang had seen many horrors following China's liberation of Cambodia after the fall of Pol Pot and the Khmer Rouge and during active service in the brief border war with Vietnam in 1979. Resilience under pressure was the single trait that separated real soldiers from the paper tigers. Kadeer had the same resilience. No matter how many times you beat him, he would never answer.

Huang nodded.

Zhang dug deep into his pockets and fished out a half-empty packet of Red Dragon.

"No!" barked Huang. He tossed a packet to Zhang. "Give him one of these."

Zhang looked at his commanding officer suspiciously.

Fancy wasting a Panda on this wretch.

Kadeer looked at Huang. The corners of his mouth twitched as if he were consciously trying to suppress a smile.

He took the cigarette proffered by Zhang and held it between dry lips. The pungent smoke warmed his chest. As he puffed on the cigarette he scanned the horizon slowly.

A pale brown haze of photochemical smog discoloured the sky revealing the location of the city centre in the distance. Sidik Kadeer focused on the smudge on the skyline and counted.

Sixty seconds to go.

As Kadeer smoked Zhang dropped back to Huang's side.

"Shall we take the bodies back to the prison when we have finished?"

Huang continued to stare at Kadeer. "See that truck at the end of the dirt road?" he said. "That's the next of kin. Or some of them, at least. They followed us from the stadium. They will remove any valuables from the bodies and stop them being defiled until the relatives come to collect them later. If their truck is big enough they may even take some of the bodies back now."

Zhang eyed the truck wondering if he should post some of his own men to watch the corpses.

"Zhang," continued the senior officer dryly, "when you get back remember to invoice the families one Yuan for the cost of the bullet."

"Yes, sir!"

Huang smiled. "It's time!"

Sidik Kadeer had run out of his. He sighed and spat out the stump of his cigarette. As he slumped forward, resigned to his fate, a movement caught his eye.

There it was! The sign he had been waiting for – expecting.

A plume of black smoke began to rise. It was far away – a blur on the horizon. Long seconds passed before the muted rumble of rolling thunder washed over him.

Kadeer closed his eyes and smiled. "I'm ready, Lord. Receive me."

***

The young woman struggled as she walked down the street to the bus stop. The heavy black jilbab effectively concealed her unusual bulk. Disguised by the trappings of her faith she could have been any age from eighteen to eighty.

Only her eyes revealed the truth.

The young woman waited at the end of the long queue. The bus to the city centre was coming soon. Still, the woman was apprehensive. Everything looked different today. She did not know if it was the rain-slicked roads, a trick of the light, or the nearly drunken euphoria she felt at this moment, but something was different. Something was not quite right. And she could not be late. Not today.

I have to make sure.

"Excuse me, sister," she tapped the elderly woman in front of her gently. "Is this the right stop for the city centre?"

The woman in front turned to face the soft voice. A small boy clung tightly to the old woman's hand.

"Yes, it is," she replied, her voice muffled through the veil. Her breath turned to a wisp of vapour as she spoke. "I'm taking my grandson to school."

The old lady gasped as she recognised the young woman. "You!" she exclaimed before biting her lip. "What are you doing here, Rebiya?" she hissed. "Everyone thinks you are dead or in hiding."

Rebiya Rouzi remained silent. She was astounded and annoyed that she had been recognised so soon. After months in hiding she assumed everyone, strangers at least, would have forgotten her face. She looked at the small boy and then back to his grandmother, pleading with her eyes.

"Not today," she said curtly. "Please, not today."

A flicker of understanding passed between the two women. The old woman gripped the child's hand more tightly. The bus rattled down the street toward them.

"Come, Umar," the old woman said to the boy. "No school today. It is cancelled." She turned to walk back up the street, as the child grasped her hand.

"Why, nana, why?" he protested. "Who's that lady?" The boy twisted and writhed to get a better look as he was led away.

"That is Rebiya Rouzi. She is a black widow," she replied. She turned to face the young woman. "Peace be upon you."

"And upon you," Rebiya replied quietly.

The ancient bus creaked to a stop and Rebiya clambered aboard. The doors closed with a hiss. As it moved off Rebiya stared out of the window watching the old woman and the child recede into the distance.

Rebiya sat down at the only available seat and looked around her. The bus was nearly full. Most of the passengers were Uygurs like herself. Small groups of Kazaks and Mongols kept to themselves. Grim-faced they all read the newspapers.

The execution of the traitors was the only story today. The state-run press – the Xinjiang Daily and the Talimu Daily - served up the news cold and bitter for consumption by the masses. In contrast, the heroic efforts of the security forces and their inevitable successes against the Uygur terrorists were recounted in hagiographical detail.

After five kilometres and countless stops the bus arrived at the terminus in the city centre. Soon it would make the return trip to the suburbs. Rebiya stood in the street as her nameless travelling companions disgorged from the bus brushing past her as they went about their daily business. She looked at her watch.

8:45. I must hurry.

Rebiya was tired. Despite the cold, she sweated with the excess weight she carried. She patted her stomach and hoped her awkwardness would not arouse too much suspicion. She waddled off toward the Public Security Bureau headquarters not far from the bus station.

The Public Security Bureau building dominated the city physically and spiritually. The twelve-storey monolith occupied the heart of the city centre, its tentacles extending unseen to every surrounding village, suburb, work unit and street committee. No inhabitant of the city escaped its influence. No one who earned its displeasure escaped. Hydra-headed, the PSB maintained an endless watch for "criminal elements" – a catch-all phrase used by the authorities to eliminate anyone who questioned their legitimacy.

Rebiya entered the lair of the beast by the main entrance. Struggling up the steps she paused occasionally to catch her breath. The building was quiet today. Most of the staff had been called up for extra duties and all leave had been cancelled in the run up to the execution.

She crossed the reception area. Its warmth engulfed her and made her sweat even more. The room was empty save for a row of cheap plastic bucket seats. The claustrophobic confines of the bare walls bore down on her and Rebiya's gaze was drawn to a small window set into the wall in front of her. The frosted glass prevented anyone looking into the office beyond.

A button, similar to a doorbell, was screwed clumsily to the desktop next to the shuttered window. A small handwritten notice ordered visitors to press it and wait.

Hesitantly, Rebiya pressed the button. A buzzer sounded far away. She knew she was already being assessed for her potential risk status by the closed circuit TV monitoring system.

The frosted glass window slid open almost immediately.

"What do you want?" the voice asked imperiously in Putonghua.

Rebiya resisted the urge to answer in Uygur, her native tongue. Falteringly, she replied in Putonghua. "I have information about Sidik Kadeer," she said.

"He's being executed today. What good is your information now?" demanded the young man.

"I know of others," Rebiya replied slyly. "Others who haven't been caught yet. They are planning an attack. A revenge attack for executing Kadeer and the rest."

The man thought for a moment. Information was always useful and this sounded important. It confirmed rumours he had been hearing for many weeks. Even so, he knew he should wait for his boss to approve an interview. But his superior was away on duty today. The man frowned; he shouldn't really let her in. Then he looked Rebiya up and down and smiled. If she caused any trouble she probably couldn't run very far.

"Wait here," replied the man. "I will open that side door and you can come through." He pointed behind Rebiya to an unmarked door.

Rebiya waited. Soon she heard the clunk of a deadbolt being drawn. The door opened inwards and the man led her through a short corridor that opened out into a large open-plan administration area. Rebiya recognised it as the area she had seen behind the frosted glass window.

Rebiya waited as the young man walked ahead and spoke to a colleague. After a brief conversation both men turned and studied Rebiya minutely. The pair approached Rebiya and she slid her hand slowly inside her jilbab.

"Who are you?" asked the senior officer gruffly.

"I am Rebiya Rouzi."

The man's eyes narrowed as he tried to remember if and when he had heard the name before.

"Mrs. Sidik Kadeer to you."

The thirty kilograms of high explosive strapped to Rebiya's body erupted in a boiling sea of orange and black flame and smoke. The pressure wave generated by the massive explosion shattered the windows and showered the streets in a rain of tiny incandescent splinters that ripped flesh to shreds. The blast radiated down the street, hemmed in and channelled by the high-rise buildings, blowing out the windows of every building for hundreds of metres. The reinforced concrete pillars supporting the weight of the twelve-storey PSB building buckled and snapped. Spewing dust and debris the ageing structure collapsed on itself.

Over the rubble a poisonous black cloud pierced the bleak winter sky. It was Rebiya and Sidik Kadeer's call to the faithful.

Three months earlier

Chapter 1

The boy sat on a large, flat boulder overlooking the valley below. From his perch he could see at least three kilometres down its length, until a giant sandy-coloured spur of rock obscured his view.

A long narrow road had been carved into the side of the gorge. Dust rose up like smoky incense from the tyres of passing vehicles and the careless wind bore its earthy offering into the tremulous haze of the afternoon sky.

Youssef had waited for half a day already. He watched the road intermittently. His mouth was dry and he licked his lips; his tongue felt rough and leathery. The water bottle had been drained hours before and dangled empty and lifeless from the woven cord around his waist.

Youssef's shalwar kameez was stained and worn with age. Repaired countless times it declared his family's poverty wherever he went. Life in the dry valley was hard, but Allah the Beneficient, the Merciful, would provide. If not on earth then surely in Heaven.

That was what Youssef had been taught and what he believed. He recited "The Opening" from the Qur'an to reassure himself.

"All praise is due to Allah, the Lord of the Worlds. The Beneficient, the Merciful. Master of the Day of Judgment. Thee do we serve and Thee do we beseech for help."

After scanning the road again, Youssef turned his gaze upward. He breathed in deeply through his nostrils; the dusty air smelt of chromite and limestone. The baking heat parched the Beluchistan plain.

They will come soon. Father says they will. When they come all will be well. We will have food and celebrations and Yasmeen and I will be able to go to school again. Sweetmeats and pastries and school - and all because Nashita has died!

A flash of light caught Youssef's eye and he spun around to face down the valley.

A plume of dirt rising into the air dissipated slowly in the gentle breeze and betrayed the presence of the expected visitors. Youssef squinted into the sun to make sure this was indeed his family's salvation.

The olive-green Land Rover Freelander, flecked with dried mud splatters and a fresh sheen of pumice-fine dust, crawled across the horizon. The vehicle bounced and bobbed, negotiating the minefield of potholes, loose scree and long-tumbled limestone blocks that greeted visitors to Yar Mohammad. After some time the Land Rover became more discernable and Youssef watched it, spellbound.

The driver and passenger appeared to be dressed alike at least from what Youssef could see through the trail-blackened windscreen. Both wore green camouflage army fatigues, sunglasses and green peaked caps. They looked as if they could be soldiers but the unmarked vehicle indicated otherwise.

There was still plenty of time. Having satisfied himself that these were the men his father had spoken about, Youssef jumped down nimbly from his aerie and ran back to the village.

Youssef reached the outskirts of the village in a few minutes. Over one hundred kilometres from the provincial capital Quetta, the village of Yar Mohammad was worlds away from that bustling town.

The main street was wide and flat but unpaved. It was empty save for the occasional bullock and donkey carts laden with hay, cloth or provisions. At the side of the road, about two metres from the imaginary kerb, a rusted corrugated iron shantytown had formerly stood. Once a hive of activity with hawkers and open-air restaurants, the stalls were all long-closed, victims of a ruinous economy and unforgiving climate. A few food hawkers remained but they opened their stalls only in the evenings for a few hours or on religious festivals.

Youssef knew the village streets well. He stepped from the main street and walked down an alleyway to his left. The labyrinth of whitewashed mud buildings was instantly cooler than the baking heat of the exposed streets. He made turn after turn past identical silent houses before stopping at a bungalow on a corner.

The wooden shutters, blue paint blistered and peeling, were closed. Hearing voices within, Youssef went around to the back of the house. Peering into the black interior his eyes adjusted slowly to the darkness. The shouts grew louder and Youssef knew his father was talking to someone on his mobile phone. Eventually he saw a shape gesticulating wildly within.

Youssef's father was agitated. The boy knew better than to interrupt him when he was like this so he slipped quietly past him to enter the kitchen to his right. As he did so their eyes met. Youssef's father, Kareem, acknowledged his son's presence with a nod.

"Yes. Yes! I understand! I have to go now", said Youssef's father disengaging himself from the demands of his caller.

"They are coming?" he demanded of Youssef.

"Yes," the boy replied. "Two of them. In a green Land Rover. They are almost here," he added looking for a hint of pleasure or satisfaction in his father's eyes.

"Good", replied Kareem. If there was excitement or expectation in his eyes it was impossible to tell. His face maintained its usual stern demeanour. "Come. We must hurry."

Youssef looked surprised. "You want me to come with you to meet the strangers?" he asked.

"Of course. I need you," replied his father. "They must come to the back entrance. Run and meet them on the edge of the village and guide them here. Go now."

Youssef was astonished. He rarely did anything with his father these days.

His job was to look after the animals and not get in the way when his father came home late from his meetings in the next village.

The boy did not know what his father did in town all day. His mother would not say anything except that he worked part-time at the madrassa. The Islamic school did not pay much and he knew that mobile phones were expensive. Not even the father of his friend Hussein had one and he had one of the biggest farms in the village. Youssef believed that the family's money came from his brother, Malik, who lived in America.

Although he did not understand how or why his eldest son had got to America all those years ago Kareem was pleased that Malik had remembered his filial obligations. Over the years the flow of money increased, a little at first, just a few dollars here and there, and later larger amounts. Now the family was receiving up to fifty dollars a month – a huge sum for the natives of Beluchistan.

It was best not to ask how Malik earned such fantastic sums, as the elder son had never excelled at any subject in the short time he had been enrolled at the village school. He had a natural affinity with animals and could always be relied upon to herd the animals efficiently in a way that Youssef had never mastered. Perhaps that was one of the reasons Kareem has been upset at Malik's departure. Just when the elder son could contribute to the farm and perhaps be relied upon to turn it around, he ups and leaves without so much as a farewell to his mother.

"Quickly! It's getting dark," roared Kareem. "They must return to Quetta before the day is through."

Youssef leapt into the hallway like a startled caracal and ran out of the house via the back door. Retracing his steps he returned quickly to his vantage point overlooking the valley.

The car he had observed picking its way through the debris of the highway was nowhere in sight.

Then he saw it.

Almost at the top of the series of switchbacks that made the ascent of the steep valley sides possible it groaned and roared, its low gears grating as it tried desperately to maintain traction on the loose chips and gravel of the slope. The vehicle made it to the top and turned towards Youssef who stood now in the centre of the road some three hundred metres away.

The Land Rover slowed to a crawl and approached to within a few metres. Lit from behind by the orange-red sun the occupants were silhouetted and black as ravens.

The SUV stopped and switched off its engine. Suddenly, the headlamps blazed and Youssef covered his hands with his eyes. He stepped to one side to escape the torpedoes of blinding white light. The whine of the electric window on the passenger side front door drew the boy's attention. It retracted fully and a uniform-clad arm extended from within and motioned Youssef to approach.

"Are you Kareem's boy?" said the Passenger. "I should have guessed. You look very much like him," he added and laughed. "Come. Get in. You can show us the way to your father's house. We are late and we cannot stay long. Damn these roads."

Youssef clambered in. The rear seating had been stowed away leaving a large flat storage area that was unoccupied except for a bundle of old newspapers. The inky black type of the *Akhbar-e-Jehan* and *Balochistan Post* had faded and the paper itself was yellow with age and exposure to the sun.

The vehicle roared to life again.

"Which way, now?" asked the Passenger turning to face the puzzled boy. Youssef saw the man clearly for the first time.

It was difficult to tell his age but he looked between thirty and forty. The poorly fitting camouflage jacket hung on narrow shoulders, while the thin and angular head and face were partly obscured by an olive-green military style peaked cap and teardrop lens aviator sunglasses. A pencil-thin black moustache traced a line across the man's upper lip.

The Driver did not speak for the entire journey. He seemed taller than his companion. Dressed identically, the uniform was tighter and the man was obviously heavier and of a more athletic build. Short, neatly trimmed black hair disappeared underneath the peaked cap. Huge hands gripped the steering wheel and Youssef could sense his strength as he wrestled the vehicle to its destination.

Within a few minutes the Freelander was parked in the dusty yard at the back of Youssef's family home. The men alighted from the vehicle and moved to the rear, where the tall silent Driver opened the drop-down tailgate while the Passenger watched nonchalantly.

The entire Abdul-aziz family gathered at the back door to watch the spectacle. Kareem stepped forward from the throng and greeted the two visitors with a hug. The faces of the three men cracked into wide toothy grins.

"Youssef!" called Kareem. "Take these newspapers and spread them evenly in the back of the car. Use them all and don't leave any gaps".

The boy twisted himself free from where he was wedged between the car's seats and manoeuvred his way gingerly into the luggage compartment. He grabbed the large bundle of newspapers and sliced through the twine that held them with his pocketknife.

In minutes a mat of newsprint six to eight sheets thick covered the interior of the Land Rover's rear compartment. Outside the men were still talking.

"We need some rope, the large board and a tarpaulin from the garage," Kareem announced to no one in particular.

The two men followed Kareem as he led the way to his workshop on the other side of the courtyard, the entrance to which faced the rear of the house. The rickety wooden door was pulled open, revealing a cavernous workshop inside.

Inside, the air was hot and stale. The skeleton of a Volkswagen Beetle appeared out of the gloom. Cannibalised for spare parts its internal spaces were now used to store all manner of boxes, jars, pots and knick-knacks Heaven knows when they might be useful.

A thick coil of rope lay in the corner like a sleeping viper. Blackened yet still supple after years of use in oil-soaked hands it was coated in a bloom of spider webs, dust and lint.

On the other side of the workshop a large wooden panel was propped up against the wall. The edges were unevenly bevelled and scored by years of knocks and scrapes.

"Help me with this," said Kareem to the Driver.

The two men manhandled the board down the side of the workshop and quickly brought it to rest against the tailgate of the Land Rover to form an impromptu ramp.

The Passenger stood in a shaded quadrant of the courtyard holding one end of the rope in his hand and coiling the remainder around his elbow, silently measuring its length.

Youssef now understood the visitors' purpose.

"Where is it?" demanded the Passenger.

"She. Not it," replied Youssef indignantly. "She's called Nashita."

The Passenger ignored Youssef and raised an eyebrow toward Kareem.

"Around the back", replied Kareem, still sweating from his exertions with the wooden panel. "I'll show you. Bring the rope. Youssef - bring the tarpaulin."

Kareem led the men around the corner. Behind the workshop lay open fields, barren now but once sown with millet, sorghum and rye. The three men walked the length of the workshop out of sight of the house.

The malnourished brown cow lay prostrate on the ground, its ribs clearly defined under its sagging fibrous hide. It might have been sleeping were it not for its staring dead eyes and swollen tongue spilling from its yawning mouth.

The pathetic creature remained tied to an iron loop bolted to the back wall of the workshop and had clearly died where it had lived. The slit where the blade had severed the throat gaped; dried blood encrusted the edge of the wound.

Pustular eruptions covered its tongue and muzzle. The cankers on the tongue had ruptured leaving bloody raw sores upon which swarming flies had begun to feed. The pustules on the lips were largely intact. Smooth and glistening between the matted hairs of the lips the slightly raised nodules appeared singly and in clumps, each about five to ten millimetres in diameter.

The soles of each foot were swollen and oozing. A thick crust of yellowish scab marked the fringes of the wounds while a thick purulent serum continued to drip onto the coarse grass. Just visible between the flies were the same nodules that appeared on the face. The udder was distended and engorged, a salmon pink fleshy balloon. Around each teat and continuing on up the sides of the mammary gland were more swollen vesicles although each was somewhat smaller than those on the tongue and feet.

The Passenger bent down to inspect the animal closely. "Good," he murmured to himself. He took a pen from his top pocket and probed the leathery pads of the cloven feet. "Excellent," he continued.

Youssef unfurled the tarpaulin as the Passenger completed his inspection. After examining the tongue and the lips for some time, the Passenger rose and turned to his colleague.

"Pay him."

The Driver reached into his jacket and took out a bulging brown leather wallet. It fell open with a flick of the wrist and familiar fringes of green peeped out.

Kareem inspected the five faded twenty-dollar notes religiously, holding them up to the light, noting the watermarks and feeling the texture of the raised ink. Satisfied he folded the bundle in half and put it into his breast pocket, barely concealing a smile of immense pleasure.

"You'll need help moving it," said Kareem, taking the rope from where the Driver had dropped it.

Lashing the animal's front and back legs together, Kareem fashioned a primitive harness that the men used to roll the carcass onto the spread tarpaulin. The cow sighed as stagnant air escaped from its lungs and fluid sloshed loudly in the rotting guts.

The men stooped as they each grabbed the hem of the tarpaulin. Heaving in unison the stiff tarpaulin began to move. Gaining momentum with every step, the few metres journey back to the courtyard was made with relative ease.

The men dragged the tarpaulin to the base of the wooden ramp leading up into the back of the Land Rover. Covering the animal with the remaining portion of the tarpaulin to form a giant roll, the Driver backed up the ramp squatting awkwardly so as not to hit his head on the lintel of the rear door.

As the strongest of the three the Driver bore the greatest load as he pulled the edge of the tarpaulin tube on to the lip of the ramp. Kareem and the Passenger manhandled the vile load, alternately pushing, rocking and pulling as the Driver maintained a steady tension until it rested in its entirety on the ramp. All three men were sweating profusely. With one final gigantic effort they hauled the beast up into the confines of the Land Rover's rear compartment.

It was a tight squeeze. The Driver could only exit the vehicle by climbing over the seats and out of the front door. Before closing the tailgate Kareem retrieved three large plastic buckets, sealed with lids, from the workshop and stowed them in the back next to the bundle.

"I prepared these exactly as you directed," he told the Passenger. "You can wash yourselves over there," he added, gesturing with a tired wave of the hand to an empty tin bath. "I'll have the women fetch you some water."

Youssef's mother and sister disappeared into the house. They returned carrying large pitchers of water, which they emptied into the bath, forming a pool a few centimetres deep.

The Passenger approached the bath first and plunged both hands into the cool water. He found a small cake of soap and began to lather vigorously. He soaped his hands and arms up to the elbow, repeatedly rubbing the skin as if to remove some invisible stain. Eventually he rinsed himself off, scooping up water with a small bowl in order to wash the creamy suds from his elbows.

The Driver likewise knelt before the bath, now milky white and greasy with soap. Being less fastidious than his companion he merely soaped his hands up to the wrists, rinsed quickly and patted dry his still sticky hands on his thighs. Standing, he pulled the front hem of his T-shirt from the top of his trousers and used it as a towel.

"We must go now," said the Passenger to Kareem. "Remember, tell no one what has happened today."

Both men turned to Kareem and in unison bowed stiffly from the neck. "Khuda hafeez", they said. "Wa'alaikum salaam."

Turning to Kareem's wife, the two strangers repeated their farewell. She accepted it with a silent almost imperceptible nod.

The Driver and Passenger returned to the SUV. Winding down the windows as far as they could to offset the putrefying smell of the interior the occupants resigned themselves to the grim task of transporting the carcass to its destination.

The car began to move away, creeping slowly around the side of the house, retracing the route described earlier to them by Youssef, who now followed on foot.

As the vehicle edged carefully out into the narrow lane the Passenger looked steadily at Youssef.

"God be with you."

Youssef stood in the middle of the lane and watched as the Land Rover disappeared into the distance.

The embers of the dying sun kissed the base of the low clouds illuminating them from within with amber and gold. The tops of the clouds darkened rapidly to indigo and purple. The billowing mass seemed almost to roar as if escaping from the gape of Hell's foundry.

Chapter 2

Paul Caine signalled left and turned into the driveway. The Animal Health Institute occupied a drab concrete two-storey building.

As a senior research scientist in the United Kingdom's premier veterinary institute he revelled in every aspect of the unending war on the microscopic pathogens of nature. It was a pity the buildings in which the war was waged appeared so depressing and unglamorous. Then again, Caine recalled, secret wars were often conducted in the most mundane of buildings. The thrill of the work being known only to those who entered their hallowed portals and who were privy to the secret dispatches from frontiers unexplored.

The car passed the gatehouse at a crawl and the ageing security guard glanced cursorily up from his tabloid and waved him through.

As virtually the last member of the virology team to arrive that morning the parking spaces nearest the front entrance had already been taken. Caine had to be content with the least muddy corner of the uneven tarmac enclosure.

The receptionist tut-tutted as Caine sauntered in.

"Good morning, Joyce", Caine announced jovially. "Not too late am I?"

"What time do you call this?" Joyce replied in mock reproach. "You're nearly late for your meeting with Dr. Reese. He'll have a fit if you're not on time. You know what he's like."

"If he asks tell him I'll be up in a minute. I've got to check in with the lab first."

"Gotcha" said Joyce.

Caine crossed the lobby and pushed open one of the stout fire doors guarding the entrance to the virology wing.

He walked briskly past the pin boards that lined the corridor. The wall was a veritable museum of virological research over the past twenty years, displaying the relics of scientific symposia from years gone by.

Electron micrographs of strange and wonderful creatures peered at him from every direction. Some delicate and spindly, others round and bloated, all of them eerily fascinating. A large photograph of bacteriophage T4 caught Caine's eye. This was the "lunar lander" bug. A virus with a stocky angular body and long spider's legs that reminded just about everyone who saw it of the Apollo moon landing vehicles of decades before. It was this bug that had inspired Caine to work with viruses nearly twenty years before when he saw it on a BBC documentary.

From the black and white photographs of the bacterial viruses the mural changed to garish computer-enhanced false colour images of newer and more terrifying vehicles of destruction. Ebola, Marburg, Hanta — the names themselves evoked a strange sense of foreboding.

The human immunodeficiency virus - HIV - was shown as a ragged translucent blue ball erupting from the sickly yellow and rapidly deflating hot air balloon of the white blood cell it had infected.

The pathogens of livestock, the institute's specialty, were next. The text of the symposium posters and abstracts that lined the walls of the remainder of the corridor charted Caine's career from graduate student to head of the department.

Caine pushed open the door to his laboratory and was thrown immediately into a barrage of accusations and retorts as he found himself face to face with his post-doctoral researcher, Jeremy Spence, pointing threateningly at his young summer student, Pamela Burton.

"I've told you before many times," screeched Spence, "always clean the balance after using it. Other people shouldn't have to do it for you and they certainly don't want their own reagents contaminated with your dregs."

"It wasn't me. I haven't even used it this morning", pleaded Pamela, flushed and stammering.

The object of their discussion, an analytical mass comparator, stood imperiously in the background. A few white crystals remained in the balance pan.

"Alright, children," said Caine in mock patronage. "We all know to clean up after ourselves, I'm sure. Pamela, be more careful in future. Jeremy, don't be such an arsehole."

Spence harrumphed away in disgust while Pamela smirked grimly as the boss's instant resolution laid equal blame on both parties.

Pamela had joined Caine's lab as an intern from university. She was studying for her Bachelor of Science in microbiology at the University of Reading and had been fascinated by animal viruses ever since Caine had visited her department earlier that year for a graduate seminar.

Normally, such seminars were dry affairs, taking place just after lunch when everyone was bloated and tired. She had diligently attended most of them either sleeping or doodling her way through to the question and answer session at the end.

It was only the animal viruses that interested Pamela - bluetongue, Newcastle disease, rinderpest, Rift Valley fever and rabies. Only the most serious diseases excited her – World Organisation for Animal Health List A diseases, to be precise. She tried to recite the phrase she had leant.

How did it go?

"Transmissible diseases that have the potential for rapid spread, irrespective of national borders, that have serious socio-economic or public health consequences and are of major importance in the international trade of animals and animal products," she sighed almost wistfully.

Of course, her interest was aroused when she discovered that Dr. Paul Caine was young, handsome and apparently unattached. When she heard after the talk that summer student positions were available in his lab later that year she applied on the spot. The seminar organiser was a friend of Caine's from his own university days and was only too happy to see one of his students taking an interest in the field. Of course he would help her write a letter of introduction. Pamela smiled at the recollection.

"Now all I have to do is get him into bed," she thought.

Jeremy Spence, on the other hand, was a toad. Although he was tall, thin and generally good-looking, his plummy accent and general disinterest in anything outside his own sphere of activities had won him few friends. He was hardworking, diligent and probably a genius in the field of molecular epidemiology – the science of determining how an infectious organism spreads and evolves by studying the genetic fingerprints it leaves behind. Nevertheless, he was not well liked in the department. Caine had hired him with grant money obtained from the European Union to study the evolution of the virus causing foot-and-mouth disease.

Following the disastrous outbreak of the disease in the United Kingdom in 2001, the Department of Environment, Food and Rural Affairs that had replaced the beloved Ministry of Agriculture, Fisheries and Food, along with counterpart departments in Europe had spared no effort when it came to finding out where this virus had come from and how it spread so quickly. Having just obtained his Genetics PhD from Oxford, Jeremy was an obvious candidate for the job.

The lab was about twenty metres long and five metres wide and divided into three areas. In one corner was an internal office not more than about two metres square, where Caine worked alone. The rest of the lab was divided into two bays separated by a floor-to-ceiling shelving unit housing the laboratory's private store of reagents and glassware.

Chunky plastic tubs of various sizes each with a sturdy easy-grip lid held everyday chemical reagents. Buffers such as Tris, Hepes and MOPS, used to stabilise the pH of chemical solutions were held in large two kilogram drums, while ultrapure agarose, used sparingly to make a jelly to filter proteins and nucleic acids, was contained in delicate pure white jars with labels of laminated gold.

The lab was well lit with natural sunlight that streamed through the bank of windows that ran the length of one wall.

Outside, the Gloucestershire countryside rolled away to the horizon. The institute was situated deep in the rural heartland of England. There were three main reasons for this. First, the activity of the institute related mainly to the agricultural needs of the country, with diseases of livestock being a major element, and it was felt that the farming community would better respect the views of the institute if it were situated in a rural setting rather than hidden in the warren of government departments in Whitehall or the ivory towers of some university or other.

Secondly, the institute worked actively on highly pathogenic organisms that could cause great economic damage in addition to considerable public alarm if they were ever to be released accidentally into the environment. Building an institute where few people lived greatly lessened this risk.

And finally, a government institute propagating dangerous organisms would be a natural target for espionage or sabotage. Any strangers monitoring the building for unusual periods of time would be identified more easily.

Caine walked through the lab to his office. Unlocking the door he flung his briefcase into the swivel chair that occupied most of the tiny office's floor space and switched on his computer.

He logged on to the server and opened his email. Thirteen messages today – mostly rubbish: home loans approved instantly, penis enlargement guaranteed, Nigerian bank official wants assistance laundering millions of dollars, a couple of internal memos from the institute admin, and, at last, the one he had been waiting for.

Caine opened the message and scanned briefly through its contents. He smiled to himself and then clicked the print icon at the top of the screen. He grabbed the single page printout and headed upstairs to Head of Department Reese's office.

Reese was the only person who made Caine sweat. He had the knack of making everybody feel as if they hadn't been working at full capacity even when they had been burning the midnight oil to get projects completed ahead of time. Caine respected his efficiency but wondered if the same achievements couldn't have been made without sacrificing his personality or charm.

Nobody liked Reese on a personal level. No one went out of their way to sit next to him in the staff canteen or chat to him about the latest football scores. As far as anyone knew, Reese had no personal interests beyond those linked to his job. He was formerly a professional veterinary surgeon, as were most of the senior staff at the institute, but his practising days were long past. Now he was a career administrator and very good at it. His ruthlessness and acumen had seen off challenges to merge the institute with other departments and had maintained the integrity of the institute as an organisation of world renown. Everyone admired him for that.

Caine rapped at the door and waited. Reese liked people to wait for as long as possible before acknowledging them. To him it was just another round of psychological ammunition in the battle to get the information he felt he needed in order to function.

Ten seconds. Fifteen. Twenty.

"Come!" barked Reese.

Caine fumbled with the doorknob and entered. Reese was seated in a well-padded executive leather armchair, silhouetted against the square window behind him. The angled slats of the half-closed Venetian blinds bathed the room in soft dappled light. Caine almost felt as if he was entering into a communion with a spiritual leader.

An empty chair stood in front of the desk and Reese motioned Caine to sit. Reese looked at Caine studiously for a few moments.

"One of the advantages of having an office window facing the car park," Reese began, "is that it gives one a fresh perspective on people's commitment to the institute."

Shit. The old bugger saw me coming in late.

"Of course, as senior management, one has a certain leeway in managing one's own time," Reese continued, "But then again, one also has to set an example to one's own staff."

"Er," stammered Caine, not quite sure where the conversation was leading, "Quite."

"Leadership comes with many responsibilities, Paul," said Reese, "Among them is respect for the established rules."

Caine looked wide-eyed in incomprehension at Reese. He had been among the most diligent of all staff at the institute. His record of publications in the scientific literature had been unequalled. No one had questioned his authority before, especially over something as trivial as timekeeping. What was the old bird getting at?

"We expect our laboratory leaders to take an active role in the international community," Reese probed. "Yet from your records I see you have only attended one international meeting this year. What was it?" he said fumbling through a pale brown folder, which Caine assumed was his personnel file.

"Ah, yes. Here it is. The First International Symposium on Viral Diseases of Livestock, in Stuttgart", continued Reese, turning down the corners of his mouth, visibly unimpressed.

"I was one of the keynote speakers," ventured Caine.

"So was Derek Foulds of Glasgow University. He wouldn't know a viral disease if he contracted one," Reese spat in genuine contempt.

"You even missed the Microbiology Union Centenary Congress in Paris, last year. This really is not good enough, Paul."

"If you remember, last year I was moving house and I missed the deadline for submitting my abstract," said Caine.

"That's no excuse. I know the entire secretariat personally. There are always ways around these things. You should have come to see me," offered Reese.

"I suppose you're now going to tell me you're not going to the San Francisco symposium?" Reese said with a hint of disappointment.

"Actually," Caine said, flapping his email printout in the air, "I received confirmation this morning. Keynote speech, all expenses paid."

"Well that is some comfort. You know, Paul, I keep my cards pretty close to my chest. That's why I'm on this side of the desk today. I know you and most other people in this institute don't like...," Reese faltered, "Don't approve of some of my methods. I like winning and I make damn sure I bet on a dead cert. That's why you're the youngest head of department in the forty-odd years this institute has been running. I don't want you to throw opportunities away when they come knocking."

And there it is, the reason for all this shenanigans this morning. He's taking an interest in my career.

"I can assure you, Walter, that nothing will distract me from the task at hand, which is to continue to ensure that AHI is the top in its class," Caine declared.

"Good. I'm glad to hear it. After all," said Reese softly, "do you really think I want to be here forever? It's no secret that I'll be moving on soon. I want to make sure that the person who comes after me has the best interests of the AHI at heart. And that means making sure that the most qualified candidate for the job comes from within the AHI itself. The last thing the people here need is a mandarin in London thinking he knows whose best to lead us. Am I right?"

Christ. He's virtually offering me the job now.

"That's why you need to lead and push yourself to the head of the pack. No more second-rate conferences and university graduate seminars for you. It's time to hit the big league. This keynote in San Francisco is just the start, I'm sure."

"I'm pleased you have such confidence in me," said Caine suddenly relieved. "I won't disappoint you."

"I'm sure you won't and I think Sean would say the same thing, if he were here," added Reese.

"Where is Dr. Coombs now?" queried Caine.

"There's a suspected case of dourine on a stud farm down in Newmarket. The Jockey Club are screaming blue murder about it."

"Dourine?" asked Caine. "That's impossible. There hasn't been a case in Britain in how long?"

"Never," said Reese. "It's almost certainly a false positive. But the Jockey Club insisted on having the top man go and confirm it. He'll be back tomorrow." Reese paused before continuing.

"So there you have it," he said planting his hands palm down on the table and shifting his weight in his seat as if to rise, effectively ending the discussion.

"Leave a hard copy of your slides on my desk and make sure you give 'em hell in America."

Caine rose and made to leave. He paused and turned to face Reese and extended his hand. Reese looked at it for a second, puzzled, before taking it and shaking it firmly. A rare moment of warmth spread through both of them before the spell was broken by the sound of a knock at the door.

"Ah, my weekly review of the post-doc's progress. Show them in on your way out, would you?" said Reese smiling. "Thanks."

Caine turned and opened the door. Two young men stood outside, carrying large black ring binders full of notes and with looks of nervous expectation on their faces.

"In you go, lads," said Caine. "He doesn't bite."

Chapter 3

It was midnight when the Land Rover arrived in the outskirts of Quetta. Turning down an unnamed street it parked outside a shuttered doorway. Reversing carefully, the Driver manoeuvred the vehicle until its rear bumper almost touched the metal screen, illuminating the worn and scratched surface with the red glow of the taillights. Only then did the shutter start to rise, the screeching of metal on metal ricocheting down the narrow deserted street.

As the shutter rose, the warm red light revealed the shadowy form of a man. The figure stepped to one side and disappeared into the void, allowing the Land Rover to back into the building. Once inside, the metal shutter was lowered again.

The Driver and Passenger stepped from the car. Both were exhausted and stretched their arms and legs, rubbing them to restore circulation numbed through hours of enforced idleness on the long drive.

A single naked bulb bathed the room in sickly light.

The room was about fifteen metres wide and ten metres deep. The bare cement floor was cracked with age and bounded by walls of grey unplastered breezeblocks. The ceiling, at least four metres high, comprised a lattice of thin stainless steel girders through which the undulating folds of a corrugated iron roof were just visible. Immediately opposite the shuttered exit to the street a flimsy plywood door led to a tiny office beyond.

In one corner stood a large wooden desk. Invoices strewn across the surface identified the premises as Rashid Fine Chemicals Ltd.

Elsewhere in the warehouse, large cardboard crates rested atop wooden pallets. On some the contents were marked clearly — titanium dioxide, potassium hypochlorite, sodium hydroxide. On others the cardboard had been ripped in places revealing anonymous grey plastic drums.

Preparations for the evening's activities had begun. The floor had been cleared and a large tarpaulin laid down. A hosepipe was connected to an auxiliary tap and a thin dribble of water escaped from its nozzle and pooled in a depression in the floor.

A block and tackle was suspended from a rail bolted to the thickest of the ceiling's supporting girders, allowing it to be dragged freely from one side of the room to the other. Next to the tap, a rough wooden bench contained an assortment of utensils and bottles.

The Passenger opened the Land Rover's tailgate. Reaching inside, he unloaded the sealed buckets and placed them carefully on the floor underneath the wooden table. During the journey, one of the buckets had begun to leak and glutinous rivulets of gore covered the outside. A congealed circular clot marked the place where the bucket had rested.

The third man approached the vehicle peering inside for a closer look. The fug that had built up during the journey assailed him. Reeling back he cupped his hand over his mouth and turned away.

"How do you stand it?" he asked.

"You get used to it," replied the Driver grimly. "Give me a hand."

Grabbing the rope truss that Kareem had made to tie the beast, the three men pulled hard. The massive bundle slid smoothly across the floor of the SUV and landed with a crump on the warehouse floor.

"Over here," said Number Three, indicating the fresh tarpaulin spread in the corner of the room.

Number Three took hold of the block and tackle and pulled it as close as he was able to the shrouded beast. He extracted a large iron hook from the tangle of ropes as the Passenger bent down to unwrap the hideous parcel. He attached the hook to the rope shackles tying the cow's legs. Number Three went to the wall and loosened the guy rope so that he could hoist the animal into the air. The Driver and Passenger followed ready to lend a hand.

The rope moved easily at first as Number Three eliminated the slack. Soon, it became taut and the Driver and then the Passenger added their strength to lift the burden. In seconds the entire three hundred kilo carcass was dangling from the ceiling.

The girders creaked and groaned in protest.

Pulling gently, Number Three guided the trussed animal to the spread tarpaulin in the corner and lowered it slightly so that its muzzle was just resting on the ground before tying off the guy rope tightly.

"That will be all," said Number Three. "I'll handle everything from here. Leave the car here and come back tomorrow morning. I will be finished by then. Take your clothes off and put them in that bag over there," he added, pointing to a black plastic refuse bag.

"Fresh clothes are on the table. Before you put them on wash yourself all over with the solution in the bucket over there."

Without a word the Driver and Passenger stripped naked and dropped their clothes into an untidy heap. The Passenger stuffed them roughly into the plastic bag, spun it a few times and tied the neck with a simple slipknot.

The Driver, naked and gleaming with sweat, walked to the bucket, which contained a pink, sweet-smelling solution that foamed slightly.

"What is it?' he asked suspiciously.

"Virkon," replied Number Three. "It's a disinfectant. I don't want you spreading disease around town. When you come back tomorrow you must wash the vehicle all over with this and also the floor. We can't take any chances. Wash your shoes with it as well before you leave."

The Driver dipped his fingers gently into the solution as if expecting them to fizz and dissolve. It felt slightly greasy and the Driver continued to wash himself all over, pausing only to wince when the solution got into his eyes. The Passenger washed himself in the same way. Both men towelled themselves dry and put on a clean shalwar kameez.

The Driver and Passenger raised their hands and bade farewell to Number Three before entering the adjoining office through the internal door. Number

Three resumed his inspection of the cow. He listened as the soft footsteps and hushed voices receded quickly into the still night.

The odour of disinfectant filled the air as Number Three, Hashim to those permitted to know his name, picked up a scalpel and began to cut. Kneeling down for easier access to the corpse, he started on the muzzle. The pustules visible in this region would be filled with virus and he had to preserve these first before attempting to work on the other tissues. Working quickly, he wielded the gleaming fifteen-centimetre stainless steel blade with the precision of a surgeon. Slicing through the tough hide and into the dermis below, he took great care not cut too close to the vesicles so as to rupture them. On the other hand, cutting too generously would result in a flap of skin containing large amounts of useless uninfected tissue, diluting its potency.

After making the initial slices, Hashim used a pair of delicate surgical forceps to lift back the skin and reveal the moist blood-red epidermis.

The skin was resilient, toughened with age, and it resisted the pull of the forceps. Hashim cut away at the interior surface of the skin where it was still connected to the underlying flesh, slicing through tendrils of collagen and elastin, freeing the layer of skin from its supporting tissue.

After some minutes Hashim had what he wanted, a flat irregular-shaped piece of skin peppered with eruptions and blisters. Carefully, he laid the coarse skin on a pad of folded tissue paper to draw away excess blood and fluid. The pad was laid in a square Pyrex dish resting on the wooden bench by his side. Kneeling again, Hashim resumed his grisly task.

Having flayed one side of the cow's face he began on the other. The lips and tongue followed. The latter was thick and heavy and stiff with rigor mortis. Several large erosions, each about three centimetres in diameter, were apparent. The surface was rough and worn and bloody. The animal must have been in great pain and probably could not eat or drink properly, thought Hashim. Maybe this accounted for the animal's dishevelled appearance.

Pressing the tongue flat on the table with one hand, Hashim took up a razor sharp filleting knife with the other and passed it horizontally through the tongue, separating its dorsal and ventral surfaces. He cut around the blisters on both sides ignoring the intact, uninfected flesh. The blisters were added to the mound of remains on the table. The leftovers were thrown on to the tarpaulin where they lay with other shards of discarded flesh and hair.

Hashim now moved on to the feet. The massive pads of corrupted flesh yielded easily to his scalpel. He sliced away at the interdigital cleft between the two great claws of the cloven hoof to better visualise the surface of the skin in this area. No blisters or erosions were present.

He examined the next foot. Immediately, Hashim noticed a large unruptured vesicle at the top of the cleft where the horn thins and becomes skin. The beige wrinkled dome, about two centimetres across, resembled a small walnut. Carefully dissecting around the perimeter, Hashim dug deep into the flesh to make sure that the virus buried in the tissue would also be liberated.

On each of the remaining feet, intact blisters and gaping bloody erosions on the surface could be seen. Hashim dissected them all out with great care and assembled the virulent mass of flesh on the bench.

Walking around the carcass, as a vulture stalks its still living prey, Hashim picked his next target carefully. The udders were warty and wrinkled. Blackened ulcers capped the teats; their sensitive coverings of skin were torn away, revealing necrotic tissue beneath. The occasional pristine white rounded vesicles could still be seen. Silently, Hashim collected both prizes and added them to his collection.

After more than an hour's toil, Hashim lent against the bench with his arms outstretched, head buried in his chest, exhausted. Rivulets of sweat trickled down his scalp and neck and disappeared beneath his collar. Underneath the bench stood the twenty-odd litres of blood, urine and milk collected by Kareem on his orders.

Hashim took a step back from his work and rested. Hands on his hips, he cocked his head to one side and gazed up at the suspended beast. The cow looked like an obscene unfinished three-dimensional jigsaw puzzle, with the last pieces to be added laid out on the table before him. Alone in the eerie half-lit warehouse, Hashim felt the hairs on the back of his neck stand up.

Crucified, bloody from its wounds, and with its sins displayed before it on the table, the beast eyed its tormentor with dull dead eyes.

In life it had provided sustenance and toil; in death its gift was damnation.

Hashim was nearly done. He went to the wall and untied the guy rope, which slid quickly through his hands, almost burning him, as the cow plummeted to the ground and landed with a thump.

Chapter 4

Exhausted by the activities of the previous night, Hashim slept soundly on a camp bed in the front office. Hidden behind the reception desk, no one would see him if they happened to glance through the window. Anyway, the office would be closed today for the Independence Day holiday.

Hashim looked at his watch. It was 9:20 A.M.

The room warmed rapidly as the sun blazed outside.

Rising from the bed Hashim switched on the air conditioner and felt a welcome blast of cool air on his face as the ageing device groaned into life. He wedged the connecting door to the warehouse open, hoping that some of the cool air would permeate through to the fetid atmosphere beyond.

In the warehouse everything was as he had left it the night before. Hashim opened some of the cardboard cartons stacked against the far wall. He groped inside and pulled his treasure free from the ocean of Styrofoam chips.

In minutes, four polypropylene spheres about twenty-five centimetres in diameter stood on the floor. The bottom half of each sphere was blue and slightly flattened at the base to form a stand. A spigot controlled by a small plastic tap emerged from one side. The upper hemisphere was transparent and moulded so as to form a handle. Hashim transferred the desiccators to the wooden bench.

Hashim attached a long length of rubber tubing to the auxiliary water tap on the wall. The other end was threaded through the iron grille covering the drain in the corner of the room. Four plastic T-junctions emerged from the rubber pipe close to where it was attached to the tap. These provided the connection points for each of the desiccators.

The infected tissue had to be dried quickly to stop the flesh decomposing and prevent the virus being inactivated.

When the tap was turned on the flow of water down the main tube sucked the air from the sealed hemispheres creating a partial vacuum. This enhanced the drying process.

The desiccators opened easily in the absence of a vacuum. The blue base was separated from the transparent cover by a thin perforated aluminium plate, which acted as floor inside the tiny spherical chamber. Removing the metal plate from each of the desiccators, Hashim lifted a large polypropylene drum from the floor and opened it.

White crystalline beads cascaded from the drum as Hashim filled the bottom half of each desiccator. Some of the beads were flecked with blue and pink. Cobalt chloride added to the beads indicated when they had become saturated with moisture. When the colour changed from blue to pale pink the beads became useless and required baking in an oven to drive off the water before they could be reused. Filling the base section nearly brimful, Hashim replaced the perforated floor and attached the cover.

Hashim checked the glass dish filled with dissected flesh. Overnight the pads of paper towels had become sodden with fluid that had wept from the skin and tissue. Peeling the paper off with his fingertips he cut the stiff and shrunken lumps of meat into small cubes about one centimetre square, and dropped them into a large glass beaker. He continued until he had filled four beakers.

Hashim wiped his filthy, numb, and foul smelling hands on a towel, leaving it streaked with blood and tiny gobs of flesh.

Removing the lid from one of the desiccators, Hashim picked up a beaker of cubed flesh and placed it in the centre of the perforated metal disk that comprised the floor. Holding the transparent dome in one hand he turned it upside down, applying a thin smear of Vaseline around the rim where a thin black rubber O-ring was embedded. He repeated this with the other desiccator units.

Taking the upper dome carefully in both hands he positioned it so that it exactly matched its lower counterpart. A little pressure applied with his hands created a seal. He attached the spigots to the T-junctions by short lengths of tubing.

At last he was ready.

Turning the tap open as far as it would go the water surged down the tubing and into the drain. The desiccators made a whooshing sound as the air was progressively sucked out. Hashim applied pressure to each of the transparent domes, watching the Vaseline coated O-ring as it turned from a dull irregular black line to a continuous circle of shiny black indicating that the seal had taken and a vacuum had been formed successfully.

The whooshing sound subsided. After several minutes, Hashim closed off the spigots, trapping the vacuum inside the desiccators. The silica gel worked more effectively under low pressure. In a few days the flesh would be completely dry and ready for the next stage.

Hashim now had to deal with the blood, urine and milk. These highly infectious materials had to be treated somewhat differently from the solid tissue.

The bucket of blood had almost completely congealed during the journey from the countryside and after being left at room temperature overnight. The dull crimson red clot adhered tightly to the sides of the bucket. Using a stainless steel ruler, Hashim scraped around the edge of the clot allowing it to fall way from the sides of the bucket. With his bare hands, he picked up the fragments of the clot and discarded them.

The residue in the bucket was a straw-coloured glutinous fluid, streaked pink with haemoglobin leaking from ruptured blood cells. The serum contained a host of natural proteins that would coat the virus and protect it from damage during the drying process.

From the original twenty litres of blood, Hashim collected ten litres of serum, which he poured into a shallow tray similar to those used by photographers to process film. The tray was filled to a depth of five centimetres. Hashim took out a large flat packet from underneath the bench and checked the label under the pallid light.

Chromatography paper, 17 Chr, 46 x 57 cm, 100 sheets

He tore the box open and tipped the contents out on to the floor. Encased in a plastic sheath lay a thick pad of virgin white blotting paper.

Next, he took a coil of plastic-coated washing line from under the bench and strung it across the corner of the room from steel eyelets screwed into the wall. Tying one end off securely, he paced out four metres letting the line thread through his fingers as the excess trailed on the ground behind him.

Feeling the rough surface of the breezeblock wall in the half-light he groped for the other eyelet. Finding it he threaded the line through the narrow hole and pulled it tight. It would have to support a considerable amount of weight and he did not want the line to sag too much. He looped the line back on itself to form a simple yet secure slipknot.

Returning to the desk he picked up his first sheet of blotting paper. It was thick and heavy; its rough slightly dimpled surface reminded him of vellum and old parchments. Holding the large sheet by its corners he stretched it taut between his fingertips and dipped it into the liquid. Immediately it began to draw up the fluid, changing colour as it did so to a pale greenish-yellow. Hashim laid the entire sheet onto the surface of the liquid for a few seconds. Leaving a dry margin of about five centimetres at the top to make handling easier he withdrew the paper from the tray.

Meticulously, Hashim had calculated his needs. The absorbent paper, 0.92 mm thick, seemed to drink the liquid. With a fluid-holding capacity of nine hundred grammes of water per square metre, the single sheet he held in his hands could absorb over two litres. As the serum was much more viscous than water, Hashim knew it could absorb not more than one litre before it became unmanageably heavy. With only ten sheets he could mop up the entire contents of the tray.

Wrapping the dry upper margin of the papers over the washing line he secured them in place with a pair of plastic clothes pegs.

He treated the urine and milk in the same way.

Working continuously in the poorly ventilated gloom, Hashim was finished by midday. As he rested the death-laden papers dried slowly.

At eight o'clock in the evening all was ready. A thick mat of yellowed wrinkled papers sat on the wooden bench. Hashim mentally calculated his load — ten papers soaked with serum, three with urine and two with milk. The milk- and urine-soaked papers had started to smell.

Badly.

Bacteria in the atmosphere were turning the urea into ammonia, while heat and oxygen had already turned the milk fats rancid. Hashim had anticipated this and come prepared. He pulled another large container from underneath the bench and inspected the label.

Activated charcoal

A cloud of microscopic black dust particles raced into the air, as Hashim unscrewed the lid. He watched as they swirled and danced in the half-lit gloom. He pulled the first paper on the pile into the centre of the table and tipped a generous pile of the amorphous black dust onto it. With his fingers working in circular motions he coated the entire surface of the paper until the charcoal had been ingrained deeply. Turning the paper over he repeated the process on the other side.

One-by-one the remaining papers were anointed in similar fashion. The massive surface area and absorbent properties of the charcoal particles effectively eliminated any odour. Taking five of the sheets together Hashim rolled them into a tight tube. The blackened parchments crinkled loudly.

When he had finished, the stiff tube was about ten centimetres in diameter. Hashim wrapped it in a large sheet of clingfilm. The charcoal would work for a while but it was not a perfect solution to the problem of decomposition. Sooner or later the smell would become overpowering.

With the wrapping complete Hashim took a large diameter mailing tube and pushed the package inside. It was a snug fit. Before snapping the plastic bung in place Hashim added a small muslin bag of silica gel and charcoal. They would help keep the contents dry and odour-free during its journey.

The remaining sheets were packaged in the same way. Hashim made sure that the milk-soaked sheets were packed together. If the smell of rancid fat or urine attracted attention, the other packages had a chance of getting through undetected. By nine-thirty, three neatly packaged tubes lay on the desk. The only hint to their contents was a few smudged fingerprints on the exterior of the brown cardboard tubes.

Hashim was startled when the Driver and Passenger returned thirty minutes later. During the course of the day he had grown used to the silence of his own company. The men had entered noiselessly through the front office and were now framed in the door of the warehouse. Both men had changed clothes since Hashim had last seen them. They now wore dirty white overalls and looked like car mechanics. They would be able to pass unnoticed in the warren of back street car repair shops, locksmiths, scrap metal dealers and courier services that occupied many of the premises in the district.

The Passenger held an object wrapped in brown paper neatly tied with string.

“You’re late,” said Hashim, a little on edge. “I expected you hours ago.”

Hashim had been working alone without food for hours now, not daring to go out, lest he arouse suspicion. As an ethnic Balti minority in a largely Balochi and Pashto speaking part of the country, he wanted to keep as low profile as possible. Even something as simple as asking for directions or buying cholay chat from a street hawker would be enough for someone to question his accent and remember his face should anyone enquire later. He was so close and had come too far to risk ruining his mission at this late stage.

"Did you bring it?"

The Passenger waved his package awkwardly in the air.

"I have spare blades, as well," replied the Passenger, unwrapping the butcher's saw and axe on the table.

"Get to work on the carcass first. I have finished with it."

The Passenger crossed the room and knelt over the beast. The head had been nearly severed when Kareem had slit its throat back at the village, so he decided to finish the job first. He set to work with the saw. The white ribbed tube of the oesophagus was clearly visible, now dry and tough as bamboo. It grated as he cut and the Passenger instinctively felt a lump in his throat. He struggled to swallow as he imagined someone doing the same to him.

Emerging from the back of the cartilage, the saw caught on the bony ventral surface of the neck vertebrae. The Passenger twisted and wiggled the blade, pushing the thick flesh to one side, so that he could bypass the bone and cut through the thin intervertebral disk instead. Tossing the severed head to one side he stood and surveyed the task ahead with a sigh. He picked up the axe.

Standing on one side of the beast, he placed his right foot on the animal's upper left forelimb and pressed down with all his weight so that the carcass gradually slid over on to its back with its legs protruding into the air.

Astride the beast now, legs either side of the belly, the Passenger bore down with the axe on the tip of the spine where it emerged from the bloody stump.

Crack!

Splinters of bone flew on to the tarpaulin.

Crack!

A wedge of flesh was dislodged and adhered to the axe head.

Crack!

A thirty-centimetre gap opened up down the animal's back.

After a dozen or more strokes the Passenger had cleaved his way through to the coccyx.

The Driver watched the performance lolled against the wall. He grabbed the remains of the dissected head by one of its ears and pulled a plastic refuse bag over it. He double bagged it and threw it on to the edge of the tarpaulin. Picking up the discarded saw he cut through the flesh of the shoulders and the haunches exposing the ball and socket joints at the top of the radius and tibia, respectively.

The Passenger wielded the axe high above his head and smashed it into the narrow gap made by the saw. With a crunch the legs started to sag under their own weight, as the splintered socket no longer supported them. As the Passenger cut, the Driver pulled and twisted. The innermost flesh of the carcass was moist and it squelched as the men continued dismembering.

With a cry of surprise, the Driver fell backwards, still grasping the freshly severed front leg. Dusting himself down, he threw the limb onto the tarpaulin next to the bag containing the head.

After ninety minutes the carcass had been rendered into a range of smaller pieces. A row of black plastic bags of various shapes and sizes sat on the tarpaulin.

Hashim was dismayed at the pleasure the men derived from the dismembering of the cow. He disliked physical violence of any kind. The intellectual stimulation, the planning and the logistics of the operation were more than enough for him. This unpleasantness was temporary and had to be tolerated for the greater good.

When the carcass had been dismembered the men cleaned the car. Using a bucket of Virkon disinfectant and a sponge the Driver washed the SUV from the inside out. The luggage storage area in the rear was especially well washed, as were the wheel arches, suspension and tyres. In thirty minutes the car was dripping wet and pristine.

Opening the metal screen briefly, the Driver drove the car out into the narrow back street. Keeping the windows and doors wide open, the cool, evening breeze wafted gently inside, drying and freshening the stale interior.

While the car was outside the tarpaulin was washed down with Virkon, rinsed with water, and rolled up. Each of the bags of flesh were splashed with a bucket of the disinfectant and loaded into the back of the SUV.

Hashim disconnected the desiccators from their umbilical cords of rubbing tubing, making sure the taps on the spigots were firmly closed so as not to break the vacuum seal. One-by-one he carried them to the car and placed them on the back seat.

Finally, after sluicing down the table and walls with more Virkon and hosing the floor, the men were ready to leave. The air was thick and moist with the slightly perfumed smell of the disinfectant. It would dissipate overnight.

By morning, when the first workers arrived, nothing would seem out of place. By timing their activities to coincide with the public holiday fewer people would be involved.

The Driver and Passenger left the warehouse by the rear exit and took their places in the car. Hashim lowered the metal screen after them and secured the door behind it.

With a final glance inside the warehouse he switched off the lights and the air-conditioner, and closed the door.

The car had crept around the narrow back alley and Hashim could hear it humming gently through the front door. Hashim got in the back clutching the mailing tubes tightly to his chest. The car powered forward into the night.

No one looked back.

They had a long drive ahead of them. It was over seven hundred kilometres to Karachi, and Hashim wanted to be at the central post office when it opened the next morning. The Karachi safe house would not be available until mid-morning. He would hole-up there for a few days while the desiccators dried out the remaining infected tissue. The Professor would have all the materials he needed to handle the residue safely.

From his seat behind the Passenger, Hashim finally felt a sense of accomplishment. His head throbbed and he was starving. Nevertheless a warm glow of pride filled his chest and his face creased into a satisfied smile. The rhythmic bounce of the suspension was soothing and Hashim drifted off to sleep. Fighting the sensation, he clung to reality for a few more seconds, long enough to reflect on how smoothly the operation had gone.

His superiors would be pleased, especially as he managed to fulfil the mission within budget. The allowance of two thousand US dollars had been well spent.

In his mind, Hashim totalled his expenses on the project.

Purchase of infected cow	$100
Desiccators (4 pieces)	$636
Silica gel (5 kg)	$115
Activated charcoal (1 kg)	$25
Chromatography paper (1 box)	$175
Mailing tubes (3 pieces)	$6
International speed post (Pakistan to Germany)	
Tubes	$41
Package	$13
Courier transport (Germany to USA)	
Tubes	$144
Package	$48
Fuel	$50
Bribe to warehouse foreman	$100
Miscellaneous (food, baksheesh, etc)	$25
Grand total	$1,478

Hashim smiled in his sleep as he calculated the cost of the damage divided by the capital outlay. The figure was astonishing. What was more, most of the equipment and reagents could be re-used.

If I fail others will follow.

Six hours later, on the Quetta to Khuzdar section of the N25, the golden sun broke the horizon. Ahead of them, in the distance, the Sulaiman and Kirthar Ranges formed an unbroken chain as far as the eye could see. They had made good time.

Still sixteen hundred metres above sea level, the interior of the car began to warm and Hashim stirred from his nap. Stiff from having to sleep in an upright position, he interlocked the fingers of both hands behind his head and massaged the nape of the neck with his palms. His finger joints cracked as he stretched.

The shadows of the low hills in the foreground melted away. Purples gave way to greys and finally to ripe yellows and greens as the landscape erupted from its slumber.

The deserted countryside was astonishingly beautiful. Wild olive trees speckled the higher slopes, whilst tamarisk and dwarf palms hugged the uncultivated parts of the valleys. Acacia, parpuk and guggul occurred in intermittent groves between the orchards of pomegranate and apricot. Stands of hawe, gorkha, and kashum grass had been left to grow and would be reaped for fodder later in the year.

Hashim wound down the window and breathed the clean air deep into his lungs. The rush of air tousled his hair and blew the sleep from his eyes. A *nambi* wind from the south blew in his face. Rain would be coming soon.

Wide-awake and happy for what seemed like the first time in months, he grinned from ear to ear.

This is why we do it.

"How long before we reach Karachi?" he called to the Driver.

"Another four or five hours."

"Good."

They would be late by several hours. Hashim didn't mind. Not now. The car sped along, alone on the empty two-lane highway.

Picking up one of the tubes, Hashim caressed it lovingly. He started to beat out a muffled tune with his fingers. The tube reverberated with the sound. A tune his mother had taught him by the fireside years ago.

Chapter 5

Philip Yeung awoke as usual at 6:45 A.M. His wife, Winnie, lay on the far side of the bed whilst Mei Ling, their daughter, occupied the middle. Philip looked at them as they slept soundly. He smiled.

God, they're beautiful.

Philip rose and negotiated the path to the bathroom easily. While his wife and daughter slept he would shower, dress and fix breakfast for himself.

The journey on the MTR underground railway from his home in the noisy and polluted back streets of Mongkok to the gleaming office of his biotech start-up company on the other side of Kowloon usually took about twenty-five minutes. On the way he read and corrected some correspondence and manuscripts, more often than not leaning against the carriage door, crushed by the morning rush hour commuters.

He couldn't wait to reach his office. The picture window faced the now disused Kai Tak airport and afforded spectacular views of Victoria Harbour beyond. On rare clear days he could see Victoria Peak in the distance. Today, however, the air was thick and muggy. A pall of smog hung over the harbour, stabilised by a slow-moving anticyclone over southern China. In the past few days that same weather system had swept in fumes and dust from the industrial heartland of the Pearl River delta immediately beyond Hong Kong's border with the mainland. By 9:15 A.M., with the sun already high in the sky, the air over the harbour had a pronounced yellowish tinge.

Philip didn't want to be outside today. The temperature was already thirty degrees Celsius and the humidity was a suffocating ninety percent. He would have to endure weeks more of this before the choking atmosphere became tolerable again towards the end of October.

The air-conditioning was humming loudly as Philip entered his office. The sweat in the small of his back seemed to freeze as he took off his jacket and draped it over the back of his chair. His shirt clung to him like a wet rag.

Philip's mail had already been delivered to his desk and lay in a neat pile in front of him. White A4-sized envelopes containing promotional offers from scientific equipment and reagent distributors lay on the bottom, destined to be unread and consigned to the oblivion of the waste-paper basket. Invoices for outstanding payments had been opened and marked for his approval. Private and confidential letters lay untouched on the top along with urgent fax messages printed out by his secretary.

As project manager in charge of research and development, Philip had a roving brief within the small company. Find a niche, an unresolved problem in the veterinary and human diagnostics field, and exploit it. The company had invested heavily in obtaining the license for a little known nucleic acid amplification assay, a rival to the polymerase chain reaction, and hoped to develop novel tests where its speed and flexibility would allow it to compete with the low cost and ease of use of the rival technique. The company had spent a lot of time researching a handful of applications and the Swiss pharmaceutical giant from whom they had obtained the license were pushing them to launch a product so they could reap some of the royalties.

Today was the Big Day. The data from the independent trial of their new foot-and-mouth disease assay was being sent from their field officer in the United Kingdom. The trial had been conducted at the Animal Health Institute in Gloucestershire, the world's top institute for veterinary diseases. A positive endorsement from them would be worth its weight in gold.

Philip flicked through the pile of mail, his eyes alighting on the fax instantly. The large shield emblem of the Animal Health Institute along with its Latin motto, *pro bono publico*, announced itself loudly from the top left hand corner of the page.

This was it.

Philip snatched it up and began to read, barely able to contain himself. Months of work and hundreds of thousands of dollars rode on the scant two paragraphs before him.

"Dear Dr. Yeung...." read Philip, "With reference to the performance of the DiaQuik Rapid Foot-and-Mouth Disease Detection System evaluated recently by the Animal Health Institute, we are pleased...."

"Yes!" cried Philip, jumping up from his seat. He punched the air in jubilation. Looking through the half-closed Venetian blinds to the outer office, he saw the other staff watching his antics with bemused fascination. Philip faced them with the fax held up in one hand and pointing to it with vigorous stabbing gestures with the other. Some of them got the message and gave the thumbs up sign. Philip continued reading...

> *...pleased to announce that, subject to adequate demonstration of the specificity and sensitivity of this system in determining the infection status of a suitable number of test animals as per recommendations of the Office International des Épizooties (OIE), this test system satisfies the basic criteria for the detection of all known serotypes of the foot-and-mouth disease virus. In particular we note the absence of interference by clinically relevant pathogens commonly confused with the foot-and-mouth disease virus. As a result, we have no hesitation in recommending this assay to the relevant committee of the OIE at its next annual meeting as an acceptable alternative to existing antibody and nucleic acid based methods of detection.*
>
> *We look forward to receiving your additional data with regard to specificity and sensitivity as noted above in due course. You are referred to Chapter I.1.3 (Principles of validation of diagnostic assays for infectious diseases) in the latest edition of the OIE Manual of Standards for Diagnostic Tests and Vaccines for information on how to collect the additional data requested.*

Please find attached an Appendix containing the results of the tests conducted at AHI. If you have any queries on any aspect of the tests, the results obtained or the methodology used, you are welcome to contact me for further details.

Sincerely,

Paul S. Caine, MSc, VetMB, MRCVS, PhD
Director, Department of Virology

Short and sweet, just the way Philip liked it.

The field tests suggested by AHI would involve at least one thousand animals known to be infected with the virus and a further five hundred known to be free from disease. Only then could statistically significant data on the diagnostic specificity and sensitivity of the new assay be obtained.

AHI had the world's largest reference bank of foot-and-mouth disease viruses covering each of the seven major serotypes or strains. The samples went all the way back to an outbreak in the United Kingdom in 1922-1924 and included every major and most of the minor outbreaks around the world since. If AHI said a new assay was able to detect the virus adequately that was just about the best recommendation available.

The relief in the conference room later that day was almost palpable as Philip relayed the information to the other senior managers and directors. Photocopies of the appendix had been circulated to them before the meeting and the heavily thumbed and annotated pages lay spread out on the conference table.

"How soon can we incorporate this data into another manuscript?" asked David Wan, the CEO and largest shareholder in AsiaBioTek Limited. A scientist and self-made businessman, Wan was always looking ways to boost the small company's credibility with potential investors

"Give me a couple of weeks," answered Paul. "I'll do it after the US conference. That way I can get some feedback from some of the FMD big boys at Ames and Plum Island."

Ames was the United States Department of Agriculture National Veterinary Laboratories Services in Ames, Iowa. Plum Island, located off the northeastern tip of Long Island, New York, housed the Foreign Animal Disease Diagnostic Laboratory, the United States' premier defence against dangerous animal pathogens.

The staff at these institutes were acknowledged as some of the finest veterinary experts in the world. This reputation was enhanced by the fact that the US had not seen a foot-and-mouth disease outbreak since 1929, despite the fact that both Mexico and Canada had only been able to control the disease decades later.

"Where was our other paper on this test published?" asked Wan.

"*Biochemistry Today*. It came out in March," replied Philip. "But that was only the preliminary data, essentially just a proof of concept. The new manuscript will be more detailed and include the results from a wider range of test samples."

"We need to push this new assay hard at the conference," continued Wan. "Make sure these results are added to your presentation. We need to convince as many people there as we can that this new test is the best – bar none."

"Does the new test really cover all the different strains?"

All eyes turned to the source of the query. Shirley Cheung, head of the cancer diagnostics division, looked up from her copy of the fax, her brow lined with a frown. "It seems the SAT-2 scores are equivocal."

"As you can see from the summary table on the last page," replied Philip, annoyed that his authority was being questioned, "all seven serotypes are clearly positive. Check the column on the far right. See? Serotype A represented by the Brazilian and Indian isolates, serotype Asia-1 again from India, serotype C from Iraq and the Middle East, serotype O from the United Kingdom 2001 outbreak and the South African Territories serotypes one, two and three – all positive. Admittedly, there were not many SAT-2 isolates in the AHI databank to test compared with the others, but the data are still very convincing. We will have no trouble selling these results at the conference."

Philip looked at Shirley quizzically raising an eyebrow, daring her to follow up her initial query. Shirley's tightly closed mouth broke into the faintest of smirks, the corners tilting up almost imperceptibly. Philip noticed and looked away, accepting her defeat graciously. Her time would come at the next meeting, when she discussed the latest breast cancer trial data, with which Philip had not been following as closely as he ought. He knew he was bound to ask a trivial question.

The sparring over, the conversation drifted to other topics and about Philip's personal preparations for the conference. Accommodation had been arranged at the meeting venue, where the other speakers would be housed, maximising the amount of time for networking between lectures. A quick Internet search produced the name of a door-to-door shuttle bus service from the airport direct to the hotel, eliminating the need to rent a car.

Philip would be gone for at least five days, and up to seven at the most, depending on whether he could swing a couple of invitations to present his lecture again to some private companies or tag along on a visit to the new National Veterinary Services Laboratory facility in San Francisco. In any case, he would be back for Mei Ling's fourth birthday.

He reminded himself to bring back a special gift from America.

Chapter 6

It was mid-morning when Hashim left the Pakistan Post Office in central Karachi. The office was busy due to a rush of customers following the previous day's public holiday.

Surface air lifted packages from Pakistan to Germany cost 775 rupees per kilo and took eight to fifteen days to reach their destination. That was too long. The virus might not survive the trip, especially in the crippling heat of the unventilated warehouses the tubes would be subjected too whilst waiting to be dispatched. International speed post was the quicker, yet more expensive, alternative. At 1,050 rupees for the same package the journey took less than one week.

After visiting the Post Office Hashim went to the Professor's house to prepare the highly infectious tissue that was still drying in the desiccators. Another twenty-four hours and they would be ready. The Professor would put him up until the samples could be processed. A phone call earlier in the week confirmed that all the necessary materials had been assembled.

Hashim did not know if the man he would visit was actually a Professor. After all, the name by which he was known to the others was also a code. Hashim – destroyer of evil. Whatever his true background, he guessed the Professor was an educated and distinguished man, judging by his general speech and demeanour from the few brief conversations they had had.

What had the Professor thought about him? The idea intrigued him during the fifteen-minute tuk-tuk ride to the suburbs of Karachi and the relatively well-to-do area of Clifton.

The Freelander was parked in the driveway of the ageing two-storey villa as the tuk-tuk pulled up outside. Hashim's colleagues had left him at the Post Office in order to deliver the desiccators.

Hashim walked to the rear of the building and rapped on the back door. A large white-haired man dressed immaculately in a freshly laundered and pressed shalwar kameez opened it almost immediately. The man smiled broadly, his round jovial face a picture of conviviality.

"My dear Mr. Hashim," he boomed. "Do please come in. Your colleagues are already here."

Hashim recognised the stentorian voice of the Professor instantly and stepped into the house. The back door led into a small but well-appointed kitchen. From the kitchen, a narrow passage led to the living room. Inside, Hashim found the Driver slouched in a chair, a half-folded newspaper in one had, a cigarette in the other. A plume of pale blue smoke curled effortlessly from its tip toward the ceiling.

The Passenger stood in one corner and raised a hand in greeting, keeping one eye on the television, which was tuned to a live broadcast of a local cricket match.

"I was commenting to your friends on how I expected you much earlier," said the Professor. "I'm afraid I must leave you now. I have a class this afternoon and then some errands to which I simply must attend. Please forgive my lack of a more hospitable welcome. In the evening I shall return and we shall talk some more. In the meantime, my home is yours. Please make yourselves comfortable."

Hashim realised the Professor was the genuine article after all. Maybe that was how he obtained the equipment he needed so easily.

The hours passed swiftly; watching cricket and drinking tea absorbed much of the time. At six the Professor returned. He rushed into the living room, breathless and sweating profusely.

"I have been talking to certain people," he stammered, barely able to get the words out, "who seem to think it would be in everyone's best interest if our involvement in this project were concluded as soon as possible."

"What's the problem?" enquired the Driver, sitting up on the edge of his chair.

"Apparently, there are rumours going around that people are being paid over the odds to report their diseased livestock to the authorities. My contact in the agriculture department says he has never seen anything like it. People are calling him up from literally everywhere demanding to be paid up front just for information on where he can find lame and diseased animals. He says there is pandemonium in the countryside. Everyone is talking about it. Under the circumstances, our people feel we have overplayed our hand and need to finish up here as soon as possible."

The Driver sat back in his chair sheepishly.

Turning to Hashim, the Professor continued, "I examined your tissue samples earlier when your friends brought them here. It is my opinion they are suitable for further processing now."

"Now?" answered Hashim.

"Now," the Professor replied firmly. "Immediately, in fact. Come with me and I will show you where to go."

Leading the way, the Professor climbed the narrow staircase to the upper floor. At the end of the hallway stood a white door.

"In there you will find everything you need. A sanitary hood, gloves, scalpel and tweezers."

"What about the icing sugar?" said Hashim.

"Yes, I almost forgot. A packet of icing sugar."

"Good. I will need an hour at the most. We shall post them tomorrow morning."

Hashim entered the room alone and switched on the light A wooden bench spanned the width of the room. On it stood a rectangular box made of transparent plastic, into which two large portholes had been fitted. Hashim sniffed. This was the sanitary hood the Professor had mentioned.

The homemade sterile chamber permitted toxic materials placed inside to be handled safely by way of airtight openings in one side to which were attached a pair of latex gloves. The operator stood outside the box, inserting his hands into the gloves, allowing him to manipulate the contents of the hood.

The desiccators sat in a row inside the box. The silica gel in the base had turned pink. It had worked. The infected tissues were now dry and ready to be processed further.

Hashim guessed the Professor had probably stolen or misappropriated the sanitary hood from where he worked, along with most of the other items he saw displayed inside the box.

An old swivel chair, its crimson fabric seat worn and tattered in places, sat in front of the bench. Hashim sat down and adjusted the height of the seat until he could see comfortably inside the box. Slipping his hands inside the limp creamy latex gloves he flexed his fingers and interlocked them pulling the sheer material tight into the fleshy areas between his fingers.

He touched each piece of the equipment arrayed before him, rearranging them minutely, getting to know their position precisely. The delicate task ahead required his utmost concentration. Positioning a flat Pyrex dish on his right hand side, he pulled the first desiccator toward him.

The sphere gasped as he turned the spigot tap and released the vacuum. Twisting the lid slightly, the greased surfaces slid apart easily. Hashim laid them to one side and gently removed the beaker containing the brown cubed pieces of tissue. He repeated the process with the remaining desiccators; each sphere inhaled deeply with a hiss as the spigot taps were turned. The rush of air into the desiccators caused the dry cubes to dance and rattle within their beakers. Hardened and mummified, the tiny irregular-shaped stones of death clinked audibly against the sides of the glass.

Hashim tipped the contents of each beaker into the Pyrex dish. He cut the largest pieces in half with a scalpel, making sure all the fragments were approximately the same size. He took great care to ensure the blade did not slip and slice through the thin membrane of his gloves. Although the virus was not transmissible to humans he did not want it escaping into the room beyond. He sifted through the heap of pebbles with the tip of the scalpel, occasionally chopping an errant cube in half. In a few minutes he was done.

Reassembling the desiccators to give himself more room, Hashim was ready for the final processing step. He opened the packet of icing sugar and emptied it into the dish burying the dried cubes. He swirled the mixture with his fingers evenly coating all the pieces.

The high osmotic potential of the sugar together with the low water content of the dried tissue would retard bacterial growth for many days, even at room temperature.

Ten empty tubes of M&Ms stood in the corner, their garish packaging providing the only flash of colour in the white-grey sterility of the room. Hashim scooped up the sugar-coated cubes and shovelled them into the mouths of the tubes. The dried tissues had lost about ninety percent of their weight, leaving one hundred grams from the original one-kilogram mass he had prepared initially. With the added sugar he would have enough material to fill all the tubes to their approximate retail weight of fifty-five grams. Before capping the tubes he checked their weight on a small electronic balance, adding or subtracting portions of the mixture as necessary.

When all the tubes were filled correctly he pushed the glass dish and equipment to one side. Hashim stretched to reach a packet of antiseptic wipes that lay on the far side of the cramped plastic chamber. He wiped his hands thoroughly to remove the sugar and to inactivate any virus that adhered to them. When he was sure his gloves were clean he sealed the capped tubes with a strip of clear tape.

Hashim was sweating now. He had worked non-stop for nearly an hour. His head throbbed and his eyes ached from the constant close-up work inside the sanitary hood.

Taking five of the M&M tubes in each hand he withdrew his hands from the box and inverted the gloves so that the tubes were trapped inside the latex. The gloves bulged and looked as if they might split. Air trapped in the fingers inflated them into bizarre sausage shapes. Hashim tied off the latex behind the filled M&M tubes with string, isolating the contents of the box from the inverted gloves. He tied a second string around the latex about two centimetres away from the first. With a pair of scissors he cut the latex in between the tied pieces of string.

The inverted gloves, each containing five M&M tubes, fell to the ground. The amputated sleeves, sealed with another tie, retracted gently inside the box.

The gloves would be packaged individually and sent to the contact in Germany, timed to arrive a few days after the tubes of treated filter papers Hashim had posted that morning.

Hashim's job was done. He sat slumped in the chair, too tired to even pick up the bloated gloves from the floor.

He looked around him. Was this where it would end - a back street house in a suburb of Karachi? The drab walls seemed to close in on him. It seemed so anonymous and indefinite.

Perhaps it was for the best. The more links in the chain the more distant were the project organisers from the frontline.

Such was always the case in a war.

Chapter 7

The FedEx truck approached the barrier. After a brief delay the heavy gate jerked upwards and the truck passed underneath. As he had done many times before, the driver negotiated the speed bumps with care and manoeuvred the slow heavy vehicle around the lazily parked cars and tight corners of the Buena Vista apartment complex.

Block 13, apartment 101. That sounds familiar.

The truck approached the rear of the complex. Block 13 was the last building on the left before the perimeter fence, beyond which lay the tall grass and muddy swamp of the undeveloped St. Petersburg hinterland.

Hector Manuel parked the truck in a vacant lot immediately next to the entrance. He gathered up the packages in his arms, climbed down from the cabin headed into the building.

Ah, yes. I know this. First floor, first door on the left. Apartment 101.

He pushed the buzzer. A dull electronic tone sounded on the other side of the door. He waited a few seconds.

Damn this heat.

The hallway and lobby were not air-conditioned and opened directly on to the resident's parking lot through a wide arched entrance.

"Come on!" he muttered under his breath and banged on the door with his fist.

"FedEx. Delivery," he called through the door.

The door opened a chink, the security chain rattling loudly, and a dark hand extended out.

"You gotta sign for it, man," said Hector, speaking more to the door than to the hand.

The door closed and reopened. A tall thin man dressed in a grubby T-shirt and jeans emerged.

"I was here last week, wasn't I?" enquired Hector.

The man did not answer but took the pen proffered by Hector and signed his name, illegibly. Hector handed over the two document pouches, each bulging unevenly in the centre.

"Anyways. I hope they didn't melt," said Hector turning to leave.

"What?" said the man, surprising Hector with his sudden outburst.

"I hope they didn't melt. It says candies on the docket. I hope you can still enjoy them, what with this heat and all."

"Oh. Yeah. Thanks," mumbled the stranger.

"No problem," said Hector, already halfway to the exit. "Jackass," he added under his breath, making sure he was out of earshot.

What have you got to do to get some response from these people?

Inside the apartment, Husam al-Din, had already opened the packages. He finally understood the deliveryman's comments when he saw the neatly wrapped packages. He scrutinised the docket carefully.

Three days from Frankfurt to Florida, not bad.

Add about five days for the Pakistan to Germany leg and the samples were less than ten days old. The infectivity would not have decayed too much, as long as the instructions had been followed.

Now it was al-Din's turn for alchemy. There was no need now for sterility or undue care. Standing on the dining room table were seven large bottles of isotonic saline solution for contact lenses and an aerosol spray gun similar to those sold in garden supply stores for applying pesticides or humidifying green houses.

al-Din emptied the contents of one of the M&M tubes into a one-pint measuring jug. He did not know what to expect and as the small hard pellets tumbled into the jug a cloud of white powder billowed up. The pile of pellets barely reached a quarter-inch in depth. Unscrewing the top of the saline bottle, al-Din poured the solution over the pile. He stirred the mixture with a spoon and the pellets swirled in the opaque milky fluid. Soon, the fluid became slightly viscous as the sugar dissolved and the pellets gradually settled to the bottom.

He would leave the mixture in the fridge overnight in order to extract the maximum amount of virus.

In the fridge a large bucket of salty water occupied most of the lower section. The thick paper that had arrived earlier in the week had been reduced to black sludge and lay at the bottom, dense and immobile. He would decant the clear liquid tomorrow.

The paper residue might still be useful.

It would be interesting to dry it out and see if it retained infectivity when dispersed as a powder.

Chapter 8

"Excuse me, er...um, Laura," Caine said, as he leaned over the reception desk. "Where exactly is the conference being held today?"

Despite being dressed identically to the other female staff in navy blue blazers and white blouses, Caine could tell from the way the uniform clung to her curves that Laura McMann, Event Co-ordination Manager, had a great figure.

"The reception and keynote speech are in the Grand Assembly room on the second floor," replied the auburn-haired beauty with unruffled calm, for what was probably the thirtieth time that day. "The afternoon sessions are in Meeting Rooms One and Two and the poster session is in Salon A, also on the second floor."

"Thank you very much," said Caine, staring deep into her eyes.

"You're welcome," she returned, her eyes widening as she arched her eyebrows slightly, anticipating a follow-up question.

"And where might I find some entertainment around here?"

"That depends on what sort of entertainment you're looking for."

"Perhaps a quiet dinner and a few drinks, that sort of thing."

"You could try calling this number," said Laura, handing Caine a business card.

"What's this," said Caine, barely glancing at it before putting it in his pocket, "A club?"

"No. My home phone number."

***

The guests mingled awkwardly in the lobby of the Grand Assembly room on the second floor of the Regency International San Francisco.

A long table had been erected in front of a pair of double doors. Two uniformed receptionists presided over a long list of names, whilst another guarded the neatly laid out rows of laminated name badges. Registration for the Fourth National Symposium on Foreign and Exotic Veterinary Diseases had begun.

Paul Caine arrived almost last and picked his way through the milling crowd toward the reception table. A man in a uniform matching those of the receptionists was filming the proceedings with a small handheld video camera. Caine detested this recent development. Not only must he suffer the bored small talk of people he did not know, but also his unconvincing grimaces of feigned interest would now be recorded for posterity.

Bugger!

Caine noted the cameraman's face and name badge and made a mental note to avoid him over the next few days. A stills photographer was also making the rounds, snapping the meeting president and committee members chatting to the delegates. This was more tolerable and Caine actually looked forward to having his introductions recorded in a few carefully contrived snapshots.

Caine recognised some of the faces, mainly those of his American and European counterparts in the national veterinary health departments of their respective countries, with whom he had regular contact, at least by email and fax, if not in person. The Asian and African delegates were mostly unknown to him. Only recently had they joined the relatively expensive international meetings and stepped up their own national disease surveillance activities. When countries were unable to afford safe drinking water for their people it was difficult to justify sending delegates halfway around the world to discuss the minutiae of vaccinating cattle and poultry.

Caine wandered around the room, half-empty wine glass in hand. He aimed for the far end of the room nearest the stage from where the keynote speech would be made later. He thought he saw the bald pate of the meeting president, Jonas Williams, shining like a beacon and he headed toward it like a moth to a light bulb. After a few yards he could hear Williams engaged in conversation, stray words filtered through the murmuring crowd.

"Surveillance…vital…exciting results…published…look forward to seeing it."

The words drifted by, Williams was deep in conversation with a young girl who earnestly took down what he was saying in a notebook. Caine smiled to himself.

The vain old bugger still can't resist, can he?

Williams' renowned love affair with himself was conducted largely through the media.

Caine turned away and immediately found himself confronted by a mound of blonde hair. A small woman was engrossed in conversation with the meeting secretary, Bill Jacobs.

"I'm so sad to hear that, Bill," she said in a warm and comforting tone.

"Thank you, Shirley. It was a relief in the end. She suffered terribly in the final months. None of the painkillers seemed to do any good."

"I don't know how you had the strength to carry on organising this meeting, though."

"I had to. It was good for me to have something else to focus on towards the end. I must admit I had a lot of help from my students, you know, for the times when I really couldn't cope."

"You're a credit to the community, Bill."

"Hear, hear," chipped in Caine, who had been listening intently.

"Paul! So glad you could come," said Jacobs, looking up and extending a large hand in greeting. Caine took it and winced at the strength of the grip.

"Have you met Shirley Novak? Assistant professor at NYU. A good friend of mine from way back."

"We met once, a long time ago, I think," replied Caine, desperately trying to remember if in fact he had.

"I was just saying how well Bill has coped since Nancy passed away," said Novak. She turned to Jacobs, "You really should try to get out more."

"I intend to," he replied. "This is virtually my last official duty before retiring. After that I'm throwing away my mobile phone and taking off in an RV for a couple of months. I'm going to see all the things I meant to but never had the chance. You know I've lived here for almost twenty-five years and I've never gotten to see the Grand Canyon. Can you imagine that?"

"That makes two of us, and I've lived here a lot longer than that!" said Shirley.

"You know they charge Canadians extra to see it?" quipped Caine.

"You're kidding, right?" replied Jacobs. "I thought that was just Mexicans?"

The group laughed, oblivious to the hum of the video camera. Panning left, the cameraman focused on the Chinese delegation.

The three men and two women looked distinctly ill at ease. Occasionally one of them would mutter something inaudible to which the others responded with sideways glances and sly nods of the head. They seemed to be looking for someone.

It was not long before Caine noticed her. Tall, slim, elegant and aloof, the Chinese girl stood out from the other members of her group.

This will be a challenge.

He walked up to her.

"Hi. I'm Paul Caine, and you're Doctor...?" he looked in vain for her name badge.

"I'm afraid my colleague does not speak English," replied a small mousy woman in thick spectacles.

Caine turned to face the woman.

"We are from the Yunnan Veterinary Institute in China," she continued. "Perhaps you would like to speak to the institute director, Dr. Li? He speaks excellent English," she added matter-of-factly.

Not really.

"Erm, yes, why not?" Caine lied.

"I am very pleased to meet you," said Dr. Li. "It is not often that I have the opportunity of travelling overseas. My work at the institute keeps me very busy."

"What fields are you working on in Yunnan?" said Caine, trying to keep up an appearance of interest. He angled himself so that he could talk to the doctor and look at his stunning female companion at the same time.

"Mainly vaccine development and manufacture. Foot-and-mouth disease, Marek's disease, and a little research on some of the more exotic viruses, Nipah, for instance."

"As I was trying to say to your colleague, here, Dr...er...," Caine floundered, hoping the director would take the bait.

"Chen," replied Li. "She is not a doctor. She is temporarily attached to my institute as..." the doctor and the beautiful woman exchanged glances, "...as my personal assistant."

Christ. They're not an item, are they?

Caine turned to face Li, hoping his incredulity was not apparent.

"Dr. Caine," said Li, "I must say I am looking forward very much to your presentation. If you would now excuse me, they are some other guests I should like to meet."

"Of course," said Caine, as the entourage moved as one past him and into the throng of other delegates.

Caine watched the tight black trouser-clad buttocks of Ms. Chen disappear into the crowd.

That is someone I need to get to know better.

After a few minutes, the crowd began to fill the Grand Assembly room. At a little under half-full, the one hundred and fifty guests still made an impressive group. There was a flurry of activity on the stage, as the meeting organisers sat down behind a specially erected table. Taking the hint, the delegates began to sit in the rows of chairs arranged in front of the stage. Clusters of people formed spontaneously here and there, grouped loosely by geographical, racial or linguistic relationships, occasionally by a shared alma mater.

Caine searched for Li and his assistant. He saw them sitting together on the far left of the hall, two rows from the back. The dappled light from the chandeliers high above draped them in shadows. They each scanned the crowd before them voraciously. Their other companions were not present. Caine turned to look for them. The mousy woman in spectacles was on the same row as her colleagues but sitting on the opposite side of the hall. One of the men in the group sat by her side. The other man was nowhere to be seen. The hall was filling rapidly.

On stage, a hotel technician assisted Jonas Williams with the angle of the microphone and demonstrated the dimmer switch. Williams tested a laser pointer by shining it on the blank screen behind him.

Caine sat in the middle of the back row in one of the few remaining seats. Ms. Chen sat to his left a short distance away. He studied her porcelain profile, the small upturned nose, chin curving delicately to a point and prominent cheekbones. Her black collar-length hair caught the light, shimmering as she occasionally turned her head to talk to her companion.

The microphone boomed and the speakers crackled in response as the opening ceremony began. Jonas Williams stood centre-stage relishing another moment in the spotlight. Two photographers buzzed around him as he prepared to speak. Caine twisted his head for a better view. He recognised the official meeting photographer. The other was a hotel employee, making sure that the hotel logo displayed prominently on the lectern was visible in all the portraits of the professor. The shots would be used later to update the conference promotional literature issued by the hotel. Williams would be pleased that his hawk-like visage would probably be seen by millions on the hotel's corporate website.

Sated for the moment, the photographers withdrew, allowing Williams to begin. He fumbled with the dimmer switch, brightening the lights in the hall significantly before finding the level he desired. A slide illuminated the screen behind him announcing the title of the symposium.

"Ladies and gentlemen," Williams began. "It is with great pleasure that I welcome you all to the Fourth National Symposium on Foreign and Exotic Veterinary Diseases. It has been three years since our last gathering and what a lot has happened since then. Foot-and-mouth disease has reared its head in Europe, although we should not forget that it has always been an endemic disease in many parts of the developing world. Highly pathogenic avian influenza continues to afflict Southeast Asia and has been documented in South America for the first time, with devastating consequences. The economic cost of these diseases is, of course, considerable, but we should also not forget the social implications of disease outbreaks. Many tens of thousands of people around the world are dependent upon rearing livestock and their welfare is intimately linked to the success or failure of our attempts to limit or control infectious disease. Any policies we implement or recommend to Governments must be with their knowledge and consent.

"This is the first time the National Symposium has been held in San Francisco and we are grateful to our sponsors, such as BioHealth Vaccines and Bentley Diagnostics for financial support, and to the Regency International San Francisco for accommodating our participants. For the record, this is the largest ever National Symposium and it is in no small part due to the efforts of my friend and colleague Bill Jacobs, who has been instrumental in building support and momentum for these meetings in the intervening years."

A murmur of approval rippled around the hall as the spotlight moved swiftly to Bill Jacobs, seated on the stage beside the lectern. He smiled thinly and raised an arm in acknowledgment. His white shirt mirrored the pale yellow of the spotlight.

"We have a packed three days ahead of us," Williams continued. "Tonight we have the keynote speech, which, I am happy to say, will be presented by our old friend, Professor Abraham Frederickson, from the Royal Stockholm Institute of Veterinary Medicine. Tomorrow and the next day we will have sessions on clinical signs and symptoms, diagnostics, vaccines and the economic implications of disease. We will also have a case study of the British foot-and-mouth disease epidemic in 2001 given by Dr. Paul Caine of the Animal Health Institute and another on the H5N1 avian influenza outbreak in Hong Kong by Dr. Lai-san Lam of the Agriculture, Fisheries and Conservation Department."

Caine smiled to himself as his name was mentioned. This was his biggest presentation yet by far. Reese was right. This is definitely the way forward.

"And finally," Williams concluded, "please make a special effort to visit our sponsors' booths and to view the poster presentations submitted by our many younger scientists. Who knows, maybe in a few years one of them will be presenting the Fifth National Symposium? Thank you for your attention."

A brief round of applause echoed around the hall, as Williams stepped down from the dais. A tall white-haired gentleman strode across the stage toward the lectern with a sheaf of papers in his hands. As Professor Frederickson prepared to speak, Caine glanced around the room again. A sudden movement caught his attention. Ms. Chen had been watching him intently and had looked away quickly. Caine stared at her. Sure enough, after a few seconds, she glanced over her shoulder at him again. Caine smiled to himself before settling back in his chair and focusing on the presentation.

The keynote speech concluded with a thunderous round of applause for Professor Frederickson, who stood to one side of the lectern and bowed deeply in appreciation. Jonas Williams crossed from the side of the stage where he had been sitting with Bill Jacobs and shook his hand. Flashbulbs popped. Formalities over, the audience rose and drifted slowly out of the exits and into the lobby for the coffee break.

Caine looked over towards Dr. Li and Ms. Chen. The doctor was alone. Li picked up his briefcase and waited for a group of people to pass down the aisle before attempting to exit his row. Caine followed at a discreet distance, hoping to see if the bee would lead him to the honey.

Li waited in the lobby for a few seconds before the mousy woman and her male companion joined him. The third man arrived a few seconds later, apparently from deep within the conference hall. They conferred for a short while before shaking their heads. The third man looked at his watch and said something to the group, who then trooped off together toward the main exit and the hotel lobby on the ground floor.

Intrigued, Caine followed. He had fifteen minutes to spare before the next session started and the absence of Ms. Chen was puzzling him.

So much for being a personal assistant.

The group of Chinese walked solemnly down the stairs separating the business floors from the hotel reception area. At the foot of the stairs they paused, as if to get their bearings, and walked into the Atrium dining area, where they sat at the table nearest the entrance and observed the passers-by. Caine followed them but continued on and walked past the restaurant entrance. He looked inside as he passed, smiling and waving to the doctor and his group, as he was recognised instantly.

Unable to find Ms. Chen in the few minutes he had allowed himself, Caine returned to the auditorium for the rest of the day's lectures. There would be plenty of opportunity later that day to track her down.

He found her in the mid-afternoon poster session. One of the smaller salons had been turned into a viewing area for the young scientists' presentations. Large poster boards lined two walls and ran back-to-back down the centre of the room. Each board was five feet square and attached to a black tubular steel frame mounted on coasters. When not in use for scientific conferences and symposia, the boards could be wheeled into storage rooms or dismantled. Now they were regaled with abstruse musings on the kinetics of viral infection, the susceptibility of mouse models to various genetically recombined pathogens, the benefits of treatments X, Y and Z for bronchitis in sheep, and so on, all lavishly illustrated with the latest computer-generated illustrations.

Young scientists, in varying degrees of sobriety, stood by the posters conscientiously discussing their research findings with whosoever happened to be passing. The session was well attended, and several times Caine had to put his hands on a person's shoulders and excuse himself as he squeezed past in order to progress further into the room.

Ms. Chen was reading a poster describing the effect of an experimental neuraminidase inhibitor therapy in racehorses infected with equine influenza. Or rather, thought Caine, she was looking at the poster. From the expression on her face it was clear she was not absorbing its content. Instead, she appeared to be listening to the conversation of the group of people behind her. As her head began to cock to one side the illusion became more apparent.

Caine glanced at the group. Three young men, one western, the others of Middle Eastern appearance, stood with their back to Ms. Chen, less than two feet away. They talked volubly about their research, comparative sequence analysis of mycobacterium isolates in Iran. A strange topic on which to eavesdrop, thought Caine, as he continued watching.

"Paul!" the voice cried.

The large flabby hand of Bill Jacobs thundered down on Caine's shoulder.

"Glad to see you're taking an interest in the young 'uns," he said. "Take these guys, for instance," he continued, waving a hand in the general direction of the three men Caine had just been observing. "Some great work coming out of the Mareshi Institute in Lahore on sheep and equine diseases. I was there a couple of years ago and the head of the institute is getting quite a name for himself."

The three men stopped their conversation to listen to Jacobs. The two Pakistanis beamed when their institute was named.

"Dr. Jacobs?" said one, stepping forward from the group and holding up a camera. "May we have our photograph taken with you?"

"Sure, fellas. Why not?" obliged Jacobs. "Come on, Paul. Get over here too."

Jacobs draped one arm over Caine and the other over the young man who had requested the photo. His partner squeezed in beside him to make a tight grouping in front of their poster. Jacobs' blue-shirted bulk filled the frame. The westerner who had been talking with them took the camera and carefully composed his shot. Jacobs and the others grinned broadly. Caine smiled weakly.

"Ok," said the photographer. "One. Two. Three."

Click.

"Thank you very much, Dr. Jacobs," the young man said, shaking Jacobs warmly by the hand.

"No problem, guys," replied Jacobs affably.

Caine looked up and saw Ms. Chen smiling at him. He smiled back, recognising the fact that she was amused at his embarrassment. Disentangling himself from the group, he made to follow the young woman, but she had already disappeared into the throng.

***

It was early evening by the time he caught up with her again. Caine spotted her sitting alone in the Washington Lounge, a secluded bar in one corner of the hotel's dining complex, occupied by stout red leather armchairs and faux colonial style oak furniture.

Apart from a couple of middle-aged suits, who sat smoking cigars and discussing corporate strategy at one end, the lounge was empty.

As Caine looked on through an ivy-covered trellis that delineated the lounge, a waiter armed with a silver tray delivered an oversized cup and saucer, a porcelain creamer, and a bowl of brown cane sugar. Ms. Chen ignored the waiter and stared at a spot on the floor a few inches in front of her.

"That's a pretty impressive cup of cappuccino you've ordered for someone who doesn't speak English," he said, by way of introduction.

Startled, the woman looked up, and smiled wryly.

"Okay. My next guess is that you're not a scientist and you don't work at the Yunnan Veterinary Institute, or whatever it is. Am I right?"

Silence.

"Tough cookie, uh? Alright. If you're looking for someone, can I help? I know many of the delegates here, if not personally, then certainly by reputation."

"Thank you. No," the woman said finally. Her voice was soft and soothing yet had an air of authority about it. Caine sensed she was stressed and keeping something back.

"Are you waiting here for someone? Perhaps I can wait with you?" he offered, sliding into the seat opposite, without waiting for an answer.

The woman clasped her hands together gently; her vibrant plum-coloured nail polish glinted softly in the subdued lighting. A small handbag sat on the table by her elbow, on top of which sat the key to her room. Caine glanced down and noted her room number from the long rectangular fob.

Her pale wrists hinted at immense strength as she turned her hands to look at her watch. The face of the delicate Gucci timepiece was protected with a metal guard, which she turned aside with practised ease. She pursed her lips.

"I'm afraid my meeting has been cancelled. As has ours," she said. Rising to leave, she turned to Caine. "Perhaps on another occasion Dr. Caine, we could have had a longer conversation."

"I'm sure we could," he replied. "I look forward to trying again tomorrow."

"You don't give up easily, do you, Dr. Caine?"

"Not if the risk is worth taking in the first place."

Chen stopped and thought for a moment. "You are quite right, Dr. Caine. The risk has to be worth taking."

With that, she turned and walked out of the lounge. Caine sat staring at the untouched coffee, wondering what to make of Ms. Chen, the Chinese group in general and the other fragments of the day's events.

He felt inside his pocket and found Laura's business card. He downed the coffee in one gulp, and looked around for a payphone.

Chapter 9

"She's a beaut, ain't she?" said the fat man, wiping his ripe red melon of a head with a handkerchief too small and too wet from previous applications to be of any use.

"Ten years old, two hundred thousand on the clock. An old couple from Arizona part-exchanged it for an Escort last month. Very dry in Arizona. Not like here. Dry as a bone, yes sir. No rust. Solid as rock." The fat man banged the nearside fender with a closed fist for emphasis.

Husam al-Din slowly circled the ageing vehicle. The Toyota Corolla had seen better days certainly, but the anonymity it afforded was almost priceless. How many of these were on the roads at any given time? He only needed it for one, maybe two weeks at the most. What was another five thousand miles to this beast of burden? He stopped at the front of the vehicle and turned to the fat man.

"Yes, I like it, but the price, is how you say, too many?" he affected the voice of a newcomer.

"Well then, let me make you a deal," the fat man replied, keen to be rid of the troublesome vehicle.

"Your two thousand dollars is going to buy you the car of your dreams, a full tank of gas and a three month all parts warranty," he grinned. The effect was like looking at a grotesque Halloween pumpkin.

"Like I said," protested al-Din. "It is a lot of money for such an old car. I will give you twelve hundred dollars."

"Whoah. Now wait a second partner, I can't accept that. I've got overheads to consider. Tell you what, call it eighteen hundred and you can drive it away right now. Can't say fairer than that."

al-Din did not want to call attention to himself by haggling too hard. The fat man would remember any unpleasantness long after he had left. Better to let him win this one. It would make him feel good, ripping off an immigrant. Give him his fun.

"Alright mister..." he looked up at the sign hanging above the office door, "Weasel..., Weso..."

"Wesolowski," corrected the fat man. "A lot of people have trouble with that. Maybe I should change my name to Smith, waddya think?"

"I have no opinion in the matter," said al-Din dryly. "Can I pay you now? I am in a hurry."

The fat man led the way into his office and sat behind a large, untidy desk. It was nice to be out of the heat and humidity of the Florida summer.

"Well, let's get some of this paperwork out of the way, shall we?"

The fat man was very pleased with himself. Pleased to be selling a turkey that had been occupying valuable space for God knows how long, pleased to be making some money out of it, and pleased to be out of the heat.

al-Din put a small roll of cash on the desk in front of the fat man, who began to scribble furiously for some minutes on a variety of papers. Eventually, he looked up and smiled broadly.

"This is your receipt," he said, tearing a rectangular slip of paper from a small book and handing it to al-Din.

"This is your certificate of ownership or pink slip, with your name recorded. I hope the spelling is correct? And this," he rummaged beneath a pile of papers, before triumphantly producing a single creased sheet with a flourish, "is your temporary registration slip. The DMV will send you the official slip in the mail in a couple of weeks."

al-Din smiled. By the time the fake ID was discovered it would be too late. "Thank you, Mr. Wes-o-loff-ski," he said labouring the pronunciation.

"You're welcome, son," replied the fat man. Everyone became his son when they paid cash.

"Do you sell maps, also?" asked al-Din.

"What? Maps? No son, I'm afraid we don't. There's a gas station over the road. They're bound to a have a selection. Where're you headed?"

"I have not decided yet," lied al-Din. "America is such a beautiful country, there are so many possibilities."

"You got that right, son. Well, you have a good time, wherever you're headed. And don't forget to recommend me to your friends, y'hear?"

al-Din shook the fat man's hand and left the office. Fumbling under the driver's seat for the lever, he stretched his legs out, creating more room for his gangly frame. He adjusted the rear view mirror until he could see the fat man propping open the main door to the office. Turning the ignition, the car started first time. Gingerly, al-Din stepped on the gas; the engine gave a hesitant throaty roar.

As he pulled slowly out of the dealer's forecourt and on to US19, al-Din noticed the fat man smiling to himself.

That made two of them.

Chapter 10

al-Din had been driving for hours. He crossed the Florida panhandle into Alabama at about two in the afternoon following his early morning departure from St. Petersburg. Bypassing Pensacola, the I-10 interstate highway took him across the foot of the Yellow Hammer State. He planned to spend the night on the outskirts of Baton Rouge, well inside Louisiana. The six hundred mile journey would take nearly twelve hours.

al-Din had packed the things he needed for his trip carefully. On the back seat sat a sports bag containing his clothes, pressed and neatly folded. An array of Publix carrier bags in the trunk contained his provisions – bottled water, instant noodles, nuts, apples, cereal-based energy bars and soda. There was enough to sustain him for at least a week. The less he was seen in public over the next few days the better.

On the passenger seat beside him sat a large insulated cool box, inside which he kept his treasure. Seven tubes of M&Ms stood upright in one corner of the box wedged between a couple of Esky Icepacks. The ice-cold blocks chilled the inside of the box, protecting the contents from the summer heat that would adversely affect the viability of the virus. Two large bottles occupied a corner each. They contained the fluid decanted from the dissolved papers sent from Germany. A large Tupperware box filled the remaining space. It was brimful with black and grey powder, the dried residue left after the virus had been extracted from the charcoal-encrusted papers.

On top of the cooler, a crisp map of the United States of America lay open revealing the southeastern states. al-Din referred to it occasionally. Outside, the endless I-10 receded in front of him, a long grey undulating ribbon.

al-Din's fingers ached from gripping the steering wheel too tightly. His back ached from maintaining a rigid erect posture. His butt ached from the uncomfortable bucket seat.

The air-conditioner was turned to maximum yet did not seem to effect any actual cooling of the interior. Sweat collected under al-Din's armpits and trickled down his back. He could feel the elastic waistband of his underpants clinging to the small of his back. The jeans grew tighter around his thighs, as the moisture made them stick to his skin and blood pooled in his legs.

The neon sign of the Baton Rouge Budget Motel shone like a beacon down the length of Constitution Avenue. al-Din had pre-booked his room by phone the previous night and informed the receptionist of his likely late arrival. At 7:00 P.M., he was not that late. Exhausted from the drive he had barely the strength to sign the register. He did not need to remember to obscure his signature; weariness performed the task admirably.

Room 12 was as uniform and anonymous as any of the other rooms in the motel. From the worn carpet in the hallway, to the peeling facia on the vanity units in the bedroom, to the faint urine smell and black mould growths in the bathroom, the word 'budget' was used in its most flattering sense. The bored look of utter unconcern on the face of the receptionist as to who he was and what he might be doing brought a smile to al-Din's face.

al-Din unloaded the cooler from the car and grabbed one of his carrier bags. Emptying the contents of the mini-bar onto the floor, he quickly transferred the tubes and bottles to the fridge. The cooling blocks were jammed into the small, inadequate ice-making compartment so they would not melt overnight.

Another long drive awaited him tomorrow, so al-Din ate his instant noodles in silence and went to bed early. Neither the sounds of the frenzied coupling in the adjacent room, nor the unintelligible arguments of the belligerent drunks outside his door, disturbed him as he slept the sleep of the damned.

The next day he awoke, refreshed. He paid cash and took an extra complimentary Danish pastry from the counter, as he checked out early. The morning rush hour had begun by the time he joined the interstate heading west into Texas.

The route had been planned long before. The I-10 carried him on to Houston. The two hundred and fifty mile drive was accomplished in a little under five hours. al-Din ate lunch in his car and stretched his legs in an air-conditioned shopping mall. A routine he expected to continue for the next few days. Another two hundred and fifty mile slog took him north on the I-45 to Dallas. Dinner passed in much the same way as lunch.

In the late afternoon, the home stretch beckoned, a two hundred mile dash due north to Oklahoma City. Anonymous towns flashed by, Ardmore, Davis, Wynnewood and Purcell. al-Din forgot them almost as soon as the names registered in his brain.

Approaching Oklahoma City, he slowed as the road passed through the southern suburbs of Norman, Moore and Del City. Negotiating the gridiron street plan with relative ease, he found the SleepyHeads Motel on MacArthur Boulevard. The thirteen-hour drive had been a killer, more for its monotony, than anything else. Every bone and muscle fibre in his body ached. The soft bed embraced him like a lover and he fell asleep instantly.

At midnight he awoke. The urgency of his task overcame his drowsiness. It was time to put aside the shallow physical desires of his body, such as sleep and comfort, and learn to condition his body to a new set of demands.

Rubbing his eyes, he stumbled to the bathroom and splashed cold water onto his face. His eyes widened and grew accustomed to the dark. Dressing quickly, he assembled his gear. Tonight he would take with him the aerosol spray gun and the container of dried paper.

The spray gun had been primed and ready for use since his first test in St. Petersburg two days before. The cubes of tissue had swollen almost to their original size. They formed an irregular-shaped clump at the bottom of the reservoir. al-Din hoped the residue would not block the inlet to the nozzle when the trigger was pumped.

Noiselessly he left his room. Although quiet, several rooms remained well lit from within and al-Din suspected that the sound of a vehicle leaving at this time would not arouse much concern.

It was only a short drive from MacArthur Boulevard to El Reno and he arrived within twenty minutes. The I-40 stretched into the distance, lined on each side by roadside diners, fast food restaurants, gas stations and budget motels - the density of each thinning as the road continued west to Amarillo.

After some miles, the nature of the businesses changed again. The world of the cattleman evolved seamlessly from the vast urban sprawl. Stores selling animal feed, farm machinery and the occasional veterinary wholesalers eventually gave way to the feedlots — the gargantuan fattening yards for America's livestock.

Although not even in the nation's top five, Oklahoma feedlots provided a healthy contribution to the $175 billion per year livestock industry. In any month, between three hundred and fifty and four hundred thousand cattle were fattened for slaughter in Oklahoma. That was a drop in the ocean compared with the bigger states, such as giant Texas with its three million head, or Kansas and Nebraska with over two million apiece.

And it was all about to stop.

There was no particular reason al-Din chose Benson and Sons Feedlots. Maybe the sign above the yard was a little more prominent than the others along the highway; maybe the street lights outside seemed a little dimmer; maybe the distance to the nearest neighbour seemed a little further; maybe the scrub nearby seemed to afford a little more cover; or maybe al-Din was simply tired of driving.

Whatever the reason, al-Din pulled off the road and switched off the headlights. He drove for some distance in darkness along a narrow gravel track. On either side of him, running for a mile and disappearing into the pitch-black night, was a series of enormous barns constructed from corrugated steel sheeting.

This was the feedlot.

Each pen held one hundred and fifty head of cattle. Docile and submissive, they had been taken screaming from their mothers and herded together for the remainder of their short lives. Their function was to eat and sleep. In a few short months they would become thousand pound monsters, destined for the fast food restaurants and all-you-can-eat steak dinners that kept America top of the world in the obesity and coronary heart disease league.

al-Din got out of the car and started to walk. With twenty pens side by side, it would not take long for him to infect them all. Even then, only one or two had to be successfully contaminated in order for all the others to be condemned.

Hugging the sidewall of one of the pens al-Din followed it around until he came to the entrance. His breath came in short rapid gasps; adrenaline and oxygen fuelled his racing heart.

Inside the pen the smell was abominable. Each animal was hemmed in by the corrugated steel of the outer wall at the back and by aluminium bars to the front and sides. The front of each stall contained a drinking and feeding trough. A thick mat of mud and waste lined the floor to a depth of about five inches. The ankles of each beast were immersed in their own filth.

The animals were sleeping. A hoarse rasping sound filled the air and clouds of water vapour wafted gently into the air as the animals exhaled.

A string of naked light bulbs snaked down the length of the pen marking the position of the central alley that divided the pen into two halves. Their weak light allowed al-Din to travel from one end of the pen to the other in a few minutes.

al-Din walked slowly down one side of the pen spraying each stall with a cloud of droplets. Occasionally, animals would be facing him directly, or drinking from the trough, in which case he sprayed them directly in the nostrils. When he reached the end of the row, he turned around and repeated the process down the other side. His index finger ached from the continuous pulls on the trigger.

In the next pen, a few yards away, al-Din adopted another tactic. He opened the container of dried paper and crumbled the matted chunks between his fingers. Grabbing a handful, he flung it into the air over the stalls. The larger pieces landed in the muck and filth on the floor. The smaller particles drifted down more slowly. al-Din was disappointed with the effect. Most of the infectious material would be wasted by this inefficient means of dispersal. Instead he dropped a handful of powder in every other water trough.

During the heat of summer, each animal drank up to twenty gallons of water per day. The slobbering beasts licked their mouths and nostrils and nuzzled each other through the bars of the stalls.

Direct contact between animals was the most effective means of spreading disease.

al-Din infected five pens with the aerosol before it ran dry. Two others had been infected with the dried paper residue. The chunks of tissue adhering to the bottom of the spray gun reservoir had gone into the nearest food trough. Nothing had been wasted. It had been a good night's work.

al-Din looked at his watch. The green spots on the dial and hands glowed dimly.

The *jihad* began in El Reno, west of Oklahoma City, at 1:45 A.M.

Chapter 11

It had been waiting in the bathroom for nearly forty minutes, alternately sitting on the toilet seat and looking in the mirror.

It.

Not he or she.

It was an animal, driven by instinct and adrenaline to act for its own self-preservation. No rational human being would do what it was now contemplating.

It sat silently, reasoning in its altered state, caressing the razor sharp nine-and-a-quarter inch stainless steel blade of the antique Bowie knife.

It wore surgical gloves to prevent its fingerprints being transferred to the porcelain and glass fittings.

The polished wooden handle of the hunting knife seemed almost to adhere to its hand. The blade would not slip or falter. The prey would not bleat or escape.

In minutes, the only real challenge to its plans would be silenced.

At first, it had been surprised by the call. The urgency in the voice was as unexpected as the source. A distant and remote research station, long ago confined to the footnotes of memory, kindled brief thoughts of panic and flight. Reason, or insanity, prevailed. It could not decide which was the more appropriate term.

"Tell no one", it argued. "Meet me in the hotel. Tell me everything and together we will inform the authorities. This heinous act cannot be allowed to go unpunished."

The meeting was arranged, but it did not attend. Instead it watched from the sidelines, stalking and ensuring the coast was clear. Confused, the quarry would wait a while before returning to its den to await further instruction. In the meantime, having let itself in, it concealed itself, waiting to strike.

The noise of the key in the lock alerted the visitor to the return of its victim. With a distant click, the door closed slowly by itself. Keys jangled as they were thrown on to the glass coffee table. Heavy footsteps crossed the room growing louder. The telephone call to the receptionist was brief and uninformative.

No. No one had been asking for him. He had no message to leave. He would try again later.

A pause. What to do now? Perhaps something to drink while he waited? The cable clunked as it was pulled out of the back of the kettle.

This was it. This was the moment it had been waiting for.

Footsteps approached the bathroom door. Its head throbbed, its heart raced, the adrenaline coursed through its veins. The handle turned. The door opened.

Slash.

A descending strike to the upper left shoulder pierced the breastbone.

Perhaps in the milliseconds available to him, Dr. Nabwas al-Jaheerah recognised his assailant and what was happening to him. If he did, he was powerless to stop it.

Slash.

A horizontal stroke across the front of the neck cut through to the windpipe.

Incomprehension. Terror. Incredulity. Reaching for his throat wide-eyed and helpless, al-Jaheerah started to buckle under his own weight.

Slash.

A plunging stroke carved the air into al-Jaheerah's back piercing the right lung.

Pain began to register and the arms started to flail but there was no sound, just a rasping from the severed oesophagus.

The hair was grabbed in the left hand and the head tilted back. In a single motion the throat was slashed from ear to ear. The jugular veins bulged and oozed blood. The carotid arteries opened and bright scarlet arcs of blood hit the wall and ceiling, splashing vibrant colour onto the previously sterile white canvas.

The chest heaved; its movements became shallower and less frequent. The head dangled at an untidy angle while the body sat in an ever-increasing crimson pool. Lips quivered in silent accusation or prayer of absolution. The eyes stared and gradually grew dull as the life force ebbed away.

The sink was filled with cool clear water and it watched as blood dripped from its face and formed tiny ripples on the surface. It was hypnotised by the swirls of colour as they danced and slowly dissipated, turning the water pink. Predatory eyes burned through the crimson mask and pierced the image it saw in the mirror.

Stepping over the body, it entered the bedroom. A small bag in the closet held a fresh set of clothes. Changing quickly, the bloody clothes were replaced by the new. On the table with the keys lay a folder and a computer disk. The evidence it had come to obtain was placed into the bag.

Still with gloved hands, it opened the door and peered out into the corridor. There was no one there. Confidently, it swung the door open wide and strode out of the room. The door nearest to room 1012 led to the emergency stairwell.

It knew that.

The door was not rigged to an alarm.

It knew that also.

The closed circuit cameras of the entire floor were out of action.

It knew.

From entering the room to leaving, forty-eight minutes had elapsed.

Chapter 12

The first day of the symposium went very well. Attendance at most of the sessions was high, intelligent questions were asked, and useful contacts made. The global networking necessary to counter the spread of disease was working.

Jonas Williams was very pleased. A flawless performance, he assured himself. Nothing stood between him and the presidency of the World Virology Union. When Election Day came next month, the other candidate, he refused to even try to remember his name, from a middle-of-the-road university in one of those obscure mid-west towns one only hears about when their school children run amok with handguns, did not stand a chance. Standing in line for the lift he was unprepared for the worst.

"Professor Williams?"

"Yes?"

"I'm Mr. Howard, the duty manager, and this is…er…"

"Detective Wayne Hobson," said the large uniformed man. "I wonder if I can speak to you for a few moments, sir? Thank you."

Hobson put his hand on Williams' elbow and guided him out of the queue and into an alcove. There was a palpable sense of urgency in the officer's manner. Williams, a man not used to being told what to do, meekly submitted to the juggernaut of the man's massive frame.

Leaning close, so close that their noses almost touched, Hobson whispered into Williams' face. The reek of cheap coffee and even cheaper tobacco was overwhelming. Williams blanched.

"Professor Williams, one of your party has met with, how shall we say, an untimely end?"

Williams stared back uncomprehendingly.

"I'm afraid he's been murdered, sir," the detective added.

"Are you sure?" stammered Williams, trying to think of something intelligible to say. The room was spinning and he was at the centre of the vortex.

"I think I know a dead body when I see one, sir. His throat's been slashed."

"Good Lord," said Williams. "Who was it?"

The detective opened his breast pocket and pulled out a small black notebook. He flipped it open and stared at it for a few seconds, silently mouthing the syllables.

"Erm..," he hesitated, "Mr. Nab…was…al…she…heara."

Williams paused for a moment, lost deep in thought.

"I'm afraid the name doesn't ring any bells with me, officer," Williams replied.

"I understand from the duty manager, here, that Mr…al…she…heara was from Pakistan."

“I must take your word for that, officer. I took a good deal of interest in the registration for this meeting, but as I say, I don’t recall this particular individual. Perhaps, Miss McMann can help you. She’s the event co-ordinator for the hotel. She will have the most up-to-date information on all the participants.”

“Yes, I know about Miss McMann, professor. She’s off duty at the moment and her computer records are not available. We’re trying to contact her now.”

“Without being indelicate, officer,” Williams said, “How will this affect the meeting? Will it have to be cancelled?”

“I think under the circumstances we can allow it to continue as scheduled. The victim’s room will be sealed, of course, and we will need to search all the other rooms thoroughly. We’ll need everyone’s cooperation for that. In addition, we’ll need to question everyone at this event. I trust we can count on you to back us up, professor?”

“Oh, absolutely, officer”, said Williams.

“We’ll start immediately. The crime scene investigators are up there already. As a foreign national is involved, the Federal Bureau of Investigation will probably send someone over to help out. My officers will start taking statements from everyone who shared the same floor as the victim.”

Hobson turned to the duty manager. “We may need to set up a temporary office for interviewing guests. Can we use one of your meeting rooms? In addition, we’ll need the names and contact details of all your staff, whether they’re on duty tonight or not. We’ll also need the contact details of former employees. Please prepare that information.”

“You don’t think it was a member of staff, do you?” said Williams, suddenly relishing the notion of being in the middle of a murder investigation.

“Happens all the time, sir,” said the detective. “Isn’t that right, Mr. Howard?”

The duty manager lowered his eyes.

“That information, please, Mr. Howard,” Hobson demanded firmly.

The duty manager scuttled away. Hobson turned to Williams. “Well, professor, perhaps I can start with you?”

***

It was just before midnight when the body was finally removed. The thick black body bag containing the corpse was strapped to the paramedics’ gurney and zipped closed before being carried, almost as if it were a religious icon, through the maelstrom of flashbulbs and jabbering TV news reporters.

News of the suspicious death had travelled quickly. The hotel staff had called the TV news hotline numbers. The lucky first caller would get a fat tip from the station as long as they had the scoop. News channel helicopters circled overhead like vultures illuminating the body bag with beams of light.

Jonas Williams loved every minute of it. He had never had this much attention in his life. The broadcasts of his interviews went out live on six channels simultaneously. Williams regretted not having a video recorder in his room.

Perhaps the reporters will send me a copy?

Williams managed to pad out the little information he knew about the dead man with plenty he didn't. The deceased scientist became "a friend", "a personal friend", or a "close personal friend", depending on the journalist to whom he spoke. From there, he went on to become "a brilliant scientist" or "an expert in his field". Later, the death would be described as "a tragedy", "a great loss" or "a personal blow". In his head, Williams had already written the speech dedicating the remaining sessions of the symposium to our "dearly departed friend and colleague". The presidency of the World Virology Union was in the bag.

The main topic of conversation at breakfast the next morning was the murder. Most of the symposium participants had been questioned, however briefly, the preceding night. The majority knew nothing; they had been out of the hotel at the time, located in a completely different floor or wing of the hotel, or had not seen or heard anything suspicious.

For the most part the police were stumped. They labelled it an opportunistic crime on a foreign visitor committed by an inexperienced thief, although probably acting with inside knowledge. The time of death had been narrowed to between 3:12 P.M., when the guest checked in and 10:15 P.M., when the maid, wishing to turn the sheets down, discovered the body. The biggest disappointment was finding that the security cameras on the tenth floor had been not been working for at least the previous month. No one visiting the murder victim in his room had been recorded.

***

Paul Caine put his tray down next to Chen Xiao Lin. "Do you mind?" he said calmly.

The woman looked up at him. Her eyes told him she was tired and angry. She said nothing.

"I take it you heard about last night's excitement?" he added, poking his fried egg suspiciously with a fork.

"I am not permitted to say anything," she replied.

"By the police? They don't mind. Half of them are being interviewed on TV now."

"Not the police," Chen replied firmly.

The mousy woman looked across the table at Caine, glowering furiously.

"Ah. I see what you mean. I suppose on days like today, it's lucky you don't speak English?"

"Thank you for understanding," Chen replied softly.

"I don't pretend to understand. I just gather you would rather be alone at the moment. If you need any help, please let me know." Caine stood, holding his tray in one hand, and went to sit at another table. Chen watched him walk away.

***

Philip Yeung spotted Caine from across the hall and walked briskly over to his table. He did not want anyone else beating him to the only available seat. This would be his best chance to meet Caine and thank him for his help in evaluating his company's test kit.

"Dr. Caine?" ventured Yeung. "It's so nice to meet you at last."

"I'm sorry, do I know you," Caine replied.

"Philip Yeung, AsiaBioTek. You evaluated our test kit earlier this year."

"Of course, Philip," remembered Caine. "Sit down and join me. How's the kit doing, selling well?"

"Well, it's early days yet. We only got your letter with the results of the evaluation last week. I'm trying to set up a meeting with some of the guys at USDA. I was wondering if you could..." Yeung's voice trailed off. He did not like asking favours from complete strangers. Most of the time he found that people were more than happy to agree to help him when asked face-to-face, but translating that promise into action when he returned home was extremely difficult, if not impossible.

"Hang on," said Caine, scanning the room. "I can see a couple of them over there, by the window. That's Jack Morris with the beard and next to him is Paul Johanssen. They're old mates of mine. Let's go and have a chat. I'll introduce you."

The room was almost empty, and the waiters had made great efforts to clear the buffet table, when the group of scientists finally got up and wandered over to the Grand Assembly room for the second day of presentations. The four men sat together through the morning session.

As expected, Williams dedicated the remaining sessions to Dr. al-Jaheerah. The delegates stood and observed a minute's silence before the first presentation of the day.

Before the first coffee break of the morning, Laura McMann took the stage and announced that the photographs of the previous evening's cocktail reception were available from her desk in the hotel lobby. Caine grimaced to himself and headed for the exit, parting ways with Yeung and his new American friends. Yeung told them he was going to find Jonas Williams.

Williams was found easily, idly perusing a poster in the mostly empty salon opposite the Grand Assembly room, sipping gently on a cup of coffee.

"Professor Williams?"

Williams looked up. Yeung stared into a blank expressionless face. What to say to one of the world's foremost experts on livestock diseases?

"My name's Philip Yeung, from AsiaBioTek in Hong Kong," he began.

"Yes?" replied Williams cautiously.

"My company develops diagnostic tests for livestock. We've just started production of a new test for foot-and-mouth disease. Perhaps you'd be interested in hearing more about it?"

"Well not at the moment, I am rather busy," said Williams somewhat testily. Nothing annoyed him more than people trying to bask in his limelight. After years of cultivating the media he was not about to give anybody a free ride to fame and fortune. Especially not by publicly endorsing a new test he knew nothing about. Williams prided himself on his ability to read people. Yeung was a chancer, and an amateur one at that; he could tell that from a mile away.

"Have you published anything in the literature?" Williams said, carefully laying his bait.

Yeung bit deeply. "Yes," he replied, "In fact we had a paper published a few months ago. Perhaps you read it?"

"Which journal?" Williams asked nonchalantly.

"Biochemistry Today," Yeung replied proudly.

Williams smiled. "That comic? Why not try a more relevant journal such as Veterinary Diagnostics or Virological Methods? I'm on the editorial board of both."

Yeung's intended product pitch was deflated instantly. He didn't expect such a cold reception and was angered at Williams' rejection of his company's novel technology. He stood open-mouthed, speechless.

"I think I must be going now," said Williams. "I'm sure to be needed somewhere. Please let me know how your new test comes along, won't you, er... Mr?"

"Yeung. Philip Yeung," he replied to Williams' rapidly retreating figure as the professor made his way back to the lecture hall.

***

The police search of the hotel produced few clues. The victim's room on the tenth floor remained sealed. The guests in the adjacent rooms had been re-housed to minimise the inconvenience to them while the police analysed the murder scene.

Coffee breaks and lunch were mostly occupied with technical talk, especially as most of the participants had never heard of Dr. al-Jaheerah, let alone knew why anyone would want to murder him. In death, the delegate from Pakistan remained as anonymous and unknown as he had in life.

After lunch, which Caine spent searching fruitlessly for Ms. Chen, he visited Laura McMann at her desk.

"I've come for my photos. Are there any good ones?"

"Well, let's see shall we?" and she bent over to look under her desk. Caine caught a glimpse of cleavage as she rummaged through a thick wad of envelopes.

"Yes. Here we are. You look pretty good in some of these," she said casually, remembering their phone call of the previous evening.

Caine opened the envelope and took out the pictures. He could not remember posing for any of them. In the first he was caught in profile as the photographer focused on Bill Jacobs and Shirley Novak. Caine nodded, not too bad. He looked pretty normal in that one, he conceded. In the second, he was caught staring at Ms. Chen as Dr. Li looked on.

Damn photographer.

"Who's that?" enquired Laura, playfully.

"One of the Chinese delegates, I think," Caine replied, keeping his composure.

"Oh, by the way. A film of the cocktail reception will be available as a VCD later this evening, if you're interested. Shall I put you down for a copy? It's included in the registration fee, but they're only processing as many as are required."

"Yes. I might as well," said Caine reluctantly, then, realising he would be able to see more of Ms. Chen added, "Can you have it delivered to my room?"

"Maybe I'll drop it off personally?" replied Laura seductively.

"I'd like that," said Caine.

"Well, I'll see you later," she smiled and winked at Caine.

Caine smiled, put the photographs in his pocket, and headed back to his room. His presentation was later in the afternoon and he wanted to check his slides and run over his notes one more time. Remembering that he had not seen Ms. Chen all morning or during lunch, Caine decided to pay a quick visit to her room. Taking the lift to the twelfth floor he eventually found her room in the dimly lit corridor.

Caine rapped on the door and waited. No response. He knocked again, louder.

"Who is it?" came the muffled voice. Caine recognised Chen instantly.

"Paul," he called. "Dr. Caine," he corrected himself.

A pause was followed by the sound of the door being unlocked.

"May I come in?"

The door opened wider, Chen stood to one side and directed him into the room with a wave of her hand.

Chen looked more tired and worried than she had at breakfast. Her beautiful dark eyes had lost their shine and become bloodshot through lack of sleep. She looked pale and drawn. She wore no makeup but still looked stunning. Caine was captivated. Before he could speak, an electronic bleep came from the bedside table.

"Excuse me," Chen said, picking up her mobile phone. "Yes? One moment please. Dr. Caine, I will take this call in the bathroom, if you don't mind? Please make yourself comfortable."

Chen walked to the bathroom and locked herself inside. She spoke loudly in a mixture of English and Putonghua, although Caine could not follow any of the conversation.

Looking around him Caine spotted Chen's passport on the bedside table. Intrigued, Caine picked it up and flipped through it quickly. Large and occasionally colourful visa stamps for a host of countries leapt from the pages - Germany, Turkey, Nepal, Pakistan, Canada and Argentina, all visited within the last two or three years. Ms. Chen was indeed well travelled. He checked her date of birth. She was thirty years old but looked much younger. Of course, her passport photo did not do her justice.

Caine was about to put the passport back in its place when a small object fell from behind the back cover. He picked it up and placed it on the table on top of the travel document. He looked at his fingertips and rubbed at the reddish brown dust that adhered to them. Puzzled he picked up the tiny black booklet again and opened it. An ugly red-brown stain covered the yellowish pages. Many of the other pages adhered to each other.

The pages were stuck together with dried blood. Human blood.

Caine knew that the booklet probably came from the dead man's room. The raised voices in the bathroom continued and showed no signs of abating, so Caine examined his find more closely. Neat Arabic script filled some of the pages. Most of the others were blank. Only one page contained anything written in English. The inside back cover read:

Regency International, S.F.
8/30
4:30 p.m.
Washington

The dead man was supposed to meet someone in the hotel's Washington Lounge yesterday afternoon. Was this the person Chen was waiting for? Did she lure him to his death or was he killed before he could meet her? Caine's mind reeled at the implication; was he sitting alone in a murderer's room?

"Dr. Caine," said the voice softly but firmly. "I suggest you put that book down immediately."

Caine froze. His heart raced and his mouth went dry. He turned red-faced with embarrassment to face the voice. Chen stood outside the bathroom door, holding a small black automatic handgun. Caine searched desperately for something to say, anything. He had nothing.

At that moment the front door erupted in splinters and a crescendo of deafening noise.

"FBI! Drop the weapon! Drop it! Now! Do it!" the voices screamed. Black clad figures surged forward. Chen was thrown instantly to the floor, her arms pinned behind her back. A uniformed figure pressed her face to the floor with his boot. A handgun was pointed at her head behind the ear, the muzzle almost touching the skin. Death was a wrong look and a hair's breadth away.

"You!" the voices rounded on Caine. "On the floor! Hands behind your head! Do it!" they commanded.

Caine obliged in terror, the blood-soaked booklet still grasped between his fingers. As he lay trembling on the floor in between the two single beds he felt it ripped from his hand as a man roughly searched his body.

After a few minutes he felt himself being raised up. He was allowed to sit on the edge of the bed. He looked over at Chen in astonishment.

This is not happening.

Chen was standing between two men who towered over her. A third, shorter, black-clad figure stood to one side pistol in hand. A hood obscured the face as violet eyes surveyed the room.

"Don't worry about me, Dr. Caine," Chen called to him. "I'll be all right. Please don't do anything stupid. They will let you go soon, I promise."

With that she was manhandled out of the room. As she was turned roughly toward the ruined front door, Caine clearly saw the shining steel handcuffs used to restrain her.

As his own handcuffs bit deeply into the flesh of his wrists, Caine turned to the uniformed man nearest to him.

"I just thought I'd mention that I'm supposed to be giving a lecture this afternoon," he said.

"Don't worry about, that," replied the man gruffly. "It's cancelled".

Chapter 13

Caine had never been interviewed by the authorities before. The experience at the FBI field office in the heart of downtown San Francisco was not at all as he expected. He did not relish the memory. After several hours he was allowed to go. He felt dirty and soiled.

This had been without doubt the most humiliating day of his life. On top of it all he had missed his presentation. Reese would be furious. As he was being escorted from the interview room he was surprised to see Chen Xiao Lin waiting for him by the front desk. She smiled as he furrowed his brow in bewilderment. Behind Chen, standing some distance away, the entire Chinese delegation waited.

"Well they certainly gave me a good grilling in there," said Caine, unable to think of a lighter topic of conversation. "I've been in there for hours. What about you?"

"Oh, I was released after a few minutes," Chen replied cheerfully. "But they're keeping my gun, though. I only have a few hours before I have to leave. I just wanted to apologise to you in person and say goodbye."

"I think I'm missing something here."

"I'm not supposed to tell you, but I was able to claim diplomatic immunity on account of my position in the Chinese embassy. To avoid any embarrassment, the embassy has acceded to the American's request to repatriate me to China immediately."

"Your position in the Chinese embassy being what, exactly?" queried Caine.

"Officially a translator. Unofficially, don't ask."

"I also put in a good word for you with the FBI. It's on account of me that you were released so quickly."

"Quickly?" Caine said, indignation and exasperation fighting for supremacy in the rising pitch of his voice. "I've been implicated in a murder. I've missed my lecture. My career may well be over."

"But was it worth the risk, Dr. Caine?" Chen answered softly, leaning over and kissing him lightly on the cheek.

"I haven't the faintest idea," Caine replied.

"Come on. We'll give you a ride back to the hotel. I have a few hours to pack. I am released on my own recognisance, but I cannot miss my flight this evening." Chen snapped her fingers and the group made their way to the exit.

"You realise one thing, don't you, Dr Caine?" Chen said, once they were all seated in the embassy limousine.

"What's that?" asked Caine.

"The person who killed Dr. al-Jaheerah was not an opportunist bungling an attempted break-in. You saw the notebook. I took that from the body before it was discovered. Dr. al-Jaheerah was meeting someone and he was killed before the meeting took place. Now the police and FBI know as well. He was targeted and murdered because of something he knew."

"So?" answered Caine, not really following.

"The killer is one of the delegates at the symposium. And he is still there. Whoever it is cannot afford to break cover and run until the meeting is over. You must be careful, Dr. Caine. Your association with me has implicated you. Your life may be in danger as well."

"Great. This just keeps getting better. My career's ruined and I'm going to die."

"Try not to be flippant, Dr. Caine. I'm very serious. Deadly serious."

"How did the FBI trace you?" Caine said, trying to change the subject.

"We were wondering that ourselves. My colleagues here think that our mobile phone conversations have been monitored. They may have overheard us discussing tactics. It is more common than you think to keep tabs on visiting delegations. We will be more careful in future."

The limousine pulled up at the hotel. The doorman held open the car door as Chen's colleagues alighted.

"I don't have much time, Dr. Caine. I will come to say goodbye to you soon. Once again, please forgive me. If it is any consolation, I probably wouldn't have shot you."

"Probably?"

"Yes, probably." Chen smiled thinly and looked Caine up and down, as if she were a sergeant major examining a new recruit. "Do you know your problem, Dr. Caine?" she said. "You don't look dangerous enough."

"I'll try and work on that. I promise."

***

Caine freshened up in his room and took a long hot shower. The steaming water stripped him of the last vestiges of humiliation and he emerged vindicated if not victorious. Within minutes of dressing Jonas Williams, Bill Jacobs and Laura McMann were in his room rescheduling his presentation to the symposium.

"As tomorrow is the closing session, I suggest we put you in straight after breakfast, pushing everything else back an hour. That would be the least painful option," said Williams. "What does everyone else think?"

"That's do-able," commented Jacobs. "If Paul can keep it to forty-five minutes and there aren't too many questions from the audience afterwards. Maybe we can shave a few minutes off the coffee breaks as well?"

"The busses for the post-symposium tour won't arrive until 3:00 p.m.," said Laura. "So a one-hour delay won't affect any of the other scheduled activities."

"That's settled then," said Williams, without waiting for Caine's input. He smiled broadly at everyone and left the room.

"How'd it go with the cops, Paul?" asked Jacobs.

"I managed to get everything straightened out in the end. I just want to forget about it. Let's just say, if that's how they treat innocent people, I really pity the criminals."

"Well, I'm glad you're back in one piece, buddy," replied Jacobs. "You take it easy now. Everyone's really looking forward to your speech tomorrow. You take care, all right?"

Jacobs slapped Caine on the back and headed to the door. Laura reached over and squeezed Caine's hand.

"I'm glad you're okay, too," she said. "It must have been awful for you. Maybe I can show you some real US hospitality tonight? How would you like that?"

"That sounds like a great idea," Caine said, genuinely touched by her concern. Laura's eyes sparkled and she gave Caine one of her winks.

"Well, I have to be getting along now. I'll catch you later, okay?"

"Thanks Laura, goodbye," said Caine, leading her to the door. He watched from the open door as she walked down the corridor to the elevator.

As Caine watched CNN, drinking a freshly made cup of instant coffee, he heard a knock on his door. He opened it to find Chen Xiao Lin casually dressed in sweatshirt and jeans. A small rucksack hung from her shoulder.

"Hi, Dr. Caine. Or maybe I should call you Paul?" she enquired.

"It's a bit late for that now, don't you think?" replied Caine, ruefully.

"As I said earlier, I must be leaving now. My colleagues will remain for the duration of the symposium. They are proper scientists after all." She smiled at the deception she had played on Caine.

"I wonder if you could do me a favour?" she added. "I don't have time to get my copies of the cocktail reception photographs. Could I take yours? I would like a souvenir of my time in America, however brief it was; I don't think the authorities will be letting me back in for quite a while."

"Sure," replied Caine, retrieving the wad of photos from his bedside table. "Although I don't know why you're bothering. They're not that good." In fact, he had only looked at a couple of them before putting the envelope to one side.

He handed her the envelope. She lifted the flap and peeked inside.

"What about this one?" she said, pulling out the picture of her, Caine and Dr. Li. "I'm sure Dr. Li will be disappointed to see you weren't paying attention to him." She giggled a sweet, charming, girlish giggle. It was the first time he had seen or heard her laugh.

"I'm sure Dr. Li has been ignored in a similar fashion on many previous occasions, especially in such company."

"Thank you for the compliment, Paul," she looked at her watch. "I really must go now. I have to check in early with the INS. Thanks again for the photos."

"No problem," sighed Caine, as he watched her walk away from him for yet another time.

At ten o'clock, there was a soft knock at the door. Caine rose and answered. It was Laura. She had changed from her uniform and now wore a tight white sweater that emphasised her curves and a knee-length skirt.

"Well this is a pleasant surprise," said Caine, beaming a smile.

"I'm not allowed in guest's rooms off duty in my uniform," she said. "So I thought I'd slip into something a little more comfortable. Do you like it?"

"I love it," he said, embracing her and kissing her full on the lips.

"Now take it off."

Stepping back, Laura unbuckled her oversized leather belt, loosened the zip on her skirt and let it drop to the floor.

Caine lay on his back on the bed as Laura sat astride him her face turned toward his. Crossing her arms, she gripped the hem of her sweater and pulled it up slowly. The tight clothing caught her full breasts lifting them slightly before they bounced free as she pulled the sweater over her head. Strands of her long auburn hair drifted upward as the static electricity dissipated.

Caine slipped his thumbs under the Lycra straps of her bra and edged them around to the clasp at the back. Discarding the bra completely he gazed upon her tight bronzed body.

He took each breast in his palms; the nipples hardened as he caressed their tips with the centre of his palms.

Laura moaned softly and lent forward to kiss him. Her tongue probed his mouth, greedy and searching.

Caine licked the skin surrounding the belly button before probing his tongue into the shallow depression. Laura giggled as her abs quivered, sensing Caine's tongue and rapidly cooling saliva.

Now it was Laura's turn. She pushed Caine away with one hand twisting him and indicating that he should lie on his back. Quickly she was astride him again sitting on his belly. Leaning forward, she kissed him hard causing their lips to bruise. She tasted a little blood – her own or Caine's she did not know or care. Sliding back, she settled in a kneeling position between his parted legs.

Satisfied that he was erect she moved to mount him. Caine guided himself in arching his back slightly to align his pelvis with hers. She was moist and slid down Caine's shaft effortlessly.

Time passed unheeded.

Caine flopped down on the bed beside Laura. Exhausted, she entwined his arm with his and rested her head on his chest. Soon they were asleep in each other's arms.

The hours ticked by. Light began to stream into the room. Caine awoke and found he was alone. He looked around. On the night table next to the bed was a note scrawled in pencil on hotel stationery.

"Thanks for a great time," it read. "Look me up, next time you're in San Francisco. Hope you have a nice trip back to England. Love, Laura. P.S. The VCD of the reception is on top of your computer. Enjoy."

Chapter 14

"Mornin', daddy."

The little girl entered the kitchen, her blonde hair tousled and unkempt from a good night's sleep.

"Mornin', sweet pea," replied her father, from behind his newspaper.

"Where's mama?" enquired the girl clambering up onto the stool so that she faced her father at the breakfast table.

"In the kitchen, darlin'. Fixin' breakfast."

The little girl spun round and focused on the open door to the kitchen. The chime of crockery being taken out of cupboards spilled out into the dining area.

"I don't want eggs. Mama, you hear? I don't want no eggs."

Mrs. Hollis appeared from the kitchen carrying a large plate in each hand, which she placed almost reverently before the man and his daughter. A large mound of pale yellow scrambled eggs sat in the centre of each, ringed by four half slices of dark brown buttered toast.

Caitlin Hollis scrunched her face.

"Aww, mama!"

"Aw, nothin' young lady. You eat up them eggs while they're good and hot, y'hear?"

The girl said nothing and picked up a fork. The steaming scrambled egg floated on an oily tide of orange-yellow butter.

"You eat them eggs up young lady and then you can come check the hogs with me afterwards. How'd you like that? Somethin' special might be happenin' today."

Caitlin pricked up her ears.

"Is it today?"

"Might be," replied Hollis, finally dropping his paper and looking at his daughter square in the eyes.

"Can I keep one of 'em, as a pet?"

"Well, we'll have to see about that," replied Hollis cagily. He did not want to get his daughter's hopes up too much; he simply wanted an excuse to get her out into the yard.

Clement Hollis had never thought of the hogs as pets, even when he was his daughter's age. They were just a means to an end. Just so much bacon on legs was how he always looked at it. No point getting sentimental over something whose throat you'll have to slit later in the year.

Hollis had worked the family farm since he was a boy. Learning everything at his father's side, he loved the outdoors. The life was simple and hard and he was glad their only child was a girl. Hollis did not want to burden a son with the responsibility of looking after a large farm. Animal husbandry was an insecure livelihood and he did not want to see his descendents throw away their futures for the sake of family obligation, or worse, guilt. This was the end of the line for the Hollis farm. His daughter was going to be a doctor, or a lawyer, or any damn thing she wanted, as long as she was away from the farm.

After three consecutive seasons in which the hogs cost more to raise than they brought in at auction, the family's fortunes rode on the sale of this season's hogs. Another failure could not be tolerated. Hollis had called in every favour he was owed and had slashed overheads. Even then it might not be enough. With no money for insurance, and vaccination for his livestock being a luxury he had not been able to afford for many years, he often wondered how much longer his luck would hold.

This time, however, things were different. The bank had issued warning letters before. Red ink was the norm at the Hollis farm. Yet, it was only at his last meeting with the bank that foreclosure had been discussed for the first time. With nothing in the pot the Hollis family were living day-to-day, bills were paid as and when required. If all went well this season he would make ten thousand dollars from the sale of his five hundred finished hogs. That would make a dent in the debt but would not clear it. It would take another successful season back-to-back with the first to see them right.

Inside the farrowing pens the immense sows lay on their sides constrained by the stout iron bars separating them from their newborn piglets. At only three pounds each, the tiny piglets would be crushed to death if they were not removed from their mothers.

Caitlin squatted down, her backside nearly touching the layer of filthy litter lining the floor of the shed, and gazed into the nearest pen. Ten squirming, wriggling cream coloured piglets lay in a heap, one on top of the other, plugged into their mother's teats, sucking contentedly.

Where the child saw new life Hollis saw twenty dollars profit per head. Caitlin looked down the aisle. Pens lined the shed as far as the eye could see. She saw the miracle of birth, new life triumphant over adversity. Her father saw two neat rows of twenty-dollar bills.

They proceeded to the last pen in the aisle. A man's head bobbed up and down. He stood upright as the couple approached.

"How's it going, Nate?"

"Fine, Clem. Just fine," replied Nathan McCreedy.

"Hi, Uncle Nathan," said Caitlin. "Are there any runts for me? Daddy says he'll let me have one as a pet."

"Did he now?" said McCreedy. "Let's take a look shall we?"

McCreedy reached down into the darkest corner of the pen. After a few seconds he emerged again, both hands behind his back. His unconvincing display did not fool Caitlin for a second, and she giggled loudly.

"Which hand?" asked Nathan.

"Left. No, right. No, left. Left," shrieked the girl, clapping her hands in excitement and jumping up and down.

"Wrong!" Nathan roared with delight as he drew both arms forward in a wide arc. Gripped firmly in each hand, was a pale piglet, streaked with mud and filth, squealing pathetically.

"Aren't they cute?" cried Caitlin. "Which one can I have?"

"It's up to you, darlin'" replied Hollis, smiling now.

One of the piglets had a prominent black patch over one eye. The other was unmarked.

"I'll take the one with the patch," said the girl. "I'm gonna call him Nelson, after the British sailor."

Hollis and McCreedy looked blankly at each other and shrugged.

"Okay, sweetheart. You take Nelson here out back and give him a good wash. You're gonna have a big job on your hands makin' sure he pulls through. Can you do that?"

"Of course I can, daddy," Caitlin replied confidently.

Hollis did not have the heart to tell her that even piglets reared naturally had a ten to twenty percent mortality rate in the first thirty days after birth. Hand-reared runts, piglets born in litters so large that the sow did not have enough teats to feed them all, fared significantly less well. Hollis would be surprised if Nelson survived another three days.

"Tonight I'll fix up a box in the kitchen so he can keep warm. Is that okay?"

"Thanks daddy," replied Caitlin.

"All right, you go on back to the house now. I'll finish up here with Uncle Nate."

Hollis waited a few seconds as Caitlin trudged back to the house, carefully holding the piglet out at arm's length. She decided she would cuddle him after he was clean.

"How's it going, Clem?" said McCreedy, sensing Hollis had something on his mind.

Hollis looked at him for a moment and hesitated, trying to see in his eyes how much he already knew or suspected.

Finally, Hollis replied, "It's bad, Nate. Real bad. This is our last throw of the dice, you know?"

McCreedy pondered the statement for some time.

"There's always room for y'all with me and Marge, you know that," he said firmly.

"Thanks, Nate. I appreciate it. You never know, we may just be taking you up on that offer soon," sighed Hollis. He reflected on his achievements over the last few years.

"You know what's funny, Nate? You work your whole life at something, try to build it up, and then it all just comes down to luck," he continued. "Is that fair? Is that how it's supposed to be?" he said, choking on the last phrase. He bit his lip as his eyes filled with tears and turned away from McCreedy in shame and disgust.

McCreedy stood silent, eyes cast downward.

After a few seconds, Hollis regained his composure and turned back to his brother-in-law.

"All right, Nate. Let's get to work," he said, managing a weak smile, but avoiding eye contact.

The blood red of the sky changed slowly to orange and yellow as the sun's disk cleared the horizon. The cloudless sky embraced the wide flat plains and the wonders of a new morning dawned over southern Kansas.

Chapter 15

al-Din arrived in Amarillo in the mid-afternoon and spent the rest of the day scouting for the best targets. This was an easier job in daylight than it had been the night before in El Reno.

Driving slowly down the roads he kept his eyes open for properties that were in relatively quiet locations or with long driveways off the main road. In the dark he could park off the main road and walk to the feedlot pens without attracting too much attention.

Only one target was required. Success would close down the entire livestock fattening industry for twenty miles in all directions, maybe more. If he failed it didn't matter. Tomorrow he was going to Kansas and then on to Nebraska. He had planned his route carefully following the main interstate highways. He would spread his poison and be gone before the symptoms had even appeared in El Reno.

But Amarillo was the prize. The small town of just 175,000 people deep in the heart of the Northern High Plains was the bustling centre of the nation's livestock industry. Its twenty-three counties produced over eighty percent of the state's fattened cattle. Nearly twenty thousand acres of feedlots in Texas housed over two million cattle at any one time. This was cattle farming on an industrial scale.

At just after 6:00 P.M. al-Din found it. The HyGain Feeders yard stood on the edge of Amarillo. Built on the three hundred acre site of a former B29 bomber runway, the yard had a capacity of around thirty thousand head. Huge open-air pens ran the length of the runway, increasing the risk of cross-contamination. With few buildings nearby the approach would be difficult but the payoff was massive.

When nightfall came al-Din returned equipped as before. A small backpack contained his spray gun, filled and primed, along with his Tupperware box of dried powder.

A concrete gully ran alongside the feeding pens. At night it was empty but was kept replenished with freshly milled feed during the day. At the back of the feedlot immense piles of corn sat outside the mill, where it would be heat-treated and steamrollered into high moisture corn feed. The gully was the target for tonight's work.

A simple picket fence topped with barbed wire surrounded the feedlot. It acted more as a deterrent than an effective barrier. With a total perimeter length of nearly three miles, there was no way that HyGain could create an impermeable barrier against undesirables.

They had had the occasional incident before. Drunks bedding down for the night, fraternity pranksters and even courting couples. Most of the previous trespassers had been caught in the act. A spate of cattle mutilations and petty vandalism had gone unsolved but they had stopped as mysteriously as they had started.

A stealthy, determined individual would have no problem gaining entry to the yard. al-Din would prove it.

al-Din warily leapt over the fence at the far end of the giant rectangular yard. The main entrance was over a mile away at the other end of the runway. Sweat soaked his shirt and he breathed heavily. The walk from his car, parked in a dirt access road parallel to the yard, had taken much longer than anticipated. Pausing to get his bearings he was surprised to see the lights in the main office come on, even though it was after midnight.

Evening deliveries of livestock were not uncommon. The cool night air reduced the stress on the animals as they were trucked across state. In the evening the temperature was in the mid-forties Fahrenheit. After some initial concern, al-Din was pleased. Any remaining staff, including night watchmen, would be diverted to the front of the yard where the holding pens for new deliveries were located. The animals would remain there until morning when they would be weighed and processed, and assigned stalls according to whether they were yearlings, heifers or steers.

Darkness enveloped the yard. The only source of illumination was the distant twinkle of yellow from the main office and the pale yellowish-green of the waning moon.

As al-Din's eyes grew accustomed to the dark he was able to make out the shape and location of the cattle pens. Guided by the snort and roar of the animals in addition to their smell he quickly found the concrete gully he had observed on his afternoon drive.

Within seconds he was on his knees and fumbling in his backpack. As the activity at the front of the yard increased al-Din dare not walk more than halfway down the main aisle lest someone on duty observe him. By then his spray gun would be exhausted anyway.

As he trudged down the side of the pens some of the animals stirred. Occasionally a bellow would be directed at him by one of the more belligerent animals. Some even approached the gully looking for fodder as he passed. Stroking the giant beasts' muzzles, he sprayed them directly in the face as he had at El Reno. Finding nothing in the gully, the animals snorted in disgust and turned away.

al-Din continued spraying the gully. When his trigger finger tired he swapped hands and sprayed into the air instead hoping that the mist of tiny droplets would be carried further.

With each breath the cattle inhaled up to twenty litres of air. In theory only one virus particle could cause infection. Breathing in an aerosol loaded with virus deep into the lungs meant that infection was almost a certainty.

As he expected, al-Din had only paced about four hundred yards down the runway before his spray gun reservoir was empty. He estimated he had exposed about one-eighth of the cattle in the yard to his virus.

With his tub of dried paper he crossed the runway and liberally sprinkled the dust into the feeding gully on the other side of the main aisle and threw it high into the air over the pens. Instead of saving the dust to contaminate other feedlots, al-Din decided to use it all up in Amarillo. He had to be sure that at least one of the targets was infected.

Satisfied with his work, al-Din surveyed the scene from the safety of the other side of the picket fence.

Two down, five to go.

Chapter 16

Refreshed from his shower, Caine dressed quickly. Putting on a crisp white shirt and the blue and red striped tie sporting the AHI emblem, he caught a glimpse of himself in the full-length mirror next to the wardrobe and shuddered.

There should be a law against wearing corporate ties in public.

Caine realised why the ties were given away as gifts to dignitaries visiting the institute; no sane person working there would wear one. A navy blue blazer ensured his complete embarrassment.

The VCD of the cocktail reception lay on top of his computer notebook. Caine groaned involuntarily. The last thing he needed was to be reminded of that event.

The police and FBI had assured the delegates that they would all be allowed to leave in time for their scheduled flights, but some were still expecting last minute complications. The group from Pakistan were particularly ill at ease, as were some of the participants from other Middle Eastern and Asian countries.

The audience had thinned considerably on the final morning of the symposium. Many delegates had decided to skip the session on the economic impact of disease outbreaks and check out early. Caine had seen a few groups doing so already when he passed through the lobby. Glancing over at Laura's desk, he saw a couple of plain clothes police officers talking with her and looking over her shoulder as they studied her computer monitor.

After his forty-five minute presentation, Caine fielded a few obvious questions and discussed at length the lessons learnt from the UK foot-and-mouth disease outbreak in 2001.

The usual polite round of applause greeted him as he stepped down from the podium. Jonas Williams shook him by the hand and escorted him to the side of the stage where he rejoined the audience in one of the many vacant seats. With the anomaly of his unscheduled appearance out of the way, the regular programme began. Caine took the opportunity to catch up on some sleep. Only the applause signalling an end to the discussions aroused him from his nap.

Finally, Jonas Williams took the stage for the closing address. Once again he dedicated the meeting to Dr. al-Jaheerah and thanked the police and FBI for their assistance. Caine looked around him and saw several new faces sitting in the audience with more strangers propping up the walls eyeing the delegates with practised ease. The investigators had sent undercover officers to monitor the remaining delegates, surmising perhaps, as had Ms. Chen, that Dr. al-Jaheerah's killer was still at large within the hotel.

The delegates meandered out of the Grand Assembly room. Caine was in no great hurry and let the majority leave before getting to his feet. As he did so, Bill Jacobs and Jonas Williams, came down the aisle toward him.

"Hi, Paul," said Jacobs. "Great speech, well done."

"Thanks."

"You heading back home, or are you staying on for the tours?"

"I'm going straight home, this year," added Paul. He remembered that the dubious pleasure of examining the scar of the San Andreas Fault in Point Reyes National Park wore off several minutes after he last saw it over ten years ago. It was not an emotion with which he wished to reacquaint himself. Neither did the Fisherman's Wharf nor the Embarcadero tourist traps appeal to him. Caine was just happy to be going home.

"Okay, bud," replied Jacobs. "You take care now. Have a good trip."

Williams nodded in approval. "Yes, Dr. Caine. Many thanks for your presentation. Your analysis of the UK situation was most enlightening. I hope we can stay in touch in the future."

Caine shook hands with Williams and watched the two men disappear down the aisle to the exit, deep in conversation.

Caine's return flight to the UK did not leave until 10:00 A.M. the next morning, so he spent his time reading, answering email and emptying the mini-bar; CNN chirped in the background, endlessly repeating the day's news.

In the evening Caine got rid of his last few dollars at a strip bar on O'Farrell Street; the smiling, trim young dancers earning money for college was in stark contrast to the sad, flabby, old women trying to pay the rent he had surreptitiously enjoyed watching whilst a student in Birmingham years before.

One thing the Americans did better than anyone was sell sex.

The dancer's antics reminded him of Laura and as soon as he got back to the hotel he called her. Within the hour she was in his arms and they spent the rest of the night together.

In the morning Laura silently helped him pack. Caine skipped breakfast so he could spend more time with her. Escorting him down to the lobby she waited as he checked out. As he turned to say goodbye, Caine saw her deep in conversation with Bill Jacobs, who was now dressed casually in Bermuda shorts and a loud Hawaiian beach shirt, indistinguishable from the fat American tourists Caine had noticed waddling around the hotel over the preceding days.

Caine was surprised and a little disappointed, having credited Jacobs with considerably more taste. Jacobs did not see Caine and he left Laura after a few seconds, waving and laughing as he sauntered off to the Atrium lounge for breakfast.

"Isn't Bill a fun guy?" said Laura, still smiling from her encounter with the big Canadian, as Caine approached, stuffing his credit card receipt into his wallet.

"Dr. Jacobs to you, young lady," said Caine with mock disapproval.

"Oh, hush!" replied Laura. "I know Bill from way back. He's brought lots of conferences to this hotel."

"Oh, yes?"

"He was here only last month. One of the Stanford sub-committee meetings, I think," Laura replied furrowing her brow. "The hotel always gives them a good deal."

"Well," said Caine with an impish grin. "I can certainly recommend the personal service at this hotel."

Laura smiled back with closed lips. She did not want Caine to think that she slept around with all the guests – only those she found handsome, engaging and unattached.

"I'm off duty this morning," said Laura. "I can drive you to the airport, if you like?"

"Only if you're sure," replied Caine. "I don't want to put you to any trouble."

"It's no trouble at all," answered Laura.

The drive to San Francisco International Airport to the south of the city was uneventful. With all his possessions carried in a light holdall, they drove to the short-term parking lot, a cavernous subterranean vault beneath the airport complex.

They walked to the international departures check-in desks arm-in-arm and in silence.

At the gate to immigration control they hugged and looked deeply into each other's eyes.

"Laura, I…" began Caine, not knowing what he was going to say.

"Shhh!" said Laura, her finger on her lips. "Let's just enjoy the moment. Whatever will be, will be," she assured him.

For the moment Laura seemed happy just to have found someone she could spend time with, no questions asked, no obligations expected.

"Go now, or you'll miss your flight," urged Laura.

It was not true. Caine had at least an hour to wait before the boarding announcement for his flight was made. Accepting the chance he had been offered to exit as painlessly as possible, Caine smiled ruefully to himself.

"Take care," was all he managed to say, before turning and heading to the nearest immigration counter.

Finding a seat in the lounge was more difficult than Caine had imagined. With an hour to go before departure the few available rows of seats had filled rapidly.

Caine was practised in the art of travelling light. Into his small sports bag he could pack his every need. He could not remember the last time he had to wait at the baggage carousel; his carry-on luggage allowed him to be the first in the line for the taxis at his destination on almost every business trip he had ever taken.

A few faces from the symposium dotted some of the rows. Their shared experience generated a tenuous bond between strangers and Caine reciprocated the occasional nods of recognition he received. Resisting the spare seats beside some of his acquaintances, Caine did not want to be reminded of his meeting just yet.

A small, frail-looking man got up from his seat as Caine approached. Taking advantage of the opportunity, Caine increased his pace and sat down in the padded chair.

Caine listened absent-mindedly to the blare from the TV mounted on a podium immediately to his left, knowing that whatever items he missed would be repeated again in another half-hour.

Federal Reserve Chairman Alan Greenspan commented today that...

Checking his boarding pass, Caine found he would be sitting in an aisle seat at the back of the plane.

A plane crash in Indonesia claims forty-seven lives; we have an update from...

Caine emptied his pockets of the detritus he had collected during the last few days, business cards from veterinary sales reps, a hotel matchbook and a lint-coated object that might once have been edible.

Yesterday's oil refinery fire in Galveston, Texas, has been successfully extinguished, more from...

Unable to decide whether he wanted to go to the lavatory or not, Caine looked around for the nearest restroom. He tried to calculate if relieving himself would compensate for the probable loss of his seat.

A suspected case of foot-and-mouth disease has state veterinary officers on alert in Oklahoma...

Caine pricked up his ears and turned to face the TV. The face of the announcer cut to a shot of the front gate of Benson & Sons Feedlot. The caption at the foot of the picture identified the location as El Reno, OK. The scene cut to a sweeping panorama of the interior of a typical feedlot – file footage from the news channel library – the camera crew would not have been allowed inside the contaminated yard.

> *A suspected case of foot-and-mouth disease was reported in the early hours of this morning at a cattle feedlot on the outskirts of Oklahoma City. Staff at the feedlot noticed that some of the animals had become lethargic and were running a fever. Some of the animals had also suddenly gone lame. Blisters characteristic of the disease were reported on the feet and tongues of two animals. Veterinary officers from the Department of Agriculture say these are apparently the classic symptoms of foot-and-mouth disease.*
>
> *The disease, caused by a microscopic virus, affects cloven-footed animals such as cattle, pigs and sheep, and has not been reported in the United States since 1929. The feedlot owners and the veterinarians stressed that other diseases can also produce symptoms similar to foot-and-mouth disease and only laboratory tests would be able to determine the specific diagnosis.*

Vaccination against the disease is possible but is not practiced, as any meat would not be able to be sold under international trade and food hygiene regulations.

Oklahoma is the fifth largest cattle rearing state in America with over three hundred thousand cattle being raised at any one time.

Tissue samples have been sent to the USDA Plum Island laboratories in New York for confirmation. Until then, local officials remain guarded about the implications for the local and national markets.

The feedlot in question has been quarantined until the test results come back; a process that is expected to take up to two days. Only then will a decision be made on market closure and other restrictions, including inter-state transportation.

Caine stood up and looked around for a payphone. Crossing the open-plan lounge to the central aisle that ran the length of the terminal Caine spotted an empty phone booth underneath the departures and arrivals monitors suspended from the ceiling.

Caine waited impatiently as the connection was made.

"Hello?"

"Dr Reese? Walter? It's me, Paul," Caine replied, hoping the urgency in his voice would help alert Reese to the importance of his call.

"Paul? What's up?" answered Reese puzzled. He was not expecting to hear from Caine until he returned to work in two days time.

"Sorry Walter," Caine persisted, "but I thought you'd like to know." Caine paused, waiting to deliver his bombshell. "There's a suspected foot-and-mouth case over here."

"What?" Reese replied. "Are you sure?"

"Well, there's a suspected case in Oklahoma. Some sort of cattle farm, I think."

Caine had never seen a feedlot in real life and had no comprehension of their size or the scale of their operations.

"Oh, really, Paul," Reese complained, irritation raising the timbre of his voice a notch. "You know as well as I do that there are other vesicular diseases that are clinically indistinguishable from foot-and-mouth. There's vesicular stomatitis, vesicular exanthema and, what's the other one…?" Reese groped for the elusive term.

"Swine vesicular disease," corrected Caine, beginning to regret calling Reese so prematurely.

"Exactly," intoned Reese.

"But this is in cattle," protested Caine.

"Okay," replied Reese, taking up the gauntlet. "Strike SVD and exanthema. Try other differential diagnoses, such as, erm, I don't know, off the top of my head, foot rot, some sort of chemical or thermal burn, maybe even bluetongue or rinderpest."

Caine was deflated. He had forgotten that merely the presence of blisters on the foot or tongue did not necessarily imply that the foot-and-mouth disease virus was to blame. Modern farmyards were awash with concentrated chemicals, bleaches, herbicides, pesticides and poisons. Animals walking into a spillage or licking residues from a freshly treated surface could easily produce symptoms resembling a vesicular disease.

Reese sensed Caine's unease.

"However, if you wish to stay for a few days as an observer. That's fine with me. Better to be safe than sorry, I suppose."

"Thanks Walter, that's just what I was looking for. They'll get the lab results back from Plum Island in two days, max. If they're negative I'll come straight back."

"And if they're positive?" Reese wanted to know what exactly Caine was planning.

"Well," Caine responded tentatively. "I thought I could liaise with the folks at Plum Island, they might be needing access to the Institute's vaccine stocks."

The Animal Health Institute was the European repository for millions of doses of concentrated foot-and-mouth disease vaccine, paid for mostly by a few European Union countries and certain members of the Commonwealth. They were to be used only in dire emergency situations. The uproar in Britain when the government refused to allow the use of these vaccine stores during their own disease outbreak crisis in 2001 was still remembered as one of the blackest days in the Institute's history. Caine winced at the memory of the numerous acrimonious meetings in the local councils, church halls and farmers' union offices, where he had to defend publicly the government's decision.

Reese was not entirely convinced. "Notwithstanding the United States' own considerable vaccine reserves," he replied, "and the fact that the Institute's own stocks belong to other countries and are not normally for sale, I find it difficult to believe that they would approach us."

"Still," Caine interjected, "I think it would be a major plus if we could have a man on the inside if it turns out to be true."

"Very well," Reese said in a guarded tone. "I'll call a few chaps at Plum Island, to see if they know anything. Better check back in at the hotel and wait it out. I'll call you as soon as I know something."

"Thanks Walter."

"Mmmm. You realise it's probably nothing. America hasn't had a case for how long?" Reese paused to calculate the date. "Nearly eighty years. They probably have the best surveillance system in the world to prevent exactly this sort of inexplicable outbreak."

"We're living in dangerous times, Walter."

"Just don't get your hopes up. It's probably nothing," repeated Reese.

The public address system crackled to life. Boarding for Caine's connecting flight to Cincinnati was announced.

"What time is it there?" demanded Reese.

Caine looked at his watch. "Nearly 10:00 A.M. You're eight hours ahead."

"All right. I'll get back to you with some info in a couple of hours. In the meantime, you can round up some of your contacts over there if there's anyone left. Get hold of Jonas Williams, he's bound to be around somewhere. Did that chap from Hong Kong turn up with his new assay?" Reese asked, referring to Philip Yeung. "Maybe you can interest them in following up with that while you're there?"

"Good idea," replied Caine, grateful he had at least been able to engage Reese on his behalf.

Cancelling his ticket at the desk in the departure lounge, Caine looked up at the speaker involuntarily as the final boarding announcement for his flight was made.

As he walked slowly away back to the main entrance searching for the shuttle buses back to downtown San Francisco, Caine smiled to himself.

I wonder if Laura will be pleased?

Chapter 17

The wait was interminable. Eventually, at 2:15 P.M. Walter Reese called back.

"Hi, Walter. What's the score?" asked Caine wearily.

"I spoke to the head of Plum Island, Eli Rosenthal, a good friend of mine. I haven't spoken to him in ages, actually," Reese answered.

"The bad news is you can't go to Plum Island, I'm afraid. There's no way around it, especially if it turns out to be FMD."

"But," offered Reese, "they have no problem with you acting as an on-the-spot investigator, as it were. Try to glean some epidemiological data to track the origin and spread of the virus. I said you were the man for the job and they took the bait.'

"Thanks, Walter. That's fantastic."

"Get yourself down to Oklahoma City pronto," said Reese. "Or should that be up? I'm afraid I don't have a map handy."

"Actually, I think it's across," corrected Caine. "Who do I need to contact when I get there?"

"Some chap in the city government. He's holding the fort until the big guns arrive. Hang on I have his name here," a rumbling sound came from the receiver and Caine imagined Reese rummaging frenziedly in his pockets. "Jackson Wilson," came the eventual reply. "Can that be a real name?" queried Reese.

"How do I find this Jackson Wilson?"

"They said report to City Hall and he will escort you around," replied Reese, now marshalling his facts confidently. "I say, this is all rather exciting, isn't it?"

Caine hung up and immediately booked a flight to Oklahoma City. Flight 866 left San Francisco at 4:45 P.M. with a one-hour stopover in Salt Lake City. Caine would arrive in Oklahoma City just before midnight.

With less than two hours to catch his flight Caine called reception and asked to be put through to Laura.

"What are you doing here?" she said

"I couldn't keep away," Caine replied smugly, then, realising he shouldn't give Laura the impression he had returned specifically on her account, added, "But I can't stay long. I have to go to Oklahoma City this afternoon. Right now in fact. I just dropped in to say hi."

"What's going on in Oklahoma City?" asked Laura.

"Haven't you heard?" said Caine with some surprise, before thinking that the occurrence of obscure veterinary diseases halfway across the country would not likely be of interest to the majority of the general public. "They think there's an outbreak of foot-and-mouth disease over there. I'm going along to check it out."

"Wow. What a coincidence, huh?" replied Laura, feigning an interest in a subject she knew nothing about. "Guess you guys picked the right time for your conference?"

"I reckon," said Caine. "Anyway, I better be going now, I have a plane to catch. You take care, okay?"

Caine gave Laura a hug and a peck on the lips. This was not the place for anything more demonstrative however much he would have liked.

"If you've got time, call me, okay?" Laura replied wistfully, as Caine pulled away from her embrace.

Picking up his bag, Caine checked out again. With a final wave to Laura he stood on the steps of the hotel and hailed a passing taxi. In minutes he was surrounded by mid-afternoon traffic heading down US101 to the airport.

Touching down at Will Rogers World Airport at 11:50 P.M. Caine was tired, having slept only lightly on the flight. With his eyes almost closing involuntarily he managed to stumble into the queue for the taxis and headed for the nearest budget motel.

On North Macarthur Boulevard, the SleepyHeads Motel seemed just right.

Chapter 18

Walking up the steps of the four-storey grey monolith of City Hall in west downtown, Caine imagined he could be anywhere in America's mid-west. The chaos of the wide, straight boulevards and avenues choked with traffic contrasted with the serene beauty of the clear blue Oklahoma skies above.

The size of the country amazed Caine even though he was a frequent visitor to the US. After flying for what seemed like most of the previous day he was still only halfway across the country. The equivalent flight from the UK would have taken him to the Middle East or beyond.

At the reception desk Caine enquired after Jackson Wilson, only to be told that he was late but expected any minute. The receptionist seemed to recognise Caine's name and eyed him suspiciously as he waited in the sparsely furnished foyer. Heels clacked backwards and forwards across the polished marble floor.

After some minutes a tall, well-dressed black man entered the building and bounded up the stairs two at a time. The receptionist flapped her arms to attract his attention.

"Mr. Wilson?" she called after him. "This is the visitor you're expecting."

Jackson Wilson, still lean and wiry despite not having played college basketball for a dozen or more years, turned to face the woman at the desk. Caine stood up and started to cross the wide reception hall to meet the man. Wilson turned to face Caine. A full head taller than Caine, he cut an imposing figure.

"Pleased to meet you, Dr. Caine. Please call me Jackson, everyone does. We're all very friendly around here."

"What exactly do you do here, Mr. Wilson, I mean Jackson?"

"Actually, I'm the city manager. I deal with the day-to-day oversight and management of all city departments – you know, fire, police, public works, utilities and what-not."

"Nothing to do with agriculture, then?" said Caine eager to get started on the suspected outbreak.

"Well not as such, although I do liaise with the other government agencies as and when required. I'm going to take you uptown to the Department of Agriculture offices right now as a matter of fact. If you need anything they can't provide, you just give me a call and I'll see what I can come up with."

"Thanks, Jackson, I really appreciate your help."

Wilson paused for a moment unsure if he should ask the question that was evidently troubling him.

"Dr. Caine, do you think it's really this disease, what's it called? Foot-and-mouth?" asked Wilson, his voiced edged with obvious concern.

"Well, I don't know until I see the animals up close and do some tests. Why?"

"Perhaps you should know that cattle rearing is the number one economic activity in this state. It's worth nearly two billion dollars per year. Anything that affects cattle affects this state, y'hear? I'd hate to see anything happen to change that."

"Well, yes. I mean, me too," Caine replied apprehensively.

"I've got a car waiting for you out front. If you'd care to join me, I'll drive you to the Department of Agriculture building. It shouldn't take more than twenty minutes."

The men left the building and climbed into a white four-wheel drive SUV emblazoned with the city seal on the front door panels. The air-conditioner sprang to life as soon as the ignition was turned. Caine tugged at his shirtfront trying to get some air circulating over his chest.

"It's gonna get hot later today," said Wilson, noting his passenger's discomfort. "May be eighty-five, ninety."

"Phew," said Caine.

"Mind you," continued Wilson, "the record's one-thirteen."

The drive down North Lincoln Boulevard ended at the driveway to the Department of Agriculture offices. The parking lot was full so Wilson dropped Caine off at the steps to the front door.

"It looks like they're all pretty busy up here," he said, cocking his head toward the parked cars. "I guess I'll have to drop you here. There's no need for me to go in. Its okay, they're expecting you. Here's my card. If you need anything just give me a call, okay?"

Caine waited on the steps, waving in acknowledgement as Wilson's car disappeared into the stream of traffic.

The atmosphere inside the Department of Agriculture was the complete antithesis of that at City Hall. Caine immediately felt a familiar claustrophobia and buzz of activity that reminded him of his own institute in the UK.

The reception desk was small and manned by a surly looking male seated behind a shatterproof glass screen. Caine wondered if it was to protect the staff from the visitors or vice versa.

Signing his name in the yellowing pages of a cheap registration book he was handed a laminated badge declaring in large black capital letters that he was indeed a VISITOR. After some minutes Caine's guide, a tall fair-haired man wearing a white lab coat, came to collect him.

"Hi, Dr. Caine?" said the man in a warm friendly tone. "Glad you could make it. Where's Jackson?"

"He's not coming. I think your full car park put him off."

The man looked puzzled for a moment then replied, "Car park? Parking lot, right? Ah, I see what you mean. Yeah, we're pretty busy at the moment as you can probably imagine."

The man pushed his way through a set a double doors that allowed access to a long corridor. Caine was reminded eerily of his own institute.

"I'm Steve by the way. Steve Gould. I'm the chief virologist around here. I hear your specialty is molecular epidemiology?"

"Yes, that's right," replied Caine.

"Well that's one area in which we're a bit thin. There's not much call for it in these parts. We usually send all our samples for sequencing to one of the reference centres, Ames, Plum Island, and so on."

The pair walked briskly down the long wide corridor toward a room at the end.

"This is our war room," said Gould cheerily.

Inside several figures sat around a large conference table talking earnestly, notepads open. A white writing board stood at one end of the room. Positioned in front of the board was an easel on which rested a large-scale map of what Caine presumed to be Oklahoma City and its immediate environs.

"Okay, guys," announced Gould, heedless of interrupting everyone's conversation in mid-stream.

Pulling a crumpled fax out of his pocket he glanced at it and said, "This is Dr. Paul Caine from England. The Animal Health Institute in," his face creased as he studied the fax in his hand, "Glow-cester-shire. Is that right?" he asked Caine hopefully.

"Gloucester," corrected Caine.

"Well anyway," continued Gould, "he's been appointed by Eli Rosenthal at Plum Island as an official observer on behalf of the British government."

Caine's eyes widened.

My, Walter has pulled some strings.

"So we're gonna show him some good ol' OK hospitality. Got that?"

A murmur slowly circled the room and all eyes were directed on Caine, who immediately sensed the need to establish the pecking order with respect to his presence. Turning, he faced his audience.

"I'd just like to thank Dr. Gould for his introduction," he began. "This is my first visit to a Department of Agriculture facility and I appreciate the time and trouble you're taking to show me around. I hope I can learn as much as possible from the experts at the front line in the short time I'll be here. I'd be happy to help in any way I can. Now I know you have a lot of important things to discuss so I won't take up any more of your valuable time. Thank you."

Caine hoped his speech would assuage any thoughts that he had been sent to usurp the local investigation. Considering that federal agencies were standing by to take over in case the virus spread, another outsider would not be well tolerated.

The introductions complete, Caine took a seat at the back of the small room. Gould remained standing at the front of the room and directed the discussion.

"Okay, may be we can take a few minutes and recap the situation for the benefit of Dr. Caine? Ted?"

The man sitting next to Caine got up and crossed the room. Standing by the easel he stabbed at the map with a pencil.

"Well, let's see," said the man, struggling to find the opening thread of his story. "Early yesterday morning, about 5:00 A.M. the night duty VO, that's Veterinary Officer, took a call from the company vet at Benson and Sons feedlot out on I-40 near El Reno. He said he had some cattle that had come down with a fever. They were lethargic with dull eyes, sort of a general malaise, so to speak. A couple of hours later, after daybreak, he calls back and says a couple of 'em also had blisters on the feet and can we come and take a look?"

"How many cattle were affected?" asked Caine.

"Around forty out of the thirty thousand head on the lot at the time".

"That's pretty quick work by the company vet, spotting so few cases out of such a large herd," ventured Caine.

"We take the health of our cattle very seriously around here, Dr. Caine," replied Gould, somewhat defensively. "Some of these guys out in the field have twenty-odd plus years experience just in cattle. They can tell if a beast is sick by smelling it."

Caine smirked.

"I mean it, Dr. Caine," Gould replied, his stern unflinching face emphasising that his claim was no idle boast.

"So," Ted continued, "Barry and Janice went over to check it out. They concurred with the company vet that the beasts were sick. Vesicles were noted on two animals and lameness noted in six others. They requested that the cattle be isolated from the rest of the stock and took pharyngeal samples with a probang cup and obtained vesicle fluid by lancing. These were sent to Plum Island by express courier," he intoned.

"Is there any possibility that the lesions were caused by chemical or thermal burns?" enquired Caine, mindful of Reese's earlier admonition.

Now it was the American scientists' turn to smile.

"Have you ever been to a cattle feedlot, Dr. Caine?" asked Gould

"No."

"There's nothing out there for miles except cattle," Gould spread his arms wide to emphasise the expanse of the operations. "No chemicals, no fires, nothing. Just cattle."

"So what's the situation now, twenty-four hours later?" Caine asked, eager to know if the mystery illness had spread.

"As of 8:00 A.M., we have six out of twenty pens with sick animals. Each pen holds about one thousand head. Of these six thousand odd suspect animals at least half have come down with fever. Of those with fever, about one hundred have vesicular eruptions on the feet or marked lameness."

Some of the people seated around the table sucked air sharply through their teeth; this was the first time the updated figures had been announced.

"Well, I don't know about you guys," said Gould, "but this looks like a full blown outbreak to me."

"Are there any results from Plum Island yet?" asked Caine.

"We still have to exclude differential diagnoses, of course. Apart from the obvious vesicular diseases, we're also looking at viral diarrhoea, rhinopneumonitis, malignant catarrhal fever and bluetongue. We're gonna have a conference call with Eli and his team at 10:00 A.M. to get the preliminary results."

"Can we visit the farm, this feedlot?" Caine interrupted.

"After the conference call we're all gonna go down there and take another look," answered Gould.

The next hour passed in a sober discussion of all the various possible diagnoses. At the end of the session, the candidates had been narrowed down firmly to a particularly virulent isolate of vesicular stomatitis virus or foot-and-mouth disease.

Just after 10:00 A.M. the conference call was placed. Gould switched on the loudspeaker and replaced the handset. The voice of an elderly man croaked from the small speaker.

"Hi, Steve. This is Eli. How's everyone doing down there in Oklahoma City?"

"We're fine Eli, nice to hear from you," replied Gould.

"Who have you got with you?"

"Of those you've met before I've got Ted Lawson, Barry Hendricks and Janice Wong. We've also got a bunch of field officers and Dr. Paul Caine from England."

"Dr. Caine?" the old man said addressing Caine directly. "Glad you could join us. Walter put in a few good words on your behalf."

"Thank you, Dr. Rosenthal. I'm looking forward to the experience," replied Caine.

"You're welcome. In addition, I believe there's a friend of yours here who would like to say a few words," added Rosenthal.

"Oh, really?" replied Caine taken aback. He did not know anyone at the Plum Island laboratories, a fact that compounded his difficulty in securing a visit to the facility.

"Hi, Paul. Is that you?" came a distinctly Asian voice.

Caine was mystified. The voice was familiar but he could not place it exactly.

"It's me. Philip Yeung," continued the voice without waiting for Caine's response.

Bastard! How did he manage to get invited to Plum Island?

"Philip! What a surprise. What are you doing in New York?" Caine replied, anger and jealously welling up inside him.

"I heard about the outbreak on TV, so I called up and offered them our company's new test. Luckily I brought along a few demo kits. It seems they were pretty interested. I flew in last night. I guess I was just in the right place at the right time, huh?"

How very fucking convenient.

"Yes, remarkable," Caine replied, seething quietly. "Let me know how it goes will you?"

"What have you got for us, Eli?" asked Gould, the suspense rising palpably with every second.

"Well," said the old man, "I hope you're all sitting comfortably. I'm afraid to say that it is definitely foot-and-mouth disease."

The crowded room let out a simultaneous gasp.

Jesus.

"I know what you're going to say next," continued Rosenthal. "Yes, I am positive."

"What's the serotype?" asked Gould, anxious to know as much as possible.

"We're working on that right now. The standard antigen detection test is giving equivocal results for some reason, so we're giving Dr. Yeung's new assay a test drive. We're also running some RT-PCR assays. We'll get the results this afternoon."

"Okay, thanks Eli. Talk to you again this afternoon. Goodbye," concluded Gould.

"Paul? For the benefit of the vets here, would you mind explaining exactly what RT-PCR is?" asked Gould, keen to get Caine accepted as a member of the team.

"Sure," said Caine confidently. "As I'm sure most of you know, viruses, like all organisms, reproduce by copying their genetic material and passing it on to their progeny. Bacteria, fungi and all other living things contain their genetic material in the form of two strands of DNA held together by chemical bonds. This property can be exploited in many rapid detection technologies. The major problem is that it is very difficult to get hold of enough DNA from a suspect sample to identify exactly what it is, so we need a method to copy it, or amplify it, many thousands of times."

"How do you do that?" asked one of the technicians.

"Well," Caine continued, "if you know the exact DNA sequence of a piece of genetic material unique to the organism you want to detect, say a bacterium or virus, you can synthesise a small piece of DNA that acts as an initiator of the amplification reaction."

"A primer, right?" said another voice from across the room.

"Exactly," said Caine, now warming to the topic. "You take your primer, some purified enzymes that can copy DNA and a bunch of the DNA building blocks called nucleotides and mix them all together in a test tube with DNA isolated from your suspect sample, whatever that may be. Then you put it in a special machine that separates the two strands of sample DNA by heating. This allows the primer to bind to the unique target gene in the organism you want to detect. By alternately heating and cooling the reaction mixture you create a chain reaction in which the enzymes copy the DNA target millions of times. After a few hours you have enough DNA to detect. We call it the polymerase chain reaction or PCR for short."

"But you said the assay was called RT-PCR," interrupted one of the staff. "What's the difference?"

"The problem is not all organisms have their genetic material in the form of double-stranded DNA. Some organisms, mainly viruses, like the viruses causing foot-and-mouth disease or influenza, contain a single strand of a related chemical called RNA. RNA is very delicate and cannot be copied easily. What you have to do is convert the RNA into DNA first. To do this you need another enzyme called reverse transcriptase or RT. Once you've converted the RNA to DNA you can use the standard PCR method. Hence RT-PCR is a way of copying small amounts of single-stranded RNA into millions of copies of double-stranded DNA. The purpose is the same, to effect a rapid detection of the organism of interest."

"That's a pretty neat trick," said one of the technicians.

"Yeah. The guy who invented it got the Nobel Prize," added Caine.

"Thanks, Paul," said Gould. "That was a nice summary. If everyone's ready, we can load up the trucks and get down to the feedlot to check how things are going."

Gould, Hendricks and Wong removed their lab coats and trudged down the corridor to the main entrance. In the parking lot Hendricks, Wong and a couple of technicians climbed into a Department of Agriculture pick-up truck and pulled away quickly. Gould and Caine followed in a second truck.

El Reno, in the western suburbs of Oklahoma City, was barely five miles from the Department of Agriculture offices and within minutes the pair of vehicles arrived at their destination.

They stopped outside the main entrance to Benson and Sons. Caine looked up and recognised the scene from the CNN newscast of the previous day.

A handful of cars and trucks from local TV stations were parked directly opposite the feedlot entrance. When the Department of Agriculture vehicles pulled up the scientists were confronted by a gaggle of eager journalists desperate for any titbit of information.

Entry to the property was forbidden by order of the Department of Agriculture.

Hendricks, in the lead vehicle, honked his horn. A figure clothed in a white coverall emerged from a small wooden office and unlatched the gate, closing it hastily as soon as the vehicles had passed inside the perimeter.

The inspection team alighted from their cars and converged on the small office. The white-clad figure approached smiling.

"Hi, fellas. Ready for an update?"

Gould turned to Caine. "Paul, this is Frank Carter, one of our veterinary officers," he said.

Carter acknowledged Caine with a nod.

"What's the situation, Frank?" asked Gould.

"Why don't we take a look around, and I'll fill you in as we go?" replied

Carter, clearly relishing this opportunity to display his knowledge.

Caine too was in his element. As a molecular epidemiologist he liked nothing better than recreating the scene from the evidence available to him. Ultimately, Caine was a detective. Instead of fingerprints, fibres and witness statements, he worked with tissue samples, extracting the nucleic acid, counting and mapping the changes and mutations in the genetic sequence, recreating the evolutionary history of a virus as its spread and slowly adapted to its environment.

It was every epidemiologist's dream to be at Ground Zero when an outbreak occurred. To describe the initial case and chart the effects on its environment was a challenge that most would never have the opportunity of enjoying. Caine almost hated himself for his enthusiasm.

Thank God for foot-and-mouth disease.

The group walked across the courtyard and onto a gravel-strewn access road running the length of the property.

"The first cases were noted in here," Carter said, leading the way to the entrance of the third pen on their left as they walked up the path.

"Let's go in and take a look," he continued.

The atmosphere inside the pen was fetid. The high roof did little to ameliorate the effects of the burning sun outside. If anything it seemed to amplify them.

The cattle were agitated and ill at ease, swaying from side to side, rubbing against their neighbours and the sides of the stalls. Muted brays and moos filled the air, as if the tormented animals sensed their fate. After the confirmation of the diagnosis by Plum Island none of the animals would leave this pen alive.

Carter moved over to the first stall and rested nonchalantly against it, his arm resting along the upper rail and the heel of one foot hooked over the bottom rail.

"We can see the typical signs and symptoms here," Carter began. "The wranglers noticed that some of the animals were restless and dull-eyed. The company vet confirmed this and took temperatures with a rectal probe, noting a high fever."

Carter pointed to a beast that stuck its head through the bars of the stall so that it faced the group, drooling profusely.

"Here we see excessive salivation typical of an ulcerated or otherwise irritated mouth. If we look inside," with a sudden motion Carter gripped the animal around the neck and prised open its jaw. The crowd gasped as he revealed a long greenish tongue with massive bloody erosions on its surface. The animal roared in pain and tried to pull away as if ashamed that its disfigurement had been made public.

"On the feet we can see typical erosions at the top of the digital cleft and around the coronary band," said Carter, making a circular motion with his finger to indicate the transition point between the hair-covered skin of the leg and the horny growth of the cloven hoof.

"How many infected animals have we got now?" asked Gould.

"First thing this morning we had confirmed infections, by which I mean vesicular eruptions or oral erosions, in six of the twenty pens. We're still working our way through the pens, but I would say that at least half of the stock here is directly affected. So we're talking about ten to fifteen thousand animals. Of course, now that FMD is confirmed, the numbers are largely academic considering that the US practices stamping out."

"Stamping out?" asked one of the junior technicians.

Carter turned to the young woman and looked directly into her eyes, "Stamping out. Every infected animal and all known or presumed contacts are destroyed as soon as practicable," he said.

"Is that really necessary?" asked the woman, astonished at the numbers involved.

"Foot-and-mouth disease is the most economically serious disease of livestock," explained Carter. "The virus can be carried by the wind over one hundred fifty miles. It can survive for six months on bedding and up to a week on pasture. On hides or in contaminated meat products the virus can remain viable for over a year. Wherever an infected animal has gone it will transport virus that could initiate another outbreak."

"Won't the animals recover?" asked the woman. "I mean what about an immune response and antibodies and stuff?"

"Most infected animals will recover from FMD, that's true," admitted Carter. "But they will never regain their capacity to produce milk or put on weight. So for fattening cattle for beef or dairy production, forget it. A farmer might as well cull his herd and start over. On top of that cattle can become asymptomatic carriers for six months or more. As soon as you mix fresh healthy beasts with disease carriers they will become targets for infection. It's an endless cycle. You must cull the herd and thoroughly disinfect before reintroducing healthy animals."

After visiting two other pens in which the cattle displayed a range of symptoms typical of foot-and-mouth disease, Gould halted the tour.

"As you can see, many of the cattle here are showing classical signs and symptoms of FMD. As we now have serological evidence of infection with confirmation by more sensitive nucleic acid tests, there is no option but to depopulate this herd."

Caine looked away and gazed over to the far side of the pen where a chink of daylight streamed in and illuminated the gloom.

Why say depopulate when you really mean exterminate?

Caine turned back to face the group. Sullen-faced they walked in silence back to their temporary office near the front gate.

"How soon will the depopulation start?" asked one of the group, as they sat in the air-conditioned comfort of the wooden hut.

"Probably this afternoon," replied Gould. "We need to get a team of qualified slaughtermen to cull the animals humanely and then arrange to transport the carcasses to a landfill site. With a herd this size, that's going to take some time."

"How will they be killed?" asked a female technician, upset at the sheer size of the task ahead of them.

"If possible we will use the humane killer. That's a special type of gun that injects a retractable steel bolt into the brain. First, though each animal will have to be stunned with an electric shock. So, there will be teams of two each disposing of about twenty-five to thirty animals per hour. If we have ten teams it will take them over one hundred hours non-stop to depopulate this yard."

"Looks like we need more people," observed Hendricks.

"I think this sort of job needs to be completed within twenty-four hours if we are to minimise any virus spread due to aerosol or fomites," added Wong.

"We may need to call in the Army or National Guard to help out," Carter said.

"Only problem is they'll be using hand guns not humane killers. The public relations are going to be a nightmare," Gould surmised.

"The army has to be used as a last resort," Caine added. "We used them in the UK in 2001 and the animal welfare people went nuts."

"I'll mobilise the Department of Agriculture offices at the county level and get them to round up some more humane killers, electric stun probes and people who know how to use them," said Gould. "Looks like it's gonna be a long night."

By midnight, over forty pairs of men were at work. As soon as one pen had been cleared they moved on to the next. Pens containing animals that had not yet displayed any symptoms of infection were set-aside until the final phase of the culling operation. The carcasses were removed by a small fleet of forklift trucks seconded from local businesses in the area.

An ugly pile of contorted carcasses lay in a heap in all the open spaces of the feedlot. The nearest landfill was many miles away. At the last moment it was considered too much of a risk to transport them in open containers such a large distance. Instead the US Army Corps of Engineers dug a large shallow groove in the earth, ten yards wide and two hundred yards long parallel to the gravel access road. The corpses were piled high and doused with aviation fuel sprayed from a container truck that drove slowly down one side of the mound.

At sunrise, an army officer clad in camouflage fatigues lit the fuse, a rolled copy of the previous day's *Oklahoman*.

The silhouettes of the onlookers appeared as black twigs against the perfect orange sphere of the fireball as it erupted from the mass grave. The orange darkened to red and finally to black as the noxious fumes moulded themselves into a mushroom cloud that boiled away leaving a colossal exclamation mark hundreds of feet high.

The pyre burned through the day and into the night, staining the air with its hideous pall.

It took four days to reduce the thirty thousand corpses to ash.

Chapter 19

Philip Yeung was worried. Since his unexpected arrival in New York he had been way out of his depth. The facilities at the Plum Island Animal Disease Center were exemplary. Whatever he needed he got, whether it be reagents for his new assay, bench space or time on the computer to analyse his data.

During a brief lull in the otherwise hectic day Philip reflected on the situation at his own company. The constant battle to allocate funds to priority projects, the hassle in clearing draft manuscripts with senior management, the unwillingness and resentment when another staff member's technician was temporarily transferred to someone else's project.

The scientists at Plum Island had a different problem. They were very polite but Yeung could sense the arrogance, the sense of superiority only understood if you have been on the receiving end of questioning and contemptuous looks for most of your life.

In Yeung's case the air of superiority he sensed was not directed at him because of his skin, but because of who he was. The outsider. The corporate scientist. The man whose only aim was to make money from other people's misery and despair. What did he care about sick and dying animals, or farmers becoming unemployed and homeless as a result? All he was interested in was patents and making money and screwing anybody else who tried to tread on his toes. Wasn't that the case?

Philip didn't have time to analyse the real reasons he became a scientist or why he travelled to New York. He was just trying to make a difference. He didn't claim to have the answer, just a small part of the puzzle.

The results of a trial run conducted with samples known to contain the foot-and-mouth disease virus — the positive controls, as they were called, looked good. The real test, however, came with the analysis of samples obtained from the Oklahoma outbreak.

The Plum Island lab staff milled around their benches casting occasional glances in Philip's direction. A large ruddy-faced technician in an ill-fitting lab coat had been assigned to escort Philip around the research centre, ensuring he visited only those areas to which he was entitled. The technician had also been one of the first to analyse the Oklahoma samples.

"I can't understand why those antigen tests didn't work the first time around," said the white-coated man to Philip.

"There's lots of reasons," Philip answered. Antigen-antibody interactions were not his strong point but he understood enough of the principles to make a stab at why they had not worked on the Oklahoma samples.

The first round of antibody testing had been unable to identify the specific serotype or strain of virus present in the tissue sample from Oklahoma. Viruses were a little like individuals of different nationalities, each one occupying a certain geographical location, but each free to circulate given the means and opportunity to do so. The three SAT serotypes for example, were predominantly found in cattle and buffalo in Southern Africa and the Middle East, while serotype O was the most promiscuous having circled the globe and finding its way into cloven hoofed animals in virtually every country.

The antibody test results earlier in the day had been equivocal, giving a positive reaction in three out of the seven serotype tests conducted. Normally, only one should have been positive. This was a problem as the emergency response to foot-and-mouth disease outbreaks sometimes made use of vaccination to protect uninfected animals from contracting the disease. As the vaccines were serotype-specific, identifying the wrong strain would mean useless vaccine being distributed to those who needed it.

"The sample came from Oklahoma right?" continued Philip. "So I guess it's pretty hot down there at this time of year? Maybe the proteins in the virus envelope degraded in the heat giving a false positive in some of the assays."

"Mmm," said the man, clearly not convinced.

"Or," Philip continued, "maybe there's some contaminant in the sample, enzymes from ruptured cells degrading the antibodies in the test tube. Or maybe the reaction mixture is just plain dirty, so the spectrophotometer can't make out if the dirt in the reaction is a positive result or not."

"Well," the man said, digesting Philip's comments, "the guys were in a rush and the samples did look pretty scummy. There might be something in what you say."

"The best thing to do in a situation like that is start over again. Purify the sample again from scratch," added Philip, glad that a human error had made his test seem more reliable.

Take what you can get.

"Yeah, they're doing that now. It won't take long. So how's your test coming along?" the man said.

"Should have the results soon," replied Philip confidently, looking at his watch. Actually he was worried, as he had received an identical sample of the Oklahoma tissue that had given the strange results in the antibody test. "I've got unique primers for all seven serotypes set up. If the viral genome is present I will be able to tell the serotype directly after the amplification result."

The amplification device sat on the bench in front of Philip. It worked silently, automatically copying the viral nucleic acid over and over. At a predetermined time, when enough copies had been made to allow efficient detection of the signal, it would switch itself off and alert the operator. A faint smell of ozone generated by the high voltage power supply drifted from the machine.

Beep. Beep. Beep.

Philip turned to face the machine.

"Time's up," he announced.

Switching on the computer monitor he imported the data from the amplification device. After a few seconds, seven traces, one for each serotype reaction, appeared on the screen. Each was identified by a different colour.

"See?" said Philip, pointing at the screen. "Six flat traces and one peak. There's your serotype."

"Which one is it?" said the man, impressed by the simplicity of the visual display.

"Let's see, the peak corresponds to primer set number twelve." Philip ran his finger down a column of handwritten figures in a black ledger on the laboratory bench. "Serotype C."

"C? Are you sure?" said the man incredulously.

"Definitely, serotype C."

A phone rang in the corner of the lab. The man excused himself and answered. After a few seconds, he said, "Let me guess. C, right?" Looking over at Philip as he listened intently to the caller he added, "The new guy's test came through a few minutes ago, that's how." The caller held the man's attention for some time. Eventually, the man put the phone down and turned to Philip.

"We gotta go down to the conference room, now," he said firmly.

"Why, what's up?" replied Philip, concerned that something was amiss.

"Because the shit just hit the fan."

In the conference room on the ground floor a large group of people had assembled. They murmured among themselves and Philip felt ill at ease, as he knew no one in the room.

Several minutes passed before Eli Rosenthal, accompanied by his personal assistant, entered. Rosenthal walked slowly and the crowd parted in deference as the old man made his way to the desk.

Sitting at one end of the immaculately polished teak conference table Rosenthal rested his forearms on the edge and interlocked his fingers. His assistant placed a slim brown folder on the table next to his left arm. Without looking at it he began to speak.

"At least once in everyone's life," he said, "we have the privilege of being tested as a nation. I am rather more fortunate than most people in this room, in that I have lived through two such occasions already. One was December 1941, when Pearl Harbor was attacked; the other was November 1963, when President Kennedy was assassinated. You may consider the events and aftermath of September 2001 as your first real test as a citizen of this great country."

Rosenthal paused, staring straight ahead, as if by force of concentration he could see through the crowd of people in front of him and beyond the back of the wall of the conference room – out into the dunes and scrub of Plum Island and further, across the water to the mainland.

"Some of you may quibble over my use of the word 'privilege'", he continued, "but I would argue that on each of the occasions I have just mentioned, the United States emerged stronger, more courageous, and more self aware of its status and obligations than it had before. We are privileged people and we should not forget it. Perhaps today is another example where we as Americans get to display our unique talents in a time of struggle."

The crowd was silent, listening to Rosenthal with rapt attention. Some looked at each other with raised eyebrows and quizzical glances, unsure as to the direction Rosenthal was heading.

"Most of you will have heard of the unusual outbreak of disease in Oklahoma yesterday and the fact that we have been doing our usual surveillance activities on behalf of the Department of Agriculture there. The results of those tests are now available. Without a doubt, the implications of the results are highly significant and that is why I have called this extraordinary meeting. I have to tell you now that the organism responsible for the outbreak in Oklahoma is the foot-and-mouth disease virus. What is more, the precise strain of the virus is serotype C."

Gasps of surprise filled the room.

"The older or more studious among you will be aware immediately of the implications of this announcement. For the benefit of those who are not, serotype C is generally found in the Old World, mainly the Middle East and central Asia. While it is certainly possible that the virus could be introduced adventitiously into this country, the size and location of this outbreak make me think that we are witnessing the deliberate introduction of an infectious agent the purpose of which is to wreak economic damage on the United States. In short, we may be seeing the first bioterrorist attack in this country's history.

"Shortly before joining you at this meeting, I reported my suspicions to the local office of the Federal Bureau of Investigation. I do not doubt that within a few hours they will be here to interview me and a few others here with knowledge of this situation. I hope you will make yourselves available for questioning. In addition, I need not remind you that one of the conditions of working at this institute is confidentiality. I won't be at all surprised if many of you receive invitations and other inducements by the news media to offer your own particular insights into this situation. I beg you to consider the consequences of your actions, especially as they might affect the ability of the law enforcement agencies to apprehend the perpetrators of this act."

Rosenthal paused and surveyed the room with a glance, ensuring the gravity of his words and the seriousness of his tacit threat had their intended effect.

"Let me finish by saying what a pleasure it is to be working with such a dedicated group of people. You are a credit to your country. Thank you."

With that, Rosenthal rose slowly from his seat and left the room, leaving it in a state of suspended animation for some seconds. Suddenly a cacophony of noise and raised voices filled the air, as conjecture and theory vied for equal space.

Philip Yeung sat silent and alone at the back of the room and wondered what it all meant.

Chapter 20

Angela Garcia strode confidently down the corridors of the Plum Island Animal Disease Center. Tall, slender and elegant the Spanish-American beauty cut a swathe through the dowdy technicians and receptionists in their crisp, white lab coats and tied back hair.

The Director's office lay at the end of the corridor. Rapping on the outer office door she entered without waiting for a reply. Inside, the anteroom was furnished simply with a desk and filing cabinet.

Eli Rosenthal and his personal assistant stood in the centre of the room. Behind Rosenthal, the door of his inner office stood ajar, yellow light from a fluorescent strip lamp overhead illuminating the interior.

"Can I help you?" demanded Dora Krantz, fixing Garcia with a piercing stare.

"Angela Garcia, Special Agent, FBI".

As she withdrew her identification, Garcia instinctively let the front of her tailored Armani jacket fall open, revealing the knurled grip of her .38 Smith & Wesson revolver.

The tactic had the desired effect. Both Krantz and Rosenthal saw the barely concealed weapon and glanced down at the floor. Their response too had been instinctive, a reflex from the dawn of man's origin. Backing down from the challenge of an aggressor in order to appease them. If Krantz and Rosenthal had been dogs they would have been cowering in the corner of the room with their tails between their legs.

"Dr. Rosenthal?" continued Garcia, staring directly into his eyes and ignoring Krantz. "You called my boss this morning. He sent me here to discuss the situation with you. What exactly are we dealing with?"

"Perhaps you had better come into my office, Miss Garcia."

Rosenthal crossed the tiny outer office in three strides and pushed open the door to his own equally small room. Quickly he rounded his desk and sat down, re-establishing his authority.

"Please sit down, Miss Garcia. How can I help you?"

"Your call was somewhat vague, Dr. Rosenthal. You said you suspected that," Garcia took a notebook from her pocket and repeated the phrase verbatim, "an act of biological terrorism has occurred." Garcia left the notebook open on her lap. "I take it you are referring to the suspected foot-and-mouth disease outbreak in Oklahoma yesterday? What do you mean by your assertion, exactly?"

"Well," began Rosenthal cautiously, choosing his words slowly and with precision, "after considering the location and size of the outbreak, and the serotype involved, I could come to no other conclusion than the infectious agent responsible had been released deliberately."

"Can we discuss these points separately, doctor?" Garcia replied, noting the information in her little book. "First, location. What's so unusual about

Oklahoma?" She smiled at the question, conjuring up images of the urban-rural divide still apparent in the country.

"Many things, as a matter of fact. First it is a land-locked state with no immediate access to traditional ports of entry to the country. An accidental outbreak might be considered close to known ports of entry for livestock, meat products or hides. Oklahoma is none of those."

"But the outbreak occurred in a feedlot," queried Garcia. "Aren't those places full of cattle sent from different farms for fattening? You have different breeds, different ages and different susceptibilities to disease. A feedlot is an obvious place to suspect an outbreak, isn't it?"

"That's very astute of you, Miss Garcia." Rosenthal was impressed. Until now he thought he had been dealing with a typical gung-ho cop. "However, feedlots are generally very strict on quarantine procedures. They require vaccination certificates to be provided upon delivery and have very experienced veterinary officers on hand much of the time. It is almost impossible to transport cattle across state from an infected farm and deposit them at a feedlot without immediately detecting something is amiss. This leads me to suspect that the virus was introduced at the feedlot itself."

"Alright," said Garcia, conceding that point. "What about size? What do you mean by that?"

"Again, something is not quite right," said the old man, delighting in showing off his theory. "The sheer scale of the outbreak is extremely disturbing. The incubation period for the virus is about three to five days under optimal conditions. If one animal becomes infected you would expect the other animals in the same stall or pen to be infected very rapidly due to excretion of very high concentrations of virus in the air and waste products. However, infection of animals in other pens is usually effected by fomites."

"I'm sorry, what did you say," Garcia replied, scribbling in her notebook.

"Fomites. Any inanimate source of infection, like clothing, shoes, tractor tyres, and so on," replied Rosenthal. "The farmer or his staff will carry the virus around on their boots and trample it into the other pens as they do their rounds. But the concentration of virus carried on someone's boot is usually much lower than in the air breathed out by an infected animal. It is a much less efficient way of infecting an animal than direct contact with a carrier. For such a large feedlot, we're talking about twenty to thirty thousand cattle being infected simultaneously; I have to suspect a deliberate application of a concentrated form of virus at multiple sites within the feedlot."

"I see what you mean, Dr. Rosenthal," replied Garcia, looking up from her notebook. "And what about this serotype thing?"

"Well this really is the clincher for me, Miss Garcia. The virus is serotype C, so it must be a deliberate attack, don't you see?"

"I'm sorry Dr. Rosenthal," admitted Garcia. "You've lost me."

"The foot-and-mouth disease virus exists as seven serotypes or strains. Each one pretty much confined to a certain geographic area. Of course, there is a huge overlap of infected areas and modern travel has made the mixing of strains a lot easier, but nevertheless, it is generally accepted that serotype C hails from the Middle East area. If it were serotype A or O I would have fewer reservations. Type A occurs regularly in South America and type O is found around the world. But C is different. It's a sort of fingerprint as to who the culprit might be."

"And the fingerprint leads you to suspect whom, exactly?"

"Well I don't know. Someone with connections to the Middle East, presumably. Besides, that's more your line of work isn't it?"

"This research centre also houses serotype C, doesn't it, Dr. Rosenthal?" queried Garcia. "Who might have access to those stocks?"

"You're quite right. Miss Garcia," replied Rosenthal, wondering when the investigator would turn on his own staff. "We have about two million highly concentrated doses of serotype C for emergency vaccination purposes. And I can assure you every single dose is secure and accounted for. In addition, there are stocks of the virus scattered throughout the building, depending on the research needs of individual staff. Again, only those people who are trained to handle it properly have access to this material. These research stocks contain either isolated nucleic acid or cell-free antigen preparations – viruses that have been chemically treated to be inactive. The only live virus is held in our level four biosecurity unit."

"What's that exactly?"

"It's a custom-built high security laboratory for handling extremely hazardous pathogens," explained Rosenthal. "There are only a handful of similar facilities in the country. Everything going in or out has to be sterilised. There are negative pressure airlocks and ultrafiltration units to treat the air. In addition, all staff must wear all-in-one spacesuits to eliminate the risk of contamination."

"That sounds good," admitted Garcia, "but what about rogue staff, people with a grudge, former employees and so on. I understand you allow pretty free access to foreign researchers, is that true?"

"Of course, it is impossible to gauge what is going on in people's minds, Miss Garcia. Certainly there have been cases where people have been dismissed but on the whole staff turnover is quite low. We are rather a dedicated bunch of people. I know you're just doing your job, but you're barking up the wrong tree."

"In addition, Miss Garcia, as a publicly funded facility dedicated to improving the world's health through the elimination of animal pathogens we are obliged to open its doors to suitably qualified researchers from other countries."

"Is there any test you can do to identify the serotype further?" Garcia asked, intrigued at the technology used to diagnose veterinary diseases.

"Indeed there is, Miss Garcia, and we are working on that right now. We will sequence some of the viral genes and compare them with other serotype

C strains from around the world stored in our reference collection. Our library goes right back to the last US outbreak in 1929. From the number and location of genetic differences in the Oklahoma strain and the reference strains we can identify the isolate most likely to be an ancestor of our outbreak virus. That will give us a likely country to narrow down your search for suspects. Beyond that there's not much we can do," Rosenthal said, spreading his arms and shrugging his shoulders in an admission of defeat.

"Well that's a great start, Dr. Rosenthal," Garcia replied, suspecting that nothing more could be done. "How long will those additional tests take?

"A couple of days at the most, probably less."

"Please let me know the outcome, won't you? In the meantime, I'm afraid I must inconvenience your staff by requesting that they submit to searches of their laboratories and personal effects. I'd also like your human resources department to put together a list of all former employees, going back say ten years? In addition, I would like a list of the names and home institutes of all the foreign workers who have visited Plum Island over the same period."

"My, that's quite a list, Miss Garcia," said Rosenthal. "I can tell you now there may be hundreds of people on it, especially the list of foreign visitors."

"You just get me the list, doctor, and let me worry about how many names are on it, okay?" Garcia replied.

Garcia had yet to formulate a suspect profile, but a disgruntled worker would be high on the list. After the anthrax scare of 2001, in which a former government laboratory researcher was implicated as the person most likely to have the means and opportunity to obtain and disseminate the deadly weapons-grade toxin, Garcia would focus initially on persons with sufficient expertise and skill to manipulate deadly viruses. Top of the list were the US government's own researchers.

"I'll contact human resources and get them to prepare the list for you. It may take a while."

"I'll expect it tomorrow, doctor," Garcia stated firmly.

Her interview with Rosenthal concluded, Garcia walked back slowly to the reception area. It was now deserted and illuminated only with a single spotlight over the receptionist's station.

Outside, the last launch from the restricted Plum Island to Orient Point had left some time before. Only a skeleton crew of security guards and night watchmen remained. Rosenthal and Krantz, the last occupants, would stay in the accommodation block reserved for staff.

A handful of twinkling lights speckled the coastline less than two miles away. They beckoned silently across the still black sheen of Plum Gut.

The FBI cutter was moored at the quayside. A man clad in black stood on the wooden pier smoking. As soon as he heard Garcia's steps on the planking he quickly tossed the butt into the water and stood up straight.

"Okay fellas," said Garcia. "We're done here. Let's get back to town."

Garcia jumped lightly onto the deck followed closely by her companion.

As the crew cast off and the cutter turned nimbly in a wake of foaming water, Garcia looked back at the squat silhouette of the Plum Island Animal Disease Center. Its remoteness and isolation gave it the image of an impenetrable fortress safeguarding the country from peril. What if its darkest and most dangerous secrets were being used against it?

A stiff offshore breeze fluttered the pennants of the craft and Garcia stared at the angular building as it receded swiftly in to the distance.

She held herself and shuddered.

Chapter 21

Gould's early morning phone call was short and direct. "We've got some more bad news for you," said Gould, his voice flecked with worry. "There's another FMD outbreak in Amarillo."

"Where's that?" asked Caine, sitting upright in his bed, searching the floor for his socks.

"Texas. A few hours down the interstate from El Reno," replied Gould dispassionately. "Looks like this thing is spreading on fomites."

"What about the wind?" asked Caine, now alert and focused. "Could that be a possible source of the infection?"

"Amarillo is about two hundred fifty miles due west of Oklahoma City. In August and September, the prevalent winds are south-southeast or south southwest. There's not much chance of a wind-borne infection travelling that far in such a short period of time. Besides, the report came in from another feedlot."

"Do you think that's a coincidence?" said Caine, picking up the concern and tacit implication in Gould's remark.

"I pray to God it is," Gould replied. "But I think we have to be prepared for the worst."

"Is it on the news yet?"

"Thankfully, no. We asked the owners not to contact anyone and they were more than happy to comply. We can't keep a lid on this for long, though. Samples are already on their way to Ames and Plum Island for analysis. The results will be in late this afternoon. We're getting a team together to take a look. We've got a plane on standby at the airport. You up for bit of detective work?"

"You bet," said Caine, leaping at the chance of more field action.

"Go straight to the airport and we'll pick you up at the information desk. We'll meet you within the hour. Bring a toothbrush, we'll be gone a couple of days."

The sky over Oklahoma was a perfect blue. Flying with the sun behind them the high plains of Texas came into view in a glorious rush of gold. In ninety minutes the Lear jet had covered a distance that would have taken six hours by road.

On board the surprisingly cramped plane along with Gould and himself, Caine recognised Carter and one of the other technicians from the trip to Benson and Sons the day before. The other faces, an assortment of veterinary officers, assistants and officials from the Oklahoma Department of Agriculture, were new to him.

"Have you heard?" asked Gould, as soon as the plane was airborne. "Eli has informed the FBI. He thinks the outbreaks are the work of extremists."

"Really?" replied Caine. While he did not discount the possibility he assumed it was far too early to credit such an outbreak to sabotage. "What makes him think that?"

"Lots of things," replied Gould. "Although it seems the fact that it is serotype C has got him spooked the most."

"Yeah, that's odd, but not impossible," replied Caine, "considering the distances that viable virus can travel."

Gould nodded silently to himself.

The jet touched down at noon at the Amarillo International Airport seven miles due east of the small city. They were met by a small delegation from the city government, including a group from the local offices of the Texas Department of Agriculture.

Small talk was relegated to a few short words of greeting while the ride into town was dominated by news of the suspected outbreak. The signs and symptoms of disease, location of the premises and number and breed of animals involved were discussed, dissected and reanalysed in minute detail.

"People in this area are gonna start getting suspicious real soon," said Bob Thornton, director of the Texas Department of Agriculture. "This is probably the biggest feedlot in the high plains," he elaborated. "They get deliveries and make despatches on almost a daily basis. If we delay any official announcement by more than twenty-four hours there's a risk we're gonna be found out by the media and hung out to dry."

"I understand we will be joined at the site by representatives from the local FBI office," added Jim Prior, the deputy director. "They must think something serious is going on."

"I think we need to wait until the results of the typing come back from Ames before we start jumping to conclusions," added Gould calmly.

As the nearest of the USDA testing laboratories, Ames was considerably easier to contact from Texas than Plum Island. Gould was betting that the Iowa lab would be able to respond quicker to the tissue-typing request.

"In the meantime, we need to follow established procedures and try to minimise the spread of this organism," said Caine. "What are your recommendations, Dr. Thornton?"

Thornton, a middle-aged man who had spent more of his career behind a desk than in the field studied the group with the look of a man about to be executed. This was his one chance to get it right. Marshalling his facts as quickly as he could he levelled his gaze at Caine and Gould standing immediately before him and began to speak. His flat Texan monotone oozed calm and logic.

"In the event of an outbreak of a disease as contagious as foot-and-mouth it is essential to limit the spread of the disease to prevent it becoming an epidemic," he said. "On suspicion of an outbreak, the immediate imposition of local movement restrictions and biosecurity measures, including the culling of animals with clinical signs is necessary."

The measured beat of his voice seemed to hypnotise his audience, dulling their senses, allowing him to elucidate the terrifying logic of disease control with ease. Pausing slightly for the barbed words to hit home, he glanced around the group, holding them rapt and expectant.

"If confirmation comes from Ames or Plum Island, full emergency arrangements must be mobilised including logistic resources, interdepartmental coordination and scientific advisory structures," he continued. "We need a rapid response team to ferry samples to the reference laboratories for confirmation; veterinary teams to investigate all premises where livestock are held; liaison between the Texas Department of Agriculture and all relevant state and federal bodies; and the formulation of a contingency plan for the immediate culling of all animals with confirmed infections as well as those on adjacent properties or those deemed to be at high risk, even if they don't have signs and symptoms."

Thornton stopped speaking, as if to take a breath. Studying the group again one by one he silently reinforced his words with a look. It was deputy director Prior who broke the spell.

"I'm afraid that after eighty years without an outbreak people are not going to take kindly to having their rights interfered with, especially in Texas," he said.

"We have to stress the extreme threat to society posed by this disease," interrupted Caine. "The economic costs, the lost jobs, and so on. It's not about invasion of privacy and taking away livelihoods."

"Agreed," said Prior. "It's just going to be a tough sell, that's all."

The group travelled the short distance to the HyGain feedlot. Its size staggered Caine. In daylight the immense pens lining the old runway stretched to the horizon.

In the forecourt just inside the perimeter fence, a high-pressure water jet had been installed. A farmhand hosed down the tyres and wheel arches of all arriving and departing vehicles. When everyone had assembled they donned disposable protective coveralls and thick green rubber boots.

Caine marvelled at the enormous piles of grain three storeys high and the conveyor belts leading from them into the processing plant. The equipment was still and silent. With the livestock now under imminent sentence of death, freshly processed feed would no longer be required.

Without listening to the preamble by Thornton and Gould, Caine drifted to the back of the group as it meandered its way through the labyrinthine yard to the cattle pens at the rear of the compound.

The early September sun was high in the sky and the air was dry and warm. The feedlot foreman and veterinary officer joined the group.

"Where were the first cases noted?" asked Caine, eager to learn how the disease had spread so quickly.

The veterinary officer was a tall and gangly man in his late fifties. His skin was dark, bronzed by constant exposure to the sun. The veins in his arms bulged like knotted cords. He turned slowly to face Caine.

"It's difficult to pin it down to one area," he said. "But it seems like the first cases were right at the back of the feedlot, up against the perimeter fence and down the western side. There were very few cases on the eastern side of the yard. Of course it's spread some since we first noticed. There're too many animals affected to bother moving them to the sickbays, so they're standing now pretty much where they were infected."

"Can you show me exactly?" Caine said, hoping the others didn't note his enthusiasm.

"Sure, but we're gonna need some transport. It's a heck of a way to walk," said the old man.

"It's okay, Paul, you go ahead," said Thornton. "We'll follow you in a little while."

Caine and the old man separated from the pack and walked toward an old Ford pickup truck parked in the corner of the yard nearest to the administration block.

"Do you think it's spread from Oklahoma City?" asked the old man warily after they had driven some distance down the long aisle separating the two rows of cattle pens.

"I'm not from round here," replied Caine, looking for some local input to the problem. "What do you think?"

"Well," proffered the old man, after a long pause. "It didn't spread on the wind, that's for sure. And it didn't come from the El Reno feedlot on trucks neither."

"How can you be so sure?"

"'Cause we're competitors, that's why," replied the old man indignantly. "Our cattle come straight from the farm and go straight to the meat packers in Hereford, Friona and Cactus. They're all in the opposite direction from Oklahoma City. Even if the trucks picked up something at the packer and brought it back with them it wouldn't be from Oklahoma City as they use different packers."

"So what you're saying is there's no way for the disease to come to HyGain from El Reno?" Caine asked, furrowing his brow at the old man's twisted logic.

"No natural way. I don't doubt for one minute that it's the same virus as El Reno. You don't have to be Einstein to figure that out."

"You think it was deliberately introduced?"

"Sabotage," emphasised the old man.

The pickup came to a stop and the two men got out and examined the cattle, now restless and irritable with fever. Caine observed the same drooling and hoof stamping he had seen in Oklahoma.

The back fence of the feedlot stretched across the full width of the yard. Beyond it lay the endless expanse of the high plains. Caine turned to face down the runway toward the main entrance far in the distance. The first cattle to get sick were next to him. The focus of the infection was this corner, farthest from the main road and nearest to the perimeter.

You bastard. You sneaked over the fence didn't you?

"What's behind the perimeter fence?" asked Caine. Tall prairie grass obscured his view.

"Just a dirt road," replied the old man. "The young 'uns use it as a sort of Lover's Lane, if you get my meaning."

You parked on the dirt track and came over the fence.

"How often do the animals get fed?"

"They feed whenever they want to really," replied the old man. "That's to say, fresh feed is available throughout the day. The troughs here," the old man pointed at the cement feeding trough running the entire length of the pens, "are cleaned out every couple of hours and fresh feed put down for them. Except at night, of course."

It's in the trough.

"What happens at night?"

"Nothing. The troughs are filled at sundown and left until sunrise when they're cleaned out ready for the first batch of the day. We take good care of our animals at HyGain."

Anything put in the trough at night is going to be undisturbed until sunrise.

Caine looked at the animals. A few poked their heads through the bars into the trough looking for food that was no longer there. Some bellowed their discomfort. Most simply looked at Caine with shallow unconscious stares. Two juvenile steers at the beginning of their hundred-day feast licked each other's faces through the bars unaware that their stay at HyGain would end prematurely.

Surrounded by the cattle licking, bellowing, coughing, and sharing their water and food in the close confines of the feedlot, Caine smiled at the simplicity of the terrorist's plan.

Chapter 22

"Looks like them folks down in Oklahoma have got it bad," Clem Hollis announced to no one in particular.

He held the inky pages of the *Garden City Telegram* so that they almost dipped into the rapidly congealing remains of his fried egg as the headlines screamed sabotage, murder and invasion.

"It's those poor folk in Oklahoma City that I feel sorry for," called Mrs. Hollis from the sanctuary of her kitchen. "All they need is another madman running around causing trouble. Do they know who done it, yet?"

Hollis studied the paper intently as if trying to lift the print from the page by force of will.

"Nuh-uh," he concluded after some time. "Says here they've prohibited livestock transport in nine counties bordering interstate-40 between Oklahoma City and the Texas border."

"Does it say anything about hogs?" Mrs. Hollis asked, her thoughts turning to her own family's welfare.

"Nope, just beef cattle," replied Hollis.

"That's good," she added, relieved.

The slam of the back door, the rush of stamping feet and the sound of giggling broke the calm of the quiet breakfast.

"Caitlin?" called Mrs. Hollis. "Is that you?"

"Yes, mama," giggled the little girl.

"Hi, sweet pea," said Hollis, "you want to come outside in a minute with me and Uncle Nate and feed the hogs?"

"Okay," trilled the voice.

Hollis smiled.

Outside in the shed, Nathan McCreedy was hard at work unloading the sacks of high protein meal from the back of the trailer. A dozen sacks lay on the dry cement floor of the shed and the same number remained on the trailer. Hollis and Caitlin lent a hand and the sacks were soon distributed evenly around the shed, waiting to be split open and poured into the feeding trough in front of each lactating sow and her litter.

The day was spent tending the hogs, hosing out the pens, scrubbing the floors and the myriad of other chores that kept Hollis and his kin tied to the farm. As dusk approached, Hollis held hands with Caitlin and together they watched the sun set from the upper window of the garage.

Caitlin often went there to watch her daddy tinker with the machinery. It was her favourite place on the farm. Warmed by the afternoon sun she could sit here and watch the fields for hours. Occasionally a prairie falcon would swoop down and take a white-tailed Jack Rabbit. At other times duskywings, skippers, and viceroys would flutter against the window.

In the twilight, Caitlin and Hollis made their way back to the house. Passing the shed, McCreedy emerged, stretching his arms. It had been a long day.

"Time to go, Nate. Everything okay back there?" enquired Hollis.

"Some of the hogs seem a bit off their feed. Reckon the mix is a little too rich for them this time. I think tomorrow we'll cut down on the high protein and mix in some regular soy meal. How's that sound?"

"That sounds about right, Nate. Thanks. That's a good job," Hollis replied, trusting his brother-in-law's intuition.

As Nathan McCreedy climbed into his pickup for the short drive to his home at the other end of Main Street, Caitlin and Hollis reached the back door of the house. They kicked off their boots and left them on the porch.

"How's Nelson doing?" asked Hollis.

"He's doing all right, I guess," she replied. "I just wish he wouldn't keep waking me up at night for feeding."

Hollis smiled. "Kids are like that, sweet pea. You did the same to us when you was a baby. It'll all work our right in the end. You'll see."

The smell of warm cheesecake filled the air as they opened the door to the kitchen.

"Smells good, mama," said Hollis.

Caitlin went to bed early. Nelson's box had been moved from the kitchen to the girl's bedroom, over the protests of Mrs. Hollis. The piglet had not made much progress in spite of the tender care lavished on him. Reared on cow's milk and some leftover baby formula the animal's failure to thrive was apparent to everyone in the family. As a seasoned veteran of the cycle of life and death on a farm, Hollis knew the creature would survive no more than three days. Perhaps it was good to learn about mortality at an early age, he wondered.

The piglet wriggled under the blanket as Caitlin held him in her arms and tried to soothe him. The saucer of milk and eyedropper with which Caitlin had diligently fed Nelson every hour during daylight and every other hour at night lay unused on the dresser.

"Not hungry, Nelson?" whispered the little girl.

Nelson looked back at her, incapable of comprehending her words of comfort.

"My, you're hot," she said, feeling his brow and comparing it with her own. The piglet struggled feebly under its blanket.

"Let's open a window for you and cool you off some." Caitlin wrestled with the stiff lock on the frame and gently eased the sash up. A breath of cool dry air spilled into the room. Nelson sensed the change in temperature and stopped his exertions briefly. Caitlin smiled; satisfied she had found the cause of the animal's discomfort.

Nelson was dropped into his cardboard box in the corner of the room with as much care as a six-year old could manage. A worn and patched pillowslip served as bedding. The animal lay still, a hoarse rasp marking each breath.

At daybreak, Nate McCreedy's pickup trundled down the narrow driveway of the Hollis farm. His breath formed a billowing cloud of vapour as he ventured out into the crisp damp air. A layer of dew adorned the few tufts of grass and goldenrods still able to sprout in the heavily used yard.

Hollis emerged from the rear of the house straining as he pulled on a thick cable-knit sweater, its dark blue appearing black in the wan twilight of morning.

"Seems a bit quiet, don't you think?" Hollis remarked, looking up into the sky as if to divine something of Nature's intent for the day.

"Still early, yet," assured McCreedy. Both men had worked the land and raised hogs for half a century between them; the subtleties and nuances of the season and the emotions of the animals could be read effortlessly with a practiced eye.

Walking to the shed it was immediately apparent upon opening the door that something was wrong. Terribly wrong. Instead of the relentless squealing and snorting of the piglets fighting to get on the teat, or the contented slurp of suckling, the pair was faced with an ominous silence. Occasionally, a sow would snuffle in the darkness.

"What's up, Clem?" said McCreedy turning to the older man.

"Dunno, Nate. Get the lights up would ya?" replied Hollis.

McCreedy fumbled by the doorframe before smacking the switch with a heavy hand. The fluorescent strip lights suspended from the ceiling by chains sputtered to life one by one. In the artificial glare of the harsh yellow light the full extent of the horror became evident.

"Mother of God," whispered Hollis.

"Sweet Jesus," said McCreedy.

In every pen the same scene presented itself. The sows lay immobile, breathing in shallow gasps, strings of saliva adhering to the corners of their mouths. Spread across the floor of the pen, or more often piled in a heap in one corner, lay the piglets. Most were dead; the others lay dying, gasping for air or writhing pathetically in their own filth.

"What the hell's going on?" cried Hollis incredulously.

Vaulting into the nearest pen, McCreedy approached the sow. The massive bulk of the white-haired American Landrace offered no resistance as he probed its flesh with his hands working his way from the hindquarters up to the head. Bending down for a closer look in the inadequate light he peered at the tip of the snout. Prising open the mouth he examined the tongue. On the front left leg, in the cleft of the hoof he saw what he was looking for. A tiny white blister the size of match head.

Sweet Jesus, no!

"It's the bug, Clem."

Hollis clambered over the bars of the stall and joined his brother-in-law. Crouching by his side he too saw the small cluster of rounded vesicles on the foot and others on the snout just inside the nostril.

Wide-eyed with horror and despair Hollis backed slowly out of the shed. Running to the house, his mind a blur, he called, "Mama, mama! Quick!

Something terrible's happened. We gotta call someone. The Department of Agriculture and the vet."

"What's wrong?" called Mrs Hollis from her vantage point on the back porch. "What's going on there?"

"It's the bug, mama. We got the foot-and-mouth disease. They're all gone," cried Hollis.

McCreedy jogged slowly across the yard and came up behind Hollis as he rested on the porch. "They're all gone," he added. "Three hundred piglets and a couple of the sows. The rest'll have to be destroyed."

Mrs. Hollis put her hand to her mouth. "Oh my goodness," she sobbed.

Hollis looked up at the sky bleeding and streaked red with the first rays of the sun and let forth a strangled guttural cry of primeval savagery. Mrs. Hollis held her husband tight to her bosom and prayed. McReedy rested his hand on his sister's shoulder.

"Daddy! Daddy!"

Caitlin Hollis' scream was almost as pained as her father's. The stairs thundered as she ran headlong down to the hallway. Still in her pyjamas and oblivious to the cold morning air, she walked through the kitchen and approached the group of adults on the porch. In her outstretched hands she carried the limp lifeless body of a little piglet.

"Nelson's dead."

Hollis looked at his daughter, tears welling in his eyes.

"I'm sorry, sweet pea," he cried, breaking free from his wife and clutching the little girl to him.

"The others have gone as well, darlin'," he said, trying to console her with the news that hers was not the only loss, nor was she to blame.

"All the hogs caught a bug and died in the night."

"I don't think Nelson suffered any," said Hollis. "Did you hear anything during the night?"

The girl shook her head mutely.

"There you are then," added her father. "Listen, sweet pea," Hollis said kneeling down and looking at his daughter in the eye, "Mama and I need to make some calls and get the authorities over here to check things out, okay? You won't be able to go to school today. Is that okay? You can help mama clean up the house while me and Uncle Nate tend to the hogs."

Confused, the girl agreed with a nod of the head.

It was three hours before Josh Gephardt, the regular veterinarian for the Hollis farm, arrived from his practice in Dodge City, twenty-five miles away.

Hollis was standing in the driveway waiting. "What took you so long?" he said, as Gephardt sat in his car with the door open, struggling to put on his rubber boots.

"Haven't you heard?" Gephardt replied. "There's foot-and-mouth disease in Garden City and back in Dodge. The whole state's in uproar."

"That right?" replied Hollis. "Guess that puts me in good company then."

"I'll be the judge of that, Clem."

The seasoned veterinarian had served the Hollis farm for many years and it would not be the first time that an owner had jumped to the wrong conclusion regarding the health and welfare of his stock.

"There's no doubt this time, Josh," answered Hollis. "They're all gone. I know the score. Sudden death in sucklings with mortality reaching a hundred percent. Blisters on the snout and feet. It's foot-and-mouth, alright."

The anguish in Hollis' voice was almost tangible. He doubted if there was anything Gephardt could say to dissuade him from his own diagnosis.

Gephardt led the way into the shed. McReedy was already inside cleaning out the pens. A neat row of tiny bodies lay on the concrete aisle outside each stall. Gephardt surveyed the scene for a few seconds. Wrinkling his brow and sniffing the air in dismay he got down to work. Approaching the first pen, he saw McCreedy's handiwork. Ignoring the wretched corpses he climbed into the stall to examine a sow that had been released from its confinement and allowed to roam the now empty cubicle.

The massive beast rooted around the corners of its cell occasionally sniffing at its prostrate offspring on the other side of the gate. To the trained eye, the sow was clearly distressed. The animal relentlessly circled the stall, searching for its young. The growing pressure in its bloated mammaries, unrelieved by almost constant suckling, causing pain and discomfort.

With his knee, Gephardt expertly immobilised the sow in one corner, pinning it against the wall. Gripping it snout firmly in one hand he turned the head toward the sky and looked down its nostrils. The glistening wet snout dripped mucus. A crop of tiny vesicles ringed the opening of the nostril. The vet grunted to himself. Still holding the wriggling sow by the head he grasped the left foreleg with his free hand. Splaying the soft cloven hoof between his fingers he rubbed away the grime and bent his head to see more clearly.

There it was, unmistakeable, a bloody sore at the top of the digital cleft. Releasing his grip the animal crashed into the wall before rearing away from her assailant.

Gephardt continued his investigation in the other pens. One by one he silently completed his examination, noting the findings on a scrap of paper. From the two dead adults Gephardt took throat swabs, preserving each in a separate screw-capped plastic tube. On the outside he wrote the date, farm location and breed of animal.

Selecting two piglets at random from different piles, Gephardt punctured the skin with a razor sharp scalpel and sawed through the cartilage of the sternum. He prised apart the ribcage, exposing the bloated grey bag of the pericardium beneath. Gephardt nicked the thin membrane with the point of his scalpel and peeled away the tissue revealing the ruby red and glossy cardiac muscle.

"See here," Gephardt called to Hollis and McReedy. The two men stepped forward and craned their necks to see in the dimly lit shed.

"What is it?" asked Hollis.

"See the ventricles, the thick muscle at the bottom?" said the vet, pulling on the discoloured walnut-sized heart so the veins and arteries strained. "Those spots and yellow streaks we call 'tiger stripes'. The vesicles and blisters can have a variety of causes, mostly other viruses. But the tiger stripes, you only see that with foot-and-mouth disease. I'll need to mail these swab samples for a definitive diagnosis but I'm satisfied this is foot-and-mouth. The piglets probably died from myocarditis – an inflammation of the heart. Under the circumstances the only thing I can do for you is to put these animals to sleep immediately. The Department of Agriculture will advise you on the correct way to dispose of the carcasses. There must be absolutely no admittance to these premises until the Department of Agriculture gives the all clear. Is that understood?"

Hollis and McReedy stared impassively at the aged veterinarian. They had expected the worst and he had not deceived them.

"I'm sorry, gentlemen," Gephardt added in a more conciliatory tone than his earlier harsh lecturing. "I truly am. If it's any consolation, the cost of slaughter and removal may be covered in your general farm insurance."

Hollis stared at the floor silently cursing his parsimony.

"If the Governor issues a state of emergency, which seems likely at the moment, you'll probably be entitled to a low cost loan to cover any necessary expenses associated with the outbreak."

Within an hour Gephardt had killed the remaining sows with a cartridge-fired captive-bolt gun.

Shaking hands with the vet on the boundary of the property, Hollis bade farewell to his old friend and watched as his car rattled down the dirt road.

By the time it reached the junction with Main Street all that remained of its presence was a lingering cloud of white dust that slowly dispersed in the breeze.

Chapter 23

It was two hundred miles from Amarillo to Garden City and the journey across the high plains took six hours by car. The Lear jet covered the same distance in less than an hour. On board were Gould and Caine. The other staff and technicians from the Oklahoma and Texas Departments of Agriculture had been sent home. Investigators from the FBI had taken their places. The friendly chitchat of like minds was replaced by a terse and unsmiling silence.

Caine picked through the stack of newspapers he had purchased at the airport whilst waiting for his armed companions to arrive. The likely chain of events in the continued spread of foot-and-mouth disease was dissected in minute detail. While the few known facts were regurgitated in every edition the identity of the culprit and reason for the attack remained shrouded in mystery. No theory however spurious was too fanciful to speculate upon.

The official acknowledgement of a bioterrorist threat had followed the news of the Garden City and Dodge City outbreaks. More than one commentator had paraphrased Winston Churchill's famous wartime remark, noting the common perception that the first outbreak in Oklahoma was happenstance, the second in Amarillo was coincidence, and the third in Kansas was enemy action. The announcement was made in a live Presidential broadcast from the White House the previous evening.

A state of emergency had been declared in the affected parts of Oklahoma and Texas. Travel restrictions on livestock were in place in a continuous band encompassing the nine Oklahoma counties west of El Reno bordering the I-40 into Texas and the twenty-three counties comprising the northern High Plains.

The cost of the outbreak was mounting daily. About eight hundred thousand independent cattle farms operated in the United States. Between them, they raised almost one hundred million head of cattle per year and generated combined annual revenues of thirty billion dollars. Now, the cattle industry was haemorrhaging cash at a rate of eighty million dollars a day. Any one of those farms could be the next target.

The stock markets were affected almost immediately. The price of beef and pork decreased as the demand for meat products plunged, even in the areas unaffected by the state of emergency.

Travel and freight counters retreated as the embargo on livestock movement continued. The demand for feedstuffs declined as animal shipments were cancelled and stock culled.

Attendance at fast food restaurants decreased significantly, particularly in the mid-western states, as unfounded fears and rumours of human infection with the foot-and-mouth disease virus and price hikes necessitated by the decreased availability of raw materials and difficulty in transporting them to the restricted zones, started to take effect.

Unemployment in many counties increased sharply as the feedlots and meat packers closed down. Dependent upon an unending supply of cattle and hogs to sate America's appetite for meat the small mainly rural communities were hit hardest by the abrupt change in client preferences.

The jet touched down in Garden City Regional Airport in mid-morning. Surprised by the large crowds of journalists waiting for them, the FBI agents formed a phalanx around Gould and Caine as they walked through the maelstrom of seething bodies, thrust microphones and lightning storm of flashbulbs as the group left the tiny arrivals hall.

A convoy of FBI vehicles drove at high speed to the site of the latest outbreak. To Caine, it was all wearily familiar. Apart from going through the motions and confirming the diagnosis and clinical signs with the veterinarians and health experts in attendance, he felt helpless – paralysed.

"I wish Bill Jacobs were here," he said eventually, almost in exasperation.

"Who?" said Gould, looking up from a slim folder of notes on the latest outbreak given to him by the FBI agents on the plane.

"Bill Jacobs. Stanford. He virtually wrote the book on serotype C in the Middle East. He spent half his life out there, wandering around collecting samples," Caine recollected. "And that was long before DNA sequencing was available. He did all his work under the microscope or in cell culture."

"Sounds like the sort of guy we could use," replied Gould. "Why don't you call him up?"

"You think?" answered Caine.

His idea had been merely idle speculation based on boredom and loneliness. Yet the more he thought about it the more the idea appealed to him. A like mind to brainstorm some of the crazy thoughts he had floating inside his head would be a useful tonic and might even stimulate a new avenue of investigation. An old friend and mentor was easily the most qualified person to ask. Despite his quickly formed friendship with Gould and the others, there remained an intangible barrier against which Caine did not like to push too hard. After all, he constantly reminded himself, he was playing in someone else's backyard and there were rules to follow.

"Sure. No problem. It's worth a shot, right?" replied Gould. "Maybe this guy, Jacobs, is sitting around now wondering, "Why doesn't anyone call me on this?" Right?"

Without waiting for a reply, Gould tapped the FBI agent riding in the passenger seat in front of him on the shoulder. The man turned with a glower.

"I need to borrow a cell phone for a minute. Do you have one?"

The FBI agent handed Gould a small chrome and black handset.

"You got the number?" asked Gould, his thumb poised over the phone's power button.

The Stanford University telephonist transferred the call to the Department of Microbiology. The departmental secretary informed Gould that Jacobs was on pre-retirement vacation and was unavailable. She did not know when he would be back.

"No problem," Caine said to Gould. "I've got his home number. Maybe he's just resting at home after the meeting."

Caine dialled the number. "It's a machine," he said after a pause. "Hi, Bill," Caine continued. "It's Paul. I guess you heard about the FMD outbreaks? I'm working with the USDA and FBI on the molecular epidemiology. Listen, we'd love to have your input so please call me if you have time. I can be reached at the..." Caine turned to Gould, raising his eyebrows, "USDA Oklahoma City, care of Dr. Steve Gould," he said, mouthing Gould's answer. "Thanks. Look forward to seeing you again. Bye."

Caine handed the phone back to the officer.

"Looks like we're on our own," said Gould. "For the moment anyway."

The convoy slowed as it approached the feedlot. A cacophony of noise erupted from the waiting hordes of journalists.

On an unseen cue, the gate to the feedlot opened as the convoy neared the premises and the three cars eased their way gently through the throng.

The vast feedlot was a hive of activity. Men in coveralls worked slowly, but precisely, in the forecourt. Several containers of fuel were parked in a shaded corner of the yard. Beside them stood a row of forklift trucks. A mechanic examined each one in turn.

A fire engine blocked their way as Gould and Caine wandered around the yard following the FBI agents. They stepped nimbly over the thick hoses that snaked across the yard and disappeared into the cavernous black interior of the nearest cattle pen.

"Where are we going exactly?" enquired Caine.

The leading FBI agent turned to face them, almost walking backwards as he spoke. "We're going inside gentlemen. My boss wants to meet you as soon as possible. I hope that's okay with you?"

"Whatever," replied Caine, too tired to argue.

The group of men passed three great pens before entering the fourth. Inside, Caine was amazed to see it had been completely cleared of cattle. The weak fluorescent strip lights common in the other feedlots he had visited were augmented by banks of spotlights powered by a generator that chugged along just outside the entrance. Bizarrely, the spotlights were all pointed downwards so they illuminated the floor. The heat and light were intense and Caine shielded his eyes as he walked by. The filth on the floor nearest the lights had begun to dry and crack under the influence of the lights, while in the more shaded areas it remained moist and pliable.

More figures clad in new white coveralls were crouched in the individual stalls examining the floor and other surfaces in exacting detail. Occasionally, someone removed a pair of surgical forceps from their pocket and picked up a scrap of something from the floor, holding it up to the light before placing it into a plastic evidence bag.

"What on earth is going on here?" said Caine.

"And you would be?" quizzed a masked figure who had appeared abruptly at Caine's elbow.

Caine turned and studied his interrogator. Obviously female from the voice, the white clad figure was tall and slim. The coveralls clung tightly to her body and her hair was tucked neatly under a disposable paper cap. Caine had seen similar hats in baker's shops and delicatessens. A paper surgical mask covered the mouth. Only the eyes were visible and Caine had never seen anything like them. An intense violet in colour, they flashed and sparkled in the light.

"I'm Dr. Paul Caine. You might say I'm with the FBI," Caine smiled and wondered if the woman was easily impressed.

"Dr. Caine," replied the woman. "Pleased to meet you." She stuck out her hand. "Angela Garcia, special agent. I definitely am with the FBI."

Garcia ripped off her surgical mask and pulled back her hat, letting her long brown locks ripple down to her shoulders. The effect was stunning and Caine stared at her for several seconds longer than was necessary. She met his stare briefly and glanced away.

Garcia held up a plastic Ziploc bag about six inches square in front of her face. It had a code number written on it in black marker pen. She pinched the middle of the bag, holding something in place between her thumb and index finger.

"What do you make of this, Dr. Caine?" she said, thrusting the immobilised speck under Caine's nose.

"I'm not sure," replied Caine, unable to tell if there was actually anything in the bag at all. "What is it?"

"I've no idea," answered Garcia, "but we found lots of it in El Reno and Amarillo. I'm curious to see if it's here also."

Garcia fumbled in her pocket and produced another bag identical to the first, this time identified by red fibre tip markings.

"And what about this?" she asked. An amorphous dark brown lump about five millimetres across was just visible in one corner of the bag. Caine reached out and squeezed it. It gave a little under the pressure before slowly rebounding to its original shape.

"Again, I can't say," Caine responded, puzzled by the questions. "Rubber, perhaps?"

Garcia smiled to herself. She enjoyed testing Caine; it underscored her authority and made him appear out of his depth.

"Do you have any leads, Agent Garcia?" Gould said, sensing a little tension.

"As you can see we are still processing the crime scene," Garcia replied, matter-of-factly.

"Crime scene?" Caine wondered if Agent Garcia wasn't dramatising things a bit too much.

"Certainly," replied Garcia confidently. "From the location, size, and serotype of the first outbreak in Oklahoma to the identical form of the outbreaks here and in Texas, I am sure this is the handiwork of the same group." She had noted Rosenthal's concerns well.

"There's a group involved?" asked Gould, concern evident in his tone. "My God, this is terrible. Do you know who is responsible? Have you done a, what's it called, a profile?"

Garcia warmed to the question. This was her first big case and she had taken special care to formulate a theory and had already sketched a profile of those responsible in her head. Now she was able to test her theory on a couple of experts before she presented it to her superiors for assessment.

"Well, I should say first that this is confidential and off the record," Garcia began, lowering the tone of her voice in a conspiratorial manner. "I'm waiting for a chemical analysis of the residues I just showed you before I can confirm any of this. I would say there are at least two men involved. One is active in performing the contamination while the other is passive and acts as a lookout and/or driver. Both men are probably of Middle Eastern origin, aged between twenty and forty, but have resided in the US for some time, probably in the southwestern states. At least one of them is educated to college level in the life sciences. Both men can drive and neither of them smoke."

Gould was impressed and said so. Caine reserved judgement. The approach was correct but too many blanks had been filled in without enough evidence. If there were terrorists roaming the countryside it would takc more than a jumped up parlour game to catch them.

Caine had a gut feeling something was wrong or had been overlooked. He remembered looking around the feedlot in Amarillo with the old man and the sense that he was standing in the same spot as the terrorists before him. He felt it; he was sure. Did Agent Garcia have the same feeling looking around the crime scene or was she just playing the game by the numbers? Surely one person would be enough to spread this disease and they did not have to be scientifically literate, just cunning.

"Agent Garcia?" A man approached the group carrying a sheaf of papers. "This fax just came in for you, ma'am," he said, handing the documents to Garcia.

Garcia stepped back from the group to give herself some privacy and leafed through the papers. After a moment she looked up at Gould and Caine.

"It's the lab report from Quantico," she said proudly. "They've managed to identify the strange residues we found. The first comprises cellulose fibres of some kind, probably filter paper, impregnated with reagent grade amorphous charcoal. The second is bovine connective tissue. In addition, both are heavily contaminated with serotype C foot-and-mouth disease virus." Garcia smiled and looked up. "I think we just found ourselves the weapon. It also directly links the Oklahoma and Texas outbreaks as the work of the same individuals.

"Have you found these residues here or in Dodge City?" asked Gould.

"Not yet but we're working on it, Dr. Gould. It's early days," replied Garcia. The presence of the residues and their identification was a breakthrough but it had not yet aided them in unmasking the terrorists.

“What will you do now, Agent Garcia?” asked Caine, intrigued as to what the next step in the investigation would be.

“Well,” said Garcia, pausing to collect her thoughts. “We’ll cross match vehicle rentals and hotel bookings between Oklahoma and Amarillo. Then we’ll identify Middle Eastern science students living in the southwest. There may be a connection between the two. In addition, we’ll follow up any reports of suspicious persons, stolen vehicles, credit card fraud in the region over the last few days to see if there’s any discernable pattern or thread.”

Caine was not convinced; Garcia’s strategy sounded too tenuous. He was disturbed by the overt racial targeting of suspects as one of the major leads in the investigation.

Another officer interrupted the group. “Agent Garcia?” said the man. “We’ve had a call from the Department of Agriculture. They have a pig farm in quarantine for suspected foot-and-mouth disease in Ingalls. That’s about twenty-five to thirty miles away. Do want to go and take a look?”

“Pigs?” said Caine, looking at Gould with raised eyebrows. “Looks like this thing is spreading further and further.”

Caine was concerned. So far the outbreak had been confined to cattle feedlots - premises where a high density of animals would help spread the disease and cause maximum economic damage. Transmitting the disease to pig farms indicated a change in approach by the terrorists. Any deviation from an established pattern would make it almost impossible to predict their next move.

“Pigs is trouble,” said Gould.

“Why is that, Dr. Gould?” asked Garcia.

“Because pigs amplify the virus tremendously,” replied Gould. “A single infected pig can shed enough virus in a day to infect a hundred million other pigs. Once one pig farm is infected it’s just about impossible to stop every other farm for twenty miles from being infected.” Gould breathed in deeply and sighed. “Yup, pigs is trouble.”

Chapter 24

Ingalls was a dot on the map. On some maps it wasn't even a dot. Midway between Garden City and Dodge City on the old Sante Fe Trail, Ingalls was a sleepy town with a population of just over three hundred.

As the FBI convoy approached the town along state highway fifty, hugging the course of the dried-up Arkansas River, low mounds of dirt were visible by the side of the road, remnants of the long abandoned Eureka Irrigation Canal.

The three-car convoy turned right onto Main Street. The main artery, less than a mile long, split the town in half before merging with the distant horizon, while the railroad track running at a tangent to the road quartered it.

At the southern end of Main Street a dirt road led off at a right angle to Hollis Farm. The entrance to the narrow side road was sealed off, rather incongruously thought Caine, by FBI crime scene tape. As they drove slowly up the road a grey FBI crime scene investigation van could be seen in the distance; a white-coated technician disappeared into the house.

Garcia and her team entered the house first followed by Caine and Gould. Clem Hollis answered some preliminary questions before leading the group of investigators out to the yard.

The dead hogs were piled ignominiously at the front entrance to the shed. Stiff and bloated the corpses looked unreal, as if hideous mannequins had been thrown carelessly in a heap. Caine could not tell if the stench was due to the filth on the floor of the shed or if decomposition had begun.

During the investigation Caine and Gould kept a low profile so as not to interfere with either the questioning of the family or the collection of evidence. For the most part, Caine accepted grimly this was another case of foot-and-mouth despite the absence of laboratory verification.

Caine decided to call Eli Rosenthal for an update. By now they would have received samples from all the outbreaks and completed the gene sequencing of many of them. He wanted to know if there was any unusual or unexpected features that would help him track down the origin of the virus. Without that, accompanying Gould on his field trips was no different from a tourist's sightseeing holiday. He was frustrated and also a little bored.

Leaving Gould inside the pen examining the stalls where the dead piglets were first found, Caine wandered back up the drive to the main road. A small crowd had gathered, kept back by a single policeman. Occasionally a car would slow, its occupants peering intently up the dirt road in Caine's direction, before moving on.

Caine approached the crowd. They drew back as he advanced as if he himself were the source of the infection.

Guessing the crowd would automatically think he was with the FBI Caine decided to bluff his way into extracting some additional information."How you folks doing?" he began, hoping his accent would not sound too many alarm bells in people's minds.

The crowd murmured their acknowledgement looking him up and down.

"I don't suppose anyone saw anything unusual in the last few days, like cars or people hanging around?" he asked speculatively.

The group turned and looked at each other. Caine could tell from their head-shaking and lowered tones that they had seen nothing.

A young boy standing across the street caught his attention. With hands in pockets and eyes cast down to the ground he glanced occasionally up at Caine with a nervous look.

What the hell? It's worth a shot.

Caine crossed the street and made his way toward the child. He half expected him to run and was surprised when he stood motionless.

"Hi," he said, as casually as he could. With no children, nephews or nieces of his own, Caine was at a loss as how to address and gain the trust of a small child.

The boy looked at him without answering.

"What's your name?"

"Paco," the boy answered quietly. "Are they going to be alright? The people? Are they going to die?"

Caine smiled. "No. They're going to be fine. But all the pigs have been destroyed."

The boy bit his lip, embarrassed about asking his next question.

"What about Caitlin?" he said, flushing slightly.

"Who's Caitlin?" probed Caine.

"She goes to my school," replied the boy. "She sits next to me. We play together. Sometimes. When her dad lets me."

Caine studied the boy some more. He wore a shirt a little too large for his skinny frame, probably an elder brother's hand-me-down. The jeans were faded, worn through in places and patched in others. The filthy sneakers had seen better days. Caine guessed that Mr. Hollis did not like his daughter playing with someone from the poor side of town. Not that the man was really in any position to complain judging by the state of his house, which was certainly in need of improvement.

"Caitlin's fine," Caine replied. "I don't suppose you saw anything unusual recently. Strangers, that sort of thing?"

The boy thought for a moment. "Si," he answered.

"Really? Like what?"

"A couple of days ago Caitlin and me was playing in the street."

"Isn't that a bit dangerous?" said Caine, before remembering that he had hardly seen a car that morning on the drive over from Garden City and the back streets of the town would have been even quieter. Paco stared back at him without understanding the question.

"All of a sudden this car pulls over and the man asks for directions. He pulled off the road too early on his way back from Dodge. He wanted to get back on fifty to Garden City."

Dodge. Fifty. Caine was losing the thread of the conversation. The boy's thick Hispanic accent did not help.

"What did he look like?" asked Caine.

"Foreigner. Dark-skinned, but not like me. Like an Arab may be. He had a short beard."

"Is that it?" Caine was intrigued but desperate for more detail.

"His friend was white though."

"His friend?"

"An old, fat, white guy."

"What kind of car were they driving?"

"A beat up Toyota Corolla. Light brown colour."

"When was this exactly?" Caine sensed this was the breakthrough he had been looking but it was essential for the times to match. If it was too recent the strangers could not possibly have infected the pigs, as the incubation period for the virus was anything from two to seven days.

"Um. Let me see," the boy struggled to remember. "Four days ago. Yeah, Tuesday, in the afternoon after school," he answered confidently. The smile on the boy's face assured Caine it was the correct answer.

Perfect.

"Do you want to come with me and tell everything you told me to a policeman?"

"Not really," replied the boy. A lifetime of discrimination and suspicion had taught him to be wary of any involvement with the authorities.

"There might be a reward."

"How much?"

"Let's go and ask shall we?"

Caine carefully shepherded the young boy past the police guarding the entrance to the Hollis farm and up the drive.

He couldn't wait to see Agent Garcia's face when he told her the news.

Chapter 25

The conversation with Eli Rosenthal was long and detailed. Over three hundred samples from the outbreaks in Oklahoma, Texas and Kansas had been received comprising mainly pharyngeal swabs from infected or suspect cattle. While only a few of the Kansas samples had been examined in preliminary antigen tests, they could still be identified as belonging to the same serotype responsible for the earlier infections. In contrast, detailed genetic sequencing confirmed that the Oklahoma and Texas viruses were indeed the same.

The viral reproductive machinery is very poor at copying its own genes and occasional mistakes are made. These mistakes are the very engine of evolution. Most of the mistakes are lethal to the virus, making it incapable of reproduction. Some have no effect, neither positive nor negative, on viral maturation or infectivity. Occasionally, very rarely in fact, a mutation arises that increases the fitness of the virus for its environment, perhaps increasing the range of tissues that can be infected or changing its response to chemical inhibitors, making it resistant to drugs and harder to eradicate.

The rate at which the virus changes can be calculated. By determining the number of genetic differences between two isolates it is possible to calculate their relative ages or how long on average it takes for one form to evolve into the other.

If the virus at Oklahoma had spread naturally by animal-to-animal contact to cause the outbreak at Texas, it would be subtly different in its genetic composition, as it would have been able to accumulate tiny changes, the errors of reproduction. If the virus had been introduced artificially at multiple sites, the virus would not have had the means to evolve and diverge. As a result, viruses isolated from the different locations would be genetically identical.

"Okay, Eli. Run it by me again would you?" Caine asked, making certain he had understood the implications.

"As you know," replied the old man in his gravelly voice, "the virus, or at least its major envelope protein VP1, evolves at about one percent per year. We know from molecular studies that the VP1 gene is about fifteen hundred nucleotides long. So every year, whenever we isolate a FMD strain of the same serotype in the same part of the world where the disease is endemic, we expect it to be about one percent, or say 15 nucleotides different from the virus isolated the year before."

"What have you found with these samples?" queried Caine.

"Well this is very interesting and supports my theory perfectly," replied Rosenthal. "There are only a handful of differences between the Oklahoma and Texas sequences. In fact, only between zero and four."

"Meaning?"

"Meaning, that the Texas outbreak was almost certainly not caused by virus originating from animals infected in Oklahoma. The most likely explanation of the similarity in sequences is a deliberate introduction of the identical virus isolate into two separate sites."

"Can you deduce the likely ancestor strain?" Caine asked, pushing the molecular evidence to its logical conclusion.

"I can do better than that," replied the old man, evident glee sounding in his voice.

"What do you mean?" answered Caine, intrigued.

"We've got it. In our bank of field isolates the most similar strain is C/Quetta/2003. Collected by a group in the Mareshi Institute in Lahore, Pakistan. I think they even published a paper on it. I'll have to check on that."

"How similar is this ancestor strain to our new samples from Texas?"

"Virtually identical. Much less than one percent, anyway," replied Rosenthal, correcting his imprecision.

"That's fantastic Eli," Caine could hardly contain his pleasure at the new information. It would give him further ammunition with which to impress Special Agent Garcia. Caine could tell she had not been impressed with his credentials or his attitude at their first meeting and he was keen to redress the imbalance.

It was thirty minutes before Caine had the opportunity to discuss his call with Agent Garcia. She had been occupied with almost hourly conference calls to her superiors.

As the case continued, the pressure on all the FBI team members grew more intense. Tempers were fraying and communication became terser as one day merged into the next. Without any apparent progress being made press speculation grew wilder as the reporters began to turn on the investigators. With each day that passed costing tens of millions of dollars in lost revenues, few members of the investigating team could expect to escape from a very public and humiliating castigation.

The report from Caine provided Garcia with her first taste of good news and she hastily arranged a press conference for later that afternoon. There she would be able to enlist the public's help in the search for the Toyota Corolla, the two men, for whom Paco Diaz had supplied an above average description, and confirm the connection between the Oklahoma, Texas and Kansas outbreaks.

As four o'clock neared, the small City Hall conference room in Garden City buzzed with activity. Garcia sat anxiously behind a desk. She was trapped between the back wall of the room and the infestation of constantly moving journalists in front of her. Her throat was dry and she sipped frequently on a glass of mineral water.

The camera crews from a half dozen local news stations had filled most of the front row of chairs barely three feet away. A cluster of gaudily labelled microphones erupted like a huge bunch of artificial flowers in front of her face. Cables snaked their way across the floor. Behind the row of cameras sat the assembled press corps from a multitude of local, regional and national newspapers — each realising that the outbreak could still be milked for several pages daily until it subsided.

At the last minute, Gould, Caine and the head of the local Department of Agriculture joined Garcia.

Paco Diaz, in his best nearly new clothes and accompanied by his father, sat on the end of the row. The journalists murmured to each other while camera shutters clicked noisily.

"Ladies and gentlemen," announced Garcia on the stroke of four o'clock, "Shall we begin?"

"Today I can announce a breakthrough in the investigation into the recent outbreaks of foot-and-mouth disease that have been affecting the south-western United States. Eyewitness accounts have identified two men we strongly suspect as being involved in these attacks and whom we wish to contact further."

As Garcia spoke, a black and white sketch appeared on a projection screen behind her. The artist's rendition based on Paco Diaz's description was remarkably lifelike. "The first man is of Middle Eastern ethnicity, approximately thirty to thirty-five years of age. He is of average height and build. When last seen he was unshaven but that may not now be the case. He speaks English with a pronounced accent." The picture disappeared and was replaced by a sketch of the other man.

"The second man is a Caucasian male aged about forty-five to fifty-five. He has a large build and is balding. He is somewhat shorter than his companion."

The second sketch was less convincing than the first. The rotund face was almost comical and combined with the lack of detail in the features reduced the effectiveness of the description.

"In addition, we are looking for the vehicle they were last seen driving," Garcia paused for dramatic effect noting how feverishly some of the reporters were scribbling in their steno pads, "A late model light brown Toyota Corolla. The vehicle was last seen on Tuesday afternoon on state highway fifty heading toward Garden City. Both men should be considered dangerous and are not to be approached. Instead, if you see anyone matching either of these descriptions you should call your local police department or the FBI." Garcia sat back and lifted the sheaf of papers she had been pretending to read from effectively signalling to the journalists that she had finished.

The questions came thick and fast.

"Who identified these men as suspects?"

"I'm please to report that the vigilant young man sitting at the end of this row provided the key piece of evidence in this breakthrough." Garcia turned and smiled at Paco who sat bewildered in his chair as the journalists and photographers closed in and peppered him with questions.

Paco retold his story almost word for word. Nervous at first he soon got used to the attention and by the end he was smiling and beaming proudly.

After a slew of questions the attention diverted back to Garcia.

"The description of the white man is quite brief compared with the other suspect, why is that?" someone asked.

"As Paco said earlier, the description of both men derives from the conversation he had with them over directions. Both men were seated with the passenger furthest away from him. All he could tell was that the Caucasian male was shorter than the driver. Actually, I think Paco did an amazing job in being able to remember so much. His information has been really useful and important to us." Garcia wanted to play up the human-interest aspect of the story. It would help divert attention from the investigators allowing them a brief respite from the constant hounding from the press. In addition, she hoped it would spur the public to be on the look out for suspicious characters.

"Any news about the car?" came a disembowelled voice from the back of the room.

"Not as yet. From a database check we can see that the Toyota Corolla is a very popular vehicle. In fact, since it was launched in the US in 1968 several million have been sold. Currently over two hundred fifty thousand new cars of this make are sold every year. We are going to have our work cut out for us to try to track down the owner of this particular vehicle simply from the computer records. That's why assistance from the public is vital to this case. We urge all members of the public to be on the look out for a light brown Toyota Corolla whether or not it is driven by someone matching the description given here."

"Where did the virus come from?"

"From a detailed analysis of the virus recovered from infected animals and from physical evidence gathered in El Reno and Amarillo, we can conclude that the virus was introduced deliberately into both sites independently. I repeat it did not spread by accident from El Reno to Amarillo. To answer your question another way, the FBI understands that the ultimate source of the virus was from southwestern Pakistan. We base this conclusion on genetic evidence provided by the USDA Plum Island and Ames laboratory analyses." Garcia was on a roll; deflecting the question, she had provided enough meat to keep the newspapers fed for another few days at least. She took the opportunity to press home her advantage. "I would also like to add that the FBI is indebted to the tremendous assistance afforded us by the United States Department of Agriculture. Their forensic analysis of the viruses enabled us to identify the source of infection."

"Will you be extending your investigation to Pakistan or other countries?"

Garcia had to tread carefully. While the scientists at Plum Island were convinced of the Pakistan link it did not necessarily follow that Pakistani citizens were involved. The virus could just have easily been stolen or obtained legitimately by scientists in another country who then passed it to the suspects.

"That is an operational matter that I am not presently able to discuss," she hedged.

It also sounded sufficiently abstruse to indicate that covert operations in Pakistan were being planned. Whatever it took to confound the suspects, if they should be watching, was a legitimate way of doing business. If, at the same time, it seemed to enhance the reputation of the agency, so be it.

"Dr. Johansen," asked a fresh-faced young man addressing the director of the Kansas Department of Agriculture, "do you have any further information about the outbreak in a pig farm in Ingalls?"

Johansen glanced at Garcia raising his eyebrows, tacitly asking if he was permitted to answer the question. Garcia nodded her assent.

"This morning we received information that pigs on a small farm in Ingalls, Clay County were showing signs of possible foot-and-mouth infection. The symptoms included sudden high mortality in suckling piglets and classic vesicular eruptions on the feet and snouts of adults. Samples were taken from both deceased and live animals and sent to Plum Island laboratory for analysis. The results of these tests are not yet available. However, based on the signs and symptoms and the proximity to a known focus of infection we are virtually certain that this outbreak is also foot-and-mouth disease. The farm has already been depopulated and decontamination is in progress."

The press conference was coming to an end. The principal message was Garcia's appeal for information, which was certain to be headline news across the country and the next day in local and national newspapers. She was anxious to return to the temporary headquarters where the avalanche of calls that would inevitably follow the first airing of the appeal would be forwarded.

The thought of filtering the deliberately false, genuinely mistaken and clinically deranged messages from the very few legitimate calls did not appeal to her. Thankfully, her team of trained professionals would be able to coach the callers into revealing as much information as possible, even if they wished to remain anonymous. If any calls seemed particularly revealing a trace could be arranged quickly.

In addition, all calls would be recorded for playback later. Apart from the information content of the message itself callers could inadvertently reveal a lot about themselves. It was not unusual for the perpetrator to call appeal hotlines either in the hope of diverting attention from themselves with misleading information or to actually implicate themselves in a desperate and convoluted cry for help. If that happened Garcia's team and a voice analysis machine would be ready to dissect the message and any background noise for hints as to the location of the caller.

Just as Garcia was about to announce the end of the press conference frenzied waving from the back of the hall distracted her. An FBI agent held a piece of paper in his hand. Garcia saw him and motioned for him to approach the desk. Easing his way past the mass of reporters and TV cameras the man leaned over the front of the desk directly in front of Garcia, the FBI logo on the back of his black jacket filling the camera viewfinders.

Garcia studied the piece of paper intently. It was a print out of an email message sent to a secure internal account from the FBI office in Omaha, Nebraska. As she read her eyes widened in surprise.

Subject: Foot-and-mouth disease in Nebraska
Date: Fri, 05 Sep 2004 15:46:05 -0600
From: Dan Godwin (Special Agent)
Organization: FBI, Omaha, NE
To: Angela L. Garcia (Special Agent)

Please be informed that suspected outbreaks of foot-and-mouth disease (FMD) have been reported in cattle feedlots in Lexington and Cozad (both Dawson County, Nebraska) today (05 Sep 2004).

At 08:00 this morning, veterinarians were called into the Western Feed Mill, (Lexington, NE) by the proprietors to investigate the occurrence of vesicular eruptions and general malaise in cattle resident on the premises. Cattle presented with high fever, restlessness, excessive drooling, sudden lameness and vesicular eruptions on the tongue and hoof. Based on the presence of these indicators a preliminary diagnosis of FMD was made. Oral samples were taken from several cattle and forwarded to both USDA laboratories in Ames, IA and Plum Island, NY.

At 09:30 this morning, the staff veterinarian at Dawson Feedlot Ltd (Cozad, NE) contacted the USDA office in Lexington directly to report signs and symptoms typical of FMD in steers and heifers.

Neither feedlot accepts cattle from outside Nebraska. In both cases the infected cattle have been resident on the feedlot for at least 30 days.

Lexington is located approx. 200 miles southwest of Omaha. Cozad is located approx. 13 miles from Lexington.

You are reminded that confirmation of a diagnosis of FMD requires demonstration of the presence of the etiological agent by prescribed tests.

In accordance with a standing directive issued by the Office of the Director, Washington, D.C., this information is provided to you in order to assist your ongoing investigation into the suspected release of biological agents in Oklahoma, Texas and Kansas.

Please contact the undersigned for further information as required.

Sincerely,
Dan Godwin
Special Agent
FBI, Omaha, NE

Garcia looked at the letter in disbelief. Just when she thought the FBI was on top of the situation, the suspects remained one step ahead, continuing their trail of destruction. The question now was whether she should relay this new information to the media. They had all seen her receive the letter and read it. It would look very odd if she turned around and said it was of no consequence. On the other hand, the information seemed to indicate that the suspects had left Kansas and were now in Nebraska. If she acted quickly maybe they could be apprehended in the vicinity of the latest outbreaks.

"Ladies and gentlemen," Garcia announced, "may I have your attention please?" She paused, to get her breath and channel her thoughts. This part of the presentation had been unrehearsed. "I have just received information from the FBI field office in Omaha, Nebraska reporting two new suspected outbreaks of foot-and-mouth disease. I must stress that these outbreaks have not been confirmed by official agencies. The outbreaks are in cattle feedlots in Lexington and Cozad, about two hundred miles from Omaha."

Caine frowned at Garcia.

Cozad. Where have I heard that name before?

Caine mulled over the unusual place name. It seemed long ago. He had never been there, he was sure. Maybe he had seen or heard about it from someone else. He drifted off, lost in his thoughts. No one had bothered asking him a question during the press conference and he wondered why he had been invited. A flash bulb popped and his mind returned involuntarily to the press conference.

"Once again, I would like to ask anyone who has seen a light brown Toyota Corolla, particularly in the Lexington, Nebraska area to come forward immediately with any information. Thank you." Garcia fixed the camera with a resolute stare and a thin closed mouth smile.

She turned to Caine when the camera flashes had subsided and the journalists had begun to exit from the small conference room to report back to their papers.

"Well, that wasn't too bad was it?" she asked. She was flushed and excited, a thin bead of sweat had formed on her temple just on the hairline. It glistened in the strong glare of a white spotlights set up by one of the TV crews.

Caine was more relaxed. Having presented reports in front of large audiences many times previously he was used to the pressure. He no longer got an adrenaline rush from such occasions. In a way he envied Garcia.

"It's getting late," he said. "Are you going to follow up that Nebraska link now or do you want to take a break for a while. It looks like you've been working non-stop since this thing in Kansas started."

Caine liked Garcia. She was cute but she was also determined and worked well under pressure. He liked that. The way she had handled herself under the spotlight emphasised her self-confidence, especially when the Nebraska bombshell landed. Caine wondered what he would have done in a similar situation. Panicked? Screamed, probably.

"Sure, I've got to follow that up," sighed Garcia. "But not in person. The FBI field office in Nebraska will send a team to cover it. I have to stay here and check out the callers who I guarantee will have seen someone matching the description in all fifty states by sun-up tomorrow." She laughed revealing an expanse of even white teeth. "Tomorrow I'll go back to San Francisco and co-ordinate things from the field office there."

"San Francisco?" asked Caine. "How long have you been working this case?"

"Since the murder in your hotel last week." Garcia replied. "You obviously don't recognise me."

"What do you mean?"

"I was with the group of officers who arrested your Chinese lady friend when she almost blew your head off," Garcia smiled broadly at the recollection. She remembered how confused and terrified Caine had looked and how relieved he had been when the door caved in and Chen was arrested.

"I'm sorry," replied Caine. "I didn't recognise you."

"Just one of the benefits of an all black wardrobe," grinned the agent.

"Say, are you going to be busy this evening? Can we go for dinner somewhere?" Caine sensed the camaraderie between himself and Garcia. She wore no ring and seemed determinedly independent, so he guessed there was no husband or boyfriend around. "Let me thank you for saving my life."

Cheap, but it's worth a shot.

Garcia bought it.

The solid pine table, stained an uneven shade of black over the years, was nestled comfortably in a discreet booth in the Dead Mans' Hand Bar and Diner on Main Street, Dodge City. Caine invited Garcia to sit so she faced the open fire. The flickering flames illuminated one side of her face leaving the other side mask-like and mysterious.

It was eight o'clock and only after Garcia had checked the latest developments with her colleagues and left explicit instructions for them to contact her if anything new or unexpected turned up did she deign to accompany Caine on his search for a suitable restaurant.

The waitress approached the table almost immediately, notepad and pencil in hand. Rattling off the greeting and list of specials with bored insouciance the girl gazed off into the distance. Caine ordered drinks while Garcia studied the menu.

"I guess steak's off is it?" she said to the waitress with a hint a smile.

"No, we got steak. Rib eye, T-bone, strip loin, you name it," replied the girl.

"Well, you can't go to cowboy country and not eat steak, I guess," said Garcia, running her eye down the list of entrees. "What about you?" she enquired, lifting her gaze from the menu briefly to look at Caine directly.

Their faces were closer now than they had been at any time since they had met. Garcia's arched questioning eyebrows perfectly framed the oval face. Her pointed chin and high angular cheekbones emphasised her slenderness.

Garcia wore black again. This time it was a Laura Ashley Revere collar two-button pinstripe jacket and matching wide leg trousers. Underneath she wore a cream silk embroidered blouse. Ruffled cuffs peered from beneath her jacket sleeves. An oversized piece of costume jewellery in a leaping leopard motif, set in rhinestones and imitation rubies, was attached uncomfortably to her shoulder. Around her neck she wore a simple string of pearls.

Caine gazed at the side of her face as she continued to read the menu. She had brushed and tied her hair back into a severe bun since the afternoon press conference, exposing her long neck. The top two buttons of her blouse were undone and as she leaned forward the dark shadow of her cleavage was just visible.

Caine ordered a ten-ounce prime rib steak. "Nuke it," he replied, when the waitress asked how he liked it done. Garcia ordered the six-ounce sirloin bleu.

They talked while they waited for their food, both stopping occasionally to sip from their drinks. Garcia was twenty-nine and had joined the FBI a year after completing her degree in criminology and criminal justice.

She was originally from San Diego where both her parents were teachers. Her father died from lung cancer when he was fifty-five and her older brother was killed by a hit-and-run driver. His death when she was fourteen sparked her interest in crime and its effect on society. Graduating top of her class, her thesis supervisor suggested she apply and further develop her skills in the detection of real crime by joining the FBI.

Garcia toyed with the idea before finally taking the plunge. The sixteen-week course at Quantico, Virginia showed her what she was capable of and tested her to the limits of physical and mental endurance. She emerged triumphant, reborn, a fully-fledged Special Agent imbued with the drive and ambition to succeed.

Garcia made no excuses for her occasionally brusque manner. She had lost count of the number of boyfriends or boyfriend wannabes who had trailed behind flailing helplessly in her dust as she towered above them intellectually. What she wanted was someone who would give her the space she needed to commit to her ideals and yet with enough of a spine to stand up to her and support her on the rare occasions she bit off more than she could chew.

Caine however was not the one for her. Garcia could tell from just one look. The way he undressed her with his eyes turned her on but lust alone was certainly not the basis for a lasting relationship. If he kept making her laugh for the next two hours she might reward him.

After an hour, the empty bottle of red wine had been pushed to the edge of the table. The conversation became louder and more frank as dreams, aspirations and broken hearts had been exposed and reburied. Like chips of flint that could be hidden but never decay, they formed the foundation for a better future.

After the second cup of rich Blue Mountain coffee, taken black with spoon of ground turbinado, and a shared portion of caramel pecan cheesecake, the couple were ready to leave. Caine got the bill as Garcia fixed her makeup. She glanced at Caine over the rim of her compact. He seemed older than his years. Although she could tell he didn't work out, the alcohol and warmth of the open fire made him seem more attractive. She hoped he could handle the ride.

The taxi ride back to Garcia's motel, where she was staying with the rest of her FBI colleagues, was a hazy memory of fumbling hands and probing tongues.

As soon as they entered the room they collapsed onto the bed. The vertical blinds were still half open and the red neon light from the gaudy motel sign by the front entrance streamed into the room. From the second floor the black sky was speckled with the distant lights of Dodge City.

Garcia lay on the bed with Caine on top of her. They kissed wildly, deeply, delving into each other's mouths, saliva and rough tongues entwining in an embrace of passion.

Sitting up Garcia slipped off her jacket and flung it onto an armchair in the corner of the room. The cream silk blouse clung tightly to her body - the imprint of her lacy bra showing through. Kicking off her shoes, Garcia undid her snakeskin belt and loosened her trousers. She stood and skipped a little as they slid down to the ground. Picking them up she tossed them across the room to the armchair to which they clung almost in desperation. Standing, the tails of the long silk blouse just covered her buttocks and upper thighs, hiding her ivory panties behind a membrane of modesty.

She approached Caine, who stood and loosened his shirt and trousers, and pulled him roughly toward her. Greedily she feasted on his lips and tongue. Her hands moved over his body — the width of the shoulders, the rounded curve of his chest and the strength of his upper arms.

Quickly she slipped her hands under his shirt and pulled it off letting it fall lifeless to the floor. Her hands moved across Caine's taut belly, the ridges of his abs just visible under the skin. Nimble fingers danced around the rim of his trousers as if deciding whether or not to proceed. With a tug the top button of the fly came loose. With her head pressed against Caine's chest one hand slid the zipper down to its base.

Kneeling in front of him, Garcia pulled Caine's trousers down to his knees, exposing his cotton boxer shorts. The bulge in the front told her all she needed to know about Caine's level of interest.

Jerking the thin shorts down, almost tearing the material in her haste, she saw her prize slowly engorge and rise as it was freed from its material constraint.

When Caine was hard Garcia rose to her feet and kissed him deeply. The aroma of his musk was on her breath and heightened their sense of arousal.

Caine loosened the buttons of Garcia's blouse. His hands roamed freely over Garcia's body — from the roundness of the hips, to the graceful curve of the small of the back and the firm ripeness of the proud breasts.

Working his way down her body, Caine licked and nipped Garcia's flesh. Fingertips pulled at the elastic; impatient hands slid the panties down to the ground.

Wrapping her legs around his back Garcia pulled herself deeper onto Caine's shaft. Her fingernails raked his back scoring the flesh from shoulder to hip.

They kissed. Garcia's tongue constantly searched and probed. She tasted meat, red wine and lust.

Garcia was exorcising her demons. Whether they were the past lovers who had betrayed her trust or the housing project ruffians who had manhandled her on countless occasions during her puberty, they became nothing – ghosts in the machine – as her passion roared forth in fury, engulfing the past and embracing only the present.

For Caine, no such demons existed. Tonight was just another adrenaline-fuelled vindication of life. Sex was the human dawn chorus. As birds of every species exulted in the twilight, celebrating the fact that they had survived another day in the struggle for existence, so humans embraced life with the same simple and direct instincts.

Caine and Garcia's frenzied bestial rutting provided the absolution both needed in a world of deceit.

At last Caine was spent.

He sank to his knees and embraced Garcia. They kissed and nuzzled each other. Closing their eyes they lay back in the bed and slept.

Chapter 26

Caine awoke early. Disentangling himself from Garcia, who lay half covered by the thin cotton sheet, he struggled to free himself from the bedclothes. A whisper of a smile remained on Garcia's face as she slept.

Caine examined himself in the bathroom mirror. A black ugly shadow clung to his face and he cursed forgetting his razor. He scraped the back of his hand across his cheek. The stubble scored the soft surface.

Caine turned on the shower and a foaming torrent of steaming water gurgled from the spout. The billowing clouds filled the small room and condensed on the mirrors. The noise of the hammering water was deafening. Soon Caine was immersed in a cloud of steam.

Garcia's obligations meant that she had to spend breakfast with the rest of her team and prepare for their departure to San Francisco. In fact only she and another Special Agent would make the trip. The others would follow up local leads developed from the press conference and travel to Nebraska to investigate the Lexington and Cozad outbreaks.

They had joked about letting Caine tag along with the FBI as a "scientific consultant", which was certainly within Garcia's authority to allow. However, they both agreed it would be inappropriate under the circumstances. In the end Caine left early and made his way to his own hotel, where he shaved, said farewell to Steve Gould and arranged passage back to San Francisco.

Garcia appraised herself with the latest developments as she flew back to San Francisco on the FBI Lear jet.

A feedlot worker at the Cozad site had actually seen two strangers on the premises. Assuming them to be veterinary officers by their clothing and behaviour he had not challenged them but had observed their actions at a distance. The two men matched the Kansas City descriptions perfectly; even down to the car they had been seen driving.

Although adding nothing new to the physical descriptions apart from clothing that could be changed daily, the psychological boost to the investigators was considerable. Garcia and her fellow officers felt for the first time that the suspects were now within reach.

Arriving in San Francisco at a little after 1:00 P.M., refreshed and buzzing from the information received in flight, the FBI agents proceeded immediately to their downtown headquarters.

The team of agents assigned to processing the calls received after the press conference began to filter out the crank messages and misinformation. Clearly, the suspects had driven from Garden City or Dodge City to Cozad. The drive was only two hundred miles or so and would have taken six hours by the most direct route.

However, it soon became apparent that none of the three hundred calls received contained any information germane to the investigation. One man was convinced he had followed the car on US283 between Norton, Kansas and Lexington, Nebraska but when interviewed personally he could not recall any details regarding the vehicle or its occupants. So it was with callers from other parts of Kansas and Nebraska on the day in question.

Frustratingly, Garcia had to be content with a success rate from the calls of about one percent. From her training she had been taught to expect no more than that. It was a miracle that these two calls had been identified so quickly. Often it took days or even weeks to filter and follow up calls received during a mass appeal for help. The worst part for Garcia was that she knew that this was as good as it would get. The number of calls would fall dramatically over the coming days, reduced to a trickle as people dithered over whether to call or not. Garcia shuddered as she thought of the number of crimes that went unsolved due to apathy.

"How's it going in Nebraska?" Garcia called to a colleague on the far side of the office. The man had a phone clamped between his neck and shoulder, the coiled wire wrapping itself around his upper arm like a runaway vine. He scribbled in a notebook. Looking up he signalled an acknowledgement with his hands as he spoke into the receiver. Garcia waited for the reply.

"Not good," the man reported eventually. "There's no trace of the vehicle since it was last seen two days ago in Cozad. A quick sweep of the motels and guesthouses in the area has drawn a blank. The original eyewitness is still being questioned but it looks like local PD and our guys have pumped him dry."

"What about the calls, Hal?" Garcia turned to the desk opposite hers where a young man was frantically keying entries into his online database.

"Nothing from the Dawson County area at all. The nearest hits are reports of light-coloured, not brown, Toyota Corollas containing one, two and three occupants. Not enough information to reach a consensus."

"What about new car registrations?" Garcia said, turning around in her swivel chair to face an elderly man in the desk next to hers.

"Well, I might just have something for you there," replied the man, as he grabbed a sheaf of papers on his desk. "I've been checking all Toyota Corolla registrations, new and transferred ownerships for the past month. On average the manufacturer sells over two thousand new vehicles per month and about four times that number change hands in the used market. So we're looking at ten thousand vehicles just over the last four weeks."

Garcia groaned inwardly. She never knew there were that many Corollas in circulation. Tracing the vehicle was going to be tough.

"Go on," she said.

"Ten thousand vehicles spread out approximately evenly over the fifty states brings us to about two hundred vehicles per state to check on. If we exclude about half for being the wrong colour and narrow down our search to the dozen or so southern states, we come down to around twelve hundred vehicles."

"Still sounds like a lot to me," Garcia replied, worrying that she was wasting manpower on a wild goose chase.

"But," answered the old man almost gleefully, "if we assume the Middle Eastern man observed driving the car is in fact the owner, we can narrow down the search using a comparison algorithm of Arabic surnames and words."

"I'm assuming you've done this calculation, or you wouldn't be looking so happy? Am I right?"

"Voila," said the old man holding up a single piece of paper fresh from the computer printer. "Seventy men of apparently Middle Eastern decent, aged thirty to fifty have registered a light-coloured Toyota Corolla in the southern United States in the last four weeks."

Garcia's jaw dropped. "Is that all?"

"It's a bit of an underestimate actually," replied the old man. "In a close-knit community many deals will be made on a handshake for cash. Also, it's still pretty easy to use a car without registering it. For quite a while at any rate," he added.

Despite the old man's reservations, here at last was a solid clue as to the identity of the man holding the country by the throat.

"Distribute this list to the relevant field offices and get them to work through it now," barked Garcia. "I want everyone accounted for this evening. I don't care if they have to drag them out of the john but I want a physical verification of ID of everyone on this list tonight."

Garcia paused; this was what she was good at, taking command and directing the forces in a battle. If she were a man, she would have joined the army.

"And another thing," she said to the old man beside her. She was calmer now and her voice quieter and more contemplative. "Fax the list over to foreign languages at Quantico. Get someone in the Arabic section over there to go through it. See if there are any unusual names. Anything that can help locate the home town or anything about these people. We know the virus is from southwest Pakistan, maybe we can make an ID based on the geographical origin of surnames or tribal affiliation or distribution."

Garcia looked at her watch. It was early afternoon. The calls had yielded a blank and the vehicle search was their strongest lead but still a long shot. On top of that, the motel search had not yielded anything useful in Oklahoma, Amarillo, Garden City or so far in Lexington, Nebraska.

Where are these guys sleeping?

"Get me a map of the outbreaks," snapped Garcia. "We need to find out what route these jokers are taking. They're not drawing attention to themselves. They're playing by the rules - obeying the speed limit, no parking tickets. The only way we're going to find them is when they need to stop. That means food, gas and lodging. We need to recheck every motel and gas station all the way down the line from Lexington to El Reno. I want to know how they got there and how long it took them. Hal? Can you take care of that?" she said, entrusting the young logistics expert with the task. "Distribute the descriptions of the men and the car to the likeliest stopping points after you figure out a potential route. Assume they had a full tank of gas when they left El Reno. It's a long drive across I-40 to Amarillo."

"Not that long," replied Anderson, unfolding a map he had prepared plotting the location of the outbreaks. He traced a line with the tip of his pen. "See? El Reno to Amarillo is only about two hundred thirty miles." The young man stared earnestly at the map. "Mmm. That's odd," he commented, tapping the end of his pen against his teeth.

"What's up?" said Garcia. She had known Hal ever since he had been transferred from Chicago as part of his rotation around the field offices. Quiet and shy he rarely made observations that were not provoking. On occasions, as with the Fox River rapist, his insight was scintillating.

"Just that the distance from Amarillo to Garden City is almost exactly the same distance. Two hundred thirty odd miles."

"Is that signifi..."

"Whoah! Check this out!" roared Anderson before Garcia could even finish her observation. "Garden City to Lexington two hundred forty miles. This guy is a regular metronome."

"Want me to tell you where the next outbreak will be?" grinned Anderson, delighted at the significance of his find.

"Surprise me," Garcia replied, letting the theory surge as far as it could before it hit an obstacle. She knew the free flow of ideas differentiated the elite officers from the plodders who merely followed orders and were unable to initiate new lines of investigation.

"The suspects seem to be trending north or west," mused Anderson. "If he's on I-80 heading west then it could be either Denver or Cheyenne, Wyoming. I'd go for Denver. There're more cows in Colorado."

Garcia thought for a moment. "Send out an alert to the Denver office," she said. "Be aware. Prime suspects in bioterror case believed heading to Denver area from Lexington, Nebraska along I-80. Arrival imminent."

Everyone in the office stopped and looked up at Garcia. Hal Anderson was especially surprised. His comment had been a quick observation and not a detailed assessment. Who could say how accurate or important it was? Many of his previous deductions had proven less fruitful than simple luck or methodical observation. Most of the time it was called being a good cop.

That Garcia had latched on to his suggestion so quickly indicated to Anderson that all was not well and the investigation was getting out of hand. He looked at Garcia. Wise now beyond her years and aged prematurely by the burden of responsibility, she remained poised and under control. How much was a façade, a delicate construction that would crumble easily if touched?

"Keep looking into that association. It can't be that easy," said Garcia, suddenly doubting her own intuition. "Factor in the make of the car, fuel capacity, miles per gallon, road conditions, weather. Anything you can think of."

Anderson returned to his desk and stared at the map. Turning to his computer he started typing. The rest of the office did likewise busying themselves so as to avoid direct eye contact with Garcia. With the media baying daily for the blood of the suspects and job losses in the service sector mounting it would not be long before Garcia's career was on the line. The entire room sensed the pressure the young woman faced. There but for the grace of God.

It would be a long time before the first reports came back from the field offices regarding the ID verification of the newly registered car owners. All Garcia could do was wait. She sat down at her desk and leafed through the transcripts of the calls to the hotline. Despite the pressure she let her mind wander back to last night and this morning. The pleasure would remain for as long as the bruises marked her skin.

Chapter 27

Caine and Laura spent a pleasant day together in Golden Gate Park. Hand in hand they walked through the Japanese Tea Garden, lingering over the ponds, sculptures and bridges scattered throughout the five-acre site.

As the day progressed Laura revealed more about her herself. She was born in Guam where her father was in the United States Air Force. The family returned permanently to the US soon after her birth. However, they were always on the move, never staying in one place for more than two years before her father was posted to a new base. Growing up this way was hard on their only child.

With no close friends for the majority of her formative years she drifted in and out of petty trouble. Running with the wrong crowd, drinking, smoking pot and casual sex were considered the norm. Of course, her parents were horrified, but her largely absent father and timid conservative mother were unable to control her.

Laura came to her senses once she moved out of her parent's house and learned to fend for herself. Gradually, sometime between eighteen and twenty, she straightened out her life, worked part time as a waitress and hairdresser to put herself through secretarial school and a hotel management course.

Moving to San Francisco five years ago was her big break. Getting a job at a smart chain of hotels was the career and psychological boost she had been working towards. Working her way up to events manager, a position she had enjoyed for over a year, was her crowning achievement.

In the cool afternoon breeze the couple found a sheltered corner, a bank of Pacific yew trees forming a natural windbreak, and sat down on the grass.

Caine was tired. They had walked all morning seeing the sights. Gamely he had trudged through Fisherman's Wharf and posed in front of the Golden Gate Bridge with Laura. He smiled at the delight Laura took when passers-by assumed they were married. Mercifully, the boat trip to Alcatraz was fully booked leaving them with a couple of hours to kill before dinner. The Golden Gate Park beckoned, an oasis of green set in the west of the city.

Now, however, he was bored. Laura's interest in him was becoming unhealthy. She enquired after his parents, relatives and details of his hometown and job. The sort of information only prospective fiancées could find interesting. Caine demurred over most of the questions, not wanting to reveal too much of his personal life and instead contented himself by ogling Laura at every opportunity.

Laura had a fantastic body, which she showed to good effect in a pair of homemade high cut denim shorts, tight white T-shirt that revealed her ample bosom, white ankle socks and a pair of white feminine brand name sneakers. A pair of sunglasses was pushed up onto her head where they sat atop a simple red hair band that kept her flowing auburn locks away from her freshly scrubbed face.

In the warm afternoon sun, Caine thought about the events of the previous week.

"Is there any word on the police investigation into the murder at the hotel?" he said, rather abruptly.

"What?" replied Laura, suddenly pulled headlong into reality once again.

"The murder last week, any news?"

"Um, no I don't think so," answered Laura, slightly annoyed how the topic of conversation had drifted back to work-related matters. "It's been in the papers a couple of times this week but the hotel is keeping tight-lipped about it. I guess there hasn't been a breakthrough. They haven't arrested anyone, I know that."

Caine wondered if the murder was related to the outbreak. A Pakistani scientist, an expert in foot-and-mouth disease, is murdered days before the first outbreak of the disease in nearly eighty years. The virus is typed and is found to come from Pakistan.

"You know Dr. Jacobs stayed in the dead man's room once," Laura said casually, flicking through a fashion magazine she had brought with her.

"Oh," replied Caine, annoyed that this irrelevant titbit of information had distracted him from his train of thought.

"Has he contacted you lately?" asked Caine. "He seems to be out of town at the moment."

"Well he did say he was retiring soon. Maybe he's catching up on his leave entitlements first," Laura replied unhelpfully.

"Perhaps I should pay him a visit?"

"When are you thinking of going?" Laura said, frowning. She didn't want her day out to be interrupted by talk of work.

"Tomorrow morning. Can you come?" Caine guessed that Laura would not be able to make it at such short notice. Still, the offer made him look as if he was interested in her company. Having a contact in a strange city was always comforting and he did not want to upset her unnecessarily.

"Rats!" she replied. "Tomorrow's no good for me."

"Oh dear," Caine replied. "Never mind, we'd just be talking business anyway."

Laura stretched out on the grass, propping her head up in her hands, an open magazine spread before her. Caine looked down from above at her yawning cleavage. He rolled next to Laura. The pair cuddled on the open grass for thirty minutes; they walked hand-in-hand back to the parking lot, blades of dried grass coating their clothing.

With the top down, Laura's convertible cruised though the afternoon traffic toward the restaurants at Pier 39. Laura looked magnificent. The rush of wind pressed the T-shirt tight to her form and the wind tousled her long hair.

Before the night was over the Queen of the Pacific enveloped the couple in its charms.

Chapter 28

Compared with the bumper-to-bumper traffic heading into San Francisco on highway 101, the drive south to Palo Alto and the Stanford University campus was more leisurely. After an hour in the crisp morning air the leafy tree-lined roads of the university town made a pleasant contrast to the twelve-lane highway to which it was ultimately connected.

Caine took the Embarcadero Road exit west toward Stanford and entered the university. He continued toward what he hoped was the centre of the campus. He found a metered parking lot and stumbled upon the visitor information centre in the Memorial Hall directly across from Hoover Tower, the university's most famous landmark.

Inside the information centre Caine found he was the only visitor. A solitary figure behind the counter busied herself with some paperwork. She looked up as Caine entered and introduced himself.

"I'm trying to find Dr. Bill Jacobs," asked Caine.

"Which department?" the woman asked curtly, eyeing him suspiciously, mentally calculating his potential risk as a troublemaker.

"School of Medicine," replied Caine. "Department of Microbiology."

"You could try to reach Dr. Jacobs at the Medical School Office Building."

"Where's that exactly?"

"Go out here and turn right onto Serra Mall. Follow it right to the end. Just as it merges with Campus Road West bear right and the Med School Offices are on the corner."

"Um, thanks," replied Caine, having difficulty remembering anything after "turn right."

Exiting the visitor centre he found Serra Mall and followed it as directed. After a short stroll through the heart of the campus Caine came to the medical school offices - a nondescript block composed of uniform prefabricated concrete slabs that looked as if it had been designed and built by someone in a hurry.

Caine guided himself to the general office on the second floor and entered. "I'm trying to find Dr. Bill Jacobs' office. I was directed here,"

"Dr. Jacobs is away on vacation. Can someone else in the department help?" replied the secretary.

"I'm not sure. You see the thing is I'm a personal friend of…"

"Paul? Is that you?" came a voice from the back of the office.

Caine turned to face the voice. An elderly woman stood in the doorway of a small anteroom.

"Margaret?" Caine replied with genuine surprise and pleasure. He stepped briskly over to her, embracing and kissing her lightly on the cheek. "I thought you retired years ago."

"They let me stay on," replied the old woman, her voice cracked and gravelly with age and a lifetime's addiction to cigarettes.

"How are you, sweetie?" Duffy said, pinching Caine's cheek as if he were a four-year old child.

"I'm fine, and you? Actually I'm looking for Bill Jacobs," Caine said, hoping to disentangle himself from Duffy as soon as possible, lest he be cajoled into spending half a day being brought up to date with the minutiae of the department he last visited fifteen years ago.

"Bill's on vacation. It was terrible about his wife, did you hear?" Duffy's voice dropped an octave, not an unremarkable feat given its current depth, and assumed what Caine took to be a conspiratorial tone, despite being able to be heard across the room. "Nothing they could do for her in the end. He watched her die day-by-day for over a year. Tragic. He's never been the same since."

"Yes, terrible I know," Caine was desperate to move the conversation along. "Can I see his room, you know for old time's sake. I saw him at a meeting in San Francisco and he said to look him up at Stanford if I had the time," Caine lied.

"I shouldn't really of course," replied Duffy. "But if I'm there as well, it should be ok."

She retreated to her office and returned with a huge bunch of keys. "One of these should fit," she announced, pushing past Caine to the door and out into the corridor beyond.

Along the corridor and up the stairs Caine walked briskly trying to keep up with the old woman. At the far end of the third floor on the west side of the building stood a varnished wooden door. On the front a Perspex nameplate lettered in black spelt out 308: Dr. W. R. Jacobs, Senior Lecturer, Microbiology.

As Duffy fumbled for the right key, Caine looked back down the dimly lit corridor. Light streamed onto the floor from a set of windows. Motes of dust were illuminated as angled beams penetrated the small square glass panes and slanted along the floor and walls.

Fifteen years? It seems like yesterday.

The door unlocked with a clunk and Caine and Duffy entered the surprisingly small office. Looking around, Caine took had to force himself to remember his first post-doctoral job.

Fresh from life in the grim industrial cities of England to the warmth of the California summer was akin to starting life anew. The university provided the intellectual stimulation he required while the absence of family and friends and openness of his new environment drove him to explore his personality. Stanford had liberated his mind and his body.

Jacobs' office bore the hallmarks of long uninterrupted occupation. A desk burdened with unmarked student scripts, draft manuscripts to be submitted to learned journals and departmental administrative circulars. The shelves bowed with the weight of heavy microbiology textbooks.

A hundred and fifty years of knowledge.

Caine tilted his head and scanned the shelf. Boyd; Murray; Brooks. He smiled at the familiarity of the volumes and was pleased that Jacobs had kept his old texts and had not upgraded instantly to the newer editions as soon as they became available. The Zinnser, now in its twentieth edition, sat at the end of the row, its thirteen hundred pages seeming to support the others.

On the desk sat an antique silver picture frame. A younger, slimmer Jacobs had his arm around his wife. They both smiled and looked into each other's eyes.

Caine remembered how Jacobs first got involved with foot-and-mouth disease. Jacobs' epiphany came on a trip to Central Asia in the mid-seventies when he saw the devastation wrought by foot-and-mouth disease. If he could find out more about the virus causing this disease the productivity of poor rural families, who depended on oxen for meat, milk, leather and labour, would be greatly improved.

Many of the families he met on his travels through the hinterlands measured their wealth by the quantity of animals they kept and not their quality. As a result, infected animals that should have been slaughtered as a control measure were often allowed to recover, inadvertently spreading disease to their neighbours and perpetuating the cycle of disease and hardship.

At Stanford, Jacobs had been research professor in microbiology, specialising in viral diseases of livestock, since 1978. When Caine arrived to begin his first post-doctoral position in 1985, Jacobs' reputation as the leading specialist in foot-and-mouth disease in Asia had long been acknowledged.

A kind and generous man, who opened his house to Caine when his university accommodation plans fell through at the last minute, Jacobs had been a personal friend and mentor ever since. Caine was sad he had not had more contact with his old friend for such a long time. He had been unaware of Nancy's illness and death right up until the time it happened. That failure haunted him and he wondered if it generated any ill feeling between the two men.

The papers on Jacobs' desk were held down with a large rubber ice hockey puck. Dented and cracked with age the heavy black object hinted at a youthful vigour in his mentor that Caine had long forgotten. He picked it up and weighed it in his hand before replacing it, careful not to disturb the papers below.

"Did Bill say anything about where he was going?" he said, turning to face Duffy who was lingering by the doorway.

"Nope, not a word," Duffy replied. "I'm not sure he'd be too interested in a vacation on his own."

"I've been calling him all week," said Caine.

"The only thing he said was he'll enjoy seeing the cowboys," Duffy replied.

"Meaning?"

"Don't ask me. I know nothing at all about sports, especially football."

“I thought Bill was a hockey man?” Caine replied, nodding to the paperweight in the middle of the desk.

Duffy shrugged her shoulders.

“Can I leave a note for Bill before I go?” Caine said, picking up a pencil and scrap of paper from the desk. He scribbled a few words and folded the note in half before wedging it under the hockey puck. “Okay, Margaret. I’m done. By the way, does he still have that place in Sausalito?”

“I think so,” replied Duffy, straightening a row of books that were leaning at a precarious angle.

The pair left the office and retraced their steps back to the general office on the floor below. Their footsteps echoed along the empty corridor.

Back in Duffy’s room the pair said their farewells with the promise that it wouldn’t be another fifteen years before hearing from each other again.

Outside in the afternoon sun, Caine walked back to the parking lot thinking about Bill and Nancy and the good times they all had together. He followed a group of students to a convenience store where he bought a supply of snacks and soft drinks for the drive back to The City.

As he waited in the queue at the checkout Caine glanced at the rack of newspapers. He picked up a copy of *The San Francisco Chronicle*, his favourite paper from his post-graduate days, and leafed through it. The back pages were awash with coverage of the new NFL season that had started the week before. Caine checked the scores for the San Francisco 49ers and the Oakland Raiders. At the bottom of the page he skimmed through the match report for the Dallas Cowboys game. Folding the newspaper he tucked it under his arm and continued to wait.

Chapter 29

The drive north to Sausalito took about an hour, a pleasant commute in the summer months but cool and damp for the rest of the year. Crossing the Golden Gate Bridge was the most spectacular part of the journey and Caine never tired of the experience.

During his days at Stanford he would often visit Bill and Nancy Jacobs in their home on the steep hillside of Sausalito overlooking the bay. From their perch on the hills of Marin County the twinkling lights of the city below enchanted every visitor.

Calistoga, Yountville and St. Helena in the nearby Napa valley provided Caine with unlimited reasons for long weekend visits. With a glass of chilled chardonnay or cabernet sauvignon the pleasures of good food and good company were magnified. Time was suspended as Bill regaled the ragtag assortment of professors, students, fellow wine lovers, and neighbours with stories of his travels in Asia and beyond.

Within minutes of crossing the Golden Gate, Caine switched to low gear and started the ascent to Sausalito. Through twisting narrow roads lined with trees he emerged on the crest of the hill. The waters of the bay below mirrored the cerulean blue of the sky. White caps danced in flurries on the water below while gulls circled overhead. A cool breeze bent the lighter branches and swept the scent of magnolia and lavender into the air.

The narrow road was quiet. In a lay-by, carved into the hillside near the summit, stood a lone vehicle. The occupant was not visible. Early in the week was the best time for uninterrupted scenic walks or wildlife observation so it was not unusual for vehicles to be left unattended for long periods. At the weekend the crowds from the city would come, choking the roads in the search for tranquillity.

On the left, cloaked by ivy, stood the heavy wooden gate that marked the entrance to "RoseLea", the Jacobs' secluded home. Passing the empty mailbox Caine approached a sturdy oak front door blackened by age yet with its heavy brass fittings gleaming. There was no bell. Caine remembered that the Jacobs' eschewed formality, more often than not leaving the front door open as an invitation to hospitality. Today, however, it was bolted firmly shut.

Caine banged on the door with his clenched fist. The deadbolt and chain on the other side of the door rattled. After a few seconds, Caine left the door and peered through the front window.

On a table inside lay a considerable amount of mail fanned out carefully for inspection. Clearly the occupant had been gone for some time for such an amount to collect unread. A stack of magazines, mostly scientific journals, lay in a separate pile.

Caine rediscovered a small path overgrown with pink lilacs running down the perimeter of the property. He emerged after about ten yards into a quiet, well-lit glade. Beyond this small apron of lawn lay a large well-tended garden that culminated in a cliff-top patio with spectacular views of the coast.

The back door, almost identical to the front, was set in an open porch, draped with variegated ivy intertwined with honeysuckle. As he approached Caine saw immediately that something was amiss.

White flecks of raw splintered wood surrounded the lock plate and hung in shards from the aged timber frame; the elegant brass door handle drooped lifelessly.

Caine paused for a moment listening for any sounds from inside, determining if it was safe for him to proceed. He did not want to encounter a burglar alone and in such an isolated location. With any luck any intruder would have fled out the back when they heard his pounding on the front door.

The door was stiff and resisted Caine's attempts to push it open. The damaged hinges groaned and the door scraped noisily across the floor as Caine pushed harder. Caine froze on the threshold, every fibre of his body alert to the slightest indication that he shared the house with another.

The back door opened into the kitchen.

The room was cluttered but cosy. An ancient wooden table that could easily accommodate eight people occupied the centre of the room. A pair of matching hand-turned wooden platters held piles of darkened fruit. Apples and pears liquefied slowly in the autumn heat while oranges and grapes sported a white-green down of mould.

The sweet alcohol-laden vapours of putrefaction filled the room.

Caine pushed the door closed behind him, lifting it on its broken hinges slightly to dampen the noise. The flagstones amplified the sounds of his steps as he crossed the room to reach the door he knew led into the hallway.

Listening carefully again before opening, he turned the handle gently. The hallway was empty. The narrow corridor linked the kitchen to the living room and study. Light from a small window in the front door was the only source of illumination.

Family portraits in complementary frames and arranged with regimental precision lined the walls. Stern-faced immigrants in their Sunday best looked past Caine, their long-dead eyes peering silently into the shadows.

In the corner of the hallway, behind the front door, an open staircase led to the bedrooms on the first storey. From his position Caine could see through the balustrade and halfway up the stairs. Satisfied that no one was loitering there he walked through the hallway into the living room.

Nothing seemed out of place. The curtains were pulled back and tied neatly either side of a large bay window. In an alcove on one side of the chimneybreast sat the TV; a thin film of dust adhered to its screen. Behind it row upon row of books soared up to the ceiling. An old battered love seat nestled against one wall, illuminated on either side by a pair of reading lamps.

An antique crucifix a full three feet across and still bearing traces of the original paint, dominated the room from its perch high up the chimneybreast. Caine remembered how Jacobs had come across it in a back street sale of

Christian artefacts in the Philippines many years ago. The anguished, tortured face of the Christ looked down on the occupants of the love seat.

A small table sat in another alcove. A vase of dried flowers stood to one side, lit from above by a single spotlight. Next to the vase sat an immense Bible. The faded tattered shards of a red silk bookmark dangled from the middle, pressed flat like a preserved wild flower.

Caine had seen the book before. The family Bible had accompanied Jacobs' great-great-grandfather on his journey to North America from England in the 1850s.

Despite the evidence of the broken door there was no sign yet that anything had been disturbed inside.

Caine made for the study. The room, a quiet cul-de-sac at the end of the corridor, contained Bill's extensive collection of California wines in addition to his library and after hours work area. It was most likely in here that a burglar would gravitate to search for hidden drawers and lock boxes.

Caine tensed as he nervously edged toward the room. The sky was bruising as twilight approached and the interior of the house darkened perceptibly casting long shadows against the walls and floor.

The door was open and Caine peered around the doorframe into the room. The disarray was immediately apparent. Papers were strewn across the floor, bookshelves emptied - their contents ripped apart and dumped into an overflowing waste paper basket or stacked haphazardly on an old battered chesterfield that dominated one corner of the tiny room. Most tellingly, Jacobs' computer was switched on; a kaleidoscopic effect screen-saver provided feeble illumination. The intruder was looking for more than just money or portable valuables. And they were still here.

The hairs stood up on the back of Caine's neck as a cold dread permeated his body. His heart raced and his temples throbbed. Turning slowly he checked behind him. Nothing. Crossing the room to the computer he nudged the mouse to reactivate the screen. The screen flickered and the psychedelic colours were replaced with text. Caine peered closer and examined the electronic document. It was Bill Jacobs' resume.

Caine scrolled through the document with the mouse. Jacobs' life and career boiled down into seventeen closely typed pages. From high school to the present day, the succinct yet emotionless tally purported to reveal all that was necessary to know about William R. Jacobs, PhD.

The resume detailed Jacobs' transfers, sabbaticals and industry consultancies in chronological order. Caine ticked off each line with a mental comment, tallying the list with his own recollections of his former boss's life. The degree of correspondence was pleasingly high and Caine allowed himself a knowing smirk as one of the few privy to the life of the real Bill Jacobs.

Still, if there was something in this document for which it was worth breaking and entering, Caine could not see what it was. The resume was simply that - a list of the comings and goings of a reasonably talented middle-aged academic. If the life story of Bill Jacobs held the key to anything it was how to respect others and have a good time doing it.

Puzzled by the logic of the burglar Caine surveyed the room for something else that might have attracted the attention of an intruder.

The walls of the tiny room were mostly taken up with bookcases lined with old, well-thumbed scientific treatises or filing boxes of correspondence. Every available space was filled with cheap picture frames containing degrees, both earned and honorary, and a mixed bag of photographs of Jacobs as a young man.

The thick bouffant hair and wide paisley ties of the late sixties and early seventies screamed out at Caine from the other side of the room; Jacobs giving a presentation to the Dawson County Stockman's Guild; the keynote speech at an international meeting; meeting the president of the Feed Manufacturer's Association; after dinner speech at the Lubbock Rotarians.

Caine remembered the pile of letters in the living room he had seen through the front window and returned to the dimly lit room at the front of the house. The weekly scientific journals Science, Nature and New Scientist were stacked neatly on one side of the table. The dates and volume numbers were visible through the transparent plastic coating. Two issues of each magazine had been delivered.

The letters were arranged on the table in a large semi-circular fan. A dozen envelopes overlapped one another obscuring the delivery address on all but the uppermost letter, leaving the franking mark in the top right hand corner as the sole indicator of place of origin and date of posting. Caine thumbed through them. The oldest letter was posted twelve days ago, the most recent just four days ago. The occupant had either brought the magazines and letters into the house from the mailbox outside, sorted and left them unopened and unread until later, or the intruder had done it himself.

Caine was puzzled and his brow furrowed in concentration. The more he thought the more worried he became. Was Jacobs dead? Was he lying somewhere in the house to be discovered later? Was that why the intruder dared disturb the mail and ransack the study, knowing the owner would not return? The feeling of fear overcame Caine again. He wanted to run, but he also wanted - needed - to find out what had happened to his friend.

The round tube of the muzzle was hard and painful as it pressed against the nape of Caine's neck. As it dug into his skin he could feel the indentation of the bore and the thickness of the barrel walls.

Stock still, Caine gripped the edge of the table and stared straight ahead. Reflected in the window in front of him he could see a vague shadow, a wraith-like figure, standing behind him. Clenching his buttocks and resisting the urge to defecate, sweat started to bead on his forehead. It ran in rivulets under his armpits.

The muzzle of the pistol jerked upward slightly pulling at the flesh as the hammer was cocked. Caine closed his eyes and tried to think of something happy and how he would rather be somewhere else.

His mind was a blank. Fear paralysed every thought. Incomprehensible terror. Maybe this was what a rabbit felt like caught in the headlights of an approaching car. Too scared to move; too scared to even acknowledge the predicament it was in.

Caine became aware of his breathing. Short gasps. His heart drummed in his chest. He couldn't swallow; his tongue seemed to enlarge, filling his mouth and sticking to his palette. Seconds away from death Caine wondered if he would be able to hear the sound of his own execution.

The warmth of human breath tingled his left ear. The cooling vapour of the exhaled air caused the skin on his neck to contract involuntarily. Tiny hairs sprang to attention on his neck.

You're in the shit this time, pal.

Chapter 30

"You're really not very good at this are you?" said the voice, as the pistol was lowered.

Caine gasped and cool air rushed into his lungs. Continuing to grasp the table for support he lowered his head oblivious to the person behind him. Gathering his strength he turned to face his would-be executioner.

"You!" he exclaimed.

Chen Xiao Lin smiled at Caine's surprise.

"Poor Dr. Caine. I'm so sorry. This seems to be becoming a habit, doesn't it?" Chen replied, arching her eyebrows mischievously.

"Might I ask," said Caine, between huge gulps of air, "what you're doing here? I thought you'd been deported."

"I'm doing the same thing you are, Dr. Caine. Trying to find Dr. Jacobs."

"Any luck?"

Chen shrugged her shoulders. She put her gun away and busied herself looking through the mail on the desk.

"Did you do this?" asked Caine indicating the piles of letters with a nod of his head.

"Mmmm," replied Chen. "What do you make of it?"

"Judging from the postmarks it seems Bill hasn't been here for at least two weeks," answered Caine.

"Bravo, Dr. Caine. We'll make a spy of you yet," replied Chen gleefully.

"Is that what you are? A spy?" asked Caine. The improbability of the question surprised even him.

Chen did not answer; she continued to poke among the letters.

"What did you find on the computer?" said Caine.

Chen smiled thinly. "Confirmation," she replied.

"Confirmation of what?" demanded Caine. "Come on, I think I have a right to know. After all you're here illegally, breaking into people's houses, poking your nose into other people's business. What's going on?" indignation at being made a fool of again by an attractive woman had made Caine angry. His pride had been fractured and his testosterone-fuelled display was an attempt to redress the balance, at least in his own mind.

He didn't see it coming.

The fist landed square in the middle of his belly and Caine crumpled like a rag doll. His legs buckled under him and he writhed on the floor clutching his stomach. A single tear ran down his cheek, as his face contorted in pain.

In an instant he was on his feet again as powerful hands gripped his collar. Caine's arms flailed helplessly as his face was pushed down onto the desk; the force of the blow sent the letters scattering. With one hand Chen pinned Caine to the table. Her other hand caught hold of Caine's arm and brought it smartly up behind his back. Wincing in pain Caine tried to stand upright but Chen's immense strength held him down. Relaxing her grip slightly, she bent down until Caine could see her face.

Calm beyond measure, almost beatific, she seemed to expend almost no energy. Bringing her lips close to Caine's ear she whispered, "Dr. Caine, the only reason I allow you to live is because you are not a threat to me – yet. If you tell anyone who I am or where I am I will kill you. Do you understand?"

Caine struggled; Chen tightened her grip and injected more venom and urgency into her question.

"Do you understand?" she repeated firmly.

"Yes, I understand," conceded Caine, his cheeks flushed and his eyes moist.

Chen released her grip as suddenly as it had been applied. Relief flooded Caine's face as he regained some of his composure. As he stood before her, Chen brushed some lint from Caine's shirt. The mercurial speed at which her attitude changed left Caine amazed.

"I guess developing lightning reflexes is included in spy training," he replied glibly.

"Please don't call me a spy Dr. Caine. I'm a patriot and my work is not made easier by people like you."

"By people like me you're referring to law-abiding citizens, I suppose?"

"I seem to think I am not the only one who broke into someone else's house," mused Chen.

"Alright, point taken. So what are you really doing here? I take it some poor bugger at the embassy took your place on the flight back to China?"

"What is it you people say about Chinese, Dr. Caine? We all look the same? I guess that can have its advantages sometimes."

"So what have you been doing for the past two weeks?"

"Investigating a murder," Chen replied.

"Whose?"

"How soon people forget! I'm sure the family of Dr. al-Jaheerah would be most upset to hear you speak like that."

"Oh, him," said Caine. "And what did you discover?"

"That Dr. Jacobs probably killed him," replied Chen.

"Bollocks!" cried Caine in astonishment.

"What was that?" replied Chen, mystified by Caine's outburst.

"Sorry. Slang," replied Caine. "It means um, nonsense, sort of."

"Well, I'm sorry to disappoint you. I know Dr. Jacobs was your friend. But don't killers have friends too?"

"Where's your evidence?" retorted Caine.

Chen thought for a moment, trying to decide on which thread of the story to begin. "Dr. Jacobs set up al-Jaheerah," she began. "He assigned the rooms to all the delegates at the conference, as part of his duties as organiser. Previously he had stayed in the same room as Dr. al-Jaheerah, so he knew the layout of the room and the location of nearby exits. He also knew that the security camera on the floor in question was disabled for routine maintenance."

Caine remembered Laura remarking that Jacobs had stayed in the dead man's room. Still, he denied the connection. "Surely this is all speculation?" he said. "None of this is hard evidence."

"al-Jaheerah was supposed to meet me in the hotel coffee shop to discuss his concerns," continued Chen. "I suggest that before he could meet me he had also arranged to meet someone else. When they didn't show up as planned he returned to his room. The meeting was a ruse to get him out of his room long enough for someone using a copy of the room key to gain access and lie in wait for his return."

"If Bill Jacobs made a copy of the room key on his last visit it means he must have been planning this for weeks if not months," protested Caine.

"So?" replied Chen. "You don't think a terrorist is capable of waiting great lengths of time in order to fulfil their goals. Most of their time is spent waiting."

"There's got to be some rational explanation to Bill's behaviour," said Caine.

"Have you seen the VCD of the symposium that everyone received as a souvenir?" said Chen, ignoring Caine's protests.

"No. Why?"

"You should watch the cocktail party segment. That was filmed on the day of the murder, wasn't it?"

"I guess," Caine replied.

"Watch it and tell me what you see."

Caine was annoyed. He came to the house expecting to see his friend and have a chat about old times. Now he was defending the greatest influence on his career from crazed talk and coincidences implicating him in murder and terrorism.

"What was al-Jaheerah concerned about? Why was he coming to see you?" said Caine, picking up on Chen's comment.

"al-Jaheerah was a mediocre scientist from a mediocre research institute. Unfortunately for him, he stumbled on something very big and very ugly. Despite the risks he did a remarkable job. Dr. al-Jaheerah was also a patriot."

"What did he do exactly?" queried Caine.

"As you know, al-Jaheerah was an expert on foot-and-mouth disease. He was the one who collected and typed the virus strain that has been used in the outbreak we are now experiencing."

"Strain C/Quetta/2002," interjected Caine.

"Exactly. Following international guidelines, as soon as he discovered the virus he sent samples to your lab in the UK and to the Americans, after which he forgot about it. Some months later, however, he became aware that his own stocks of the virus had been tampered with. No one in his institute would take responsibility. On his own initiative, he discovered that the head of the institute was a member of an extremist Islamic group with contacts across central Asia. What Dr. al-Jaheerah feared was that this group, or others like it, would use the threat of biological warfare as a bargaining chip in negotiating favourable terms for Muslim minorities in neighbouring states. Chechnya and Russia, that sort of thing.

"So how did Chinese, how shall I put it, special interests, get involved?" Caine said, careful not to upset Chen again.

"Through our network of contacts in Muslim groups in China, we were able to show that al-Jaheerah had been correct and that contact between the Pakistani radical group *Justice under God* and Islamic secessionists in China had already been made. It was simply a matter of time before the virus was used within China. We contacted al-Jaheerah several weeks ago through our embassy in Pakistan and asked for a meeting to provide more information. He said he was too frightened to meet in Pakistan and so we agreed to use the international symposium as a cover. But it looks like someone got to him first."

"What extra information was he supposed to provide?"

"The name of the group's contacts in China, in addition to the rest of Central Asia. China is a big place, Dr. Caine. While we have infiltrated many groups we can't be expected to keep track of all treasonous and destabilising activities."

"That's a bit melodramatic, isn't it?" Caine replied.

"Secession is a serious crime in China, Dr. Caine. We are surrounded by enemies. A country's strength lies in its unity. Those who promulgate secession are traitors who seek nothing less than the destruction of the People's Republic. We cannot allow that to happen."

Caine did not buy China's concern for internal stability as a motive for its interest in the terror group. Larger issues were at stake. Destabilisation of weaker Muslim-led countries by spreading rumours of an Islamic bioterrorist plot would maintain Chinese hegemony in Central Asia for many years to come. Demonising a religious minority would allow the government to impose unfettered control over the civil rights of both the minority and, by extension, the majority populations within China.

"Who are you afraid of?" asked Caine. "Who's going to break away from China?"

"It's not a question of fear, Dr. Caine," replied Chen. "It's about maintaining harmony through unity. We must always be on guard against those who would create instability for their own selfish ends."

"I take it you mean Tibet?"

"Not necessarily. Tibet enjoys a high degree of autonomy along with religious freedom."

Caine snorted. "Who then?"

"There are elements within some of the other autonomous regions in China who capable of abusing their power to create disunity."

"Such as Muslim regions, like Xinjiang, for instance?"

"You know about Xinjiang?"

Chen was surprised to find a westerner familiar with the less travelled regions of China. She had lost count of the conversations she had had with foreigners about the magnificence of the Great Wall or the timeless splendour of the Forbidden City, as if they were the only two things to see in the most populous country on earth.

"So you will know that separate languages and religion are not necessarily grounds for independence," Chen persisted, determined to have her say. "These things can exist quite happily within an autonomously administered province. China has hundreds of ethnic tribes and dialects yet they co-exist very well together without constant claims for homelands of their own." Chen paused, suddenly aware it was not an appropriate time to try and persuade Caine of China's realpolitik in Central Asia. "Have you ever been to Xinjiang?" she said, changing tack.

"Yes, I once collected samples of foot-and-mouth disease virus there," said Caine. "Clandestinely, of course."

During his PhD studies Caine backpacked through Xinjiang, where the central authorities had always vociferously denied any reports of foot-and-mouth disease outbreaks. Managing to smuggle a handful of biopsy samples from infected cattle back to his lab, he proved they had been infected with the virus. However, because of the manner in which the samples were collected, he was never able to publish his work. Consequently, his findings languished unread in the only six copies of his PhD thesis he could afford to publish.

"Maybe I'm a bit of a spy after all," he added.

"But foot-and-mouth disease does not exist in China, Dr. Caine. You must have had a wasted journey."

"Just because China does not fulfil its international obligations and report all the outbreaks of livestock disease occurring in its own borders does not mean these diseases do not exist," Caine replied, pointedly. "As a member of the OIE, the international animal health organisation, China is required to inform other members of disease that may affect world trade in animals and their products."

"I can assure you that China fulfils all its international obligations," replied Chen.

"Considering that foot-and-mouth disease has been reported in every one of China's neighbours, including Hong Kong, Korea, Taiwan, Russia, Pakistan and the others, it is inconceivable that the country is free of the disease. Small outbreaks have been reported in isolated areas such as Tibet and Hainan over the years and even in Guangdong in 1986. But sizeable outbreaks in more populous regions have never been acknowledged officially."

"We are a very developed country, Dr. Caine. All our animal diseases are prevented with vaccines," countered Chen. She had no knowledge of veterinary practices but she was aware of the availability of vaccines to treat a host of diseases.

"I suppose you are aware that vaccine production facilities are a recognised source of infection? Vaccines incorporate the killed virus in order to stimulate the immune response. If the virus is not killed properly during the manufacturing process it can persist in the vaccine and actually spread the disease it was meant to prevent."

Chen's face crinkled in a scowl. She could not argue the point further; she did not have the factual ammunition necessary to shoot down Caine's thesis. Caine smirked in triumph as Chen paused.

"Okay," continued Caine, "so I guess al-Jaheerah was going to give you the names of these Xinjiang contacts who were going to blackmail China into allowing a breakaway Islamic republic. Am I right so far?"

"Something like that."

"And you think Bill Jacobs killed him before he could tell you."

"And removed any evidence al-Jaheerah had brought with him," added Chen. "Remember, I searched al-Jaheerah's body. All I could find was his notebook. Everything else had been taken."

"So you think something might be here?"

"It's a possibility."

"What makes you think that al-Jaheerah didn't make a copy and leave it at home in Pakistan? Maybe you should be looking there as well."

Chen raised her eyebrows and smiled at Caine, silently indicating that alternative possibilities for the location of the data had been considered.

"Oh," said Caine, as he suddenly understood Chen's knowing glance, "I see. I guess I'm in the middle of a big international conspiracy."

"Watch your back, Dr. Caine."

"You said you had confirmation of Bill Jacobs' guilt," asked Caine. "What did you mean by that?"

"I shouldn't tell you of course," said Chen guardedly, "but from what I gather from his resume he had sufficient knowledge of Central Asia to be a useful contact and source of information for the terrorists."

"Holidays in Tashkent are hardly grounds to implicate him in a global conspiracy to overthrow China," retorted Caine.

"Nevertheless," continued Chen, "I will report my findings to the appropriate authorities and doubtless they will act upon them to neutralise any perceived threats."

"I doubt if the FBI will welcome your reappearance after the last stunt you pulled."

Chen looked at Caine silently. Her black eyes stared out, piercing the wan light in the room like a cat, boring into Caine's skull. She attempted to gauge Caine's thoughts toward her and her theories on Bill Jacobs' treachery from the nuances of his facial gestures. Chen was puzzled by Caine's poker face. Did it show awe, incredulity or mere incomprehension?

"When you say appropriate authorities, you mean in this country?" Caine asked, now nervous over the possible meanings of Chen's ambiguous statement.

Silence.

"Or do you mean Chinese authorities?" Caine continued.

Chen arched her eyebrows as the light caught her high cheekbones. In her tight black outfit her pale skin shone like a sickly moon in the darkened room, giving her head a ghostly, disembodied look like a genie or will-o'-the-wisp.

"Neutralise the threat means someone is going to kill Bill Jacobs first before he does anything, is that right?" Caine's voice was rising, and he was almost hysterical. Still Chen remained silent. Her presence was unnerving and Caine backed towards the door to the corridor.

Chen stood before him. In the shadows she slowly unbuttoned her black coat. As the front flap fell open the holster of her pistol could be seen glinting in the reflected light. The knurled handle of the gun nestled in the hollow under Chen's arm.

"Not you! God, not you!" cried Caine, now terrified. If Chen could kill Jacobs, who knew little or nothing about her existence or activities in the US, she would have no qualms about killing him, someone who now knew all her secrets.

Caine ran. He prayed that in the darkness he could remember the layout of Jacobs' house after all these years and escape before Chen caught up with him; he had no doubt she would be able to kill him with her bare hands.

Caine ducked out of the door into the corridor. Running back to the kitchen he headed for the partially open door and into the back garden.

Chen sighed, buttoned her coat and followed at a leisurely pace.

In the garden Caine sprinted down the path to the cliff top, where he hoped the path that climbed part way down the steep cliff still existed. It led to a private viewing area that Jacobs had carved out of the hill and where he had erected a bench. Caine vaguely recalled the story of how the bench had been 'rescued' and restored from the San Francisco parks department.

Stumbling over fully-grown and newly planted shrubbery that he did not know was there and could not see, Caine made his way to the bottom of the garden. Muddy and gasping with fear he strained to hear if Chen was following. He heard nothing except his own terrified keening.

The moon was full and low in the sky. Looking up Caine noticed he was silhouetted against the night sky. Hurling himself to the ground he crept toward the edge of the cliff. Thick tufts of grass covered the undulating slope. Occasionally his hands or elbows sank into the turf, as a concealed hole suddenly appeared, the remains of a long disused rabbit warren or gull's nest.

After some minutes of frenzied groping he came across the steep descent to the viewing area. A series of notches, six inches apart and barely eighteen inches wide had been cut into the hill. The climb down was treacherous during daylight; at night it was suicidal.

On the slope adjacent to the steps iron rings had been embedded into the rock and strung with thick nylon twine. Blindly searching the cliff face with his fingertips Caine found the first of them, worn smooth with frequent use. Holding the ring tightly for support Caine felt for and found the nylon rope.

The cold wind gusted up the slope and he could hear the waves crashing eighty feet below. Leaning back slightly to maintain his balance and stepping softly Caine descended the first steps easily. Confidence growing with every step, he increased his speed fearing that Chen was not far behind and would soon discover his means of escape.

Thick moss grew over some of the rock notches and Caine guessed that Jacobs had not used this path for some time. Halfway down Caine paused for breath. He felt the rock face; its cool hard surface was reassuring. Just as he was about to continue a flutter of wings and a great caw pierced the air. A large double-breasted cormorant bolted from a natural rock alcove, forcing Caine to take a step back. As he did so he lost his footing and slipped.

Landing on his backside he immediately pitched headfirst over the cliff. As he stumbled he grasped at anything that might break his fall, clumps of grass slipped through his fingers as the momentum carried him forward. Just as he was about to disappear over the edge he scrambled to find a handhold.

Crevices and fissures dissected the rock ledge into which the steps were carved. Caine jammed his hands into the nearest crack, his fingers screaming in pain as they carried the entire weight of his body. Instantly, he brought his other hand on to the ledge to take some of the load. His plunge into the sea averted, Caine dangled from the cliff. Scuffing his shoes along the unseen face of the cliff beneath him, he tried to get a toehold with which to boost himself back onto the ledge.

The pain extended up his arm as the long wait to find a support took its toll on his muscles. Swinging gently Caine managed to snag one foot onto the ledge. He breathed a sigh of relief as his aching arms were given a respite. He hauled himself fully onto the narrow rocky outcrop, where he floundered gasping for air. Hugging the rock for comfort he stared down into the black sea, as the distinctive odour of salt spray and rotting seaweed assailed his nostrils.

After some time the realisation that Chen was probably not looking for him convinced Caine to try to make it back to the garden. Exposure to the cool sea air for much longer would drain his body of energy. If he remained where he was during the night it would get colder, darker and more difficult to return. He chided himself for his fear and his over-reaction to Chen's mute threat. Too wary to stand, he bloodied his knees as he unceremoniously retraced his steps.

Peering over the crest of the cliff Caine looked back toward the house. The lights had been switched off. Caine hoped Chen had found what she wanted and departed. Still straining to listen Caine hunched up and stepped quietly back to the house, using the dense shrubbery as natural cover.

At the edge of the glade immediately outside the broken back door Caine paused and listened as he straightened himself up. Sensing nothing he walked calmly to the back door. It had been pulled back roughly in place. Holding the handle with one hand and lifting at the same time to counter the effect of the damaged hinges Caine applied his shoulder to the door.

Crack!

The doorframe above Caine's right ear erupted into splinters. Instinctively he ducked whilst continuing to push hard on the door. It opened enough to allow him entry and he dived into the now darkened kitchen. Slamming his body hard against the door it screamed shut.

Remaining slumped against the door Caine cowered in terror. Fearing that another bullet would pierce the door he leapt to his feet and ran through the hallway, bounding up the stairs two at a time until he reached the relative sanctuary of the upper hallway.

Caine opened the door to the guest bedroom, which he knew had a view of the back garden and crept toward the window. The curtains were open and Caine hoped that the sniper below could be observed unseen. However, after some minutes there was still no sound or movement from the garden. Caine exhaled deeply.

In the distance Caine heard a noise. The still night air carried the sound faint but distinct; it was the sound of an engine turning over. It was not his own car in the driveway at the front of the house but that of a vehicle some distance away. Racing to the master bedroom, with its views of the front road, Caine jumped on the bed and peered out of the window.

Two parallel beams of light moved in synchrony toward the house from lower down the hill. As the vehicle approached and tore past at high speed Caine realised that it was the small red car he had seen in the lay-by on his way to the house. Once again Caine ducked as he fancied that the driver cast a look in his direction.

Exhausted by fear, Caine flopped down on the bed. He was safe for the moment. Chen was off to track down Jacobs using whatever information she had obtained searching his computer.

In the morning Caine would thoroughly search Jacobs' house himself and then call the police to report the break-in.

In the meantime, he had to call Laura and explain why he would not be coming home. He wondered what he would say without alarming her unnecessarily.

Bill Jacobs was always famous for his welcomes and tonight was no exception.

Chapter 31

Garcia was exhausted. She had spent a caffeine-fuelled night in a series of teleconferences with FBI field offices around the southwest United States as they tracked down, in real-time, the suspects on the list of car owners.

In the preceding thirty-six hours fifty-five suspects had been accounted for and eliminated. A further two had been added to the list after more information became available. Only seventeen now remained unaccounted for.

After the first round of door knocks had failed to elicit a response from the homes of the remaining suspects court orders were obtained to effect immediate forced entry on the grounds of suspicion of aiding and abetting terrorist activities.

The first of these actions was scheduled for 10:00 A.M. that morning. Garcia awoke from a doze at her desk and checked her watch. One hour to go. Closing her eyes she continued to catnap. Before she managed to drift off to sleep the phone on her desk trilled quietly. In the silent office, darkened by drawn shades, Garcia snapped to attention and fumbled for the receiver buried under the profiles, maps and computer projections collected during the investigation.

"Garcia," she answered wearily, rubbing her temples firmly with her long bony fingers.

A soft voice replied, "Special Agent Garcia? This is Tariq Habib from the Asian languages section at Quantico. I believe you recently sent me a document for examination?"

"Yes, Dr. Habib," replied Garcia, now fully erect in her chair. "It was a list of Arabic names, I just wanted an opinion as to whether any of them seemed," she paused, acutely aware of how racist the question appeared to someone from a similar culture as the suspects, "well… suspicious."

"Mmm," replied Habib, "I see."

As a former assistant professor in Asian languages, with a particular preference for modern dialects of Persian, Habib's talents as a translator and interpreter had been much in demand following the Gulf War and the September 11, 2001 attack on New York and Washington, D.C. Poached from a small university in the mid-west he was persuaded to join the combined fight against terrorism by a strong sense of patriotism to his adopted home and the generous resources at his disposal. Still, the automatic and implicit sense of bias against his fellow countrymen that occurred every time he was asked for help rankled.

"From the list provided to me, Agent Garcia, there appear at first to be no peculiarities. Most of the names are fairly standard family names typical of many Arab and Muslim dominated regions around the world."

"Well," replied Garcia with a hint of resignation, "I guessed that might be the case. I'm sorry to have wasted your time."

“Actually,” said Habib, “I said there appeared to be no peculiarities. One entry on the list interests me. The name Husam al-Din stands out.”

“In what way?” asked Garcia, flicking through piles of papers on her desk to find a copy of the page she had had faxed to Quantico. At last she found it. The typed list of seventy names, with the additional two entries tacked on the end in her wide looped handwriting, was creased and worn. Yellow highlighter strokes and pencil crosses marked where most of the entries had been checked and eliminated. Scanning quickly down the list of names she found Husam al-Din. The name was circled in blue; he was one of the seventeen suspects who had not been questioned.

“The name is unusual,” continued Habib. “I suspect a westerner might assume that al-Din is a family name, whereas in fact, Husam al-Din in its entirety is a given name. There appears to be no family name at all for this individual. Is this name correct or am I missing some information?”

Garcia quickly checked her list. “That’s all the information I have, Dr. Habib. You must assume that that is the correct entry as obtained from the Department of Motor Vehicles in Florida.”

“In that case, Agent Garcia, you may have a problem.”

“In what way?” replied Garcia, adrenaline surging through her body in a rush of excitement and anticipation.

“The name is mostly associated with medieval Arabic governors and sages, around the time of the Crusades. Bronze coins from that period attributed to Husam al-Din Yuluq Arslan, for example, are still collected today. As it stands, Husam al-Din alone means ‘Sword of the Faith’.”

“Thank you, Dr. Habib. You’ve been a great help.”

Garcia replaced the receiver in its cradle and stared at it for a few seconds. Picking it up again she called the reception desk.

“Helen, call the airport. Have them fire up the Lear jet and file a flight plan for St. Petersburg, Florida. I want it ready to go within the hour.”

Garcia was pumped; she lived for the thrill of the chase and now she had the scent of blood in her nose.

“Forward all calls to my cell phone, I want to keep up to date on this morning’s take downs,” she added, referring to the forced entries scheduled for later that day.

Slamming the phone down, she picked up her bag and a sheaf of papers from her desk and ran through the office to the reception.

“Get hold of the Tampa field office, have them liaise with local PD. Make sure there’s a Crime Scene Investigation unit on stand by. I expect there’ll be a lot of forensic work to do. I’ll call them with details once I’m up in the air. My ETA is about seven hours from now,” she said glancing at her watch. “Make sure they wait until I get there before going through the door. I want to see for myself what this son-of-a-bitch is up to.”

Chapter 32

Caine spent a restless night in Jacobs' old house. Despite seeing Chen depart at high speed the night before he had difficulty assuring himself she would not return in the middle of the night and finish him off. He was exhausted from lack of sleep.

Respect for his absent host meant Caine slept in the smaller guest room rather than in the more comfortable master bedroom. Even then he did not undress and get under the covers, merely kicking off his shoes and slipping under the counterpane. The unheated house chilled him to his bones and he awoke cold, hungry and irritable.

After breakfast, Caine searched the house systematically. The kitchen, upstairs bedrooms and living room yielded no clues as to where Bill Jacobs was, why he was missing, or why Chinese agents should be searching for him. The unopened letters in the living room revealed nothing.

In the middle of the morning Caine examined the den in detail. Straightening the pictures and bookcases was the easy part. A quick examination of the torn books produced nothing of interest. They comprised standard texts from a variety of subjects that would not be out of place in any university professor's bookcase.

In the corner of the room, under an old armchair, Caine saw it. The tote bag from the conference in San Francisco sat unzipped and gaping. Jacobs had returned home since the conference ended over a week ago. He must have dumped his bag and then left almost immediately, a fact supported by the unopened mail dating from that time.

The black canvas holdall with the conference name and logo stencilled in white on one side was surprisingly heavy. When he opened it Caine saw why. A thick bound volume of speakers' abstracts and presented papers took up most of the room. A supplementary book of advertising flyers and junior scientists' poster summaries added to the bulk.

As he pulled the books out into the daylight he noticed a red-brown stain on the edge of the pages. The colour had seeped from the edge of the page almost to the spine. He had seen the stain before in al-Jaheerah's notebook in San Francisco; it was blood.

As he rummaged deeper into the bag Caine found Jacobs' copy of the souvenir VCD. Chen's suggestion regarding the disk came to mind and Caine looked about for something on which to play it. Jacobs had no VCD player but Caine guessed the disk drive on the computer would be compatible.

The computer was still switched on from the previous evening and Caine slipped the disk into the CD drawer. Double-clicking an icon on the screen started the movie.

The film was a distinctly amateur affair. A crude title slide introduced the contents. The first scene began immediately with a babble of different voices as the cameraman moved through the crowd of people. The backs of people's heads moved in and out of focus as the cameraman walked through the teeming mass. Occasionally he would stop and eavesdrop on a conversation, moving on as the participants noticed him and fell self-consciously silent.

The scene was repeated for several minutes. It was some time before Caine could put the activities into context. The only item of note was a rather stilted discussion between Jonas Williams and Bill Jacobs about how pleased they were to be hosting the latest symposium. Caine couldn't help feel embarrassed for Jacobs. The early scenes of the film showed the guests assembling before the cocktail reception on the first day. Chen had warned Caine specifically to watch this segment.

The cameraman focused on the beautiful Chinese girl amidst a group of men. She stared back into the lens, smiling thinly. Caine shuddered. He found her no less beautiful now than when he had first seen her. But how looks can be deceiving. Caine himself entered the frame and introduced himself to Chen, his questions being diverted to the elderly professor. As he feared, the cameraman had caught Caine's surreptitious ogling of Chen.

Damn!

Was this what Chen had been talking about? Caine was sure she had meant something else. He let the film run with the volume turned to the maximum as he continued his search of the den. The rumbling and distorted sounds from the computer's inadequate speaker were strangely comforting to Caine. The distant sounds of human voices chased away the fear and loneliness of the isolated house.

Tidying up the shredded books as best he could and replacing them on the shelves allowed Caine to better negotiate the confines of the tiny room. Every nook and cranny was searched meticulously. During his exploration it became apparent that Chen had done the same the previous night. Doubtless she had taken anything of value to her investigation.

On the computer, the film progressed to the keynote speech by Professor Frederickson. Caine looked up just in time to see the Professor take the stage. Jonas Williams and Jacobs were just visible in the background; the grainy image from the dark interior of the auditorium did not make it easy to determine whether there was anything else of interest in the picture. Caine clicked the fast forward button and the image jerked forward a few frames at a time.

After a few minutes, Frederickson's speech finished and Caine clicked the play button to resume the film's normal speed. The camera panned from Frederickson to Williams as the latter got up and crossed the stage to shake the speaker's hand. Caine stopped the film at this point and rewound it a few frames. He did this several times until he was satisfied he had not missed anything.

Son-of-a-bitch.

Intrigued, Caine sat down at the desk and watched the remainder of the disk. When the cameraman wandered around the poster session Caine studied the screen minutely. He smiled as he saw Chen eavesdropping on the Pakistani group.

The embarrassing photo opportunity with Jacobs, Caine and the naïve young Pakistani scientists was replayed. Caine looked into Jacobs' eyes as he stared deep into the video camera. The look of calm and self-assurance was sublime. Caine played the scene over and over confident he had now seen what Chen had referred to in their conversation.

Son-of-a-bitch.

Caine stopped the disk knowing it did not contain any further information useful to his investigation. He returned the disk to its thin card envelope and slipped it into his breast pocket.

The trawl through the remains of Jacobs' possessions proved to be a distressing affair for Caine as Chen had thoughtlessly trashed too many shared memories in her ruthless search for evidence of Jacobs' involvement.

A scattering of paperbacks formed the lowest layer of the detritus underfoot. Like an archaeologist piecing together history from layers of broken pottery shards, so it seemed to Caine that he was revealing more of Jacobs' life with every freshly exposed document.

The books Caine found were not academic texts but popular fiction and non-fiction titles that Jacobs' used to while away the hours of a Sunday morning in his cliff top retreat. Among the expected titles on gardening and North American wineries, a couple of other books stood out.

Caine picked up an epidemiological treatise discussing how and where the next human plague would originate. Intrigued, Caine idly thumbed through the account with some interest before casually tossing it into a nearby box he had prepared to help with his tidying.

At his feet lay another book purporting to reveal details of human history hidden in coded references in the Bible. Among the author's claims was that the assassination of Israeli Prime Minister Yitzshak Rabin had been foretold in biblical code. Caine knew that the work had been discredited as similar results were obtained using other large texts, such as *War and Peace* or *Moby Dick*. Soon he tired of the nonsense and threw the book into the box. As he did so a small piece of paper fluttered to the ground. It had been secreted within the book and became dislodged as it flew through the air.

Caine stooped to pick it up thinking it was only a shopping list or the like. It was an ATM receipt on the back of which were scribbled a series of letters and numbers.

Studying the paper closely Caine's brow furrowed. The list read:

Zep 1-2-3
Ex 9-3
Nos 14-12
Lev 26-24

Caine guessed the numbers were biblical references, mostly from the Old Testament, if he recalled his primary school RE lessons correctly, although he also reminded himself that Zep 1-2-3 could refer to the first three Led Zeppelin albums, which considering Jacobs' eclectic interests was also a legitimate possibility.

Caine walked to the living room. The sun streaked through the windows and illuminated the massive crucifix piercing it with parallel shards of light. In contrast, the alcove holding the family Bible was deep in shadow; the precious text protected from the harsh rays of the sun.

The page indicated by the red silk marker seemed as good a place as any to start so Caine delicately prised open the book with his thumb. To his surprise, the marker was laid at the beginning of the Book of Zephaniah. Caine looked at the scrap of paper again. With his index finger at the top of the page he traced the text pausing at the superscript verse annotations until he found chapter one, verses two and three.

> *I will utterly consume all things from off the land, saith the Lord. I will consume man and beast; I will consume the fowls of the heaven, and the fishes of the sea, and the stumbling blocks with the wicked: and I will cut off man from off the land, saith the Lord.*

Caine stared at the words barely comprehending their meaning. It was some time before he turned to the front of the book to find the next reference on the list - Exodus chapter nine, verse three.

> *Behold, the hand of the Lord is upon thy cattle which is in the field, upon the horses, upon the asses, upon the camels, upon the oxen, and upon the sheep: there shall be a very grievous murrain.*

To Caine the word murrain had a specific meaning. It was a veterinary term less common now that at the turn of the century indicating a variety of diseases of cattle, such as anthrax, foot-and-mouth disease and babesiosis. Its medieval meaning was more disturbing – pestilence.

Anxious now, his palms sweating, Caine searched for the third reference, which he took to be from the Book of Numbers. Fumbling with the thick pages in the heavy book he eventually found the relevant passage.

> *I will smite them with the pestilence, and disinherit them, and will make of thee a greater nation and mightier than they.*

Caine shook his head in dismay. What did this mean? The jumble of phrases seemed at once threatening and yet at the same time slightly ludicrous, as if some schoolboy was playing a prank, breathing life into ambiguous texts by interweaving them into a semi-coherent plot. Disheartened, he searched for the last term on the list in chapter twenty-six of the Book of Leviticus.

> *Then will I also walk contrary unto you, and will punish you yet seven times for your sins.*

The book closed with a thump. Resting his hands upon it Caine's head drooped. A sense of exasperation and incredulity swept over him as he contemplated the verses. Numb with doubt, Caine tried to remember a time when he did not love and respect Bill Jacobs.

Betrayed and frightened Caine now had to make a choice. At the back of his mind was the thought that the list was a coincidence or a mistake and unrelated to the events unfolding around the country. In his heart he suspected the truth. Carefully folding the paper he stuffed it into his shirt pocket where it lay next to the VCD.

In the den, Caine picked up the bloodstained conference proceedings he had found in the conference tote bag.

Caine took a last look around the house before calling the police and leaving an anonymous tip about the break-in at the house. It would be a long time before anyone came to check it out, leaving him plenty of time to make an unhurried exit.

The sun was high in the perfect cloudless blue sky as Caine started his descent from Sausalito to the bay. For the first time in his life the Golden Gate Bridge failed to inspire him as he crossed its rust red span.

Caine had always been overawed by the technological prowess of the bridge builders. Now he knew that the knowledge to conquer nature was a double-edged sword; it could always be turned against those who wielded it.

By mid-afternoon, he was back in Laura's apartment. A hot shower and change of clothes cleansed his body but the fear and disappointment remained. As he lay on Laura's bed staring at the ceiling fan as it rotated slowly he pondered if and how he would break the news to the authorities. Eventually he resolved to call Agent Garcia. For the moment however, sleep claimed him.

Chapter 33

After a spate of phone calls to set up a meeting with her colleagues in Tampa, the location of the FBI field office nearest St. Petersburg, Garcia caught up with her sleep.

The persistent drone of the engine and the claustrophobic confines of the jet increased her desire for rest. The clatter of her cell phone vibrating against the polished veneer of the tiny writing desk eventually roused her from the slumber.

"Garcia," she replied, wincing at the bright light that flooded into the cabin. At forty-one thousand feet the jet cruised in clear blue skies high above the clouds.

"Special Agent Garcia, this is Helen," said the receptionist from the San Francisco FBI headquarters. "I have a call from Dr. Paul Caine. He says it's an urgent matter. Shall I put you through?"

"Yes, please, Helen. Thanks," replied Garcia, wondering what Caine wanted.

"Angela? It's me, Paul. How are you?" said Caine, his voice distant and tinny, distorted by the satellite connection. A time delay of a few seconds between question and answer added to the sensation of immense distance.

"Paul, I'm fine. What's up?" she asked.

"Listen," replied Caine. "I've got some important news. I think I know who's behind these outbreaks. I think it's Bill Jacobs."

"Jacobs? From the conference?" said Garcia, disbelief apparent in her tone. "Are you sure?"

"I went to his house. He wasn't there, so I poked around a bit. I found bloodstains and biblical references to a plague."

"Whoah! Hold on there, partner!" said Garcia. "I hope you're not telling me you broke into someone's house? I hope you didn't take anything or disturb any evidence? Tell me you didn't."

"Er, well actually," Caine stammered. "It seemed very important that someone look at this stuff, especially the bloodstains. I think you should check Bill's hotel room to see if you can find any similar stains."

"Paul!" Garcia was incredulous. "You realise that anything you find and take without permission can't be used as evidence? How could you be so irresponsible?"

"I didn't want anyone destroying it before it could be analysed. Can I give it to you for testing?"

"That's going to be difficult. I'm following up a lead in Florida. I don't know when I'll be back. Take it to my office and they'll deal with it."

"I'm really worried about Bill," said Caine. "He's been missing since the conference ended and he kind of matches the description of one of the suspects in the case you're working on. I'd really hate it if he were involved."

"Paul, we checked out all the conference delegates during the murder investigation. They were all clean. I'm sure you have nothing to worry about."

"Did you take swabs of Jacobs' room for traces of blood?"

"I'll have to check," replied Garcia. "Probably not unless there was an obvious sign of a struggle or staining," she added.

"Can you have someone check his room at the hotel again? I really think it's important." Caine was almost pleading with Garcia.

"I'll try, but I can't promise anything. I'm all tied up right now."

"How many outbreaks have there been so far, I mean distinct foci?" asked Caine.

"Um, let me see," replied Garcia. "El Reno, Amarillo, Garden City, Dodge City, Lexington and Cozad," she said, counting them off on her fingers. "Six I guess, why?"

"There's going to be another. There will be seven outbreaks in total," said Caine.

"How do you know that?" demanded Garcia.

"It's all part of Bill's plan. The biblical quotes he uses specified seven punishments. There's only going to be one more. We need to find him before he does something terrible."

"Get your stuff to the FBI now," Garcia stated firmly, hoping to placate Caine. "I'll order a re-test of Jacobs' hotel room. Okay?"

"Okay, thanks. I'll have all the stuff there later this afternoon," said Caine, relief flooding him. "Angela, whatever you're doing over there. Take care, okay."

"Thanks, Paul. I'll be careful. I promise."

"Oh, and another thing," Caine wanted to mention Chen's interest in Jacobs' but didn't know how to broach the subject. He paused. "I think there's someone else interested in Bill Jacobs as well. When I went to visit him his house had already been broken into and searched."

"Well, all the more reason for you to give up what you found," said Garcia. "Make sure you give a statement to the officers as well when you get there, okay? I want to know what you've been up to while you were away." Garcia's mischievous smile translated to a rising lilt in her voice and Caine sensed she was toying with him. He thought of their night together and then his return to Laura, and blushed.

"Well you know me," he said sheepishly, "always up to something."

"I'm sure," said Garcia softly. "Anyway, It's nearly time to land now, so I'll keep on top of what you've told me and get back to you later, okay? It may be a couple of days so don't start worrying till then. Got it?"

"Thanks, Angela. I appreciate it, I really do." Caine was embarrassing in his gratitude, almost pitiful, and Garcia winced at the sentiment.

The line clicked dead just as the descent into St. Petersburg began. Garcia's ears popped and she looked out of the window. The time difference added three hours onto her day. It was now early evening and the city lights dotting the highways and strip malls spread like coloured ribbons across the flat Floridian landscape below.

The sword of justice was about to be pitted against the Sword of the Faith.

Chapter 34

The cicadas chirruped in the hot moist night air as the unmarked van approached Buena Vista Apartments. The automatic barrier rose slowly and the vehicle advanced into the yard. Behind it followed a smaller grey van, also without distinguishing marks. Quietly the two vehicles drove to the end of the apartment complex and parked some distance away from Block 13. The vehicles switched off their engines and headlights.

The rear door of the larger van opened silently and eight men dressed entirely in black emerged. The only sounds were the dull rustle of their uniforms, the thud of boots as they hit the asphalt of the parking lot and the chink of metal on metal as they released the safety catches of their assault rifles. As the shadowy figures swarmed toward the building in single file the only reason they did not melt completely into the night was the luminous yellow letters on their backs. The FBI had arrived.

Between them, six of the men sealed off the entrances and exits closest to the targeted apartment. Two other officers prepared to enter. One held a battering ram, a heavy steel pole sufficient to render the flimsy plywood of the front door to splinters with a single blow.

With her handgun drawn Garcia signalled her readiness to the others. Her companion swung the battering ram back and plunged it forward engaging the door slightly above and to the left of the keyhole.

The door disintegrated as expected, the battering ram penetrated the hollow structure and became embedded in the wooden matrix. As the door flailed open the ram disentangled itself and Garcia ran into the opening.

"FBI! Drop your weapons!" she called into the gloom. There was no response. "Lights!" she shouted urgently. The officer immediately behind her slapped the wall and the fluorescent strip light above their heads flickered to life.

The pair was standing in the kitchen, which opened out into a sparsely furnished lounge and dining room. At the far end of the room wide glass doors led out into a communal inner garden and pool area.

Cautiously, Garcia and her partner searched the apartment. Only when they were satisfied that the place was empty did they return to the living room. The generously proportioned room contained a small sofa, a TV, a dining table and four chairs.

The table was strewn with documents - maps, AAA travel guides and reams of paper covered with blue and black handwritten notes. To one side sat a telephone.

"This is it," said Garcia, as she pulled off her protective facemask. "Get CSI in here."

The man whispered into a small radio secured to the lapel of his jacket, "It's clear for CSI."

Seconds later, three figures in white coveralls entered the apartment.

Elasticated cuffs sealed the wrists and ankles of their uniforms. On their hands they wore thin cotton gloves. Their heads were shrouded with a fine mesh hairnet, while N95 respirator masks obscured their faces. At the threshold they paused one after the other and slipped their feet into a pair of plastic shoe covers. Each carried an aluminium suitcase. Without a word they moved quietly about the apartment, each focusing on one room or area.

From the bathroom, hair and dandruff embedded in combs, plugholes and soap dishes were collected along with fingerprints from glassware and porcelain; from the kitchen, utensils and food containers provided a ready source of fingerprints. Together they could be used to build a profile of how many people frequented the apartment. The bedroom delivered used laundry and fibres from clothing left behind in the closet in addition to pubic hair from bed sheets.

At Garcia's request one of the team dealt immediately with the dining table and its horde of papers. After some preliminary photographs to record the undisturbed scene the investigator removed the documents one by one and placed them carefully into transparent plastic envelopes.

A white oblong evidence label was taped to each envelope. The collecting officer filled it in using permanent marker, recording the case number, item number, date, time, a brief description of the item collected and the location where it was found. Finally he authorised each label with his initials.

Garcia waited anxiously as each piece of paper was documented meticulously. Despite her impatience she remembered the way she had admonished Caine earlier in the day about his laxity in collecting evidence from Jacobs' house.

Looking over the investigator's shoulder as he stooped over the desk Garcia had a bird's eye view of the evidence. She scrutinised each page before it was laid flat in a cardboard box for further analysis at the laboratory.

Fingerprints, fibres and inks could all be analysed in detail. Microscopic spores and pollens embedded in the matrix of the paper might reveal the time of year and location where the blank paper and maps were purchased. The rate at which the ink dried could reveal the order in which the pages were written and so document the sequence in which events had been planned. In this way, last minute changes to a schedule could be differentiated from long established plans.

Fibres from the writer or other occupants of the room could identify what they wore when the pages were being composed. DNA extracted from shed hairs or skin cells left behind on fingerprints could identify the sex and race of the author.

The fingerprints themselves would be invaluable. Entered into a database they could be matched with any person who had previously been arrested or charged with a crime. Mountains of barely visible evidence could be collected that would betray a man and his crimes.

By 10:00 P.M. the team had finished. A small crowd of residents had assembled in the parking lot as the forensic team filed out of the apartment bearing boxes and bags of evidence.

The thirty-minute drive back to the Tampa FBI field office on Zack Street was emotional. The team were in exuberant mood as it was clear that a major breakthrough had occurred. Everyone would share the glory. Garcia was especially pleased, as it was her idea to check the names on the list with a linguist that had led to the targeted operation. The textbook entry and search would also be acknowledged in her report.

For the moment, the priority was to analyse the documents. Those were the key that would determine the extent of the damage the terrorists would wreak on the country.

By eleven o'clock, Garcia herself was wearing a white coverall and facemask studying the documents intently alongside her forensic team colleagues.

"You can run the complete range of tests later," Garcia. "I want to know where the next attack will be." She scanned the documents arrayed on the table before her, still sheathed in their plastic folders. Spreading them with her fingertips she concentrated on a large-scale map of the mid-west United States. Circles and arrows were clearly visible; dark blue and black swirls delineating targets and directions of travel. The depth of the ballpoint impressions in the paper indicated to Garcia a deep-seated hostility and seething hatred on the part of the author. They had been made by the hand of a focused individual who would stop at nothing to achieve his goal, even if that led to his death or martyrdom.

There were no dates or annotations on the map — nothing to indicate when the attacks had been planned or when they were to occur. Garcia picked up the map and followed the red ribbon of the interstate as it passed through Kansas. Dodge City and Garden City lit up like beacons, twin swirls of black in the bottom corner like an unfinished doodle of a pair of spectacles. Lexington and Cozad to the north looked like a penny-farthing; Cozad, small and almost insignificant, cowered at the foot of its larger neighbour.

Turning the map over, Amarillo leapt off the page circled in black in the midst of the high plains. A straight line, thick and heavy, parallel to interstate 40 completed the barbell shape with El Reno circled at the other end.

"Six outbreaks, six circles," announced Garcia. "Where's the seventh?" she asked aloud staring at the map, willing it to give up its secret. Garcia had discussed Caine's theory at length with her colleagues in Tampa.

"You still think your contact is right and that this thing is all wrapped up in some biblical mumbo jumbo?" asked the man who was examining the documents.

"I don't know," Garcia replied. "He was scared and concerned enough to be right. His list of biblical quotes sounded convincing to me. I need to check with the profilers at Quantico to be certain. At the moment though, I think it would be prudent to continue as if this pair haven't finished what they set out to do. They haven't been caught and realistically we are no nearer to catching them now than we were a few days ago."

Garcia looked at the men in the room trying to conceal her disappointment and frustration. Glancing from face to face she stared each man in the eye daring him to challenge her. Instead, all she saw were faces held rigid with determination, a latent confidence that science would identify the culprit and that, as humans, the suspects' fallibility would inevitably lead to their downfall.

After reading through the notes it was clear that the seventh location speculated by Caine was not mentioned. Exhausted, Garcia excused herself and returned to her hotel room, leaving the night shift to examine the documents in detail. Perhaps they would have news for her in the morning.

From her hotel room she called the profiler at Quantico for an update on the biblical quotations Caine had delivered to the San Francisco field office.

"Isn't it past your bedtime, sweetheart?" said the fatherly voice. Dan Bradford, the senior profiler at Quantico had been very kind to Garcia during her time at the academy. Patient and considerate, he was well respected by both senior and junior staff. Upon graduation, Garcia had kept in touch. Suspect profiling was an art and she wanted to learn more from the master. Besides, she always knew that one day she would be working with one of her favourite teachers again.

"I could say the same to you," replied Garcia, trying to hide her tiredness behind a mask of civility. "Do you have anything for me?"

"Educated, white male, over forty, and of European descent," announced Bradford authoritatively.

"How so?" queried Garcia.

"The quotes are from the Authorised King James Bible," replied Bradford. "Have you ever read it? It's a bitch. Give me the New American Standard Bible any day. To me, it looks like the guy knows his way around a Bible. He reads it regularly and understands it, hence educated. Nobody just goes out and picks up a King James on a whim. This is a family heirloom. I guess he has been reading this version for quite a while, probably his whole life. If the author of the note is indeed involved with the outbreaks, which have occurred at all times of the week, the perpetrator is either unemployed, on vacation or retired, which seems to indicate he's older rather than younger. He's likely to be single, as he can move freely around the country without arousing suspicion or concern from a spouse or significant other. He could be divorced or widowed. As it's the King James Version and not some bowdlerised heathen text, he's probably European – possibly British or Dutch descent. Selecting passages to make codes is the work of a male as opposed to a female, who tend to get to the point a bit quicker. Am I wrong," he teased Garcia.

"Anything else?" probed Garcia.

"He's devoutly religious and Protestant Christian, although that's pretty much a given," Bradford replied. He was treading water, waiting to see if Garcia would let slip some more information on her suspect before moving on. "On that basis, you could deduce that he is somewhat conservative in his thoughts and personal habits, indicating a meticulous, cautious nature." Bradford lowered his voice and spoke carefully, imbuing his words with a subtle malevolence. "People driven by religious faith are often very persuasive and cunning. Be careful not fall under their spell."

"Thanks for the warning," replied Garcia, drawn herself to the potency of Bradford's spoken word. "What can you tell me about the passages themselves?"

"They're all Old Testament, mostly the Pentateuch."

"It's gonna be just like Sunday school again," said Garcia.

"The first passage from Zephaniah describes a vengeful God punishing the wicked for their sins," began Bradford, his voice calm and oozing authority. "In the Bible, Zephaniah refers to God punishing the people of Judah for their religious sins. Out of context like this it can refer simply to the coming of a great catastrophe that will affect all people." Bradford paused before continuing.

"The second passage is from Exodus and describes one of the plagues that afflicted Egypt for Pharaoh's refusal to liberate the Israelites. It is interesting that the word 'murrain' is used today specifically to refer to foot-and-mouth disease. This is the only passage that indicates the author of the note anticipates the current situation and so may be linked directly to the outbreaks." Bradford coughed to clear his throat.

"The third passage is from the Book of Numbers. The verse describes God reassuring Moses of the coming victory over the Egyptians. However, our man could be trying to indicate that the present order will be overthrown in favour of a new group, of which he is a member or with whom he is affiliated." Bradford coughed again, and Garcia heard him take a sip of water and guessed he had been honing his analysis for some time.

"The final passage is perhaps the most interesting," said the old man. "The narrator in Leviticus is for the most part God Himself. In the book He describes the various dietary, sacrificial and priestly duties associated with worship. At the end of the book, from which our verse is taken, He describes the punishments meted out to those who disobey Him. So it seems that the author of the note actually sees himself as God or the initiator of the events he has described in the previous passages. Disobey him and he will punish you – apparently seven times. Given that he has not made any demands that we are aware of it seems that we, society or the US Government or whoever, have disobeyed him already and as a result we are being punished."

"So he could be our man?" Garcia queried. She wanted a different perspective on the evidence, fearful that her judgement had become blunted or jaded during the past few days.

"On balance," replied Bradford carefully, "I am satisfied that the author of the note has sufficient knowledge of the nature of the disease outbreaks and should be sought immediately for further questioning. How was that?" he concluded.

"Thanks, Dan. That was great, very informative," replied Garcia. "Is there anything else you can tell me from the note?"

"Sure, the handwriting indicates a right-handed male. I'm working on a photocopied image. I assume the lab is working on latent fingerprints and DNA analysis of any cellular material left behind by the writer on the original. In addition, I understand the note is written on an old ATM receipt, in which case you may be able to trace the writer from the security camera records of the relevant bank from the date and time imprints."

"Yeah, thanks. We're working on that."

Garcia was pleased. Not only had she re-established a friendship with an admired mentor but also she now accepted that Caine's fears had proved correct.

The problem now was finding out where they were. It was four days since the last outbreak in Nebraska. Even in a beat up Toyota Corolla they could have covered quite a distance since then. Finding the intended target for the next and, as Caine seemed to think, final outbreak would be an immense challenge.

Even with these myriad thoughts pulsing through her brain, sleep overwhelmed Garcia. This was a problem she needed to tackle anew in the morning. Perhaps then the night shift forensic team would have some good news for her.

With leaden reluctance Garcia stripped and pulled her crimson silk pyjamas, now bunched and creased, from the small Gucci travel bag she had brought with her. Only after glancing over at the door to check the deadbolt was in place and securing the safety catch of her .38 automatic pistol did she succumb to the urge to crawl between the stiff linen sheets of the king-size bed.

Within seconds of turning out the lights she was sleeping soundly, too tired to dream.

Chapter 35

At 8:15 A.M. Garcia arrived at the Tampa field office. After an untroubled sleep she was refreshed and keen to get started. The office had just opened and administrative staff were still arriving. Garcia flashed her badge and handed her gun to the officer beside the metal detector before passing through. She re-holstered her weapon and walked through the doors into the investigators' offices at the back of the building.

Even this early in the morning there was a tangible buzz in the air. Several people turned their heads as she walked through the door, looks of expectancy on their faces. Garcia sensed it immediately; triumph, a burden lifted. All that remained was to plot the minutiae of the arrest.

"You're late," beamed one of the elderly agents, clearly the person in charge of the office. "We've been burning the midnight oil just for you."

"And?" replied Garcia.

"We got a lead on the seventh location. It just came in."

Garcia was puzzled, the documents she spent so long poring over the night before contained no hint of the final location. The man turned toward the wall and the large white marker board on which was mounted several pieces of paper held in place by magnets.

Garcia recognised some of the pages on the board. Newer pages covered the older ones forming a mosaic of evidence. The last page, mounted in the centre of the board, held the eye as if it were the final piece of the puzzle. The sheet contained a single handwritten word.

The paper had been photocopied and enlarged many times exaggerating the loops of the handwriting, revealing tiny breaks in the stream of ink as the ballpoint tip left the surface of the page for infinitesimal fragments of a second as it was pushed and pulled in all directions. Black and fuzzy as if it had been sent repeatedly through a fax machine, Garcia could barely read it. Maybe it began with a 'G' and ended with a 'y', that was about all she could make out. The letters in between ran together in an undulating squiggle.

"I don't recognise this," said Garcia drawn to the page without the man speaking of it.

"We just got that a few minutes ago," replied the man. "We studied the maps. The six locations we think were the focal points of the foot-and-mouth disease outbreak were all clearly marked. They are definitely the work of one man or group," he said confidently. "The smaller outbreaks surrounding those foci are not listed, probably because they were derived from the initial infection by movement of people, machinery and livestock, indicating that they were caused accidentally."

"So at least we can now link them all together," said Garcia. "Good work. What about the other documents, what do they show?"

The man took a deep breath, arched his back and exhaled. "We analysed all the handwritten documents. At first there was no mention of a seventh location. Then we tried ultraviolet and infrared to see if we could find any latent ink stains. Nothing. Eventually we put everything through the electrostatic document examiner."

Garcia arched her eyebrows, asking the question silently.

The elder man smiled and obliged. "The documents are mounted on a special platform and held in place by a partial vacuum to stop them shifting about. Then we place a thin sheet of plastic on top a bit like a sheet of Glad Wrap you use in the kitchen. The vacuum sucks the plastic onto the paper. A tiny electric current is applied to the plastic sheet to charge it and black powder, like photocopier toner, is poured over it. After we remove the excess with a brush the black powder collects in small pits and depressions on the surface of the paper. We use it to reveal latent handwriting - the impression of words written on paper resting on the document we are examining."

"What did you find?" asked Garcia.

"This," said the man triumphantly, pointing at the piece of paper in the middle of the board with the index finger of an outstretched hand. The gesture was both defiant and accusatory.

"What does it say?" queried Garcia, the black fuzzy snake refusing to reveal its secret under her gaze.

The man paused and shifted his weight to his other foot. "We're working on it," he replied, looking away from Garcia. "It's obviously written in haste. Preliminary analysis suggests it is consistent with other handwriting collected at the scene, so it's definitely written by our man. After he wrote it down it seems he removed or destroyed the original."

"But we don't know what it says?" Garcia asked, impatiently. She did not have that much time. Not only was there the risk that the terrorists would strike again soon but her career and reputation were at stake. She had fought with her superiors to be assigned to this case and she would be damned if she was going to let it slip away from her on the homestretch.

"We sent it to the handwriting analysis specialists at Quantico to see if they can do any better. We should have an answer in a couple of hours. Stick around for a while and I can fill you in on what we've been up to."

The man picked up a thick manila folder from his desk. He led the way down a short corridor to his office. As they walked Garcia's mobile phone rang.

"You go ahead, Mike," she called after the man, "I've got to take this. Garcia," she barked into the mouthpiece. From the corridor, she walked absentmindedly into the nearest room and sat down at a long polished conference table.

"Agent Garcia? This is Special Agent William Fung from the San Francisco field office. You ordered an examination of room 1012 at the Regency International hotel?"

"Yes, that's right. I'm sorry to trouble you," Garcia replied. "I don't suppose you found anything did you?" she said, her voice ripe with expectation.

"You had a very good hunch, Agent Garcia," replied Fung. "We found traces of blood in the seams of a drawer in a bedside table and on the floor of a wardrobe. In addition, we recovered carpet fibres from near the entrance that tested positive for the same blood group, O Rhesus negative. It looks like someone stored bloodstained clothing in the room and made attempts to clean it up afterwards," he speculated. "However, the blood seeped into crevices and imperfections in the woodwork and into the dark-coloured fabric at the bottom of the wardrobe, so it would have been very difficult for anyone to observe and remove," he added. "We wouldn't have found it if we hadn't been told where to look. We analysed the DNA in the blood using our standard short tandem repeat polymerase chain reaction and it matches the murder victim, Dr. al-Jaheerah. There is no match with any of the profiles in the CODIS database. Is that enough information for you at present, agent Garcia?" Fung concluded.

Garcia smiled broadly. "That's great news, Agent Fung. Thank you very much." Garcia hung up and punched the air in celebration. Jubilant, she relayed the information to her fellow staff.

Special Agent Mike Zelek's analysis of the document evidence was thorough. After an hour he had finished and Garcia had a fuller grasp of the techniques involved and the findings of the team.

Also in the meeting were the hair, fibre and pollen specialists, who concluded that only one man had lived in the flat in recent weeks, corroborating neighbour and other eyewitness testimony.

"So there's no link between this Husam al-Din character and Jacobs, apart from our single eyewitness in Garden City nearly a week ago?" said Garcia. "So where the hell are they now?"

Garcia paced the room. Photographs of al-Din had been obtained from his drivers licence application at the Florida Department of Motor Vehicles. A recent picture of Jacobs could be obtained from countless sources. They would be released alongside the sketch description in the next press conference scheduled for later that day.

Garcia wanted to light a fire under the suspects and make them believe for the first time that the FBI was now calling the shots. She could do that only by revealing in advance the seventh and final target, nullifying the element of surprise that the suspects had enjoyed for so long.

To Garcia it seemed as if they were casual terrorists, travelling by day – commuting, almost, to commit their acts of terror. If this casual approach was not part of a plan and reflected their actual demeanour there was a chance local residents would pick them out in good time.

Garcia could not hope to be so lucky. A strategy needed to be in place before she could act. As the minutes ticked by the final outrage was being planned if it had not already taken place.

Garcia's mobile phone vibrated silently in her pocket.

"Garcia. Who's this?"

"Hi, Angela, it's Hal," said Anderson, calling from the San Francisco field office.

"What have you got for me, Hal?"

"I've been re-examining the data about the various outbreaks," the quiet young man replied. "I thought the best fit was distance; remember we found that about two hundred fifty miles was a good approximation? Well, now I'm not so sure. I was crunching my numbers, mileage, gas consumption, weather conditions, and so on, and I suddenly thought it was something simpler."

"Go on," said Garcia.

"It depends on the road. You can go two hundred fifty miles in about four to six hours. El Reno to Amarillo, Amarillo to Garden City, Garden City to Lexington, they all fit. But suppose they stop for some other reason, illness perhaps? Maybe the driver or his passenger gets car sick, or they are diabetic or need to rest or take medication that makes them unfit to drive? Maybe they dare not drive for longer than six hours?"

"In that case, how far can they go…?"

"From Lexington, Nebraska along all possible routes in six hours?" said Hal, finishing Garcia's question.

"Right, smartass," Garcia replied.

"Technically, they could cover most of the mid-west," explained Hal, "but last time we discussed this, we said they might be heading west along I-80. Six hours down that road could be anywhere from Laramie, Wyoming to Fort Collins, Colorado. That area in general."

"Any word from Colorado police or FBI about the alert we posted a few days ago?" asked Garcia, anxious that some of the lines of enquiry she instigated would bear fruit.

"I'll check and get back to you on that, ok? How's it going over there?"

"I'm just waiting on the handwriting experts to get back to me on something," replied Garcia, suddenly tired and irritable.

The morning had started well but now the investigation had become bogged down again. She dreaded the upcoming press conference and how she would spin out the few facts into a positive message that the perpetrators were close to being caught. The press would sense her lie, read it in her face. Her stomach started to knot and she felt nauseous. Stress had never bothered her much before. In fact she thrived on it. But this was different; there was a sense of helplessness in the air, a desperation that could not be exorcised by glib exchanges and confident smiles.

The substance of the investigation was lacking a foundation, something on which she could hang facts and quantities. She returned to the sanctuary of the disused conference room. Alone, she cupped her head in her hands, her face obscured by her long chestnut brown hair. No one would see the tears she told herself.

"Agent Garcia?" The woman's voice startled Garcia and she looked up suddenly. Immediately, she knew something was wrong. The look in the woman's face told her so. Garcia snuffled and reached for a tissue to dab the corners of her eyes. The tissue stained black with mascara.

"Shit," she muttered under her breath and reached for the compact in her handbag.

Uncomfortable, the woman paused before continuing. "There's a call for you in Special Agent Zelek's office. Can you come through?"

"Can I take it here?" replied Garcia, reluctant to see anyone while she was redoing her makeup.

"Um. There's no phone in here, ma'am," the woman said sheepishly. "The room's being renovated."

Garcia looked around her. The walls had been stripped of decoration; hooks surmounted square white patches on the discoloured wall, the ghosts of maps and pictures long removed.

Garcia frowned. "Tell him I'm coming," she replied. As the woman disappeared, no doubt to inform her colleagues of what she had seen, Garcia hurriedly checked her eyes and packed her handbag.

"Here she is now," said Zelek into the receiver. He cupped his hand over the mouthpiece, "Colorado PD, Larimer County."

Garcia turned down the corners of her mouth, equally surprised and puzzled.

"Hello? This is Special Agent Garcia. Who am I talking to?" she said.

"Hello, ma'am. This is Sergeant Charles C. Calhoun, Larimer County PD," the voice was stentorian and authoritative. "I believe I have some information for you with regard to your investigation," he continued. "I spoke to a gentleman in the FBI field office in Denver and he suggested I talk to you in person."

"Yes, Sergeant Calhoun," Garcia responded. "Do you mind if I put you on the speaker phone, so my colleagues can listen in?"

"You go right ahead. It's not often I have the opportunity of discussing things with other agencies. I appreciate the chance."

"You're welcome, sergeant," Garcia replied, warming to the kindly charm of the police officer.

"Well, ma'am," Calhoun began, "we recovered an abandoned vehicle that matches the description of the one issued by your agency a few days ago." The sergeant paused as he consulted his notebook. "It's a beige 1992 Toyota Corolla with a Florida dealer's license tag."

Zelek and Garcia exchanged glances. Garcia smiled. Zelek winked at her.

"The vehicle was abandoned outside Bulger, Larimer County. That's an old ghost town about twenty-eight miles south of Cheyenne on the old Overland Trail. The car was driven into a gully between the shoulder of the southbound lane of highway 87 and the railroad track. Looks like it's been there for several days. An engine driver called it in but it took us a couple of days to locate it. We ran a check and it is registered to one Husam al-Din, who I believe you folks are looking for?"

"Indeed we are Sergeant Calhoun," replied Garcia. "Has the vehicle been impounded?"

"Well," answered the policeman, "we considered having a tow truck come in and take it to Fort Collins for you. We didn't want to risk messing things up, so we left it alone. The back is all full of trash mind, so there'll be plenty of evidence, fingerprints and the like."

"Trash?" asked Zelek. "What do you mean exactly?"

Calhoun paused unable to define trash more precisely. "Trash. Garbage. Food wrappers, Coke cans, you name it. Looks like someone's been using it as a hotel for the past month."

"Bingo!" said Garcia. "That's why there's no motel receipts. They've been sleeping rough."

The door to Zelek's office opened after a light tap on the door and a young fresh-faced man stuck his head into the office, clinging to the doorframe with both hands.

"We got a name," he announced. "Greeley or Grierly, something like that. We're plugging the various spellings into an online gazetteer right now," he said.

"Pardon me, ma'am," said Calhoun, his voice almost drowning in the flurry of activity that followed the young man's announcement. "There's a Greeley in Colorado, not forty miles from here."

"Do they have stockyards there?" asked Garcia.

"Are you kidding me, ma'am?" replied Calhoun incredulously. "InterCon have two yards down there, each with about one hundred thousand head of cattle."

"That's it," said Zelek firmly. "That's the target."

"How long will it take to get to Greeley?" demanded Garcia. "I need to get there today."

"You can fly to Denver and then drive on to Greeley," replied Calhoun. "It can't be more than an hour, although there may be a small regional airport closer."

"It's over fifteen hundred miles to Denver from here," said Zelek. "If you leave now in the Lear jet it's gonna take at least five hours."

"I need to get there tonight," said Garcia. She had rarely been this determined. This was her only chance to make up some ground on the terrorists. If an attack was imminent she wanted to be on the spot.

"Mike," said Garcia calmly, "get the jet warmed up for me and file a flight plan to Denver. I'll need a car at the other end to get me to the field office. I'll need to brief the SWAT team. And fix me up some accommodation in Denver. Nothing fancy."

In the air Garcia contacted the Colorado Department of Agriculture in Lakewood to inform them of the potential threat. In a conference call with the state Commissioner and Deputy-Commissioner for Agriculture, Garcia lobbied hard for a suspension of all livestock trade statewide until the threat was eliminated. After a heated exchange, the officials agreed only to restrict travel within Weld County, in which Greeley was located, for a period of forty-eight hours. Disgusted, but unable to force their hand without further evidence, Garcia accepted.

Now Garcia faced a dilemma. She wanted to proceed with the press conference as planned and identify Jacobs and al-Din as the prime suspects. In addition, she wanted to announce that Colorado, specifically Greeley had been identified as the next likely target. That would allow law enforcement and residents to be on the alert for the suspects. However, such a move would also tip off the suspects and might precipitate a final assault for which the authorities were unprepared.

After agonising for some time, Garcia decided to delay the announcement of the suspects' names but indicate that they had moved on to Colorado in general. Mike Zelek would handle the press conference by himself, allowing him to describe in detail the forensic evidence obtained from the apartment, saving Garcia from any public embarrassment over the failure to apprehend the terrorists.

From her discussion with the Colorado Department of Agriculture Garcia discovered that Weld County housed over six hundred thousand cattle at any one time on twelve hundred beef and dairy farms. In addition, there were more than two hundred and fifty thousand pigs on two hundred pig farms. The county was a prime target for anyone wanting to spread foot-and-mouth or any other livestock disease. Contacting the farms individually in the next few hours to query them about suspicious characters or vehicles was a daunting task.

Recognising the need for local input to focus the search, Garcia contacted the FBI field office in Denver again. Assuming the last target would be the most spectacular, she asked the staff on duty to draw up a list of the biggest farms, those that housed livestock numbering tens if not hundreds of thousands. She hoped that would reduce the list from nearly fifteen hundred operations to just a handful.

The sun was going down as the plane landed at Denver International Airport. The drive to the downtown FBI field office in Stout Street with the local officers was a sombre, joyless affair.

By 10:00 P.M. Garcia had briefed the officers of the tactical units as to the description and modus operandi of the terrorists. She did not expect them to be armed but would likely resist arrest and try to escape. The staff continued their briefing after Garcia left, familiarising themselves with the layout of several farms identified in advance as prime targets.

In her modest hotel room on the edge of Greeley Garcia checked and rechecked her handgun. In the dark she loaded and cocked the heavy weapon before gently releasing the hammer and emptying the chambers. This was her physical mantra, her pressure release valve in times of extreme stress. Eventually, in the small hours, she drifted off to sleep.

Awaking early she pounded out her fear on the running machine in the hotel's fitness centre. The gruelling monotony of the endless track reflected her insecurities about the way she had handled the investigation. No matter how hard she kept running she never seemed to get anywhere. Sweating heavily, she jumped off the track and jogged over to the sand-filled punching bag, letting fly with a powerful right hook. The thick leather crumpled under the impact and the bag swayed gently on its chain. Garcia's knuckles tingled.

Things were about to change.

Chapter 36

The man alighted from the taxi and set his black leather attaché case on the ground. He gazed up at the painted sign above the threshold. The taxi slipped away as the man hesitantly approached the entrance.

This would be his biggest test. Surprised to get this far he relished the daily digest of news about his work. Thousands of jobs lost, hundreds of businesses closed or suspended, travel restrictions imposed over large swathes of the country. And the money! Unimaginable, incalculable quantities of money had been lost. The thought brought a rare grin of pleasure to his face.

As he approached the front door he saw his reflection in the giant oblong of smoked glass. Looking dapper in a new suit, clean-shaven and with combed hair, Husam al-Din made quite an impression.

The door opened into a spacious foyer. The muted pale crimson of the carpet contrasted with the eggshell white of the walls. On the right stood the reception area; a large curved desk greeted visitors, behind which sat two forty-something secretaries.

Directly opposite, another glass door opened onto a small courtyard. A single corridor running left to right bisected the foyer.

al-Din took a deep breath and walked toward the reception desk. One of the woman, freckled and brunette, looked up at him as he silently crossed the lobby. Appraising him instantly she grinned broadly flashing a toothy smile as he approached.

"Welcome to Great Western Breeders," she said, her voice containing no trace of an accent just a grating, over-eager attitude to please. al-Din disliked the woman at once. "How may I help you?" she intoned.

Grinning like a fool al-Din fumbled in his jacket pocket for one of his business cards. "My name is Ahmed. I am here to see your Mr. O'Dell," he said in a precise clipped manner handing the card to the woman. With his mouth dry from continuous practice in the back of the taxi his tongue seemed stiff and unresponsive. He hoped no one had noticed. The attaché case was heavy, leaden in his hand and al-Din chided himself for not practicing with it more.

"Well," said the woman, flirting like a schoolgirl, "I'll just see if our Mr. O'Dell is available. Is he expecting you?" she lifted the telephone to her ear and pressed a button.

"Of course," al-Din replied tersely. "I have an appointment at 2:15 P.M."

The receptionist did not comprehend the slight and fanned herself with Ahmed's business card, an ineffectual means of cooling but it enabled her to show off her ring-less left hand with a well-practised casualness. The woman spoke briefly on the phone and turned to al-Din. "Mr. O'Dell will see you right away, Mr. Ahmed," the woman said coyly. "Please go right in," she added, indicating the corridor that ran behind the reception area. "It's the second door on your left." She watched al-Din as he walked stiffly down the corridor. Switching the briefcase awkwardly to his other hand he knocked on the door and entered.

"Nice butt," said the other woman, a plump peroxide blonde.

"Hey, hands off his butt. I saw him first," she said before they both broke down in giggles.

The office was small and functional and almost exactly as al-Din had imagined. As O'Dell rounded his desk and flopped into his chair al-Din scanned the room. The window, although obscured by a half-closed Venetian blind, looked out onto the processing yards beyond. The sounds and smells of high intensity pig farming filled the room even though the windows were closed.

The office could have been anywhere; the tiny square room was painted an anonymous blue-grey, the floor carpeted in an industrial shade of brown. It looked like a prison cell. The desk contained the detritus accumulated after many years into a long sentence.

A cheap plastic in-out tray was full; most of the correspondence lay in the 'in' section. A chipped mug with 'world's greatest Dad' stencilled in bright cartoon colours, overflowed with pens and pencils; a stapler gaped liked a floundering bass.

O'Dell was a fat man. Studying the desk intently, al-Din saw the customary family photographs; the sort men use to remind themselves why they stick with dead-end jobs. A plastic faux silver frame with a smiling moon bas-relief in one corner contained a picture of a plump woman cuddling a plumper child.

"Pigs," said al-Din.

"I'm sorry?" said O'Dell, as he adjusted the height of his chair. "What was that?"

"I've come about your pigs. You said over the telephone that you were interested in our new line of feed," replied al-Din, slipping into his act

"Yes, indeed," said O'Dell, surprised at the speed with which his visitor began business talk. O'Dell liked afternoon meetings for the opportunity to while away an hour shooting the breeze. "We've been considering a host of options in that direction," he lied, "so when one of our consultants suggested you to us we naturally called you up to see what you could offer. I must say I had trouble getting into your website, so I don't know a lot about your company's history."

"Really?" replied al-Din. "I will report it to the appropriate person. We are a new company, formed only last year. We use biotechnology to produce high protein feed for animals. It is very good."

"That's very interesting," said O'Dell. "As you may know the diets fed to gilts and sows in this area are generally a vitamin- and mineral-fortified mixture of corn and soybean meal. How does your feed compare in nutritional composition, for instance?"

"Obviously, the dietary requirements of your animals varies depending on whether they are gilts or gestating or lactating sows," replied al-Din.

He had memorised most of Jacobs' script but he was still uncomfortable in the role of salesman. If he had to ad-lib any of the conversation he feared immediate exposure.

Concentrating hard, he continued. "We have a range of feed tailored to different conditions," he said, focusing on the nameplate at the front of O'Dell's desk. When he dared to look up he saw the fat man leaning back in his chair, his head resting on the interlocked fingers of his hands. Dark stains of sweat discoloured the underarms of his shirt. "The protein content ranges from twelve to fifteen percent, and the lysine in particular is from natural sources, not synthetic, so that it is absorbed more efficiently."

"What about trace minerals?" asked O'Dell.

"Our feed is high in calcium and phosphate to help alleviate demineralisation in sows with large litters. In addition, we have biotin supplements to prevent hoof damage in gilts."

"At the moment we use a lot of local grain in our feed. Do you think that is appropriate?" O'Dell asked.

"Well," al-Din replied, trying to remember what Jacobs had said on the subject, "grains in this area might be low in selenium, copper and vitamin E, which is of concern to gestating sows, so we have increased the level of these compounds in our feeds."

The meeting was going well. O'Dell nodded his head and al-Din began to relax. Still, his primary concern was gaining access to the yards.

"Might we perhaps continue our discussion as we tour your facilities?" he said, hoping to mask the urgency in his voice with civility.

"Why certainly," said O'Dell, pleased and surprised to be getting the opportunity to stretch his legs. "You can leave your jacket and briefcase here if you like, they'll be perfectly safe."

The comment struck al-Din like a thunderbolt. "No!" he said in alarm. Reacting to his own panic he added more quietly, "I mean, no thank you. I would prefer to take it with me, if that is alright with you?"

"Whatever," replied O'Dell unconcerned. "You'll need to wear a hard hat though, company rules." He walked over to a filing cabinet where two scratched and obviously well used hard hats sat atop one another. "There you go," he said, handing al-Din the cleaner of the two helmets.

O'Dell led the way out of the office and back to the reception stopping briefly to inform one of the women where they were going. The brunette stared at al-Din wide-eyed and smiled.

The two men took the rear exit from the reception area into the intense heat of the small courtyard. A narrow alley led to the yard proper. The air was filled with the pungent aroma of pig filth. Rotting faeces, straw and mud mingled together to form a putrid clay that adhered instantly to almost every exposed surface. After twenty yards the hems of al-Din's trousers were damp and discoloured. The leather uppers of his shoes were similarly stained, the laces trapping sagging lengths of filth-encrusted straw.

A crop of giant hangars filled the sky as they trudged through the mire. Covering over twenty acres, Great Western Breeders was the largest pig breeding facility in northern Colorado housing one hundred thousand pigs at any time.

Outside the cavernous shed into which they were heading diesel generators chugged away in the background, their noise filling the air. Acrid exhaust fumes added a pale blue tint to the air, as they powered the various machines scattered around the yard.

High-pressure water hoses lined one wall; an array of black coiled snakes dozing in the shade of the yard entrance. Their angular metal nozzles were slung haphazardly from hooks and looked like cobras ready to strike.

Overhead, suspended metal cables ran the length of the yard, forming a continuous loop driven by one of the generators. Mounted in the ceiling at each end of the shed was a turntable. The large wheel with its grooved rim guided the thick metal wire and held it in place as it performed its endless circumlocution. Attached to the belt at distances of about ten feet were steel poles, each terminating in a large vicious hook. As each pole approached the turntable their momentum caused them to swing out stiffly. The poles continued to oscillate back and forth menacingly as they rounded the corner; the size of the swing gradually diminished until, after about ten yards, they once again hung limp and lifeless. Red lines painted on the ground, long obscured by filth, defined an area in which it was forbidden to stand on account of the danger posed by the barbed shafts.

At the front of the shed a forklift truck arrived bearing a heavy load. The pallet was set down slowly next to a raised wooden frame just inside the entrance and the vehicle reversed and disappeared into the maze of narrow alleys that divided the sheds. A workman standing on the oak platform grabbed one of the poles and deftly inserted the hook into the steel ribbon bindings that held the contents of the pallet in place. After a brief pause the pallet rose a few inches off the ground swaying slightly as it was carried down the length of the shed. Another workman walked alongside, holding the plastic-coated pallet as it crept slowly along, its immense weight causing the cables above to sag. The generator and cables whined in unison, a high-pitched shriek, protesting against the sudden burden imposed upon them.

"What's going on there?" asked al-Din.

"That's the pulley system for the feed," replied O'Dell. "The forklift's too noisy and dirty to use near the hogs, so we rigged up this overhead wire system. It works pretty well."

Loaded with fifty-pound bags of feed the pallet weighed over a ton and moved slowly. In the central part of the shed the cable sagged so much that the pallet scraped the floor and the wrangler alongside had to use all his effort to keep the bulky object in motion. At the desired point of delivery the workman pulled a crowbar from a pocket in the leg of his coveralls and knocked the hook clear of the ribbon. The pallet fell to the ground with a clump. At the same time the steel ribbon containing the load snapped with a crack and unravelled swiftly, whipping through the air. O'Dell put his arm in front of al-Din to stop him dead in his tracks as the workman ahead ducked instinctively. The ribbon of thin steel, black and slightly polished, lay on the floor buckled and lifeless.

"Easy fella," said O'Dell. "That thing'll take your face off if you're not careful."

A couple of bags of feed that had been dislodged by the impact lay against the foot of the pallet, their contents bleeding from a split in the seam of the multi-layered paper.

The farrowing pens ran along both sides of the shed. It was the first time al-Din had seen animal stalls in daytime. His previous nocturnal visits had been hurried affairs. Now he could take his time and choose his location carefully.

The two men continued their tour. al-Din discovered that the company not only raised the pigs on site they also processed them. The next shed housed the abattoir. O'Dell guided his visitor away by the elbow.

"We've got an annual sanitation audit coming up in a couple of days," he said by way of explanation, "and the abattoir manager has asked any non-essential staff to stay clear for a few days so the place is spotless. You know how things are," he added with a sly wink.

al-Din smiled, feigning understanding, and let himself be guided deeper into the maze of towering sheds. Shortly, they arrived at a third shed, identical to the others.

"This is the processing area," explained O'Dell. "When the pigs have been slaughtered and dressed next door, they come here to the blast chilling facility. The carcasses need to be chilled quickly to inhibit bacterial growth and to turn the flesh into meat. As you may know, when an animal is killed and exsanguinated the lactic acid levels in the muscle tissue rise lowering the pH. We need to chill the animal from blood heat to about five degrees Celsius in around twenty-two hours. Any quicker than that leads to a toughening of the meat texture."

"How do you chill the carcasses?" asked al-Din, keen to keep the man talking as long as possible.

"Forced convection," replied O'Dell over the noise of the machinery. "We have very large turbines that draw air cooled to minus forty degrees Celsius over the carcasses at speeds up to fifteen feet per second."

"Can we go in to see?" enquired al-Din.

"Believe me," said O'Dell, "even on a day like today, you wouldn't want to be in there. You'd freeze to death in minutes."

al-Din nodded in appreciation, impressed by the scale of the facilities. "What happens next?" he asked.

"After the carcasses are cooled, they're used for processing as needed,"

O'Dell explained. "We generally run at least a week ahead of schedule, so we always have a stock of chilled carcasses on hand in case we have problems at any other stage of the process. The present situation is a case in point. The animals out on our suppliers' farms are being culled because of this damned foot-and-mouth," he spat the words out vehemently. "On one hand, supply is short because of the lack of animals for processing. On the other, demand is weak because of travel restrictions and health concerns."

"Does processing occur in here?" queried al-Din.

"Heck, no," chortled O'Dell. "It's far too cold in there. See that conveyor over yonder?" he said pointing to a short flat platform connecting two sheds together. "That's for transporting the chilled carcasses next door. That's where the processing proper takes place."

They had walked a long way from the main entrance and al-Din wondered whether he could find his way back alone if necessary. The briefcase was uncomfortable in his hands. Several of the workers in the yard stared at him as he passed mutely, noting his ethnicity, his clothing and the accessories he carried. He could feel their burning accusatory eyes boring into him. He resented them; lips quivering, he recited silently the sacred words of the Prophet.

For surely if they prevail against you they would stone you to death or force you back to their religion, and then you will never succeed.

O'Dell stopped and turned to face the visitor. "This is the processing factory," he said with genuine pride. "This is where we make a full range of meat products, both our own brand and under contract for some of the country's biggest retailers. You'll probably recognise most of them." A thick muscular arm pushed open the door.

Instantly, the noise and smells were different. The dull thumping of muted equipment heard outside became a deafening roar, a crescendo of contrasting sounds. The conveyor belt hummed along, its cargo of chilled cadavers, yellowing on the outside and red ripe on the inside, passed by - looking oddly statuesque as they traversed the factory.

Expert butchers de-boned the carcasses, razor sharp electric knives whirring. Hunks of flesh fell onto a short conveyor and were transported up to a large stainless steel hopper into which they were deposited. Any meat that dropped to the ground was swept up at intervals and added to the mix in the giant container. Other machines cut, diced and pulverised the flesh. No part was wasted. Finely shredded, skin, eyeballs and testicles could be labelled, safely and legally, as meat. Flavoured with monosodium glutamate, salt, dextrose and corn syrup, no one would be any the wiser.

Inside the hopper, a giant Archimedes screw mixed the rendered pasty grey flesh with soy meal, colour enhancers and chemical preservatives. The giant screw, eighteen inches in diameter, sat unseen at the base of the hopper. Turning at sixty revolutions per minute, the screw efficiently turned the ingredients into a homogenous mass and delivered it to the next stage of the processing stream.

al-Din peered inside. The sickening sweet aroma of uncooked meat permeated the air.

"Neat isn't it?" beamed O'Dell. "One batch and we can make sausages, pie fillings, pates, meat spreads, you name it," he continued, spreading his arms wide as if encompassing the world's entire variety of different meat products.

"Wonderful," replied al-Din through clenched teeth. "Where is it all going," he managed to say, careful to avoid breathing in through his nose whilst indicating with outstretched hand the shiny writhing mass as it disappeared slowly, drawn down by the screw.

"Once it's been mixed here, it gets piped into sausage casings," explained O'Dell. "This hopper and screw arrangement is mobile. We can mix the paste and deliver it to whichever product line is running," he elaborated. "Today, it's sausages; tomorrow it could be meat pies. That's the beauty of it."

al-Din paused, satisfied he had seen everything he needed. There were no more animal sheds this far back. He needed to return to the farrowing and fattening sheds at the front of the complex.

"Thank you, Mr. O'Dell," said al-Din smiling at the fat man. "This has been a very informative trip. Perhaps we can return to your office and discuss my company's products in more detail. I'm sure they would be happy to provide a small sample at reduced price for evaluation purposes. How does that sound?"

"Well that sounds mighty generous, Mr. Ahmed. Let's go this way." O'Dell led the way to a small entrance in the side of the building. Alarmed, al-Din stumbled after him.

"Can we go back to see the pigs?" he asked impatiently. Then, realising the odd nature of his request, added, "I…I want to see… see how the… pigs are…." al-Din was lost, flummoxed by the rapid change in direction.

"Fattened?" said O'Dell. "Checking what mix we give our stock, eh, Mr. Ahmed? It's a good salesman who checks on his competitors. I like your style. No need to be shy about it, come right out and say it. That's what folk are like round these parts. No problem, we can reach the fattening pens through here as well," he said, continuing in the direction he was going.

"Right," said al-Din recovering his composure. "Fattened. Are you using a soy-based meal or what?" al-Din skipped behind the fat man trying to keep up. The grip on his briefcase tightened.

The time was near.

Chapter 37

The heat was not the worst part. It was the smell. The gigantic InterCon feedlot twelve miles outside Greeley was the size of a small town. One hundred thousand cattle were packed a thousand to the acre on the immense site. Each animal deposited fifty pounds of manure and six gallons of urine per day on to the thick brown clay that comprised the floor of the pen. Four hundred tons of shit and six hundred thousand gallons of piss daily - and Garcia was downwind of it.

Behind her as she leaned against a fence, the seething mass of brown cattle mooed and grunted. Mostly they ignored her, rooting with their moist snouts for the concrete feed trough at the side of the stall. Slipping their heads between the vertical guardrails that separated them and kept them from jostling unnecessarily for the plentiful feed, they munched peacefully, oblivious to their fate.

Stifling the urge to retch, Garcia looked down the two thousand yard perimeter of the feedlot. She could not see the far end. The undulating ground, the beginnings of a mid-west heat haze and dust kicked up by the stomping cattle obscured the horizon. As she gazed into the distance with her binoculars the futility of the operation was evident.

Garcia had only twenty men at her disposal to contact the sixty targets in Weld County identified as the largest and most productive cattle and hog farms. The only comfort she could draw was the fact that all her team were within forty miles of one another such was the concentration of the feedlots. Weld was the richest agricultural county in Colorado, contributing over one billion dollars annually to the state's economy.

The farm managers' dislike of the FBI presence was apparent and early reports from some of her men indicated that the other team members could not expect a warm welcome.

The teams of two carried photographs of Jacobs and Husam al-Din in addition to the original sketches. They were to ask every watchman, receptionist and farm hand on duty if they had seen anything or anyone suspicious in the last three days.

Each team had been given three addresses to work through. The farms and feedlots had been carefully selected to minimise travel time. Despite this, Garcia did not expect to hear from any of her officers for most of the day.

Garcia made sure she assigned the prime targets to herself. The two giant InterCon lots were five miles apart on the northern edge of Greeley, sufficiently downwind to minimise the impact of the horrific stench they generated.

After spending the first four hours of the morning at the larger of the sites, she had hastened to the second, still not immune to the smell. She and her team of four, double the size assigned to the targets considered less significant, had not identified anything out of the ordinary. The daily feedlot routine of arrival, sorting, slaughter and processing had continued in the usual manner without interruption. The only aberrant aspect was the county-wide ban on transportation initiated at Garcia's behest that came into force at midnight, which resulted in livestock filling the fattening stalls to overflowing and trucks standing idle, prohibited from loading up and shipping the processed meat around the country.

While the other members of the team were interviewing staff, Garcia was monitoring the perimeter, finding the weak points, imagining she was the terrorist trying to break in.

It would have been easy. She had been walking outside now for fifteen minutes and had not seen another human being. Occasionally a forklift truck or small van could be seen in the distance delivering feed to the furthest reaches of the feedlot. At other times a farmhand walked past, head down under a wide-brimmed hat to keep off the blazing sun. In the early afternoon, Garcia had only the cattle for company.

The trill of the phone startled Garcia and the animals closest to her. They reared up and tried to move away but their necks were held firm between the bars of the stall and they were so closely packed they could do nothing except snort in contempt. They eyed her suspiciously until they could no longer remember the reason for their fear and settled down to feed again.

"Hi, Angela. It's Don Bradford." The reception in the flat open countryside was clear.

"Yes, Don," replied Garcia. "What's up?"

"I've been through some of the information provided by our folks over in San Francisco about our Bible thumper," said Bradford. "I spent a few hours going over it and it makes disturbing reading. This guy is really on the edge and I think he's looking for a way out."

"You mean kill himself?" asked Garcia.

"I think he's just looking for an excuse," the ageing profiler continued. "We got a look at his personnel files from Stanford and found a resume on his home computer. He has personal links to every one of the outbreaks from Oklahoma to Greeley."

"Such as?" asked Garcia, wanting to know more about her quarry.

"In '77 he taught courses at the College of Veterinary Medicine in Stillwater, Oklahoma and ran field trips to the El Reno livestock auctions. From 1982 onwards, he's been an honorary member of the Texas Cattle Feeders Association, based in Amarillo. In the mid-seventies, he did a lot of epidemiological fieldwork in southwest Kansas, based around Garden City and Dodge City. For a time, his wife worked at the Garden City Community College. He's got honorary doctorates from Nebraska State University for his contributions to livestock vaccination and was a veterinary consultant for AgroTech West based in Lexington. He bought property in Cozad and rents it out. AgroTech West was bought out a few years ago by Laing Webster based in Greeley and they kept him on as technical consultant."

“If he had links to all these places himself why does he need an Islamic fundamentalist partner?” Garcia asked.

“I think the use of foot-and-mouth disease as a weapon of terror is all Jacobs’ idea and did not originate as an Islamic plot,” replied Bradford. “Jacobs decided to cash in his chips and make as much trouble as possible. If we look hard enough I think we’re gonna find that it’s Jacobs who made the first move, that he was the one who contacted the Islamic militants.” Bradford measured his speech so that the implications of his words had time to sink in. “I think it’s more likely that he is the one with the necessary substantive contacts in the Middle East underworld,” he continued. “I don’t believe there’s a group of fundamentalists in Pakistan with the kind of connections with United States academics and virologists needed to pull this off. Jacobs needs a fall guy and some exotic virus. He’ll tell them what to do with it for maximum damage and, psychologically at least, erase his past.”

“What was that?” asked Garcia, bewildered by the profiler’s reasoning.

“Many of the targets are not obvious or legitimate when one considers their national significance to the cattle and pig rearing industries in America,” explained Bradford. “The only connection is Jacobs. They are important to him. By destroying these he is indirectly toppling himself. Eliminating his achievements one-by-one is psychological suicide. When that is complete, all that remains is physical suicide.”

“Does Jacobs have a history of mental illness?” asked Garcia.

“Believe me,” replied Bradford, “Jacobs is very seriously disturbed. However, I think a good measure of his warped reasoning can be attributed to a bout of clinical depression over his wife’s death last year. We found Prozac prescriptions in his house. Mentally, he’s running on empty, coasting. I really think Jacobs is going to kill himself very soon.”

Garcia was not convinced. “Dan, you can’t just go through Jacobs’ resume and cherry pick the significant events and shoehorn them into a theory,” she said. She’d worked hard to crack the case with scientific evidence and she did not want her success to be obscured by a forensic psychologist retrofitting the data and claiming the crimes were all predictable in advance. “You could go through his CV and find links to all sorts of crimes if you looked hard enough”, she claimed, attempting to usurp her mentor’s theory. “So what is al-Din’s role?”

“al-Din is definitely the patsy in this operation,” explained Bradford. “Remember Jacobs’ biblical quotations? There will only be seven deliberate outbreaks. That is a requirement. It is non-negotiable. I wonder how many arguments Jacobs had with his collaborators in Pakistan over this issue; how long it took him to persuade them that that would be enough?” Bradford was calm and measured in his replies; he sensed that Garcia was less than pleased with his eleventh-hour assessment of the situation. “In addition, you should also consider that Jacobs is a devout Christian, a fact he probably concealed from his partners in crime. Nothing would please him more than to lay the blame for his activities on what he considers to be a false religion."

"Boy, he's not afraid of making enemies is he?" said Garcia.

"I guess if you're going to kill yourself, it doesn't really matter that much," the old man replied, managing to smirk through the unpleasant implication of his comment. "So how's it going over at the Laing Webster lots? Any joy?"

"Laing Webster? We're at the InterCon yards. I'm surprised you can't smell it over the phone," replied Garcia.

"Remember what I said, the most prominent target is not necessarily the true target. As far as I can tell from his resume, Jacobs has no connection with InterCon. What are Laing Webster's holdings in Greeley? Can you find out? I think that would be a more productive approach."

"Thanks, Don," she said casually. She did not want to indicate to her mentor that she had not considered the possibility. "I'm looking into it." A sudden feeling of dread came upon her, manifesting itself as a tightening, a knotting in the pit of her stomach. Garcia rang off and immediately called the FBI tactical co-ordination centre operating out of the Greeley police department headquarters near Lincoln Park.

As the connection was being made, Garcia started to walk back to the parking lot. She had wandered some distance from the car, surveying the flat plains and perimeter fences for signs of sabotage.

"Hi, this is Agent Garcia," she said, as the operator at the police station handled the call. "I need to speak to someone on the Operation Moses team; preferably someone with local knowledge. Quickly, please." The urgency in her voice translated well over the phone and she was transferred instantly to the operations room.

Moses had been the natural choice of codename for the search for Jacobs and al-Din. Not only did it reflect Jacobs' Old Testament quotations, the wandering of the terrorists over the heartland of America mirrored Moses leading the Israelites across the desert. Moreover, the reference to divine plagues conjured up by the ancient leader had a particular resonance with the taskforce assigned to hunt down the perpetrators.

"Agent Garcia? Can I help you?" a young man's voice, calm and controlled, answered the call.

"Laing Webster," said Garcia firmly. "What companies do they run in Greeley?"

"That's going to be difficult to find out without going through the company directory at City Hall or the Laing Webster annual report," the man said. "Hang on a minute," he added. Garcia heard muffled voices in the background before a hand was clamped noisily over the receiver. Seconds passed. "Great Western and Beauchamp," the man announced suddenly. "Some guy in the office knows people over there."

"Which is bigger?" asked Garcia impatiently, sensing she was on the right track.

"Beauchamp is a cattle yard; Great Western is mainly hogs," replied the man. “I’d say Great Western is the biggest and most well known.”

“How far is it from my present location? I’m at InterCon, the Eaton yard not Ault,” she added, distinguishing between the company’s two giant feedlots.

“Six miles north from you on highway 85,” came the reply.

“I’m on my way there now,” said Garcia, jogging to her car. “Have the team scheduled to visit Great Western meet me there,” added Garcia, careful not to let her impulsive decision disrupt the rest of the investigation.

Grinding the gears in her Buick LeSabre, gravel sprayed against the other cars in the parking lot as Garcia sped away. Barely pausing to check for traffic as she exited the farm Garcia turned the steering wheel sharply and continued north.

The highway followed the railroad track. On her right, between the arrow-straight paved road and the iron-stained flints of the railroad track, the regularly spaced telegraph poles stood like sentinels. Each pole caught her eye as she sped past and she blinked instinctively as the totems blocked out the sun for infinitesimal fragments of a second. The effect was hypnotic.

In a few minutes the small town of Ault appeared on the horizon, dominated by the other half of InterCon’s investment in Weld County.

Near county road 86, halfway between Ault and Pierce, the odour changed perceptibly. It was no longer the overpowering humus-like aroma of fermented cattle dung; instead, the sharp acrid tang of pig manure was unmistakeable. It emanated from a series of red-roofed hangars in the distance. At sixty miles per hour, it was another two minutes before Garcia entered the Great Western Feeders yard.

Garcia pulled up on the turning circle adjacent to the main entrance and stepped lightly from the car. Straightening her jacket and adjusting her shoulder holster for comfort she pushed open the smoked glass front door.

The brunette receptionist watched Garcia walk across the foyer toward her. “May I help you?” she asked politely. She did not smile.

Garcia pulled her FBI badge from her pocket and laid it on the counter face up for the woman to see. As the receptionist stared at the ornate silver shield dumbfounded, Garcia placed the photograph of al-Din next to it.

“This man,” she said narrowing her eyes and staring at the woman. “Have you seen him recently?”

The woman stared at the photograph. Enlarged to three times its size from the driver’s license original, the lighting and resolution were poor, making the subject appear darker and older than he was. Despite this the likeness was remarkable.

“He’s here,” the woman replied breathlessly. “Oh my! He’s here.”

Garcia stared back at the woman in disbelief. “Are you sure?”

The receptionist fumbled for the business card al-Din had given her. “He gave me this,” she said handing the object to Garcia. “He said his name was Mr. Ahmed. He had an appointment and everything.”

“Where is he now?” asked Garcia, lowering the tone of her voice and putting the badge back into her jacket.

“He’s out in the yard with Mr. O’Dell, our sales and marketing manager,” replied the woman anxiously. “They should be back soon, they’ve been gone awhile.”

“Can somebody show me the way?” queried Garcia.

As she spoke, the main entrance burst open and two men rushed in.

“Agent Garcia,” said the first, “we got here as fast as we could. Is everything okay?”

The FBI agents were a welcome sight for Garcia; she did not relish tackling al-Din alone.

“Call for back up, this is it,” she said calmly. “He’s here.”

The taller of the men, lean and angular, with short blond receding hair turned away and spoke into his walkie-talkie. The other man, stocky with more rounded features, drew his weapon and released the safety catch.

“Which way?” demanded Garcia of the receptionist, who had blanched visibly.

The small woman raised a pale skeleton-thin wrist and pointed to the back door leading from the foyer to the small courtyard.

“Through there,” she said. “It leads to the fattening and processing yards.”

The three FBI agents ran through the door and into the sweltering heat. The courtyard was empty and they continued at a brisk walk though the narrow passageway leading to the fattening yard.

In the distance, they saw the opening to the cavernous hangar-like shed. The black yawning hole obscured all activity that might be occurring within. In the foreground, figures moved freely going about their assigned tasks.

The taller man split from the other two and headed to the side of the building, checking for alternate entrances and exits. Garcia and the stocky agent approached the front entrance. The weak fluorescent strip lights overhead barely generated enough light to illuminate the floor.

Beside the parallel rows of stalls used to fatten the pigs two figures were only just visible in the depths of the shed. Garcia drew her badge and gun. The figures were some distance apart. One man, fat and casually dressed, leaned against a stall. The other thinner, unusually well dressed and carrying a briefcase appeared to be talking on a mobile phone.

Garcia tried to adjust her breathing. Shallow and irregular, the adrenaline was surging through her veins and her heart pounded. Licking her lips she tried to swallow in a vain attempt to soothe her dry mouth.

Raising her gun, she clasped her other hand onto her wrist for support and to stop the shaking.

“Husam al-Din! FBI! Stop right there!” she called.

Chapter 38

The walk back to the farrowing yards seemed quicker to al-Din now that he was more familiar with the layout of the immense feedlot. Following O'Dell, but not too closely, al-Din prepared for his final act as America's most wanted terrorist.

Feeling in his pocket he fondled the curved cheek plate of the handcuffs. The blue carbon steel was smooth and polished. At twelve ounces, the handcuffs were sturdy enough to resist all attempts to interfere with his plan. Unseen, al-Din bunched his fingers together and inserted them into the opening of the bracelet. When he was sure O'Dell was out of earshot he snapped the ratchet closed with his other hand. It locked with loud clack. al-Din flinched at the sound and looked up. O'Dell had not noticed and continued to lead the way back to the farrowing pens.

Closing the handcuffs required the use of his other hand and al-Din had to swing the briefcase wildly to accomplish the task. He hoped others had not observed his awkward movements. Breathing deeply, he withdrew his hand from his jacket pocket. The handcuff hung limply from his wrist; the bracelet gaped like a mouth, the serrated edge of the free ratchet resembling the bared fangs of a wild animal.

In his haste, al-Din had tightened the first ratchet too far. The metal pinched his flesh and tore the hairs from the skin around the wrist. The pain would focus the mind, he told himself. Besides, it would not last long.

Transferring the heavy briefcase to his shackled hand al-Din swiftly closed the free cuff around the handle of the case. It was done. The unfashionably long sleeves of his jacket obscured the cuff around the wrist; fingers clasping the grip hid the cuff around the handle.

al-Din activated the trigger incorporated into the briefcase handle. A satisfying clunk told him the mechanism had been actuated correctly.

Closing the gap on O'Dell, al-Din managed to smile as the fat man turned to see where he was. Obligingly, O'Dell held the door open for his guest to enter first.

"Well, here we are," he said, "back to square one, more or less."

al-Din feigned interest in a nearby pallet of feed touching it with his free hand and tilting his head to read the list of ingredients. Stepping back he put his hand in his pocket and pulled out his mobile phone.

"Excuse me, Mr. O'Dell," he said, examining the phone briefly and putting it to his ear. "I think it's my head office. I'll have to take this."

"You go right ahead son," O'Dell replied. "I'll just rest up over here." He walked a few feet away and propped himself up against one of the stalls. The inhabitant was preoccupied in suckling her litter and did not object to the man's presence.

al-Din nodded his appreciation and turned away. He retreated to the end of the row, his finger on the trigger. Outside, in the distance, two figures approached.

The ten-ounce compressed air canister hissed almost imperceptibly from deep within the briefcase. As it did so a fine mist, a deadly aerosol, emerged from a small hole in the side of the case. Casually aiming the spray into the stalls as he walked slowly down the aisle, al-Din turned and crossed to the other side of the narrow path to infect the stalls opposite.

O'Dell looked up and saw al-Din deep in conversation, impatiently walking up and down. He smiled, pleased that his own bosses never made him that nervous.

A sound made the fat man turn around. Two strangers, well dressed in black, were approaching quickly down the gangway. Raising himself from his slumped position he stepped into the middle of the narrow passage effectively blocking it with his bulk. He raised his hand, palm outward as if he were a policeman halting the flow of traffic. His brow furrowed in concern as the guns were drawn and the silver of the badges caught the light. Looking over at his visitor and then back at the strangers he guessed the reason they had come.

"Husam al-Din!" barked the woman, gripping her gun with both hands and advancing toward her target. "FBI! Stop right there!"

O'Dell stepped aside and turned to face the young man with whom he had spent the past two hours. "Son of a bitch," he muttered under his breath.

al-Din looked up and his eyes widened in surprise. The intrusion was unexpected; but he was prepared. Dropping his useless phone into the filth on the ground, he ducked and headed for the door at the rear of the shed through which he and O'Dell had just entered. The door opened outwards and al-Din leapt toward it pushing against it with all his strength. He did not hear the first shot or the splintering of wood as the doorframe disintegrated above his head.

Almost immediately, al-Din encountered the tall thin FBI agent and caught him off guard. Dazed by the sudden opening of the door in his face the agent was pushed back against a wall by al-Din's momentum as he exited the shed. Before he was able to react al-Din swung the heavy briefcase up with both hands, intent on using it as a cudgel. The sharp corner hit the agent across the bridge of the nose rupturing it instantly in a spray of blood. Swinging back the other way the second blow caught him across the temple and he doubled up in pain. A third blow with the edge of the case crushed his windpipe. al-Din left the man clutching his throat, his face and clothing stained with blood.

Running up the passageway al-Din headed toward the next farrowing shed. As he fled, the pounding of footsteps behind him could not be distinguished from the racing of his own heart or the throbbing in his temples from the sudden exertion.

The second shed was identical to the first except now he was at the front entrance rather than the back. Above him, the overhead cables screamed as a pallet of feed made its way sedately to the rear of the building.

Climbing the few steps up to the wooden platform used to secure the pallets to the metal poles attached to the overhead cable, al-Din pushed the attendant workman away with his case and watched him topple backwards down the steps.

The second FBI man rounded the corner and burst into the shed, gun drawn. He did not see the barbed spike bearing down on him until it was too late. Impaled through the shoulder by the metal pole the man dropped his weapon and screamed in agony as he was lifted, feet kicking empty air, and transported down the aisle. As the man passed the platform and drew level with his attacker, al-Din arched his eyebrows and smiled.

With only seconds to spare, al-Din jumped from the platform and ran down the aisle, easily overtaking the dangling FBI agent and the suspended pallet of feed some yards ahead. Using it as cover he evaded Garcia's second shot, which ripped open the bags being carried into the shed, sending bullet-sized pellets of feed arcing through the air.

Racing to the back of the pen al-Din headed instinctively for the rear door. Around the corner, lay the blast chilling plant. Ignoring the warning signs he barged impulsively through the door, the cold stung his eyes and burned his skin. The moisture on his shoes froze instantly adhering them to the floor. Yanking his feet free he continued running to the end of the building dodging between the gutted carcasses suspended from the ceiling by shiny steel hooks. Vents in the ceiling and floor pumped out ice-cold air and the din of the turbines drowned out all but the loudest sounds.

As he searched for the exit at the rear of the building, the hind leg of the pig closest to him erupted, sending shards of flesh and splinters of bone into his eyes. Putting up his free hand to shield his face he turned and saw Garcia, pistol raised, mere yards behind him. She ducked behind a suspended carcass and al-Din guessed she would try to use them as cover to work her way toward him. A shadowy movement in the hazy fog, generated as moist outside air came into contact with the dry cooler interior, confirmed his suspicions.

al-Din retraced his steps to face his stalker head on, hiding behind a parallel row of chilled corpses. He was level with her now and saw her, gun in hand, peering into the frozen void ahead. He ran toward her pushing a frozen cadaver into her side. The hundred-kilogram mass knocked her down. The sound of her gun clattering to the floor was lost in the drone of the turbines.

As she put her hand out to brace her fall the bare skin froze on contact with the textured steel surface. Instinctively she pulled back ripping away skin and flesh leaving a bloody red wound. Instantly anaesthetised by the searing cold and rush of adrenaline Garcia felt nothing. Clawing at her assailant she saw him disappear into the mist ahead of her. Knowing that she had to get out of the building to live she followed blindly.

A shaft of light guided her way. Far to the right a square hole was cut into the wall through which ran a conveyor belt. As this was the only exit she could perceive Garcia stumbled toward it and clambered up onto the slowly moving surface, lying flat as it entered the narrow square tunnel that led into the next building.

Lying supine on the green rubber belt Garcia craned her head back to see where she was going. The noise of the turbines subsided and the temperature increased perceptibly. As it did so her hand started to throb. Garcia became aware of a whirring noise, a buzzing that sounded as if it came from an electric drill.

As she emerged from the tunnel the whirring got louder. Suddenly he was upon her. The twelve-inch razor sharp blades of the electric knife scythed through the air toward her face. Rolling away from the serrated weapon Garcia dropped from the conveyor onto the floor. The smell of blood and minced flesh assaulted her nostrils and adhered to her face and hair. The electric knife caught the edge of the conveyor ripping the thick rubber belt to shreds and sending a shower of white-hot sparks cascading through the air.

Garcia sprang to her feet as the blade came at her again; this time thrust through the gap under the conveyor. Now, for the first time in her long quest, she met her assailant face to face. His eyes were demonic and filled with hate; his lips were stretched wide, teeth bared in a skeletal grin. Again he thrust the lethal blade toward her. Garcia relaxed. al-Din could not reach her. The conveyor belt acted as a barrier and the power cable of the knife was only a few feet long. Quickly, Garcia looked about. To her right stood a shelving unit containing an array of squat black plastic drums each about six inches tall and four inches in diameter. A small square label indicated their contents. Garcia grabbed one, ripped open the cap and flung the contents into al-Din's face.

White odourless crystals of propyl gallate filled the air like a miniature snowstorm. His eyes stinging, al-Din dropped the knife which instantly ceased its whining. As he stepped back and tried to wipe his tear-filled eyes Garcia leapt up on to the conveyor belt and launched herself at him.

The pair fell to the ground in a heap. al-Din wrestled with his briefcase and managed to bring it up in front of his face to avert the first of Garcia's blows. With both hands he dragged the case smartly across the side of her head and sent her reeling on to the cement floor.

With a few seconds' advantage al-Din clambered up the aluminium scaffolding supporting the vast hopper and Archimedes screw arrangement. Pausing for breath in the narrow alleyways that linked the various pieces of apparatus together he searched for Garcia.

al-Din could see very little through the criss-cross metal framework supporting the heavy processing equipment. Finding a small set of steps that led to a higher level he ascended, hoping the additional height would give him an advantage in his search for the troublesome agent.

Garcia had beaten him to it. Lying in wait behind a control panel she could see al-Din clamber the steps, his briefcase snagging the handrail awkwardly on the final step. Delivering a smart kick to his chin he fell backwards down the stairs, landing in a heap on the lower platform. Exhausted and in pain herself, Garcia plunged headlong down the stairs straddling the prostrate form of the winded man.

Grabbing his lapels with both hands she pulled him up and brought her face close to his.

"Where's Jacobs?" she gasped.

The man smiled, recognising the name, but remained silent.

"Tell me," screamed Garcia. "Do you know where he is?"

"I know everything I need to know," replied al-Din cryptically.

"Bullshit," shouted Garcia. "You don't know anything."

al-Din smiled almost serenely. "Only three things are unknown to man," he said. "The source of his next meal, the hour of his death and the true name of Allah."

Garcia held the man's head as blood filled her hands. al-Din had cracked his skull as he fell on to the cast iron platform.

Laying him gently on the ground Garcia wiped her hands on her jacket. As she did so the raw wound on her own hand flared up and she winced in pain.

The fist caught Garcia square on the chin and sent her staggering backwards. al-Din had only been able to use his left hand because of the impediment caused by the briefcase, so the blow was not as heavy as he would have liked. Still, it served its purpose. Scrambling free of the FBI agent, al-Din mounted the stairs again toward his original destination.

Now on the uppermost level of the processing unit he had a clear view of the factory floor in all directions. He searched for the nearest exit. Beside him the conveyor belt bringing freshly diced flesh from the cutters below delivered their load into the wide-open mouth of the stainless steel hopper. Deep inside the hopper, hidden by the vast writhing mass of churning meat, the giant rotating blades of the Archimedes screw could only be heard.

A noise behind him made him turn. Garcia was on the platform, bloodied and bedraggled; her eyes were filled with as much venom as al-Din's had been.

"Where's Jacobs?" she demanded.

"Go to hell, FBI," retorted al-Din, stepping backwards along the narrow ledge.

"I'm not letting you go," said Garcia. "You either tell me here or in custody," she gasped.

"I think we both know that is not going to happen," replied al-Din, maintaining his slow backwards walk and eyeing the platform to his right, mentally calculating the easiest way to descend to floor level.

al-Din stopped walking; the end of the passageway halted his progress. Now less than six feet apart, he and Garcia stared at each other - the hunter and the hunted, predator and prey. Garcia had run out of options. Alone and unarmed, this was her best chance of apprehending the suspect and extracting the information she needed from him. If he had the chance to flee again he might kill himself or be killed by other officers on the chase.

Sensing her tactics, al-Din edged forwards, hoping to reach the steps leading down to the lower platform before Garcia cut him off. If he was going to die he was ready to take someone with him.

al-Din saw it first; its bronzed body perfectly disguised against the iron floor. The thirty-six inch pipe wrench was propped against a railing. The jaws were open to their fullest extent; a hideous grinning mouth capable of crushing bone. Stooping swiftly al-Din snatched up the object with his free hand, its seventeen-pound mass heavy and unwieldy in his grasp. Rested, armed and confident he strode toward Garcia swinging the iron club from side to side, cutting the air like a sabre. Gripping the railing for support Garcia flinched as the cudgel swooped through the air and landed with a clang next to her hand. The entire platform shook with the impact.

Flinging herself at him Garcia managed to grab hold of al-Din's arm and prevent him from aiming another blow at her. The pair rolled onto the narrow platform. Every sharp edge dug into their flesh as they careened about the equipment. Using the briefcase to protect him from Garcia's fists, al-Din rained blows upon her body. Racked with pain Garcia struggled to respond. A punch, one of many she aimed blindly at al-Din's face, found its target. Reeling backwards, al-Din responded by bringing his briefcase up to head height. Depressing the trigger in the handle a virus-laden mist stung Garcia's eyes.

With no escape Garcia's only recourse was to attack and she timed her challenge for when al-Din was at his most vulnerable. As he raised the club to its highest point she sprang forward, ramming him in the chest with all her strength. Unbalanced al-Din toppled backward and over the railing. As he fell he let go of the wrench, which plunged into the hopper and disappeared into the undulating mass of flesh. Seconds later the Archimedes screw let out a hideous screech of metal on metal as the tool was swallowed and digested by the ceaseless mechanical teeth.

The briefcase was wedged in the railing; the handcuffs providing the only support for al-Din as his body hung over the hopper. The metal rim of the cuff dug into his flesh. His body hung limply too exhausted and frightened to move.

"Where's Jacobs?" Garcia demanded.

"Fuck you," spat al-Din.

Garcia nursed a cut lip with the back of her hand. "You said you didn't know the source of your next meal," she said. "Look behind you."

al-Din squirmed like a worm on a hook. The briefcase slipped a fraction of an inch between the railings and al-Din gasped in pain and surprise as he inched closer to the pulverised flesh below.

"Where's Jacobs?" Garcia reiterated firmly.

"Go to hell!" retorted al-Din, triumphant in his defiance.

"You said you didn't know the hour of your death," mocked Garcia unsympathetically. "It won't be long now."

al-Din and his briefcase were out of reach. There was nothing Garcia could do but watch. al-Din clasped his free hand over his aching wrist attempting to provide some kind of relief to the enormous strain on his body. As he did so the briefcase slid free from the railing and al-Din plummeted into the centre of the hopper.

Buoyed up momentarily by the ocean of flesh his body soon began to sink, drawn down by the inexorable pull of the Archimedes screw operating in darkness inches below his toes.

"For God's sake stop it!" he cried. "Stop the machine!"

Garcia wearily looked about her for the bright red emergency stop buttons that she knew were scattered around the factory. She couldn't see one. By the time she looked back into the hopper al-Din was already waist-deep and sinking further.

al-Din looked up at Garcia wide-eyed in terror silently pleading for help.

The pitch of the motor changed as al-Din's foot, complete with shoe, was wrenched off and dragged into the swirling screw. The screaming echoed around the cavernous factory and seemed to last for ever.

Writhing, squealing like an animal, al-Din's fight against the machine was futile. It did not stop him struggling. Beating the surface of the fleshy mass in which he swam, clawing at the air and scratching his nails down the seamless sides of the metal casing, his battle against death was short.

The briefcase was the last item to be dragged into the machine's maw. With a crunch that resonated from deep within its belly, the briefcase and its deadly contents was consumed by the insatiable beast. al-Din's blood mingled quickly with the rest of the lurid pink meat.

Garcia peered over the edge of the railing into the hopper. "You said you didn't know the true name of Allah," she muttered under her breath. "Ask him yourself."

Chapter 39

"We got him," shouted the young man from the far side of the room, slamming down the phone whilst scribbling on his notepad. He tore off the top page and crossed the room to where Garcia sat, bruised and bandaged.

It had been twenty-four hours since her encounter with Husam al-Din. The news of his death had electrified the country. The killing of the terrorist brought a palpable sense of relief to the nation. The cattle industry representatives were particularly pleased; the traditionally conservative organisations were unstinting in their praise and best wishes towards the authorities. Financial analysts predicted that the stock markets would rally on the back of the good news.

As a result of the storm of media coverage, Garcia had been inundated with requests for interviews. Mindful of the need to project a favourable image of the agency, Garcia's bosses at the FBI were keen that she appear on camera as soon as possible after al-Din's death. The fact that she was both female and from a minority was a golden opportunity that proved irresistible. Several interviews had been arranged and taped during the morning and would air on news specials over the next few evenings.

Garcia's injuries were not extensive. A preliminary examination by dermatologists indicated that the skin that had been torn from her hand probably would not require a graft. A cracked rib from the repeated blows with the wrench was heavily strapped with bandages so much so that she found it difficult to inhale deeply. Tiring easily, she sat at her desk and rested most of the day. An opened bottle of prescription painkillers stood in prominent view on the desk, almost as if it were a trophy of her exploits.

The heavy make up used during the recording sessions that morning disguised many of the small scratches to her face but could not obliterate the thick lip she sustained from al-Din's fists. Avoiding the mirrors would be her daily chore for the next few days. She did not feel pretty.

Garcia's colleagues however, were ecstatic. Having one of their own take down a prime suspect single-handedly was the highest tribute that could be paid to their courage and resourcefulness. Fielding calls from the FBI's Director and Assistant-Director personally, Garcia felt both elated and humbled at the attention. In reality, and as she had told her high-level well-wishers, she just wanted to get back to the job and ensure that all the loose ends were tied up.

The biggest loose end was finding out what happened to Bill Jacobs.

The young man approached Garcia's desk and reached out with the piece of paper. Garcia winced as she leaned forward to take it from him and the man looked away in apology.

"What's this?" said Garcia, studying the paper intently.

"It's from Jacobs' credit card company," replied the man. "He used his card to rent an RV in Wellington, Colorado three days ago. That's less than five miles from where the car was found abandoned. It ties in with how long Larimer PD think the car was left before its discovery."

"Okay," mused Garcia. "So they abandon the car, walk to Wellington and rent an RV. al-Din continues alone or is dropped off at Greeley. So where is Jacobs now? Is he sitting around waiting for al-Din to return? Unlikely if he's been watching TV in the last twenty-four hours. We need to go back to this Wellington RV dealer and pump him for info. Any volunteers?" Garcia scanned the room, wondering if one of the junior staff would actually fall for her suggestion. "Sue," she said, turning her attention to the officer seated opposite, "call Sergeant Charles C. Calhoun in the Larimer County P.D. and have him mosey on down to the, what's it called again?" she said to herself, studying the young man's handwriting, "RV Heaven, and have him find out more about these strangers in town." Garcia's affected cowboy accent raised a few smiles around the office. "I want to know what vehicle they're travelling in and if they indicated at all where they were headed after Greeley. Jacobs has disappeared and it's imperative we find him. He's suicidal and could be looking to hurt some more people if he decides now's the time to say goodbye."

The roomful of officers mulled on Garcia's words for a few seconds before setting about their tasks.

It was after 6:00 P.M. when Sergeant Calhoun reported back.

"Yes, Sergeant," said Garcia, taking the call as soon as it arrived. "What did you manage to find out?"

"Well ma'am," replied the elderly man in a voice cracked with age, "two men did approach the RV Heaven premises on the afternoon of September 9. The owner recollects that the white male was overweight and sweating profusely, as if he had been exerting himself. I think that would tie in with him having walked down highway 87 from Bulger. The owner also recalls that the white male did all the talking and quickly settled on a brown 2000 Jamboree, which he rented for ten days at one hundred twenty-nine dollars per day. He paid a five hundred dollar deposit by MasterCard, with the balance due on the return of the vehicle. The vehicle registration is papa-zulu-uniform-two-four-niner."

"Did they say anything about where they were headed?" asked Garcia anxiously.

"No ma'am, they did not," replied Calhoun. "Although the owner says that when they drove out of the lot they headed south down I-25, which would be the quickest way to Greeley."

"Thanks for all your help, sergeant," said Garcia, the air of despondency in her voice was clear.

"You're welcome ma'am," replied the older man. "And may I just say what a pleasure it has been serving such a fine officer as yourself. I saw your picture in the paper after what that... that... well I don't like to use such words in mixed company ma'am, but looking at what he did to you just made my blood boil. It's been an honour and privilege to be of service to you."

Tears welled up in the corners of Garcia's eyes as she listened to Calhoun's tribute and she remembered her deceased father and brother. Would they have been so proud? Of course they would she told herself. Quietly, almost imperceptibly, she thanked Calhoun and replaced the receiver.

Snapping out of her malaise Garcia tasked one of the junior staff with searching for Jacobs' RV.

Garcia could do nothing more. With innumerable campsites in Colorado alone to search, it could be weeks before any further news of Jacobs was forthcoming. In addition, she doubted he would be returning the rented RV, convinced it would soon become his coffin. Perhaps someone should inform the owner? She smiled at the thought. Slumped at her desk, she waited for a miracle.

Chapter 40

Caine looked at himself in the mirror. The stubble clung to his jaw and rasped as he ran his fingertips over it. Yellow crusts of sleep peppered the corner of his eye and adhered to the short lashes on his lower lids. He winced as he saw the damage Laura had done to his back with her nails. After a slow methodical shave and a long hot shower he was ready to face the world again.

Laura was downstairs in the kitchen preparing breakfast. Today, as she had every morning, Laura jogged the half-mile to the grocery store to pick up some fresh milk and the morning paper. She would walk back briskly. The return trip took twenty minutes tops. When she arrived, glowing from the exertion, the grey baggy sweatshirt she wore to disguise the bounce of her ample bosom would be damp with sweat. Usually that would be an excuse to strip off and jump in the shower with Caine. After last night's activities he wondered if either of them had the strength for a morning session.

In the bedroom Caine picked up his crumpled shirt from the floor and sniffed the armpits. Good for another day at least.

Laura was reading the horoscopes when Caine at last descended for breakfast. Still only 7:30 A.M., Caine had adapted quickly to Laura's early-to-rise early-to-bed philosophy.

"Good morning, Mr. Sleepy," Laura smiled.

Caine said nothing but smiled and sat down opposite. The solid pine breakfast table comfortably held the assortment of breakfast accoutrements in addition to the large morning paper, whose various sections had spilled out where Laura had dropped it.

"Whoah!" exclaimed Caine, as his attention was caught by the screaming headline.

FMD BIOTERRORIST KILLED
Greeley, CO, manhunt ends in death

Picking up the paper Caine devoured the news, turning the page eagerly to follow the story inside. The article was illustrated with diagrams showing the location and layout of the Great Western Feeders building, the FBI chase through the feedlot and photographs of the scene of al-Din's death. A prominent photograph of Angela Garcia being led to an ambulance, her hand and head heavily bandaged, dominated one of the pages devoted to the story.

Caine was stunned. He guessed a lot might have happened since he last spoke to Angela. He never thought she would be hailed as a national heroine within a week.

"Paul?" said Laura, sweetly.

"Mmm?" replied Caine, engrossed in the article.

"I'm due some vacation," she said, wondering if Caine would be angry at her suggestion. "I thought maybe if you extended your stay here a few days, we could go somewhere nice?"

"Such as?" said Caine, slightly irked that Laura made him lose his place in the article.

"I don't know," she added. "Away from the city. Somewhere drier. Arizona maybe. They've got London Bridge in Lake Havasu City, if you're homesick," she suggested politely.

Caine arched his eyebrows, surprised and disgusted in equal measure.

"Las Vegas is only a few hours away," continued Laura, hoping to entice Caine to stay a little longer with one of her suggestions.

Caine continued to read the paper, not really listening to Laura. He scoured the article for references to the plot he had discovered. There was no mention that Bill Jacobs was a co-conspirator, nor was there any mention of the biblical quotes.

"What about the national parks?" Laura said, oblivious to Caine's lack of interest. "Some of them are very nice this time of year. Sequoia. Death Valley. Grand Canyon."

"Grand Canyon?" Caine looked up form his paper. Where had he heard someone mention that place before?

You know, I've lived here for twenty-five years and I've never gotten to see the Grand Canyon.

Caine put the paper down on the table reached over and cupped Laura's face in his hands. She smiled at his tenderness. Leaning across the table he kissed her gently on the forehead.

"I have to go," he said. "It's important."

Laura could tell that Caine was not joking. Her bottom lip quivered and she flushed. "Is it me?" she asked, her throat choked with emotion. "Was it something I said?"

Caine shook his head. "It's me. I have to go. There's something I have to do. I can't tell you why. Trust me, it's very important. Maybe in a few days you'll even read about it in the paper."

Rising from the table he walked into the kitchen. Laura remained seated. She stared at the discarded paper and wondered if it had any connection to Caine's sudden decision to leave.

Retrieving his wallet and passport from the kitchen table he left by the back door. Stony-faced and determined, he did not look back. Laura followed him into the kitchen but did not speak. Caine caught a glimpse of her as he left, the pleading in her big brown eyes left him aching, wishing he could do something to placate her - to take her up in his arms and say it would be alright.

He could not lie to himself or to her. Tomorrow, or the day after, he would face the toughest challenge of his life and he did not want, could not afford, any distractions, however well intentioned, that might interfere with his preparation.

Walking down the driveway he could feel Laura's eyes through the living room window willing him to return. He felt cold and empty as he trudged through the cool damp morning air. Halfway down the road he hailed a passing taxi.

Chapter 41

Armed only with a credit card and wearing just the clothes in which he stood, Caine didn't know if leaving Laura to pursue a hunch about Jacobs was a good idea or not. In the back of the taxi to the airport, he was in a daze. He knew that he was going to leave Laura at some point, so it was probably better for all concerned if it was sooner rather than later. Still, he mused, he could have done a better job of telling her. Laura would not understand why he had to leave until she saw it on the TV news and only then if Caine's wild, spur-of-the-moment idea was correct. He had plenty of time to dwell on his misgivings as he waited in the airport lounge.

The quickest way to the Grand Canyon was to fly to Las Vegas and then catch a tourist shuttle to the tiny Grand Canyon Airport at Tusayan, a few miles from the entrance to the National Park. Caine made the necessary arrangements. Leaving at 10:55 A.M., the American Airlines flight stopped en route at Los Angeles during its five-hour journey.

Before his departure Caine bought a few travel guides and maps of the Grand Canyon region, which he perused during the flight, locating suitable hotels and finalising his travel plans. At Las Vegas he decided to call ahead to the hotels in Grand Canyon Village to see if any rooms were available. Mid-September was peak tourist season and it was likely that all the rooms would be booked solid.

It also occurred to him that Angela would like to know his whereabouts and what he was about to do. Doubtless she would have her own theories. He remembered the way she had chided him the last time he had tried to intervene. Caine smiled at the recollection and had to remind himself that he had been right on that occasion.

The plane landed more or less on time. With twilight approaching, the sky near Las Vegas turned from pure cobalt blue to purple within the space of a few minutes. The clarity of the dry desert air extended visibility for miles. The city lights were not yet coming on as the plane approached and the gridiron pattern of roads in the city centre dissipated at its fringes, trailing off into the desert and disappearing into the creosote, blackbush and Joshua trees of the Mojave Desert and Utah Badlands.

As he passed through the arrivals hall on his way to the taxi stand, Caine looked around for a phone booth. A poster for Scenic Airlines, the only commercial carrier flying to Grand Canyon Airport, was displayed prominently. Caine noted the counter location and continued his search.

The Holiday Inn Express Grand Canyon was located one mile from the park entrance and half a mile from the airport; it was the best choice available given the time constraints. Caine called ahead and booked a room for two nights.

Despite the evidence, Caine still hoped he was wrong about Bill Jacobs. Caine had told himself constantly throughout his journey, recounting as if it were some kind of personal mantra, that the trip was a waste of time.

The wait for the connection, the last scheduled flight of the day, to the tiny airport that served the Grand Canyon National Park, was spent mostly staring at the floor. Flight 1739 left at 5:30 P.M. The de Havilland Twin Otter Vistaliner, a twin-engine propeller-driven plane, looked small and fragile compared with the 747's on the apron in the distance.

A gaggle of people assembled in the far corner of the departure hall. A group of teenagers on their first vacation away from their parents made the most noise, trying to out-compete each other with their shallow form of bravado, bullshit and profanity. An elderly couple, retirees on the trip of a lifetime, frowned at them from a safe distance. A young couple, engaged or just married, Caine could not tell which, were engrossed in their own public expressions of devotion. The man caressed the girl's face as she stroked his hair. The elderly woman beamed at them. Caine frowned; all nineteen seats on the small plane would be filled.

In the darkness, the flight to the Grand Canyon was uneventful. The small plane bobbed and lurched riding the pockets of rising air and hugging the fringes of the few high clouds. As Caine looked out of the window on the brief seventy-five minute flight, he imagined he could see the Grand Canyon below him. All he saw was the reflection of the plane interior in the oversized picture windows. Below him the great chasm yawned, a vast black hole, silent and immutable - an ageless scar on the face of the earth.

At Tusayan, Caine walked to his hotel. With no baggage and no overcoat, the crisp clear night air was sufficiently cold to make him shiver. After checking in he ate dinner in the hotel restaurant. Deciding he needed a change of clothing he visited the local mall where he purchased a sweatshirt and underwear.

Guilt, fear, or simply the desire to rekindle a friendship, made him call the FBI field office in San Francisco to leave a message for Angela. It was short and sweet. He was checking up a hunch, perhaps something to do with Bill Jacobs. If she was interested and had time she could find him here.

Bored in his hotel, Caine decided to take a walk around the village. The small community of fifteen hundred people lived in a cluster of streets bordering the edge of the canyon. The majority of the villagers were employed in the retail and service sectors serving the National Park.

During the early evening Caine sat on his bed, the local Yellow Pages open on his lap, as he called every hotel in the Grand Canyon area asking for Bill Jacobs. Perplexed and slightly pleased, no one of that name had registered in the last twenty-four hours.

Tired, and with his throat sore from constant talking, he went to bed early, intending to get up the next day in time to watch the sunrise. For the moment, sleep claimed him and he passed the night in undisturbed slumber.

The shriek of the alarm clock at 5:30 A.M. pierced the silence of the room and Caine awoke with a start. Bleary-eyed he stumbled into the shower. After a quick shower and a shave he was ready to face the new day. The new sweatshirt itched.

The walk to the canyon's entrance was spellbinding; the road was nearly deserted and the forest lined a path for Caine to follow. It was as if he was on a runway leading to the vast chasm.

The amber rim of the sun warmed the sky above the horizon imbuing it with crimsons and yellows, melting the harsh purple-black of the night. Gradually, the spectacle began to unravel and Caine was surprised at the size of the crowds that had come to watch. Distracted from his search for Jacobs he was entranced by the dawn breaking over the canyon. The creeping sun slowly illuminated the walls and rims of the canyon, banishing the shadows to the darkest and most impenetrable recesses of the buttes and temples that peppered the great abyss.

Standing alongside the rim, soaking in the vast cliffs and colours, Caine recognised nature's colossal power over humankind. Looking around he saw the awe in people's eyes as they drank in the intoxicating splendour of the scene before them. The canyon was by definition a void of land, yet it had become a tangible thing, filling people with hope and wonder, and the urge to explore.

The landscape was rugged and raw; the jagged walls of the canyons were striped with rainbows of ever-changing mineral colours. Juniper trees and ponderosa pines clung to the sides of the immense ravine, and banana yuccas sprouted defiantly along its rim. Even the native animals seem rugged; mule deer, bobcats and coyotes lurked in the canyon's niches.

Caine stood on the South Rim, the most popular part of the park. Directly opposite, ten miles distant across the enormous gulf that confronted him, stood the North Rim. Both areas supported mature forests of ponderosas, allowing sufficient sunlight for mountain grasses, wildflowers and oak. Descending in elevation, the trees diminished in size and desert-friendly plants of a hardier nature began to thrive. Sagebrush, gambel oak, ponderosas, quaking aspen and Indian paintbrush gave way gradually to pinyon pine, Utah juniper, Mormon tea, brittlebush and Apache plume.

Eventually, as the sun rose and its disk cleared the horizon the colours of the rocks became bright and harsh, the subtleties of texture lost in the glare. The crowds dispersed, heading back to the campsites and hotels for breakfast or to get a head start on the hiking trails.

Starting at the South Rim, Caine headed down Park Loop Drive and West Rim Drive where he discovered exceptional lookout points over the canyon. He followed the Rim Trail, a partially paved track that provided an easy hike along the canyon's edge, stopping at Hermit's Point and other historical sites along the way.

Caine did not have time to cover the entire park. He had to think like Jacobs. Where would he go? An ageing overweight man rekindling memories of a lost wife would not tackle the harder paths. Even the Bright Angel Trail, the most popular route descending to the Colorado River, would be too difficult for him. On the other hand, gentler trails leading to Desert View and the Watchtower allowed hikers to take in views all the way to the Painted Desert and Utah's Vermillion Cliffs, and might appeal to someone like Jacobs.

Caine had underestimated the size of the task ahead of him. He would have to use a different strategy than simply trying to bump into Jacobs at the popular tourist spots.

Having established that Jacobs had not checked in to any of the local hotels, at least under his own name, that left the campsites and RV compounds as the only alternative lodging. Knowing that Jacobs enjoyed the finer things in life, he could not believe that his ageing mentor would willingly accept shared or tented accommodation under any circumstances. A well-appointed RV on the other hand would provide both the comfort he desired and the anonymity he required for his task.

Satisfied that he had found another plausible seam of information to mine, Caine trudged back to his hotel, where he could rest and eat. The Visitor Center would have ample information on the location of the nearest RV sites around the Grand Canyon.

Within minutes he found what he needed. The only RV site within the Grand Canyon was Trailer Village, one mile south of the Visitor Center. With only eighty-four sites available, Caine imagined it would not take him long to find the missing Jacobs.

Immediately after lunch, Caine went to the small business centre in the hotel. He logged on to the Internet and found the official website for the meeting in San Francisco he had attended a few days previously. He scanned quickly through the homepage noting the various sub-headings: message from the Chairman, committee structure, scientific program, registration, and abstract submission – the usual digest of a large international meeting. Using his mouse, Caine clicked on the committee structure page. A flowchart of how the meeting secretariat was organised appeared on the screen. At the top, enclosed in a rectangular box, was the name Jonas Williams. Underneath, in block capitals were his title and university affiliation. The second tier of the organisational pyramid contained two boxes, Bill Jacobs and Peter Reynolds along with their title, Vice-president. The third tier contained the names of the committees the president and his deputies oversaw.

Caine scrolled the mouse over the name of Bill Jacobs. It lit up as he did so, indicating that it was linked to another page. He clicked the highlighted name and was immediately transferred to a page containing a brief welcome message from Bill Jacobs and a description of his duties during the meeting. As expected, a high-resolution portrait of the man, in suit and tie, filled a sizeable portion of the screen. Caine isolated the image and saved it to the computer's memory. Opening a new word processing document he inserted the figure into the file, adjusted the size, and printed it out. A few feet away the laser printer whined into life and Caine heard the familiar scuff of paper being drawn into the machine.

With his freshly minted wanted poster Caine headed to Trailer Village. In the early afternoon it was mostly deserted, the occupants enjoying the natural amenities available to them. Again Caine had underestimated the size of the task. Despite space being at a premium, the RV site had been designed to minimise interference from neighbouring vehicles. Considerable distances separated each vehicle and its electrical hook-up from the next. In addition, it looked as if all eighty-four spaces were occupied. The search would take longer than expected.

In the distance Caine spotted a group of youths. There were about four or five of them sitting outside a decrepit RV, lolling on deck chairs.

They did not look up as Caine approached softly over the close-cropped scrub grass and boot-worn dirt patches.

Caine was nervous. He didn't like talking to strangers especially when the age and cultural differences between them were as wide as the canyon he had just explored. Caine fingered the folded picture of Jacobs in his trouser pocket for reassurance.

"Er, hi fellas," he said, cautiously.

The young men stopped talking and turned as one to look at the new arrival. Caine addressed the man nearest to him, who even though he was seated was obviously the tallest member of the group. The man was pale; his hair was so short Caine found it almost sinister. In addition, he had a tattoo on his shoulder - a black star and the name of what Caine took to be a rock band although the lettering was too indistinct to read. A glint of sunlight highlighted the stud embedded in the man's right nostril.

The man cocked his head to one side in order to get a better look at Caine who towered over him.

"What's up, dude?" the man replied. As he spoke the shiny metal barbell piercing his tongue flicked briefly into view.

Caine was so entranced by the bizarre spectacle he could barely initiate a conversation. Remembering the picture in his pocket he pulled it out and unfolded it.

"I'm looking for someone," he said, spreading the paper flat in his hand and pointing to the portrait with a thick finger.

"You a cop?" said one of the other youths, a burly teen propped against a tree, nodding vigorously to music playing on his earphones.

"No," replied Caine firmly. "I...he's my father," he blurted. "He's got Alzheimer's and I think he's wandered off somewhere." Caine was impressed at the scale of his fabrication. Very plausible. "I was wondering if you might have seen him wandering around the park?"

The tall youth turned to the rest of the group. "What about it, you guys? Any of you seen this fella?"

"Nah."

"Uh-uh."

"Sorry, man."

"Hey, maybe the ladies will know," said the tattooed youth, visibly straightening up and smiling as a group of three females laden with brown paper grocery bags approached.

The girls, all dreadlocks and tie-dyed ripped T-shirts, ambled up to the group of young men. The men parted and formed a semi-circle into which the women walked, dropping their heavy loads onto the grass.

"Munchies and brewskies, everyone," cheered one girl, ripping the ring-pull off a can of cheap non-descript lager and taking a noisy slurp.

The bags clunked and crinkled as the supplies of beer and potato chips were disgorged to form a messy pile. The cans of beer were distributed quickly among the group. Those that remained were transferred to a battered icebox the size of a small car.

"Who's your new friend?" laughed one of the girls; a pointy, rat-faced girl with a crew cut who Caine thought was probably a lesbian.

"The guy's looking for his pop. Got Alzheimer's. Any of you seen him? He might be wandering around the park somewhere."

The girls craned their necks to take a closer look at the picture. "He looks familiar, sure," replied one, a tall surprisingly beautiful young woman.

"Really?" replied Caine earnestly. "Where was he?" The urgency in his voice startled the girl.

"Well, I don't know if it was really him," the girl backtracked, not wanting to raise false hopes. "But he looks like a guy we saw in the store back there. Right Cassie?" she said, turning to the rat-faced girl for confirmation.

"Erm, may be," replied the girl hesitantly. Then, "I don't know though."

"Tell you what, man," said the tall youth. "We'll keep an eye out for him and if we see him we'll let you know. How does that grab you? Can't say fairer than that."

"Yeah, thanks," said Caine, desperate to head off to the grocery store to check out the sighting. He took back his picture, folded it carefully and thrust it back in his pocket.

"Where you staying?" asked the youth.

"Holiday Inn. My name's Caine."

"Nice," nodded the man thoughtfully. "See you around Mr. Caine. I hope you find him okay." The man saluted Caine with a half-finished beer and his colleagues did likewise, wishing him their best.

Caine smiled and walked away in the direction the girls had come, assuming it was the way to the grocery store.

"Freaks," he muttered, under his breath.

Chapter 42

Caine crossed the RV park to the Visitor Center. The wide flat path was well maintained. It had to be. Over five million visitors came to see the Grand Canyon every year. To Caine it seemed a majority of them had arrived at the same time.

The Visitor Center and its immediate environs buzzed with activity. Children and adults whizzed past on bicycles, exploring the car-free stretches of road within the park; young couples and families with small children tramped through the forested trails that led to the more accessible vantage points. Groups of young men and women, strangers the night before, had paired up and were taking in the stunning vistas together. Holiday romances, as ephemeral as the mayflies that skimmed the surfaces of the quieter reaches of the Colorado River far below, would blossom and wane as the week progressed.

Inside the Visitor Center Caine looked around quickly for Jacobs. He picked up a map of the park and pretended to read the back of it as he systematically searched the aisles of books and pamphlets. Discarding the map close to where he found it he left and continued on to the shopping mall.

As he walked down the aisles of a convenience store Caine grabbed a few essentials he might need if he had to stay a few more days. With his trove of razors, shaving gel, instant noodles and bars of chocolate he approached the checkout. The queues in all four lanes were of equal length and Caine anticipated a long wait. He took the opportunity to scan the lines of waiting customers for any sign of Jacobs. There was none.

Soon Caine was halfway down his line. A movement caught his eye — a flash of white as it passed the window in front of him. Looking up Caine saw a large man ambling past the front of the store. The figure stopped outside the store as if deciding whether or not to go inside. Caine could see nothing of the man's features as large advertising posters filled the window and obscured his view.

After a few seconds the figure moved on. As it came into full view Caine was astonished. It was Jacobs! He was sure of it. A neat white Panama hat sat atop the man's head disguising the bald pate, but the full figure, ambling gait and hang-jowl profile were unmistakeable.

Convinced it was his quarry Caine excused himself from the queue and dumped his intended purchases in a large bin intended for discounted items. As surreptitiously as he could manage in full view of the public, Caine edged toward the exit and popped his head outside. The man had disappeared. Pausing to double-check in the opposite direction Caine left the shelter of the store exit and sidled down the wall. Peering around a corner Caine again spotted the fat man walking slowly up the path to the RV park. He carried a small carrier bag from a drug store also located in the mall.

Jacobs continued on his way oblivious to the presence of his pursuer.

Caine walked behind maintaining a distance of at least twenty yards at all times.

The path weaved gently in and out of the trees and at times Caine was not in direct line of sight of his former mentor. As they approached the entrance to the RV park, the shelter provided by the trees decreased significantly. The path became straighter and eventually merged with the paved road. The final twenty yards were flat and open and afforded no cover. At the end of the path, Jacobs paused to let a newly arrived RV negotiate the entrance. Caine stopped and waited. Jacobs turned slightly so that he was in profile. Any sudden movement from Caine and Jacobs might spot him in the corner of his eye.

Jacobs was sweating heavily and Caine thought he looked awful. His skin was clammy and his face was bright pink. Sweat stained the light coloured polo shirt and the trousers sagged at the rear as if he had lost a lot of weight since he last wore them.

When the RV had passed the gate and disappeared into the park, Jacobs resumed his walk. He did not follow the path but instead cut across the grass separating the semicircular loops of road, large concrete lay-bys carved out of the sparse pine copse, that had been set-aside for the RVs. Crossing onto one of the loops, Caine could see it was a dead end. Apart from the three RVs parked on this small section of road there was no other way to go. A rustic fence made from solid pine logs and chicken wire formed a boundary a few yards beyond. This was it! Jacobs lived in one of these three RVs.

Jacobs walked past the first two and stopped in front of the third, a compact brown-coloured model. The door was unlocked and Jacobs fumbled with the handle and disappeared inside. Caine made a mental note of the location and returned to his hotel. He wanted to call Garcia again and find out what he should do next.

When he called the FBI field office in San Francisco the receptionist seemed to be expecting his call. Evidently, Garcia had retrieved the message he had left the night before. The receptionist gave out Garcia's mobile phone number and made Caine repeat it back to her. She told him he should call her immediately.

Propped up against the headboard of his bed Caine dialled the number.

"Garcia. Who is it?"

"Hi, Angela. It's me," said Caine, genuinely pleased to be hearing Angela's voice again. He had not spoken to her since the incident in Greeley and he was anxious to know how she was doing. "What's up?"

"Hi, Paul. Any luck finding Jacobs?" asked Garcia directly. After disposing of Husam al-Din she was keen to close the case once and for all.

"Not yet," lied Caine. If Jacobs was involved Caine wanted to be the first to confront his old friend and colleague. Whether he was involved or not, Jacobs deserved some measure of respect and trust for his long years of friendship. If Caine could not give him that, no-one could.

"I don't suppose I need remind you that he is wanted for the murder of Dr.

al-Jaheereh during the conference?” Garcia did not like to reveal confidential information to unauthorised people but Caine was intelligent enough and close enough to the case to warrant an exception. “We found traces of the victim’s blood in Jacobs’ room,” she continued. “He should be considered armed and extremely dangerous.” Garcia sensed that the forceful way she expressed herself might alienate Caine rather than bring him round to her way of thinking. Softening her tone, she added, “Whatever your past relationship with this man, remember he is very disturbed and not rational. He’s not the man you think he is.” She heard Paul sigh at the end of the line. She couldn’t tell if it was understanding or exasperation. “Paul,” she urged finally, “please tell me you’ll be careful and you won’t try to do anything stupid. You might regret it later.”

“I promise,” said Paul. “I won’t.”

Liar.

“Any way,” continued Garcia, “when this is all over maybe we can get together again. I guess you must be headed back to the UK soon, right?”

Caine’s job at the Animal Health Institute seemed a lifetime ago. So much had happened in the last two weeks. He wondered if he could ever get back in to the routine of lab work and stuffy scientific meetings.

“Surc,” rcplicd Cainc. “I’d love to.”

“I’m sure I’ll see you soon,” said Garcia. “Keep in touch. And take care.”

“Yes, dear,” answered Caine, gently mocking Garcia’s almost motherly concern.

When he hung up Caine had an empty feeling. He sensed his meeting with Jacobs would be the last time he would see his mentor alive. His mind went over all the things they had said and done together over the years. The debt he owed to Jacobs was incalculable. Now he had to face him down and extract a confession, or at least an explanation for his involvement in recent events, and try to get him to give himself up.

Caine went to bed at ten o’clock. He needed an early start in the morning so he could stake out Jacobs’ RV. Even now he had no definite plan mapped out. He would have to play everything by ear.

Caine had pre-set the alarm for 5:10 A.M., one hour before sunrise. That would give him enough time to wash and dress and get into position long before Jacobs himself had risen.

By morning the cool night air permeated the hotel room. As Caine clambered from beneath the thin cotton sheets gooseflesh immediately began to rise on his upper arms. Outside, wisps of mist in the still air clung to a few hollows in the pine forests. Soon the warming rays of the sun would stir the air just enough to melt them.

The TV news stations all carried the progress of the investigation into the foot-and-mouth disease outbreaks although it had now slipped from first place in the list of the day’s lead stories. The spread of the disease at Greeley had been contained by the immediate slaughter of all animals on the Great

Western Feeders lot. After two days, the process was still continuing. Funeral pyres stacked with the stiff bloated corpses of hundreds of otherwise healthy cattle burned through the night. Daylight brought no respite from the infernos and an acrid pall hung over the town.

The FBI spokesman intimated that the spread of the disease was now under control following the death of Husam al-Din and the case would be closed completely upon the imminent arrest of his accomplice. To Caine's surprise there was still no indication of the suspect's name, the location of the continuing search or the biblical quotes defining the limit of the outbreak.

Caine stopped at the shopping mall and bought some snacks for breakfast, which he ate on his way to the RV park. The sun was beginning to rise and Caine began to feel its warmth on his back as he watched the ponderosa pines change colour from a dark foreboding blackish-green to more cheerful hues, softening their distinctive conical, almost triangular, silhouette. Squirrels clung to the bare trunks and scurried between the branches pausing to nibble on exposed patches of inner bark.

As he entered the RV park Caine noticed that many people were up and about. His presence would not be considered unusual. Retracing his steps of the previous afternoon he returned quickly to Jacobs' RV in its secluded cul-de-sac. Caine retreated into the fringes of the pine forest a few tens of yards away and selected a suitably large tree with which to support himself during his vigil. He slumped down resting his back against the ridged bark of a giant ponderosa pine, two feet in diameter and at least one hundred and fifty years old.

In his isolation Caine experienced more readily the beauty and majesty of the park and its natural inhabitants. The dense layer of brown pines needles underfoot gave off its distinctive aroma and reminded Caine of childhood family Christmases.

Caine was awoken from his slumber by the slam of a door. Jerking awake he looked up. Jacobs was leaving! Looking at his watch Caine realised he had been asleep for at least thirty minutes. It was now 7:30 A.M. and his prey was stirring.

Wearing knee-length shorts, sandals and a comfortable old sweatshirt Jacobs stepped down from the cabin.

Caine twisted his neck from side to side to loosen the stiffness from his unintended nap. He watched as Jacobs walked gently down the path toward the Visitor Center. Caine guessed he was shopping for breakfast supplies or to purchase a newspaper. In any case, Caine imagined he would return shortly as the old man was certainly not equipped for a day's hike.

When Jacobs had disappeared down the tree-lined path Caine made his move. He guessed he had about twenty minutes at the most before Jacobs returned. Approaching the RV he tried the handle to the door. As expected, it was not locked. Caine mounted the step and squeezed into the narrow vehicle.

Inside, the RV was surprisingly well furnished; maple veneers covered all the surfaces giving it a warm homely feel. In the tiny kitchenette Caine saw a microwave and small electric hob. In the corner of the living area a TV equipped with satellite capability enhanced the feeling of a home away from home.

Caine did not know where to start or for what he was looking. "Evidence," he kept telling himself. "You must find evidence that Jacobs is involved." Yet, what did he expect to find — a bloodstained knife?

Methodically, Caine started in the driver's cabin. Instantly, he found a road map. The page was open at northern Colorado. Greeley was circled in blue ballpoint. A piece of paper with what Caine guessed to be important highway exit numbers slipped out of the pages of the map and fluttered to the floor of the cabin. He picked it up and silently checked the numbers off on the map one by one. They described the route south from Greeley along I-25 to Denver and then along I-40 to the Grand Canyon. It was a long drive, over nine hundred miles. On the dashboard was a receipt for a trailer park in Sante Fe. Jacobs had stopped overnight on the way.

Climbing into the living area from the driver's cabin, Caine looked around and searched for anything unusual. The sofa was clean and tidy; a couple of newspapers and magazines were stowed neatly in a rack beside the TV. In one corner sat the carrier bag Caine had seen Jacobs carry the previous day as he followed him back from the store. Caine opened it and peered inside; the rustling of the polythene was amplified by the silence of the room and Caine's guilt at his stealthy entrance.

Tipping the contents of the bag out on to a small coffee table Caine rummaged through the packages. They were all medications of one kind or another. He did not recognise the brand names, so he looked for the generic name. With training in chemistry, pharmacy and veterinary medicine, he could identify most drugs easily. Mentally he checked them off — oxycodone for severe pain, dihydrocodeine and coproxamol for moderate pain, simvastatin for high cholesterol and enalapril for high blood pressure. Jacobs was a walking pharmacy.

For a man as overweight as Jacobs, Caine understood the need for drugs to regulate his high cholesterol and hypertension. The prescription painkillers were more puzzling.

Caine searched the bedroom. In the tiny desk drawer he found some more papers, mainly letters. The franking mark on one envelope in particular caught his eye. The name Mercy Hospital, Carmel and a prominent crucifix were emblazoned across one corner in blood red ink. Intrigued, Caine pulled out the single typed sheet and read it quickly. When he had finished he sighed and replaced everything as he had found it.

As Caine made his way through the RV from the bedroom at the back to the driver's cabin he saw Jacobs' notebook computer half concealed under a cushion. He looked at his watch; still a few minutes left.

Quickly, he flipped open the slim machine and switched it on. After a few seconds the screen flickered to life. The screen-saver was the same picture of Jacobs and his wife Caine had seen in Jacobs' office at Stanford. The couple stared back at him and Caine could almost feel their sense of betrayal.

Clicking on the 'My Documents' icon Caine scanned the list of folders that appeared. The one-word descriptions and acronyms Jacobs had used to describe the contents of each file were fairly easy for Caine to decipher. STU referred to Stanford University. A brief look at the contents of the folder assured him that he was correct, as it contained sub-folders dedicated to the various university Senate committees in which Jacobs was involved.

STUDENTS listed the personnel files and confidential progress reports of his numerous undergraduate and post-graduate students. VACATIONS contained digital photos of previous holidays. The last image was dated over two years previously, before Nancy Jacobs' illness had left her bedridden.

The word ZEPHANIAH leapt from the screen. Caine opened the folder with interest. It contained several files. The sub-file NUMBERS drew his attention. It consisted of a series of digital images of various documents. Courier receipts, invoices, expense claim forms and the like. Caine enlarged one of the pictures. In late August a package left Karachi for Frankfurt. From there it was sent to an address in St. Petersburg, Florida.

Puzzled, Caine moved on to the next file. It contained more digital images. Caine recognised the picture of Dr. al-Jaheerah instantly. Several other photographs, taken clandestinely, caught him from different angles. Copies of his hotel registration form and correspondence with the organisers of the scientific meeting were also included.

Caine was sweating. He didn't have much time. The last file, JUDGES, contained a list of names, addresses, photographs and contact numbers. The majority of the images, scans of passport-style black and white photos, were of glum, surly dark-skinned males. The names of the men pictured were of Central Asian origin.

Is this what Chen was looking for when she broke into Jacobs house that night? Were these the organisers of the plague; the men Chen accused of plotting to destabilise China's Muslim-majority western provinces?

A noise interrupted Caine's musings. It was not the sound of the cabin door opening but it sharpened his mind all the same and urged him to leave as soon as possible. Switching off the computer he returned everything to its place as best as he could remember. With one last look at the interior he climbed down from the cabin and slammed the door. As he reached the safety of his vantage point and settled back down to his vigil, Jacobs appeared through the trees. Under his arm he carried a thick newspaper. In the other hand he had a small paper bag of doughnuts and a sealed cup of coffee. Balancing them precariously in one hand he opened the door and climbed in.

Caine watched intently for a few minutes anxious to discover if his presence had been detected. After a few tense minutes he rested back against his tree and waited.

Chapter 43

Caine's stomach growled in protest as he continued his vigil. The wait for Jacobs to make a move was interminable. Propped up against his tree for several hours Caine was surprised that no one had spotted him. He wondered how long it would be before someone noticed the odd man sitting in the fringes of the forest staring off in to space and called the park rangers to investigate.

At 2:30 P.M. Jacobs emerged from the RV, dressed exactly the same as when he had entered earlier that day. A gentle afternoon breeze rattled the wiry stems of the pine trees and Jacobs adjusted his hat, planting it firmly on his head, before setting off in the direction of the Visitor Center.

Caine gratefully rose and stamped his feet to improve the circulation to his lower limbs. Cautiously, he set off in pursuit.

After some minutes Jacobs arrived at the Visitor Center and Caine observed him from a distance. Checking his watch, Jacobs turned to look down the road, putting his hand to his brow to shield his eyes from the glare of the sun. He waited impatiently, hands on hips, as if exasperated. Caine watched as Jacobs spoke briefly to someone standing nearby. The stranger replied and Jacobs nodded, appearing to thank the man before checking his watch again.

In a few minutes a small crowd had gathered. Evidently they were all waiting for the same thing. The sound of gears grating alerted the group to the arrival of the bus. Caine was annoyed and swore under his breath.

The regular Park Service shuttle bus left at fifteen-minute intervals and travelled down West Rim Drive to Hermit's Rest and back. Caine could not board the same bus as Jacobs without giving himself away. If he followed on the next bus he might never find Jacobs. There were eight stops between the Visitor Center and the Hermit's Rest terminus and Caine would not know if or where Jacobs alighted.

Just as Caine was wondering what he should do a second bus chugged its way up the road and came to a rest behind the first. The doors opened with a hiss and a stream of tourists got out. They wore expensive cameras and broad grins of satisfaction. The short drive was one of the most popular features of the park. Due to the demand two buses left every fifteen minutes.

Waiting until he saw Jacobs get on the first bus Caine made his way to the second and sat in the front row adjacent to the driver. He could see the passengers alight from the bus in front more easily. Within minutes both buses were bouncing along the road toward the first stop on the twelve-mile round trip.

The views were exceptional and were enhanced by the clear air and slight breeze. Caine had no time to enjoy them, as he was engrossed in watching the bus ahead. After a few hundred yards, red taillights from the vehicle in front indicated that it was slowing down. Caine waited in his seat as he watched some of the passengers get off, while others who had been waiting by the side of the road boarded. Caine watched intently, waiting for Jacobs to make his move.

After an hour they had nearly reached the end of the route. The penultimate stop was Pima Point, a spot that Caine knew from his map offered unprecedented views of the canyon. Here, at last, he saw Jacobs leave the bus.

Jacobs crossed the narrow road to the barrier that marked the limit of the viewing area and peer over. When he was sure Jacobs was engrossed in the view Caine stepped from the bus. There were only a handful of people at this stop. A few couples walked hand in hand or took photographs of each other overlooking the magnificent panorama. Caine tried his best to put some distance between himself and Jacobs but the confines of the narrow viewing area made it difficult.

A pile of stones had been erected to form a crude henge. Each column of cobbles, three feet in diameter and eight feet high supported a single rough-hewn granite lintel upon which was carved the name Pima Point. Caine observed Jacobs silently from behind one of the uprights.

With a small knapsack strung across his back Jacobs waited until he thought he was alone; the other visitors enjoyed the view or waited near the bus stop for the next shuttle. The old man clambered over the grey metal poles of the safety barrier and climbed down on to the gently sloping apron of rock that led to the precipice beyond.

Caine walked briskly to the barrier and looked over. Twelve feet below him, reached by a series of treacherous-looking steps, was the remains of a trail. The abandoned path ran along a ledge that demarcated a sheer drop to the Colorado River over a mile below. In places the path was eroded and great holes peppered the trail making it impassable. In others, erosion from above had littered the trail with mounds of scree and loose rock.

The ground was warm underfoot. The dying afternoon sun dipped toward the horizon drenching the ground in amber, ochre and tawny shades of yellowish-orange, softening the sharp angular textures of the rocks and adding an ethereal dimension to the canyon as if the ageless natural monument were a living breathing entity.

Caine watched as Jacobs gently made his way along the path. Looking around exactly as Jacobs had to check that the coast was clear, Caine gingerly stepped over the barrier and jumped to the first of the age-worn steps cut into the face of the canyon wall. In seconds he had descended to the level of the path, nearly losing his footing as the weathered gravel slipped and rolled under the soles of his sneakers.

Stealthily, he walked slowly and deliberately after Jacobs. The path, about twelve to eighteen inches wide, hugged the canyon wall. To the left, the apron of scree extended up to the road at an angle of about forty degrees. The slope was punctuated irregularly by small creosote bushes, sagebrush and scrub grass.

To the right lay a stunning view of the North Rim and Kaibab Plateau ten miles in the distance. The plateau formed a straight line separating the land from the sky. The flaming sun lit up the rocks and the sky mirrored the russet reds and browns of the canyon walls so that it was almost impossible to tell where one ended and the other began. The stone temples Shiva, Osiris and Isis, immense fortresses of natural rock carved out of the earth over aeons, guarded the approach to the far rim of the canyon.

The path followed the natural contours of the rock; fissures, crevices and other weaknesses in the strata determined the rate of erosion of the canyon wall and hence the width of the track.

Jacobs was out of sight, having disappeared around a bend as the path curved gently around to the north. Caine quickened his step as much as he dare. He recalled his terror as he clung to the cliff face at Jacobs' house during his moonlit escape from Ms. Chen. The drop that night was eighty feet. This time it was over five thousand. His palms began to sweat at the memory.

As he rounded the bend, he saw Jacobs a few yards away. The path had broadened considerably forming a flat promontory about five yards wide. Beyond this natural lay-by the path continued along the canyon wall.

Jacobs sat on the ledge, his feet dangling over the edge. His back was to Caine as he approached. Caine stood and watched him for a few moments. The old man seemed completely at peace. Disturbing him seemed impertinent, even disrespectful. Eventually, Caine resolved that he had no choice. People had died, the country was in chaos and Jacobs was partly responsible. Caine and everyone else needed some answers. He hoped Bill would open up to him as a friend.

Caine advanced, cringing as his light steps crunched the gravel. Jacobs was too absorbed in his thoughts to notice. Caine stopped less than six feet away.

"You know they charge Canadians extra to come here?" he said.

Jacobs stiffened and his shoulders pulled back, clearly surprised by the intrusion. He swivelled round and brought his legs back up on to the ledge. Looking up at Caine he smiled broadly.

"I thought that was just the Mexicans?" he replied.

"Hi, Bill. What's up?"

"Paul," replied Jacobs, "I'm so very glad to see you. I wondered if anybody I knew would figure it out. I'm so pleased it was you."

"Figure it out?" Caine was upset by his friend's flippancy. "You think this is a game or puzzle?"

"Isn't it?" answered the old man. "Life's the biggest puzzle of all, don't you think?"

"Your friend's dead," said Caine, referring to Husam al-Din.

"I don't doubt it," replied Jacobs. "Although I must say I haven't really been following the story. How did you find out about my involvement?"

Caine cast his mind back. When exactly did he first suspect something odd about his friend? He should have suspected something when Laura mentioned that Jacobs shared the same room as al-Jaheerah on a previous occasion. But he didn't. He should have believed Chen Xiao Lin when she told him Jacobs was the killer as they searched his Sausalito home. But he didn't. Not really. He was only convinced when he watched the VCD in Jacobs' house and Garcia confirmed the presence of al-Jaheerah's blood in Jacobs' room in the San Francisco hotel.

"Lots of things really," replied Caine. "The Bible quotes, perhaps. And some things that an FBI friend of mine found out, you know, forensic stuff. Oh, and the fact you changed your shirt after killing al-Jaheerah."

Jacobs nodded thoughtfully.

"Nice touch, I thought. The Bible quotes," he said cheerily. "Took me ages to find them."

Caine smiled. He had always appreciated Jacobs' schoolboy humour. It was one of the strategies they shared in coping with the absurdities and pressures of life.

"I went to your office in Stanford to look you up after the conference. I thought we might do lunch together. Catch up," said Caine wistfully.

"That would have been nice," admitted Jacobs. "Thanks for the thought."

"I spoke to Margaret Duffy. Haven't seen her for a long time."

"She's a game old bird, isn't she?"

"She said the last thing you told her was that you'll enjoy seeing the cowboys. Was that a reference to something in particular?" asked Caine.

Jacobs said nothing, but arched his eyebrows, silently demanding Caine to think of the answer for himself. For a moment Caine was twenty years old sitting by his mentor's side trying to answer a complex question on microbiology.

"Dodge City?" said Caine. "You met up with this al-Din character at Dodge City."

Jacobs clapped his hands in congratulation. To Caine the gesture was slightly patronising.

"I went to your house in Sausalito, as well," said Caine, hoping that by keeping Jacobs talking he would start to feel more relaxed and able to talk about his involvement in the epidemic still burning across the country. "Someone else was there too. A woman. A Chinese spy."

"My, my," replied Jacobs. "What did she look like?"

"Tall, pretty. She was posing as Dr. Li's assistant from the Yunnan Veterinary Institute at the conference."

Jacobs nodded as he recognised Caine's description and smiled at the deception that had been played on him.

"You think you know someone and then…" his voice trailed off.

"She broke into your house searching for something. That's where I found the quotes from the Bible."

Jacobs nodded again.

"The police and FBI know it's you, Bill. They'll find you eventually. You can't run and hide for the rest of your life. Is there anything you want to say? In confidence."

"Do you think it's possible to love someone too much?" said Jacobs.

"Erm, I don't think I'm qualified to answer," replied Caine, not expecting that his question would elicit such a response.

Jacobs snorted and smiled. "When Nancy died I thought I would die too. Really. Life suddenly had no purpose, no reason. What was the point of waking up in the morning in a cold bed in a cold house? No one to talk to or ask you how your day has been. For people like me, Paul, from my generation, that means a lot. I think that's something people in this day and age don't appreciate too much. And the way she died was really terrible. She was in pain, Paul. Screaming, agonising pain. In the end she was begging me to kill her. Begging me. Can you imagine?" Jacobs closed his eyes and relived the horror of those days and weeks, gripping his thighs with clenched fists until the knuckles turned white. "For months she lived like that. None of the doctors could do anything. The painkillers didn't work. If there was anything I could have done to help her I would have done it."

"I know you would, Bill," reassured Caine.

"Then the insurers refused to pay. All three of 'em. Said we didn't inform them about her pre-existing medical condition. Like we were trying to screw them out of money. After I buried Nancy, I said fine. To hell with them. To hell with everybody. You don't believe Nancy Jacobs existed? Maybe Bill Jacobs doesn't exist either. Now I've got my own time-bomb ticking away inside me, may be I should do something about the whole goddamn situation. What do you think, eh Paul? Good idea?"

"What's wrong with you, Bill?" asked Caine, pretending he had not read the diagnosis in Jacobs' RV earlier.

Jacobs smiled grimly. "Inoperable pancreatic ductal adenocarcinoma," he said, almost with relish. "I'll be dead in three months. Maybe sooner."

"I'm sorry," said Caine, staring at the ground in front of his feet.

"Why? It's not your fault."

"It must be very painful," asked Caine, remembering the painkillers in Jacobs' carrier bag.

"Damn right," relied Jacobs, wincing at the thought. "Played hell with the travel plans. Had to keep stopping every few hours to get some rest."

"How did you get in touch with the group in Pakistan?" asked Caine. If Jacobs was going to kill himself he at least wanted to make sure he had something positive to tell Garcia.

"Hell, I know lots of people over there from way back. They all know people who know people, if you know what I mean," Jacobs replied with a wink. "It's not difficult finding somebody who wants to do what we did. The problem is finding someone discreet who can support you and misdirect anybody who comes snooping around. For that you need money – *baksheesh* they call it over there, and connections."

"Are there any others like you in America?" asked Caine, thinking about the file of mug shots he found on Jacobs' computer.

"I'm sorry, Paul," Jacobs replied, "I can't tell you. It's not your job to find out these things. Leave it to people who know what they're doing."

"You sound like Ms. Chen, the Chinese spy," smiled Caine.

"I wish I could make her acquaintance," said Jacobs. "Looks like we have a lot in common. I know it's against doctor's orders, but do you want to crack open a beer and take in the sunset before we go? I guess that's why you came? To take me in?"

Caine looked at his old friend, perched on the ledge looking up at him. The years melted away and he became the same kindly man who cracked jokes and shared indiscretions in his Stanford office and cliff-top home.

"Sure, why not?"

"My bag's over there, behind that rock," said Jacobs, gesturing to a boulder a few feet away. "Get it for me would you?"

Caine turned and stepped toward the rock. As he reached the large sand-coloured boulder, the deception dawned on him.

He turned around to face Jacobs. The ledge was empty. Jacobs' wide-brimmed hat was propped against the stump of a dead sagebrush. A chill breeze whistled up the side of the slope.

It took thirty-eight seconds for Jacobs' body to hit the canyon floor five thousand feet below.

Caine crossed to the ledge. He picked up the hat and held it to his chest as he stared over the chasm to the North Rim in the distance.

The setting sun plunged the canyon into darkness. A blanket of red, streaked through with velvety oranges and vibrant purples swept over the great rift from the west.

Caine looked down into the abyss.

"Goodbye, Bill," he said.

Chapter 44

The canyon walls amplified the roar of the rotor blades as the helicopter took off. Inside the passenger compartment lay the battered and bloodied corpse of Dr. William R. Jacobs.

At first light, few observers were present apart from those assigned by the Park Service, Coconino county PD and the FBI.

Angela Garcia watched from the wide gravel flood plain wincing as the deafening noise of the engine reverberated around the canyon. The noise abated as the helicopter rose vertically and turned slowly to climb out of the deep chasm.

The sweeping metal rotor blades pushed up concentric rings of waves in the sluggish pool of water that bordered the fringes of the Colorado River. As they spread from the centre they diminished gradually to become mere ripples. In seconds tranquillity had returned to the Grand Canyon.

Later that morning, after the formalities had been completed and she had filed her field report, Garcia visited Caine in his hotel room.

"You okay?" asked Caine, as she stood in the doorway.

"I'm fine. What about you?" she replied. Her hand was still bandaged heavily but the abrasions on her face had mostly healed.

Caine shrugged his shoulders.

"I'm sorry about Dr. Jacobs. I know he was a friend of yours."

"Have you searched his RV yet? I can show you where it is."

"That's why I came."

"He's got…" Caine bit his lip. He was going to tell Garcia about Jacobs' computer and the file of names and photos of terrorist suspects, but thought better of it. After her previous admonitions, he did not want to reveal to Garcia that he had been inside Jacobs' RV and searched it for himself.

"He's got what?" asked Garcia.

"He's got satellite TV and a great view," replied Caine.

"When did you find out he was here?" probed Garcia.

"Erm, let me see," said Caine. He had to fix the time after his last phone call to Garcia. "Late Saturday night. I bumped into him outside one of the bars. We had a few drinks and a chat."

"One of our profilers at Quantico said he might be suicidal," said Garcia. "I suppose I should have told you in case he tried to do something stupid and take you with him. I'm sorry."

"That's okay," replied Caine.

"How did you know he would come here?" asked Garcia. "It's a pretty wild guess."

"I remembered something he said at the conference. Things he wished he had done when his wife was still alive. I thought if he was in hiding he might come here."

"Good guess. Well done."

“Why did you believe me that he might be here?” countered Caine.

“Instinct,” replied Garcia. “You know him better than anyone. You can’t beat inside information. You’ve got to grasp anything that will give you an edge. We had people staking out his homes in Sausalito and Nebraska and his office at Stanford. Never underestimate how stupid people can be. He might have tried to brazen it out. Sometimes, the best results come from luck rather than planning.” She turned to face the door. “Shall we go?”

Garcia led the way out of the hotel and into the parking lot. An unmarked car was waiting, its engine running. The driver acknowledged Garcia with a nod as they approached the vehicle and climbed into the back seats.

They chatted about Jacobs’ background on the short drive to the RV park. The car slowed and parked opposite the brown RV about ten feet away. Just as they were about to step from the car a violent explosion rocked the vehicle. The windows of the RV shattered with a high-pitched squeal, bowed outwards, and showered the car and its occupants with a rain of jagged glass fragments. Plywood and fabric debris was catapulted high into the air and strewn over the park. A mushroom cloud of orange flame and acrid black smoke billowed up, towering over the skeletal remains of the shattered vehicle.

“Son-of-a-bitch must have booby-trapped the thing,” shouted the driver over the roar of the flames.

Caine gulped. What if it had gone off when he searched the RV himself?

Garcia and the driver approached the burning wreckage ducking and weaving in and out of the smoke and flames trying to see if anything could be salvaged, but the intense heat and poisonous fumes drove them back.

Caine was surprised yet secretly pleased amid the chaos and confusion. At least he didn’t have to worry any more about Jacobs’ complicity in other plots, as whatever evidence he may have kept had been destroyed. Caine could safely deny ever seeing the file naming the other conspirators. Jacobs could die remaining merely a suspect rather than as a known terrorist. Caine owed him that.

As he sat on the grass verge bordering the narrow lane Caine thought about all that had happened during the past three weeks. He wondered what the old man might have said to anyone who asked for an explanation. Caine smiled at the probable answer.

Not my job.

Chapter 45

The coffee tasted good. Perhaps she would have another. That would give her time to finish writing the postcard. She hoped the address was sufficient: Dr Paul Caine, Animal Health Institute, UK.

She smiled and stretched her legs; she looked good in shorts. The men in the restaurant were all admiring her, secretly of course, lest their wives and girlfriends notice.

The rooftop patio of the restaurant was not in a particularly good location. It overlooked the RV park and was not a popular choice with the park visitors. But it was more than sufficient for her needs. A few minutes more and she could leave. The unmarked FBI car had just passed by and would be arriving at its destination soon.

The transmitter was hidden deep inside the shell of her mobile phone. It was so powerful she did not need to be in line of sight. Anywhere within a one kilometre radius would be just fine.

She looked at her watch and craned her neck in a vain attempt to visualise her distant target. A little longer — now! She pressed the send button. There was no sound; she was too far away. She watched from her chair by the railings.

The black plume of smoke rose slowly, majestically, from the midst of the trees. After a few seconds a distant rumble, like faraway thunder, rolled over the park. A murmur of concern rose from the crowd of people in the restaurant. They rushed to the window for a better look before running downstairs or on to the balcony to see what was going on. In less than a minute she was alone.

A crisp five-dollar note was left on the table, wedged under the demitasse. It would more than cover the price of the coffee.

Chen Xiao Lin closed the laptop computer, thrust it under her arm and walked out. She had ten minutes to catch the last mail collection of the day.

Epilogue

Translated from *Awami Awaz*
Karachi, 3 September
Burned out car abandoned

The charred remains of a green Land Rover Freelander was found on the southern outskirts of Karachi yesterday. The car was reported missing by the Go!Karachi rental company seven days after it was due to be returned. Upon investigation, the name and address supplied by the final client on the rental agreement was found to be false. No trace of the occupants was discovered. Police suspect arson and appeal for witnesses to the dumping of the vehicle and subsequent fire to come forward.

Translated from *Qaumi Akhbar*
Karachi, 10 September
Another headless corpse discovered

The headless corpse of a man in his mid-thirties was discovered in a monsoon drain in western Karachi last night. The victim's hands had been tied behind his back. A police spokesman said the body was too badly decomposed to allow fingerprint analysis. Police have classified the case as homicide. Last week, two bodies mutilated in exactly the same way were recovered from monsoon drains in a similar location. Police are unsure if the cases are connected. The physical descriptions of the men do not match any of the reports of missing people lodged with the police during the last two months. A spokesman said police were investigating the possibility that all three victims were in some way related to a recent spate of gang-related deaths associated with gambling activities. No arrests have been made in relation to any of the deaths.

Time
20 September
On the trail of the terrorists

The FBI is currently investigating the identity of Husam al-Din. A DNA profile obtained from the terrorist's remains in Greeley, CO and entered into the FBI's CODIS database revealed no match. Further analysis of genetic markers, known as short tandem repeats, using the polymerase chain reaction indicate with high probability that the man was ethnic Pakistani, probably from the Balochistan region. While it is certain that Husam al-Din is a fictitious name, FBI Arabic scholars reported that the name means "Sword of the Faith", the true identity of the man in question is likely to remain a mystery. No information is available on how Husam al-Din managed to enter the United States and obtain false identity documents.

USA Today

San Francisco, 30 September

President honors agent

The President yesterday honored a local FBI agent when he presented Special Agent Angela Garcia with a meritorious conduct certificate on his scheduled visit to the Bay Area. Agent Garcia, who has also been promoted, was recognized for her involvement in stopping last month's foot-and-mouth disease outbreak.

Business Post

Technology section, 10 December

The rapid foot-and-mouth detection test produced by Hong Kong biotech company AsiaBioTek Ltd was evaluated fully by the United States Department of Agriculture in the weeks following the US foot-and-mouth disease outbreak earlier this year. Their report will be forwarded to the biotechnology committee of the international animal health organisation, Organisation International des Épizooties, who will further report to the society's Annual General Meeting in May next year. Shares in AsiaBioTek rose thirty-six percent on the back of the news and are expected to make further significant gains if, as expected, the method is adopted as an official test for the disease.

San Francisco Chronicle

Announcements, 14 December

McMann – Fuller

Dennis and Margaret McMann of Westlake, San Francisco are pleased to announce the engagement of their only daughter Laura Jane (29) to Michael Sean Fuller (42), the eldest son of Vernon (deceased) and Patricia Fuller of Palo Alto.

Scope: The official newsletter of the World Virology Union

Volume 37, issue 4

Williams elected

Prof. Jonas Williams was elected President of the World Virology Union by a landslide majority of 1269 votes to 323, defeating incumbent Prof. Sam Atholt. Prof. Williams was said to be delighted at his surprise win, but refused to comment on whether his high profile during the recent foot-and-mouth disease outbreak in the USA earlier this year had influenced the voters. He will serve a two-year term.

Postcard

Undated

Greetings from the Grand Canyon!

Dear Paul,

I hope this reaches you ok.

Thanks for showing me around the Grand Canyon. You were a very good guide (even if you didn't know it)! I'm sorry I couldn't stay longer and say hello. My friends in China are looking forward to receiving the gifts I got for them. Bill's computer will be very useful for my work! Please thank him for me. I hope we can meet again some day under more pleasant circumstances.

Best wishes,

Chen Xiao Lin

XXX

P.S. You were right. It was worth the risk!

Daily Telegraph

London, 24 November

Amnesty 21, the organisation monitoring the rights of political prisoners around the world, yesterday decried the renewed Strike Hard campaign against internal dissent in the People's Republic of China. Of particular concern was the recent announcement from Beijing that over 40 ethnic Uygurs from the western province of Xinjiang had been arrested and held incommunicado since mid-September. They are said to be high-ranking members of a secessionist group in the largely Muslim province and are being held on explosives, conspiracy and treason charges. The Chinese government had recently expressed difficulty in penetrating the tight security of such underground groups and the latest success has been presented as a major intelligence coup. All those arrested face the death penalty if convicted.

Further reading

The foot-and-mouth disease virus (FMDV) is the most infectious pathogen of animals and the most economically damaging. The use of FMDV as a bioterror weapon has long been considered a possibility. The events described in this book are based on fact. The following resources may be of interest to readers.

Brown C. Vulnerabilities in agriculture. Journal of Veterinary Medical Education 2002; 30(2): 227-229.

Musser JM. A practitioner's primer on foot-and-mouth disease. Journal of the American Veterinary Medical Association. 2004; 224(8): 1261-1268.

Grubman MJ, Baxt B. Foot-and-mouth disease. Clinical Microbiology Reviews. 2004; 17(2): 465-493.

Sutmoller P, Casas Olascoaga R. The risks posed by the importation of animals vaccinated against foot and mouth disease and products derived from vaccinated animals: a review. Revue Scientifique et Technique (International Office of Epizootics). 2003; 22(3): 823-835.

DeHaven WR. Factors to consider when using vaccine to control an exotic disease outbreak. Developmental Biology (Basel). 2003; 114: 281-289.

Donaldson AI, Sellers RF. Transmission of FMD by people. Veterinary Record. 2003; 153(9): 279-280.

Hietela SK, Ardans AA. Molecular weapons against agricultural vulnerability and the war on terror. Journal of Veterinary Medical Education. 2003; 30(2): 155-156.

Gibbs P. The foot-and-mouth disease epidemic of 2001 in the UK: implications for the USA and the "war on terror". Journal of Veterinary Medical Education. 2003; 30(2): 121-132.

Collins RA, Ko LS, Fung KY, Lau LT, Xing J, Yu AC. A method to detect major serotypes of foot-and-mouth disease virus. Biochemical and Biophysical Research Communications. 2002; 297(2): 267-274.

Printed in the United Kingdom
by Lightning Source UK Ltd.
102589UKS00001BE/7